THEIR GAZES LOCKED AND JESSIE FORGOT EVERYTHING BUT THE MESMERIZING BLACK EYES ABOVE HER.

Tony lowered his head, brushing his mouth softly against hers. He didn't want to stop, but he knew he had to now or he wouldn't be able to stop at all.

Jessie sat frozen, stunned. The sensations tumbled through her body like a mountain stream swollen from the spring thaw.

As Tony rose to slip into the wagon, he paused. "Don't look so stricken, Jess. It was just a kiss."

But it wasn't just a kiss, and Jessie, wrapped in the welcoming, magical darkness, knew it.

It was a beginning.

Harper
Monogram

Susan Kay Law

Journey Home

HarperPaperbacks
A Division of HarperCollinsPublishers

This is a work of fiction. The characters, incidents, and
dialogues are products of the author's imagination and
are not to be construed as real. Any resemblance to
actual events or persons, living or dead, is entirely
coincidental.

HarperPaperbacks   *A Division of* HarperCollins*Publishers*
            10 East 53rd Street, New York, N.Y. 10022

Copyright © 1993 by Susan K. Law
All rights reserved. No part of this book may be used or
reproduced in any manner whatsoever without written
permission of the publisher, except in the case of brief
quotations embodied in critical articles and reviews. For
information address HarperCollins*Publishers*,
10 East 53rd Street, New York, N.Y. 10022.

Cover illustration by Aleta Jenks

First printing: July 1993

Printed in the United States of America

HarperPaperbacks, HarperMonogram, and colophon are
trademarks of HarperCollins*Publishers*

10 9 8 7 6 5 4 3 2 1

*To the men in my life: Matthew, Nathaniel, and Ian,
for teaching me enough about love that I could write
about it.*

Prologue

He had been betrayed.

At first he could not believe even the evidence before his eyes. It could not be true! To lose everything, and lose it to the one he would have—indeed, had—trusted with his life. Later, when he could no longer deny the truth, there was one question that reverberated in his head again and again, like a heavy mallet driving a stake through his soul: *Why?*

He had no answers. He looked at his parents and his sisters, gathered there with him, and knew they also had no answers.

"I have to go. I have to find him." With those words, he left. They let him go, to seek answers and solace where he could.

He strode down the broad steps of his home, where he had lived all his life, where there had always been comfort and warmth and contentment. He went to the stables and saddled his horse, hoping to dull his pain and anger by doing what he had always loved most.

And so he rode. The land he flew over was green

and new with the onslaught of early spring, its vibrancy at odds with the chill in his heart. He remembered when they had explored this land together, as children discovering the world and youths discovering themselves. It was all familiar, the gently rolling hills, the bluish tinge in the green grass, the majestic horses grazing there. The air was filled with the sweet scent of magnolia and the call of songbirds welcoming the reborn world. Still, he heard only the question in his head: *Why?*

The steed followed a familiar path, flying over bushes and fences to reach the river. Though it was not wide, the stream was lovely, its banks carpeted with tiny lavender and white violets. The man pulled his horse to a stop and dismounted, stroking the horse's velvety nose and heaving sides, whispering a word of apology for pushing him so hard.

The man followed the river until it curved sharply. There, where it undercut the banks deeply, he stopped. Hidden behind the large dogwood bush, whose white blossoms dropped petals to the ground like a light dusting of snow, was the entrance to a cave. It had always been their secret place. As boys they had played there endlessly, creating worlds peopled by pirates, thieves, and dragons. As young men, it was where they had confided the secrets, hopes, and dreams they had dared share with no one else.

It was not dank and gloomy inside but warm and cozy. He sank to the sandy floor, propped an elbow on a knee, and rested his head in his hand. He could almost hear the echoes of past laughter bouncing off the rock walls.

His eyes slowly adjusted to the darkness. It was then that he saw it: an envelope, starkly white against the earth. He took it out into the sunlight, ripped it open, removed the single sheet of paper inside, and began to read.

I knew you would come. After all, it all began here. And you, who always had everything, would have to have answers, too. I want you to know why. It was because of her . . .

1

Antonio Winchester pulled his big chestnut stallion, General, to a stop on top of a small rise just outside of Council Bluffs and surveyed the wagon train sprawled out on the flats below. There were perhaps fifteen wagons, gleaming white like freshly bleached sheets in the warm May sun. It was a small train, but that was good. They could move much faster than larger, more cumbersome ones.

Even with so few vehicles, the scene below him was one of disarray. Each wagon had its own livestock and equipment, all arranged in haphazard fashion, grabbing whatever bare ground could be found. Horses stamped and snorted, children ran underfoot, and people shouted at both with equal gusto.

With a sigh, Tony pushed up his shabby, wide-brimmed hat, squinted his eyes, and searched the chaos for some semblance of organization or leadership. He didn't particularly want to join the train. What he wanted was to ride west as hard and fast as he could. But riding west was a dangerous business in

1853, even for someone as skilled in taking care of himself as Tony was, and being in a caravan would help increase his odds of getting to California in one piece. That was one thing he intended to do.

He had to.

It wasn't as if joining the train would increase his comfort on the trail, he thought as he turned to check the packhorse trailing behind him. He wasn't planning on traveling in a wagon himself. On the other hand, perhaps he could charm some woman into cooking for him. Cooking wasn't one of his talents. But charming women—well, that was another thing entirely.

Tapping his heels lightly against the horse's sides, he sent General down into the midst of the confusion. He scanned the crowds, looking for the leader of the wagon train or a likely candidate for cook. His attention was caught by a young woman walking across the camp with a purposeful tread. Her hair, arranged in a simple knot on the back of her head, gleamed red-gold in the sun. Tony figured it was the color normally called *strawberry blond,* but somehow that seemed too weak a description for it. Her simple gingham dress could not hide the trimness of her figure, nor the enticing sway of her hips, as she passed. Something about the way she moved reminded him vaguely of . . .

He shoved the memory away. It was just too damn painful. But guilt never seemed to him to be a particularly constructive emotion, and after eight years he'd become pretty adept at ignoring his—most of the time, anyway.

Tony quickly dismounted, tied General to a nearby bush, and moved to follow the woman, hoping she was as beautiful close up as his glimpse of her had led him to believe. He had nearly caught up with her when she stopped to speak to a burly, shaggy-haired man. Just close enough to overhear their conversation, he couldn't suppress a smile as an idea began to form.

Perhaps he had found both of the people he was looking for in one place.

"Excuse me, sir, are you Tom Bolton?" she asked.

"Yup, sure am. What can I do for ya?"

Jessie paused to consider the man in front of her before she answered. Tom Bolton was of only average height, but he gave an overpowering impression of strength. His legs looked sturdy as the trunks of good-sized trees. His beefy arms were folded across a formidably broad chest. His head was covered with a great growth of bushy hair, as dark brown as the rich Iowa soil. There was little of his face to be seen, as most of it was covered by a thick beard, and the rest by heavy eyebrows which sprouted with little regard for uniformity of length or direction. He would have been a forbidding figure, except that his eyes did not look hard, only determined. It was easy to see why he was called "Buffalo" Bolton. All in all, he looked like he could get her to California safely.

"I'm Jessamyn Johnston. I'm going west, and I'd like to join the train. I was told you were the captain and therefore the one I should see." Jessie extended a hand.

Tom pulled one huge palm down the length of his beard before he reached forward and shook her much smaller hand. His eyebrows lowered as his gaze swept her dainty frame from head to toe.

"Where's your husband?" he asked.

"My husband?"

"Yeah, your husband," he said. "You're not coming with us unless you've got a husband. No single girl is allowed to travel on the train by herself."

Jessie lifted her chin. "Do you mean to tell me a perfectly competent woman—"

"Look, ma'am, I'm the captain, and it's my job to see we all get through quickly and safely. It's a lot of hard work going overland, and I ain't lettin' anybody join the train who can't carry his own weight. It ain't safe for everybody else. No woman could handle the trip herself. Sorry, Miss Johnston, but you're going to have to find somebody else."

Tom turned, lifted a large flour barrel from the ground, balanced it on his shoulder, and began to walk toward a big wagon near the edge of the camp. Jessie felt panic and anger begin to well up within her. She needed to get to California, and this was the last train leaving Council Bluffs this spring. How dare he think she couldn't take care of herself! She'd been doing it for most of the past three years, and taking care of her father besides. She alone had managed to bury her father, sell her house, travel from Chicago to Iowa by train and steamship, and buy, outfit, and learn to handle her own rig.

Jessie was used to being alone. She'd had to be. It was better that way.

She ran forward to place herself in Buffalo's path.

"Mr. Bolton, please, I must speak to you about this!"

Tom had his head down, watching for gopher holes so he wouldn't stumble into one, and he nearly lumbered into Jessie before her voice stopped him. He set the barrel on one end upon the ground, braced one hand on the top of the barrel and another on his hip, and glowered at her.

"I'm mighty sorry I can't help you, Miss Johnston, but ain't no way you're gonna change my mind. I've got a lot to do before we leave tomorrow, and right now you're keepin' me from my work. So please, get out of my way. Next time I won't ask so nicely."

"I assure you, Mr. Bolton, I am quite capable of handling my wagon and my team. I see no reason why—"

The rest of Jessie's sentence was lost when an arm spun her around and hauled her roughly against a solid chest, squashing her face against the coarse fabric that covered it. She automatically tried to push away, but the arm held her so tightly, she could scarcely breathe.

"Jess, honey, everything arranged?" a deep voice rumbled from the chest. "You must be Tom Bolton. I'm Tony Winchester, Jess's husband. Pleased to meet you. What time are we leaving in the morning?"

Jessie gasped, struggling to look up at the obviously deranged man holding her. She had no idea who he was or what he was doing, but by the time she was done with him he would be sorry he had chosen to play his games with her.

"Her husband?" Buffalo sounded confused. "I thought she was single."

"Did she *say* she wasn't married?"

"Well, no, but—hey, wait a second, you said your name was Winchester. She said her name was Johnston."

"What?" Jessie had finally gathered enough breath to let out the word in a shriek, but she couldn't seem to find any other words to express her outrage.

Tony gave her a quick, tight squeeze, willing her to remain silent.

"Hush, sweetheart, we'll talk about it later." He winked at Tom. "Well now, Bolton, we're newlyweds. Guess she's just not used to her new name yet."

Tom eyed Tony, weighing his explanation. The man seemed sincere enough. Hell, what business was it of his, anyway? As long as the woman was taken care of, it didn't much matter to him how. He had more important things to worry about.

"All right, then. Welcome to the group. We'll have plenty of time to get acquainted on the trail, but right now I got lots to do. You have any problems or questions, just ask. There'll be a meetin' after sundown tonight, last chance to get organized before we head out. See ya then." Tom hoisted the barrel again and stomped away.

The arm around her loosened, and Jessie pushed

hard against the chest with both hands. Her release was so sudden that she stumbled back, almost falling before his hand reached out to steady her. She lifted her head, getting her first look at the man who had so boldly accosted her and claimed to be her husband.

He was the most gorgeous thing she had ever laid eyes on. His thick, wavy hair was so black that the highlights gleamed midnight blue in the sun. His skin was deeply bronzed, his cheekbones high and broad. Jessie supposed his strong, straight nose would be termed Roman, and his jaw was square and strong. He was tall; her eyes were barely level with his wide chest. All in all, he was so handsome that just looking at him was probably enough to cause most women to stutter. Thank heavens she was stronger than that.

"W-w-what in the S-Sam Hill do you th-th-think you're d-d-doing?"

"Look, Jessamyn—that was your name, wasn't it? —you want to get to California, right? I've got a way that you can, but you're going to have to give me chance to explain. Where's your wagon? It'd be better if we were alone. If somebody hears us, it's not going to work."

Jessie looked into his eyes, trying to discern what he was talking about. His eyes were so dark that it was impossible to tell where iris ended and pupil began. Rather, the color just continued to deepen and deepen as it reached the center. It was impossible to read anything in their depths.

Would it hurt her to hear what he had to say? She had to make this journey; there was nothing left for her here. She decided to give him a chance.

"I'll listen. I'm not making any promises, but I'll listen." Jessie whirled around and stalked toward her wagon, wondering if she should hope that he didn't follow.

He did. Jessie rounded the back corner of her wagon, away from the rest of the camp, and turned to find him close on her heels. She took two steps back and placed both fists on her hips.

"Talk."

Tony bit his tongue to keep from smiling. She was every bit as delectable up close as she was from a distance, but she was undeniably furious. Her eyes fairly shot blue sparks, and the smoothly curved cheeks bloomed chili-pepper red with color. Her full, rose-pink lips were tightly compressed, as if she was holding the angry words inside by sheer will. This would have to be handled delicately if he wanted her to agree to his proposition, and suddenly, he wanted her very much to agree.

"Look, there isn't any wagon train that's going to let a single woman come along. The men are all afraid they'll end up doing your work for you, and they're not going to believe it when you say you can handle it yourself. So the only way you're going to get to California, short of going to New Orleans and buying ship passage 'round the Horn, is to get yourself a husband —or at least appear to."

The man was clearly crazy. There was no other explanation. "You lunatic! I have no intention of marrying—"

"Jessie, I said you have to *appear* to have a husband. You know, get somebody to play the part."

"Oh sure." Jessie waved her hands in wide circles. "And you're a desperate actor just begging to pretend to be my husband."

Tony bowed deeply with a theatrical flourish.

"You're not suggesting we fake being married," said Jessie. It wasn't a question. He was leaning back against the wagon, a thumb hooked in the waistband of his tight buff buckskins, which hugged his long, solid thighs. She abruptly refocused her gaze on the much safer sight of the white canvas wagon top. What was the matter with her? Just the thought of being married to a man like that—even if it was a sham—

was almost too unsettling to contemplate. "You're not serious, are you?"

"Yep. No one has any way of knowing if we're really married."

"Why?"

"Why would I want to help you?" At Jessie's affirmative nod, he continued: "I was planning on joining the train, too, but I'm only traveling with a mount and a packhorse. It would be more comfortable for me, when the weather gets bad or I need to carry extra provisions, if I had use of a wagon. Besides, I'm not much good at cooking and sewing and washing. You could take care of those kind of things for me, and in return I'd help you with the heavy stuff—driving the team, fixing the wagon, things like that."

Jessie was suspicious. It seemed an ideal solution—and that made her immediately distrustful. The last few years had taught her the truth of the old adage that anything too good to be true usually is not. There had to be more to it than he was saying; nothing was that simple. But what other choices did she have? "Are you sure those are the only 'wifely' duties you're interested in?"

"I swear to you—" Tony stood straight and placed his right hand over his heart. "I'm capable of controlling myself. I've never had any trouble finding someone to attend to those particular wifely tasks. Of course, if you find you can't control yourself, I promise I'll do my best to cooperate."

Jessie glared at him. He was arrogant, he was insufferable, he was . . . handsome. His eyes were twinkling now, like a man who knew secrets—her secrets—and found them utterly amusing. She reached over, picked up the rifle that had been leaning against the wagon waiting to be loaded, and ran her hand slowly over the barrel.

"Let me make one thing perfectly clear. If I agree to this . . . arrangement, any part of your body that touches part of mine," Jessie leaned closer, pronouncing each word clearly and slowly as if to make sure any idiot could comprehend, "is a part of your anatomy you are never going to have to worry about again. Understood?"

"Understood!"

He was smiling at her now. By Lucifer, the man had dimples! It was almost impossible to mistrust a man who had dimples. Worse, she had the disconcerting feeling that he knew it. There was no reason in the world why she should believe him, but that was exactly what she was going to do.

"Mr. Winchester, you've got yourself a wife."

2

Tension was palpable in the camp as the sun traveled lower in its arc through the sky. It was a time for second thoughts as people worried about the journey ahead. As always, the familiar was less frightening than the unknown, and these people were preparing to leave everything they had known.

A harried mother paused in her inventory of foodstuffs as visions of green California hills and free land were interrupted by images of arid deserts and rapid, unfordable rivers. A young man, dreaming of still-hidden gold while cleaning his rifle, tried to ignore nightmares of Indian attacks. Into a small boy's fantasy of warm sunshine and endless fields to play in intruded harrowing thoughts of rattlesnakes and bears.

As people scurried about, packing and repacking provisions, debating over what to take and what to leave, and frantically trying to predict what would be necessary and what expendable, nerves frayed and tempers shortened.

Tony spent the day looking over Jessie's supplies

and trying to become friendly with his new "bride." He was satisfied with the results of the first endeavor, but in the second Jessie thwarted him at every turn. Since they were to spend most of the next five months together, he thought it advantageous for them to become at least comfortable with each other—although he had hopes for a much closer relationship than that. Whenever she paused in her labors, he sought to start a conversation with her, but she always remembered another task she had to attend to and rushed off. He applied his charm full force, with no result—a rather novel experience for him. If he didn't know better, he'd suspect she disliked him. But that seemed improbable, likable fellow that he was.

When he turned to her preparations for the trip, he was pleasantly surprised. It seemed that he had managed to hook up with a practical woman, a creature most rare in his experience. Her wagon was smaller than most, solidly built of aged hardwood. The wheels were wrapped in iron, and the arched ribs were covered with a double thickness of sturdy, well-oiled sailcloth. The vehicle was well stocked with food supplies of all types: flour, bacon, beans, dried fruit, coffee, potatoes, sugar, rice, even pickles, and a few gallons of wild-plum preserves and blackberry jam.

Jessie had shown remarkable restraint for a woman in her selection of personal items to bring along, and as a result the wagon was not loaded down with heirloom furniture and treasured china pieces. In fact, the lack of keepsakes seemed almost unnatural. There was a good collection of the necessary tools and several spare axles, spokes, and wheels. Jessie had only four oxen instead of the usual six, but they seemed sound, and her wagon was light enough to be pulled by only one yoke if absolutely necessary. She even had a milch cow, a placid, snuff-colored creature which could be pressed into service as a draft animal if need be.

Tony was pleased. It was clear that his arrangement

with Jessie was going to make his trip immeasurably more comfortable. If she was a halfway decent cook, he would certainly eat better. When he coaxed her into a more agreeable mood the trip might be tolerable after all.

Well, he might as well give it one more try now. He gave his horses, pastured with the other animals, one final check and decided they'd probably be fine. His horses weren't used to staying outside overnight, but they were going to have to start.

It was almost time to meet with the other men. They were going to make plans for the trip, pass the rules every member of the train must follow, and elect a council. Usually, they'd also elect a captain, but Buffalo Bolton already had that job.

He ambled back to Jessie's wagon, nodding to the people he'd already met, stopping to introduce himself to the ones he hadn't. He was going to be spending a lot of time with these people, so he figured he might as well start getting to know them. Now if he could just do the same thing with Jessie.

She was scurrying around her wagon like an excitable little squirrel trying frantically to gather nuts before winter. She poked her nose into crates, peered under stacks of boxes, and rummaged in piles of clothing, occasionally consulting a large sheet of paper she clutched in her hand.

"Hello, Jessie," he said. "What are you working on now?"

Her spine stiffened. He was back, him and his irritating I-want-to-be-your-best-buddy voice. She didn't buy it for a minute. It was like a panther pretending to be a cuddly little housecat. She knew the claws and the teeth were there; she just hadn't found them yet.

"Well, I suppose it is rather difficult to figure it out." She wondered if he'd even notice the sarcasm. "I'm checking my supplies against my list. See?" She held up the white paper.

"What a great idea. Could you use some help?"

Sarcasm apparently had no effect. Perhaps outright negation would be more effective.

"No."

"I'm a very useful fellow, Jessie."

"I'll just bet you are."

"Why don't you give me a chance, *cara*?"

Because he made her nervous. He'd been popping up all day, offering to help, smiling that darn irresistible smile. Nobody could be that cheerful, helpful, and good-natured. It was unnatural.

"That's fine, Tony. I know where everything is. You'd just get in the way."

"Oh." He grinned, showing rows of beautiful, perfect white teeth. "Well, if you change your mind, just let me know."

"I won't." She wasn't sure how much more of his friendliness she could take without dumping something over his head. She returned to her list and checked off two more barrels of flour and six bags of sugar.

He was still there, leaning comfortably against the side of the wagon, arms crossed casually over his chest as he watched her work.

She turned to face him.

"Was there something else you needed?"

"No."

A bolt of cotton and two lanterns were checked off.

"What is it, then?" She wasn't going to lose her temper and yell at him. Still, she had to get rid of him somehow. She couldn't concentrate when he was around; she was too conscious of the fact that he was there.

"I just stopped to let you know that I was heading over to the meeting."

"And you thought it was necessary for me to know this?"

"Well, of course, *cara mia*. A considerate husband

always lets his wife know where he his and what time
he's going to be home."

She closed her eyes to shut out the sight of his gorgeous, smiling face. It didn't help. When she opened
her eyes, he looked even more amused.

"Tony, I'm not looking for a considerate husband.
I'm just looking for one to get me to San Francisco.
You are under absolutely no obligation to tell me
where you are going. I don't want to know, and I don't
care to know. I am completely uninterested in your
whereabouts."

She sounded rude, even to herself, yet she wanted
to discourage him from seeking her out unless absolutely necessary. She couldn't put up with his friendly
charm all the way to California. She'd go insane . . .
or she'd fall in love.

Jessie wasn't sure which would be worse.

"I'll let you know anyway," Tony replied. He
wouldn't consider his attempt at friendship a success,
but at least she wasn't indifferent to him. She was far
to fiery for that. "After all, I expect you to keep me
informed."

"I certainly will not!"

His grin disappeared. "Jessie, on this trip, your
safety is my responsibility. I need to know where
you're going to be."

Her lips compressed into a thin, determined line.
"No one is responsible for me but me. It's been that
way for a very long time, and it's not going to change
simply because you feel like pretending to be a protective husband."

"Regardless of what you think, I feel responsible
for you," he said. "This isn't the city. We're going to
be heading into wild country, Jessie. It's dangerous
out there. I have to know where you are, and if I say
something isn't safe, you're going to have to listen to
me. It's called survival."

"I'm perfectly capable of taking care of myself."

"You will not go off without telling me."

"I'm not planning to take any stupid chances, Tony. I am a reasonably intelligent woman."

"Intelligent, yes. Reasonable . . . that remains to be seen. Out there, Jessie, any chances are stupid chances."

"You have no right to dictate to me!"

"Until we get to California I am your husband. Your safety is going to be my concern whether you like it or not. If you don't agree, we can call this off right now."

Jessie glared at Tony's set face. He wouldn't.

Maybe he would. He was going to get there anyway. Darn, she needed this pretense more than he did.

Hopefully he'd get tired of playing protector soon. Then she'd be able to go ahead and do as she pleased.

"All right," she said. "I won't do anything remotely dangerous unless I clear it with you first. Good enough?"

"Good enough."

The grin was back.

Tony strolled slowly away, humming happily.

The sky began to deepen to indigo, and the scent of wood smoke wafted on the cooling night breeze. The darkness forced people to stop their frantic labor and turn their attention to their growling stomachs. In the glow of cook-fires they tentatively began to get acquainted with the strangers who would be their companions for the long journey.

Jessie was preparing beef stew for supper, viciously chopping carrots, potatoes, and onions as her stomach quivered with nerves. She tried to concentrate on getting to California, seeing Jeremiah and David again, and not on all the disasters that could occur on the way.

It was bad enough that she had been compelled to

enter this odd agreement with Tony Winchester to get there; she couldn't dwell on the possibility that they might not make it. And what would happen when she arrived? Jeremiah would be happy to see her, she was sure, but perhaps she should have warned him she was coming. The mail service going west was undependable, though, and she probably would have shown up long before any letter she sent, anyway.

It was just as well she had not written. Then he would have been watching for her arrival. If J.J. ever found out about this farce with Tony, Jessie had no doubt he would lock her up until her change of life. A protective older brother could be an annoyance.

If J.J. found out, so would David. Jessie's heart skipped a beat at the memory of her brother's best friend, the hero of her youth. David Marin had warm hazel eyes, tousled sandy curls, and a gentle heart, so different from her volatile brother. If David knew she was pretending a marriage that didn't exist, he would certainly think her improper, if not downright loose.

Jessie dumped the vegetables into the stewpot where beef was simmering in broth. She was already having second thoughts about her hasty decision to go along with Tony's scheme. Earlier that day she had decided that the best way to get along with the man was to spend as little time with him as possible. They were already fabricating this nonexistent matrimony; to allow any more intimacy was only asking for trouble.

She was not convinced that he had no intention of trying to take advantage of the situation. Most men would, sooner or later. If he had any notions, she was planning to stomp on them right quick, like she did to the spiders that persisted in crawling out of the corners of the old house where she had grown up.

She had Tony pegged, all right—a rogue, through and through. She knew the type well enough. Her brother was one of them—a man who enjoyed a woman for the moment, ran the other way at the first hint of expectations, and couldn't understand why their former lovers were hurt by it all.

The stew was cooking nicely now, bubbles rising to the surface of the thick brown liquid where they popped with a small *blurp*. Jessie sniffed at the rich aroma rising from the pot, and her stomach growled in response. She was hungry; it had been an exhausting day, and this was her first opportunity to relax. She wiped her hands on her linen apron and tried to stretch out the stiffness she was beginning to feel.

An odd prickle of uneasiness ran down the back of her neck. Out of the corner of her eye she saw a man standing in the darkness just beyond the edge of the firelight. His gaze rested on her breasts, where the thin cotton fabric pulled tightly while she arched. She immediately dropped her arms and crossed them protectively. The flickering flames gave her only brief glimpses of him, just enough to see he was tall and lanky, with eyes nearly as light as his hair. He continued to stare at her rudely, smiling lecherously all the while.

He took a step toward her, bringing him fully into the light, and she moved a little further away. He was younger than she'd thought at first, probably not much older than she was. But he had done nothing to her, so why was she so jumpy? It was his eyes, she decided, pale, flat eyes, eyes that stared at her covetously, without a flicker of warmth or compassion. Eyes that made her feel like a mouse in that instant before a snake struck.

Jessie spun around, turning her back to him and busying herself stirring the stew as if it were of the greatest import. It was some time before she dared peek behind her again, and with a sigh of relief she realized he was gone. If the man was part of the train, which he likely was or he wouldn't be there, it was going to be a long trip. There was something about the way he looked at her. She instinctively knew she would have to be wary.

Walt watched her. Jessie, he thought that was her name. He'd noticed her first thing when he had come into camp that afternoon, and he'd been keeping an eye on her all day. She sure was pretty. Feisty, too, and determined. He could tell by the way she moved: quick and confident.

She was the reason he'd decided to go to California. A woman like her, anyway. He'd always wanted a woman like her but had never managed to make one notice him. He'd always been too poor, or not quite good-looking enough, or not quick enough with his tongue.

With a woman like that, Walt knew, his luck would change at last. How could a man not be lucky with her at his side? He'd find gold for sure. Oh, he knew he was a few years late. The gold rush was petering out. But somewhere in California, he just knew there were some of those pretty yellow rocks waiting for him. Then it wouldn't matter anymore that nothing he'd ever tried had worked out. It wouldn't matter that his folks couldn't seem to scratch a living out of that poor, broken-down farm, and that he hadn't managed it either. It wouldn't matter that every woman he'd really wanted had never looked at him twice.

No, in California it wouldn't matter anymore, 'cause he'd have the only two things a man ever needed.

Gold.

And a woman like that one.

3

Jessie tested the vegetables in the stew. They were tender. More than ready to eat, she fetched a tin bowl and spoon.

"Hello there!"

Jessie was just reaching to serve herself a portion when the greeting interrupted her. She looked up to find a woman about her own age coming toward her. The woman was a bit shorter than Jessie and slightly plump. When she reached Jessie's fire she plopped down on a nearby crate. She had masses of brown curls, shining chocolate eyes, a turned-up nose, and a wide smile. Jessie returned the greeting and was unprepared for the rapid torrent of words that spilled out of the woman in response.

"I'm Virginia Wrightman. Call me Ginnie—everybody does. You must be Jessamyn Winchester. I met your husband on his way to the meeting. He walked over with my Andrew. Tony told me all about you, and I'm so happy to meet you. Andrew and I are newlyweds, too, just like you and Tony. I wasn't sure if there would be anyone for me to be friends with, but here you are! How long have you and Tony been married? Andrew and I have only been married a month. Why are you going to California? We're from here in Iowa, but Andrew is a second son, and we wanted our own place. He's a farmer, you know. And say, I know I shouldn't say this, being just married and all, and I do love my Andrew, but that husband of yours is really somethin', isn't he? I just knew you would be as beautiful as you are. Oh, I know this is going to be grand fun!"

Jessie's mind and heart both began to race frantically. How could she answer those questions? What could Tony have possibly said about her? Was she going to be found out before the trip even started?

"Oh, I'm sorry!" Ginnie waved a hand in apology. "I'm getting ahead of myself, aren't I? I asked too many questions; I'm always doing that. Andrew says I could outchatter a magpie. I'm just so happy that there'll be another woman my age along. My friend Ladisa went to California three years ago with her Cornelius, and she wrote me that the train was mostly men. She was awful lonesome. There are some things you can only talk to another woman about, don't you agree? Men just aren't much good for chatting. I swear, sometimes what I say to Andrew floats in one ear and flies out the other, like the space in between was as empty as my grandpapy's whiskey bottle."

Jessie bit her lower lip to keep from laughing out loud. But Ginnie was expectantly awaiting a response. Jessie nodded, wondering just what exactly she was agreeing with.

"Won't you stay and have supper with me?" Jessie asked. "I was just getting ready to eat. There's plenty, and I'd sure appreciate the company." It had been a long day. If there was anyone who could keep her mind off of what lay ahead it was this effervescent woman.

Ginnie looked aghast. The brevity of her answer indicated just how shocked she was. "You're not waiting for your husband?"

"Oh . . . well, I . . ." The thought had never occurred to Jessie. A proper wife would wait for her husband, wouldn't she? "Tony didn't know when he'd be back, so he told me to go ahead and eat when I was hungry."

"My, my, he certainly is considerate, isn't he? Maybe he'll rub off on Andrew a bit. I love him dearly, you know, but sometimes he's just the teeniest bit single-minded. Why, occasionally he even interrupts me when I'm speaking!"

She couldn't help it; unable to hold it in any longer, a giggle escaped. Jessie gave up the struggle and let out a peal of laughter.

A few yards away, Tony froze in mid-step. He and Andrew Wrightman had been returning from the meeting, strolling along the darkened path when the sound of Jessie's merriment reached them. No breathy, feminine twitter, it was a full, rich guffaw. Tony felt a spark ignite deep within; it was a laugh full of life and passion, the laugh of a woman whose feelings ran deep and real, a woman who had no room for artifice.

Jessie jumped when Tony's arms encircled her from behind, pulling her back against him while he planted a soft peck on her cheek. She immediately tried to pull away; his nearness was just too disconcerting to deal with, but Tony held her fast while he bent to whisper in her ear.

"We're newlyweds, remember? I'm not supposed to be able to keep my hands off of you, and you're supposed to love it—and I assure you, you would." He straightened and spoke in a louder voice to Ginnie Wrightman. "I see you two have met."

It was embarrassing, Jessie thought, to be hauled around like a bag of flour. That was why her heart was pounding so hard she'd be surprised if Tony couldn't hear it. She was angry at the way he took advantage of the situation, that was it. It had nothing to do with the way he felt against her back, warm and solid and real. The reason she couldn't draw a decent breath was that he held her too tightly, not because his hands were gently rubbing her waist.

"Oh, yes, we met," Ginnie replied. "I just trotted right over and introduced myself and we've been busy getting acquainted ever since. She's exactly like you described her, Tony. I just know it's going to make things so much easier to have friends along." She jumped up and grabbed onto Tony's companion with both hands. The man was of medium height, squarely built, with a shock of straight, straw-colored hair, eyes the color of much-washed chambray, and features saved from plainness by the friendliest smile Jessie had ever seen. He was looking at Ginnie with an odd mixture of tolerance and love. "And this here's my Andrew."

Jessie smiled. "I'd guessed it must be."

"I'll introduce you properly another time. But now, if you'll excuse us, I'm going to go feed this man. I'm dying to hear what plans were made, and he needs to keep up his strength. We'll see you both tomorrow, and if we can help with anything, holler!"

"Are you sure you won't stay and eat with us?" Jessie asked, figuring that Tony would have to behave if there were other people around.

"No, no, I've got supper all ready, can't see it going to waste. 'Sides, I'm sure the two of you would like to be alone. I'm looking forward to getting Andrew to myself, too. Haven't had much chance of that, living with his family since we been married, then all the commotion getting ready to go. Now, you have fun tonight, ya hear? Might be the last good chance for a while. I imagine we'll all be too worn out the next few days for much evening entertainment!"

"Ginnie, my girl, there's always plenty of entertainment when you're around." Andrew threw an arm around his wife and gave her an affectionate squeeze. "Mrs. Winchester, it sure was a pleasure to meet you."

"Call me Jessie, please. After all, I'm sure we'll have plenty of opportunity to get to know each other over the next few months."

"O.K., then, Jessie. We'll see you in the mornin'." At that, the couple turned and left, arm in arm, wending their way between the wagons and among the supplies and equipment that still littered the ground.

As soon as the Wrightmans were out of sight, Jessie pushed Tony's arms away and stepped out of his embrace. She smoothed her apron and reached a hand up to pat her hair. She felt as nervous as a young girl at her first dance, unsure of how to deal with this man she was bound to for the duration of the trip.

"Ah . . . are you hungry?"

"If that stew tastes half as good as it smells, I just might eat the whole thing, pot and all."

Jessie gave a tense little laugh. "Pull up a crate and I'll get you some, then. It's not much of a dining room, but I guess we'll get used to it."

He wished she didn't seem so uncomfortable with him. He didn't mean to make her nervous or angry, but he always seemed to be doing both. He wanted her to be as easy with him as she'd been with Ginnie.

"Jess, I don't expect you to wait on me."

"That's all right, I know where everything is. You sit, I'll be just a minute."

So Tony sat, crossing his ankle over his knee, and watched her preparations. She moved rapidly, collecting a bowl of stew, cutting two thick slices of bread, spreading them generously with sweet butter and delivering them to him before going to pour him a tin cup of coffee. Her motions were fluid and economical, and he found he enjoyed simply watching. He tasted a large spoonful of the stew. It was meaty and rich.

"Jess, this is terrific. I'm beginning to think that this arrangement of ours is going to mean I'll really enjoy this trip." In a lot of ways, he added to himself.

Jessie looked up to find him watching her intently. His eyes did not flicker for so much as an instant when they met hers, and his dimples were in full force. She dropped her gaze quickly. For some reason she couldn't seem to keep her thoughts in order when she knew he was looking at her like that.

"Ginnie asked a lot of questions."

Tony chuckled, a deep, resonant sound. "I imagine she would."

"I wasn't sure how to answer without giving anything away. I didn't know what you had told her. What did you say to her about me?"

"Only that we had just gotten married, that she would like you, and that you're about the prettiest woman in three states."

"You're better at deception than I am."

"Except for a minor legal technicality, it's all true."

Jessie didn't dare look at him this time; she knew he was still staring at her.

"Tony, if we're going to keep up this hoax, we're going to have to learn a bit more about each other. I'll never pass another inquisition from Ginnie."

"What do you want to know?"

"Oh, the basics to start with—your family, where you're from, what you do for a living."

"O.K., the short version. I grew up in Kentucky. My family has a place called Winchester Meadows, where we raise horses. I have three sisters—Catharina and Anna-Maria are older than me. Angelina is the baby, she's only eighteen."

"You're Italian?"

"My mother is." At his pause, Jessie looked up to

find his eyes twinkling like those of a little boy who was plotting to filch a cookie from the cookie jar. "When my father was first starting Winchester Meadows, he went to Europe to look at breeding stock." His dimples deepened. "He brought home my mother."

Before she could stop herself, Jessie smiled, a beautiful, pure smile. To Tony, it was like the sun breaking over the horizon after a long, stormy night. He'd known he could make her do that sooner or later.

"You seem very fond of your family. Why are you leaving?"

His grin faded, and his voice was flat when he answered her.

"I have business in California. With any luck, it won't take too long."

"You're not planning on staying?"

"No."

"This is a mighty long trip to make if you're just going to turn around and go back."

"Sometimes a person doesn't have much choice." Tony took a large bite of the soft, yeasty bread, chewed, and swallowed before continuing. "What about you?"

"I've lived in Chicago all my life. My dad was an attorney. I never knew my mother; she died of a fever shortly after I was born. My brother Jeremiah—everybody calls him J.J.—is five years older than me. He went to California four years ago to look for gold, and Daddy got consumption the next fall. He died last November. There wasn't much left for me in Chicago, so I decided to go find my brother."

She recited the facts unemotionally, her voice flat and expressionless, as if she were speaking of someone else.

"I'm sorry, Jessie. It must have been tough for you, being alone there with your dad while he was sick."

She echoed his words. "Sometimes a person doesn't have much choice."

They ate the rest of their meal in silence.

Jessie knelt in the wagon, smoothing linens over the feather bed on top of the hair mattress, which fit snugly in the bottom. She was bone tired, her muscles aching from the day's exertions, and looking forward to a good night's sleep. She was glad she had made room for the mattresses. Many people hadn't, but Jessie had chosen to leave other furniture behind rather than sleep on a hard surface. The trip would be strenuous enough; she knew she would be grateful for a comfortable bed each night.

Tony lifted the back flap of the wagon cover. He paused, admiring the shapely rump pointed in his direction as Jessie stretched to reach the far corner of the bedding. She was wearing a voluminous white cotton nightgown that covered her from neck to toe, but the flimsy material stretched tightly across her backside as she bent. He braced both hands on the rough-board side of the wagon and vaulted into the wagon bed.

The wagon quaked with his motion. Jessie started and turned to face him while he tied the puckering strings on the back flaps.

"What are you doing here?"

"What do you think I'm doing here? I'm going to sleep with my wife, of course."

The pearlescent moonlight streamed through the front of the wagon, and in the semidarkness Jessie could clearly make out Tony, kneeling and untying the lacings at the throat of his ivory muslin shirt. She felt a constriction in her chest, as if she were wearing a corset pulled too tight. Her voice was a thin screech as she forced out the words.

"Not on your life!"

"Where else would I sleep, Jessie? Do you think anyone would believe we were just married if we slept apart the whole trip? People get to know each other real well when they're traveling together, *cara mia*. Somebody would be sure to notice. We have no choice; we have to share a bed."

"You can sleep on the floor."

"The floor?" He looked around at the boxes and crates and sacks piled nearly to the ceiling, crowding the bed from all sides. "Honey, there is no floor."

"Oh." She searched for another solution—any solution—that wouldn't require him lying down next to her. "We could shove a couple of crates together, maybe."

"You want me to sleep on a couple of crates? Jess, no way in hell am I spending the next several months, after working my tail off all day long, sleeping on a couple of hard, splintery crates." He pulled the last shirt lace free. "But I promise you, I've never laid a hand—or anything else—on a reluctant woman. Besides, I'm too bushed to do anything but sack right out tonight."

He sounded so calm, so unruffled, so danged . . . reasonable about it all. Jessie steeled herself to be reasonable, too, until he whipped off his shirt and reached for the buttons on his buckskins.

Jessie closed her eyes, squeezing them shut as tightly as she could, repeating a litany to herself: I will not look, I will not look.

"What the devil are you doing now?" she asked.

"I'm taking off my clothes so I can go to sleep."

"Tony, if you expose any more pieces of your body, I swear to God I'll shoot them off."

"I don't like sleeping in clothes. It's uncomfortable."

"I'll guarantee you're going to be a lot more uncomfortable without them."

He conceded with a sigh. "Oh, all right, I'll keep my pants on."

Jessie dared a peek, cautiously opening one eye, then the other. Perhaps she could survive this after all, as long as she didn't look at that wide, bare chest. He had all kinds of bulges—nice big ones—on his arms and chest and—

He flopped down on the bed. On the right side. Her side.

"You're going to have to move."

Tony lifted his head, linked his hands behind it, and settled himself more comfortably. "Why?"

"Because that's my side of the bed."

He couldn't resist; she was so easy to fluster. "I wasn't aware that you had enough experience sleeping with someone to have a preference for a side."

Jessie felt a blush heat her cheeks, grateful for the darkness that hid her rising color.

"No! It's not that—of course not. It's just, at home, that side of the bed was next to the window. I like to sleep on my right side, and that way I faced the fresh air."

"But there's no window here."

"I know that!" she snapped. "But I'm accustomed to that side, O.K?"

"Nope, sorry, I've got to have this side."

"Oh, for pity's sake. Why?"

"I'm right-handed."

She paused for a moment, perplexed. "What on God's green earth has that got to do with it?"

"I'll show you." He turned on his left side, facing the center of the mattress, raised his right hand, and grinned. "When I turn this way to face a woman, my right hand is free to . . . be useful. If I'm on the other side of the bed, I'm lying on my right arm, and I'm not quite as proficient with my left hand."

That was all it took. She could feel the anger bubbling up, rising within her, waiting to spill over right onto his arrogant head.

"You are an idiotic, conceited gorilla! You're the vainest person I've ever met, though I can't for the life of me figure out what you have to be proud of! You haven't got the chance of a corncob in a sty of ravenous pigs of ever, *ever*, using your proficient hand on me! This is my wagon, that is my bed, and you're going to give me my side or I'll . . . I'll pluck out every hair on your obnoxious head one by one!"

"Oh, all right, *mia poco incendio.* Be my guest." His voice was resigned, barely hiding a note of amusement as he slid to the other side of the bed.

Jessie flounced down on the bed, turned on her right side, and pulled the blanket high over her shoulders, trying to get as far away from Tony as possible. It was a futile effort. Although the mattresses took up the full width of the wagon bed, they were only about four feet wide, simply too narrow for her to ignore him. She was acutely aware of his warmth seeping through the fabric of her nightclothes, the brush of his body as he settled himself, and the sound of his steady breathing. She was sharing a bed with a man for the first time in her life; the thought was unsettling enough that, despite her fatigue, sleep eluded her.

Tony obviously had no such problems.

Jessie was still ordering herself to relax when Tony emitted a string of loud, undignified snorts. Great, just what she needed. The man snored like a bull moose with a bad head cold.

What came next was even worse. Tony flopped over, his hard chest close against her back, and threw an arm over her. Jessie froze. His hand was perilously close to her breast.

Enough was enough. Jessie jabbed her elbow sharply into his ribs.

"Get back on your own side!"

"Umm . . . sorry," Tony mumbled groggily and rolled back to his side.

She waited tensely, but when he didn't move again she gratefully snuggled under the blanket and allowed herself to drift into slumber. She wasn't so deeply asleep, however, that she didn't notice when Tony cuddled up behind her again.

This time she tried kicking him. It took three hard strikes of her heel against his shin before he retreated. Only a brief time passed before the rumbling snores resumed.

When Tony moved behind her once more, Jessie began to wonder if he was really asleep. She knew he was just trying to annoy her, the clod. But how was she going to find out if he actually was awake?

"Tony?" she whispered.

No answer. She had to think of something he would certainly respond to if he was listening.

"Tony . . . I want you to wake up and kiss me. I can't stand it any longer . . . I need you."

Still no answer, not so much as a twitch. He must really be sleeping after all.

It was clear to Jessie she wasn't going to get any rest if he kept rolling over on her all night long. Carefully, she eased his arm off her, stood up, tiptoed around the foot of the mattress, and lay down on the left side. She'd let him have the right side, just this once. It was better than being bothered all night long.

Hidden by the darkness, Tony gave a victorious smile.

4

If everyone in camp had been filled with apprehension the night before, the morning brought, instead, anticipation. They were headed for a new life! Whatever their reasons for going, whether they were traveling to something or trying to leave something behind, it was a time for excitement.

Jessie was not immune to the hope that beat in everyone's heart. To her, being coherent before eight o'clock in the morning was a challenge tantamount to carrying her gear to California on her back. But today she had managed to get up before sunrise with a minimum of struggle, milk Wilhelmina, and fix breakfast while Tony packed up the remaining supplies and hitched the oxen. Even though she was sure she could have handled the trip on her own, she admitted it was rather handy to have someone to share the work—although there was no way she was going to let him know that.

Jessie was stowing the clean plates and mugs in the grub box affixed to the back of the wagon when she heard hoofbeats pounding behind her. Swirling dust filled the air, and she felt hot breath gusting on the back of her neck. She spun as Tony leapt off the horse, her eyes widening at the size of the stallion only a few feet away, his withers even with her nose. She would have ducked away, but the wagon was blocking her only avenue of retreat.

"Is that overgrown animal yours?"

Tony chuckled, running a hand down the horse's neck and patting it affectionately.

"Yep, this is my baby, General."

"Baby? Isn't he sort of . . . big?" Jessie was not at all sure she liked the idea of having this monster in close proximity for two thousand miles.

Tony strolled to the back of the wagon and secured his sturdy roan packhorse. Jessie edged closer to him, trying to keep Tony's body between her and the huge stallion. If someone was going to get the stuffing kicked out of them by those lethal-looking hooves, it wasn't going to be her.

"Actually, he is big for a horse. He's a shade over seventeen hands, and most riding horses who are that large aren't sound, but he comes from good stock. He's the first horse I ever broke and trained all by myself, back when I was sixteen."

"Is he safe?"

"Absolutely. He's the most intelligent horse I've ever known, and he's extremely well mannered, if I do say so myself. Come on, you can touch him. He especially likes pretty ladies—takes after his owner, I guess."

Jessie gulped and took a tentative step forward. She hadn't had much experience with animals in Chicago. It had taken her two weeks of steady practice before she felt comfortable driving her oxen, and they were pretty dull creatures, usually doing whatever they were told. Reaching out a hand to stroke General's dark, velvety muzzle, she admired the copper sheen the fading pink light of the dawn highlighted in his deep red coat.

"He's beautiful. Are all the horses you raise like this?"

He left the packhorse with a light slap and moved to stand close behind Jessie, close enough so she could feel his chest against her back, and she wondered if her sudden agitation was due to the proximity of the horse or the man.

Pride was evident in Tony's voice as he answered. "No, not all, but they're each special in their own way. Actually, most of the other horses are thoroughbreds. They're the best horses for racing, although not very many people know it yet. General's a quarterhorse. He's not quite as fast in a typical race, although he's quicker in a short sprint and he's got much more stamina over the course of a full day of riding. He's bigger, and you can see how muscular he is in his chest and gaskins." Tony stroked each part as he talked about it. A faint note of sadness entered his voice as he continued, "I don't know if a thoroughbred could survive a trip like this."

"Everybody ready?" Buffalo bellowed the question so it was heard all down the line of wagons.

"I'd like to ride in front for a while and check things out if you don't mind. Are you sure you can drive the team yourself?" Tony asked.

Jessie was already clambering into the front seat and reaching for her whip.

"I'm sure."

Tony swung up into the saddle. "Tell me when you get tired and I'll take over." A slight signal sent General galloping forward.

Jessie watched him ride away, admiring the way he and his horse moved as one, as fluid as the ballet dancers her father had once taken her to see.

"Westward, ho!" The traditional call echoed down the line.

And so it began.

Jessie was ambling alongside her wagon, whip in hand. There was no need to hurry, for the oxen plodded along slowly. She had already discovered that riding in the wagon wasn't nearly as comfortable as it sounded. The trail the train followed was deeply rutted by the wheels of previous travelers. Since the wagons had no springs, each bump and hollow was quickly transmitted to her backside. Although she had tried padding the bench with two folded blankets, she still preferred walking.

An assortment of pots and cookware hung from hooks on the hoops of each wagon, swaying with the motion of the rolling vehicles and causing a continual, discordant clanging. Even after such a short time, the sound had become familiar, as much a part of the rhythm of each day as the creak of the wheels, the rustling of grasses, and the calls of the drivers.

It was a glorious day. It seemed as if the vivid azure of the cloudless sky and the piercing gold of the sun had streamed down and blended to become the vibrant green of the endless prairie grass. There were deep yellow black-eyed Susans and stalks of tiny, nameless white flowers waving with the grass in the constant wind, gentle today.

On the second day of their journey it already seemed as if everyone had fallen into a routine. The first day had been slow going. Driving the oxen took some practice, as the teams were not guided by reins but merely by verbal commands and the crack of a whip over their heads. Most of the travelers were farmers and already proficient teamsters, but the two clergymen and the trio of young city men with belated gold fever had had a difficult morning. Jessie was glad she had had the foresight to get used to her team before attempting the trip.

The train had barely left Council Bluffs the day before when they had had to cross the Missouri River. The river was too deep and wide to ford easily, so several years earlier the town, then called Kanesville, had built a ferry to cross the river. The town's bid to replace Independence, Missouri, further down the river, as the major jumping-off point for overland travel had been successful; but even with the ferry, crossing the river was difficult.

The wagons had been loaded on a flatboat and the wheels blocked to prevent them from rolling into the water. Women and children rode in the wagons, led across the river by ropes pulling from the opposite bank. Although several husky men strained on the guidelines, the current was sufficiently strong that the boats ended up several dozen yards downstream and had to be laboriously towed back up to the landing point.

It was worse for the livestock; they were expected to swim across. A group of cattle and horses were tied together to prevent one from being washed downstream. The animals, too, were guided across by ropes, but Tony and some of the other men had chosen to swim with their animals to calm them.

It had taken all of the morning and a good portion of the afternoon to get everyone to the western side of the Missouri. Jessie could only guess how long the crossing would take for the huge trains of seventy-five or a hundred wagons that sometimes attempted to travel together.

A shout from ahead interrupted Jessie's reflections now and called the train to a halt. They couldn't be stopping already; it was only midafternoon.

"Jessie! What do you think's goin' on?"

Jessie turned to see the Walker twins running toward her. Samuel and Susannah were four years old; their parents, Mary Ellen and Stuart, were a soft-spoken, gentle couple who owned the wagon that was just behind Jessie's in line. Mary Ellen was six months pregnant. Jessie didn't understand why they had chosen to make the trip at this time, although no one else seemed to think twice about it. She had never been around children much, and the twins' enthusiastic charm and never-ending questions had already captured her heart.

Jessie bent down and took a small hand in each of hers. The twins had angelic faces spiced with cinnamon freckles and topped with caps of near-white curls.

"I'm not sure," Jessie answered. "Do you think we should go find out?"

The twins' response was to take off, running as fast as their chubby little legs could manage. Jessie hurried to follow.

As her wagon was only the third in the line, they didn't have far to go.

"Jessie, look!"

They had reached the Platte River.

The river was immensely wide and shallow, its color the dull brown of dead oak leaves. It appeared to be made up of many smaller streams, which haphazardly joined, separated, and joined again like the strands of a fish net as the river slowly meandered through its broad, flat bed.

"We're really on our way now," Tony said as he came up behind Jessie, removing her sunbonnet before placing his hands on her shoulders. She had a small mole, the size and shape of an apple seed, on the back of her neck, and he wanted to reach out with his tongue and test the texture. Would it be smooth or rough? Resisting temptation, he rested his chin on the top of her head and inhaled deeply, enjoying the sweet fragrance of rosewater soap that emanated from her hair, intermingling with the grassy smell of the plains.

Jessie knew the journey would now begin in earnest. This river, too muddy and alkaline to be used as a source of fresh water, would be the pathway they would follow for almost half of the trip. There was good vegetation along both banks of the river, although they would follow the north side until they reached Fort Laramie. According to Tom Bolton, who continually consulted his guidebook, *Route and Distances to Oregon and California, with a Description of Watering Places, Crossings, Dangerous Indians, etc.*, the trail north of the Platte was less frequently used, reducing the danger that the fodder had been overgrazed by the livestock of the travelers who had used the trail before them. The streams that fed into the Platte would provide a steady source of fresh water, the most precious commodity on a journey.

Jessie shaded her eyes with her hand, seeing the bluffs on the far side gleaming pale in the bright sunlight. Tony's hands on her shoulders were as warm as the rays beaming down on them.

"Jessieeee!" Samuel was tugging hard on her skirts.

"What is it, Samuel? You don't have to pull on my dress to get my attention."

"Yes I do. I asked you sixteen times already but you din't answer. Is that the Plattey River? Mama says the Plattey is gonna take us to a new life."

"Oh . . . I'm sorry I didn't respond the first time. Yes, that's the river, but it's called the Platte, not the Plattey."

"Is it gonna to take us to a new life?"

It was Tony who answered as his gaze caught and held Jessie's. "Samuel, I think this trip will give us all a new and better life."

5

Where was she? Tony dropped the two field-dressed sage grouse on the ground next to the campfire. Jessie had already started supper; the cookfire, in a ten-inch-deep trough to protect it from the ever-present wind, was burning, and there was a large black pot of beans simmering over it. But where was his wife?

His wife. It was strange how accustomed he was getting to thinking of her in those terms. Tony had never really thought about having a wife. He had always enjoyed women too much to consider limiting his attentions to just one, but in the week they had been on the trail he and Jessie had developed a very satisfactory working relationship. Each went about their business, doing their tasks well and quickly, asking little from each other. If a real marriage worked like this it might not be completely terrible.

About the only problem he had was his enforced celibacy. He could tell already that this was going to be a mighty long trip. Five months was longer than he had ever gone without a woman since puberty. But everyone on the train lived in too close proximity for him to start an affair. Also, each woman was somebody's wife, daughter, or both, and a dalliance with one of them would cause a lot more problems than it would solve.

That left Jessie. As it was, he was having a hell of a time getting to sleep each night. Every time she slid into bed next to him he felt a hot stab of desire in his groin. It would have been embarrassing if Jessie wasn't too innocent to notice.

And she was innocent. He was sure of it, and that was precisely his problem. He had no intention of taking a virgin, a woman who would expect promises he couldn't keep. He had tried that once.

Even after eight years, the thought of Liza caused a spear of guilt to sear his gut. There was no way in hell he was ever going to do that to a woman again, especially not to Jessie. He liked her too much to inflict himself on her. She deserved better than that.

No, he'd stick to women who knew what they were getting: a good time and a simple farewell. Problem was, there didn't seem to be any of those kind of women around.

Tony raked his fingers through his hair and looked around the wagons, already circled for the night. They'd been making good time and had stopped early today to give the men a chance to hunt and the women to do the washing. He figured the men got the good end of that deal. There were some definite advantages to having a wife.

He spotted Ginnie Wrightman and Mary Ellen Walker strolling between two wagons and went to speak to them. If anyone knew where Jessie was, they would. The three women had struck up a fast friendship.

"Ginnie. Mary Ellen." Tony nodded to each woman in turn. "Have you seen my wife?"

Naturally, it was Ginnie who answered. Her hair was damp, and each hand held the end of a long length of linen towel that was draped around her neck. She tilted her head back to look up at Tony.

"Oh, honey, we've been having the greatest time. We got done with our wash quick as a wink. We were so hot from standing over those wash kettles we just decided to go swimming. We found the prettiest little bend just upstream a ways, all shaded with bushes and the bottom nice and sandy. We took turns watching so we'd have some privacy and we all just jumped in and cooled off."

"Where's Jessie then?"

"She was having such fun she just decided to stay a little longer. She said she was going to rest a bit and dry off in the sun and—"

"Is she there alone?" Tony broke in. His mother would say interrupting was impolite, but he couldn't wait through another one of Ginnie's rambles.

"Well sure, honey, she—"

By this time she was speaking to Tony's back as he ran off in the direction they had come from. Ginnie giggled, cupped both hands around her mouth, and shouted after him.

"I know what you're in such a rush about, but you can slow down! I think she already has all her clothes back on!"

If anything, Tony speeded up, swearing under his breath as he followed the stream bed, a prickle of fear running down the back of his neck. The little fool, didn't she realize she wasn't safe out here by herself? There were wild animals, and maybe wilder people. Bandits weren't unheard of, and this was Pawnee country.

He knew she thought she could take care of herself. Maybe she could in the city, but this was hardly Chicago. *Dio,* what if something had happened to her?

There was so much commotion back at camp that nobody would ever hear her scream.

He wasn't used to worrying about people. He didn't like it much, and when he found her, he'd make damn sure she wouldn't make him worry about her again. She'd stay in camp where she belonged if he had to tie her to a wagon wheel.

Up ahead Tony could see a large clump of gray-green bushes marking the small bend in the stream. He couldn't see through the dense foliage, and the air was unnaturally quiet. Cautiously slowing his steps, he crept toward the bushes. He couldn't just go barging in. If someone was there with Jessie, he wanted to take him by surprise. Needing to get a fix on the situation before making his presence known, he dropped to his belly, peered under the dusty leaves, and let out a sigh of relief. Jessie was safe.

Annoyance came flooding back as quickly as it had left. Jessie was lying on her back in the sun, an arm flung over her eyes, apparently asleep, and vulnerable to any bypasser, whether animal or man.

What should he do? He knew she was too stubborn to listen to him if he just told her to be more careful. He'd already told her twice to stay close to camp unless he was with her. No, talking wasn't going to do it. She obviously needed a demonstration if he was going to get anything to sink into that lovely, stubborn head.

Tony reached up to work free the knot of the large kerchief tied around his neck.

The warm sunlight shone down on Jessie, making her feel drowsy and content. It was seldom that she had a chance to relax. The trip thus far had been a lot of work, but it was going very well. She and Tony had pretty much managed to stay out of each other's way. They hadn't really gotten to know each other better, but that was just fine with her. If they got closer she might start to like him more, and God knows, with a man like Tony that was just asking for a broken heart.

It was typical in camp for the women to rise at four o'clock and do chores and fix breakfast before waking their men to eat and head out before seven. But after the near disasters caused by Jessie trying to function at that time of the morning—she'd managed to set her skirt aflame one morning while building the cook-fire, and another day she'd tried to milk Beauregard the ox instead of her cow—Tony had taken over most of her morning chores, allowing her precious extra time asleep. He'd even attempted to fix breakfast, but one taste of half-raw, half-charred bacon and rubbery fried eggs had convinced them both that cooking was one chore best left to Jessie, even in a less than alert state. As it was, he took a fair amount of ribbing from the other men about spoiling his new bride by doing "woman's work."

He was an unusual man. He never seemed to get angry. When she had been so upset at the recalcitrant Beauregard that she'd declared they were all having roast beef for supper, Tony had stepped in, defused her temper with a joke, and gotten the stubborn Beau moving again. While other men drove their teams with shouting and profanity, he did it with calmness and humor. He seemed so carefree and unfettered, she wondered if she imagined the brief shadow of pain she sometimes saw in his eyes. Everyone seemed to like him, he—

A heavy weight was thrown across her chest, forcing the breath out of her lungs. Before she could react, a cloth was tied tightly over her eyes and a rough hand clamped over her mouth. Oh, God, what was happening? She couldn't see, she couldn't breathe, she couldn't think. Jessie tried to fight the wave of terror clenching inside her; it seemed as if some wild creature was trying to gnaw its way out of her stomach.

Suddenly the weight was gone, and Jessie was

hauled roughly to her feet. When she could breathe normally, a little bit of the fear left her. At least her brain was beginning to function again. Think, Jessie, think, she told herself. She didn't know what was happening, but she knew her only chance was to stay in control.

An iron-hard arm wrapped around her, pinning her own arms at her sides and clutching her tightly to a solid chest. Jessie tried to squirm free but it was like being in a vise. She went still with shock as the hand covering her lower face was removed and she felt a mouth, hard and hot, on hers.

Oh, God, no! Who could it be? An image loomed in her mind: Walt Morrison, one of the gold miners, the man who had been watching her the first night in camp. She forced the thought away. She'd worry about who and why later. Now she needed to get away. What was she going to do?

Before J.J. had left for California he had taught her a bit about self-defense, saying that since he wouldn't be around to keep her out trouble she was going to have to learn how to protect herself. He often told her the best defense was a good offense, and the best offense was a surprise attack.

Jessie went limp in the man's arms, fighting revulsion as she forced herself to kiss him back.

When Jessie relaxed in his arms Tony forgot everything. He forgot all about teaching her a lesson, forgot all about swearing to leave her alone, and forgot all about her not being his kind of woman. He remembered only that he had wanted her since he met her. The momentary flash of surprise at her willingness was quickly replaced by a surge of passion, hot and sweet. He had known it would be like this, that the feel of her in his arms would be soft and compelling, that she would taste like spiced wine with honey, intoxicating and addictive. He pulled her tighter against him, tilting his head and slipping his tongue into her mouth, delving deeply, feeling—

Pain. Pure, unadulterated pain. He jumped back, startled, when he felt her sharp teeth clamp down on his tongue, drawing blood. But he didn't move quickly enough to prevent her knee from slamming into his groin, causing an intense wave of nausea.

When the man's hold on her loosened Jessie quickly scrambled away, tearing off her blindfold and diving for the pistol she had left on the grass near her towel. She grabbed the gun, spun around, and, with a shaking hand, aimed it at the man curled on the ground with one hand to his mouth, the other between his legs.

It was Tony.

"Tony! What in God's name were you doing?"

Tony weakly flapped a hand her, taking deep, gulping breaths, unable to answer. When he swallowed, the taste was salty, metallic.

Perplexed, Jessie kept her gun leveled at his chest. Although she realized she didn't really know him at all, she never would have thought this of him. She waited, one toe tapping a rapid staccato beat on the ground. Finally she could stand it no longer. Hurt or not, he was going to have to explain himself.

"Well? I distinctly remember you saying you never forced yourself on unwilling women. Decide to try something new, did you?"

"Damn it, Jess, what the hell did you do that for?" His injured tongue slurred the words.

"I was trying to protect myself!"

"Damn, that hurts."

"You deserved every bit of it!"

"Honey, I'm not sure any man deserves that. Hell, Jess, I wasn't trying to attack you, for Christ's sake. I just wanted to prove to you it wasn't safe out here alone."

"Not safe for who?"

Tony managed a wan smile. "I knew you wouldn't take my advice—"

"You got that right."

"I know you think you can take care of yourself, Jess, but—"

"I think I just proved that I can."

"Did you have to be so, well, vigorous about it? I'm not sure I'll ever be the same again."

Jessie smiled reluctantly. "Serves you right if I did permanent damage. I probably did the women of the world a favor."

"The women of the world will never forgive you."

Jessie snorted in disbelief.

"Would you please sit down? For some reason it inhibits my sparkling conversational abilities when someone is standing over me with a gun."

Jessie grudgingly sat down next to him, unwilling to give in to his humor when he hadn't apologized to her satisfaction. She braced her arms behind her and stretched out her legs, crossing them at her ankles. Tony finally unrolled and sat up, looking at her intently.

His voice was low, his usual amusement absent. "Jessie, I am sorry. I probably shouldn't have tried that particular method of instruction, but I couldn't think of any other way to make you realize you can't go wandering off by yourself. Just because you were able to protect yourself from me doesn't mean you will always be able to do so. After all, I didn't really want to hurt you. Others wouldn't have the same restraint. When Ginnie told me you were alone I kept imagining the most terrible things."

"You were worried about me?" she asked softly. It had been so long since someone had tried to protect her.

"Yes."

She dropped her gaze to the small river, unwilling to let him see her confusion. There seemed to be some unknown force pulling her to him, leaving her wishing for things that could never be.

The stream was clear, as brown as a fawn's coat, speeding up as it swept around the bend. The sun glimmered off its surface, sending a multitude of sparks dancing over the tiny ripples. Jessie plucked absently at the long, emerald grass which grew along the banks.

She was so beautiful. He admired the clean curve of her jaw and the impish tilt of her nose. Her sable lashes, tipped with gold, had lowered, hiding her eyes, but his memory filled in the details; they were blue-gray, like a thin veil of high clouds drawn across the summer sky. There were glints of red fire in her shiny golden hair, hinting at the fire in her personality.

Her laughter, her caring, and her anger she shared freely. Her pain she kept buried. He sensed it was there, but she schooled it in tightly. She was unwilling to talk about her past, but then again, so was he.

Jessamyn raised her eyes to find Tony still staring at her. "Is there a smudge on my face?"

"No."

"Then why are you staring?"

"I'm counting your freckles."

"I do not have freckles," she returned, wrinkling her nose and self-consciously rubbing a forefinger across its bridge.

"Mmm-hmm. Eleven." Tony tapped the tip of her nose lightly before he rose to his feet and extended a hand toward her. "I think I've recovered enough to walk back. Ready to go?"

He pulled her up in one swift motion. If either of them noticed that he held her hand a few moments longer than necessary before releasing it, neither one commented.

6

Tony strolled back to his wagon, whistling. He had just performed his evening ablutions, and his jet hair was still dripping, his shirt thrown over his bare shoulder. It was early to turn in—the sun was just beginning to set in a fireball of mingled carmine, fuchsia, and tangerine colors—but he had drawn early morning watch, and he planned on snatching a few extra hours of sleep.

Besides, if he was lucky, he'd be asleep before Jessie came to bed. He'd been unable to block this afternoon from his mind as completely as he would have liked. While he had worked, currying his horse and oiling his saddle, recollections kept returning, unbidden, of how she had felt in his arms, how soft her lips were, how warm her breasts were, pressed against his chest. He would come out of his reverie with a start to find his hands had gone still in their labors and his work only marginally advanced from the last time his thoughts had drifted. He knew he wouldn't be able to sleep tonight if she was lying beside him, close enough to touch if he made the slightest movement. His body would betray him. He prided himself on his self-control, but it wasn't *that* good.

Tony hoisted himself into the wagon, ready to throw himself onto the welcome bed. A small gap in the front flaps let in just enough light to make out the crates and bundles, boxes and trunks packing the interior. The only clear space was the area where the mattresses lay.

It was occupied. How strange. Jessie never went to bed before the moon was high in the sky, but there she was, curled on her side in a ball, her arms wrapped tightly across her stomach, her eyes shut.

Was she ill? Concerned, he scrambled over the supplies, ignoring the damage to his shins, and dropped to his knees beside her. Placing his palm on her brow, he tested for fever.

Jessie opened one eye. Tony's skin was still slightly damp from his washing, and it looked burnished in the soft light. Jessie thought she should be accustomed to his bare chest by now. Even if she wasn't, feeling as lousy as she did, she shouldn't be worrying about such an inconsequential detail as Tony's penchant for wearing as few clothes as he could get away with. Still, she couldn't seem to stop the automatic acceleration of her heart.

"I don't have a fever." Jessie's voice was soft.

"Sorry, I didn't mean to wake you."

"I wasn't asleep."

"What's the matter, Jess? Do you want me to fetch Harriet?"

Harriet Bolton was as petite as her husband was large, but she was a whirlwind of efficient activity. She had faded red hair which she claimed had gained more gray with the successive births of each of her eight children—children she managed, for the most part, to keep in line because she had more energy than any of them. Since the train lacked a doctor, Harriet was the next best thing. Her healing skills were good enough that few people she treated ever felt a physician could have done any better.

Jessie shook her head, tendrils of hair falling over her pale face. "I just don't feel well. Please go away. I'll be better soon."

Tony didn't go away, but he was perplexed. "If you're sick you should let Harriet take care of you."

"There's nothing she can do."

"I know it can't be something you ate because we had the same supper. You don't feel warm. Is it your head?"

"Yes, that's it. I have a headache."

"Really? Then you should let me get you something for the pain. Although if it's your head, why are you all curled up in a little ball? I would have thought it was your stomach. Oh . . ." his voice trailed off as the light dawned. "I see . . . you have a *headache.*"

Jessie's moan was as much one of embarrassment as pain.

"Oh, God, do we have to talk about this? Can't you just leave me alone?" she mumbled.

"Let me help you, *cara.*" Tony slipped down behind her, curling his body around hers, and began to rub her stomach gently. Jessie weakly tried to push his hand away, but he was insistent, and she was in too much pain to really care.

"What are you doing? I told you, my head hurts."

"Yes, I know. You have a headache." Let her call it a headache if it made her feel better, although he didn't understand her insistence. He figured that after years of going through this every month, women would stop being embarrassed about it. After all, it wasn't as if the continued existence of the human race didn't depend on it. "Now be quiet and let me help you."

"You think you know everything about women, don't you?"

"I have three sisters, remember? They're all rather, ah, vocal when they are disturbed about anything. Believe me, when one of them is hurting, everyone within ten miles probably knows. Besides, my father used to do this for my mother when she had . . . a headache. Are you feeling better now?"

She was, even though she didn't plan on telling him that. The warmth of his large hand seeped through the thin cotton of her nightgown. His rhythmic massage was relaxing her muscles, lessening the tight knot that clenched her abdomen, and his bare torso pressed against her back distracted her from her pain. Unconsciously she wriggled closer to her source of comfort.

Tony clenched his teeth, willing his manhood to behave itself while hoping that Jessie couldn't feel him swelling against her buttocks. Didn't the woman have any idea what she was doing to him? He was pricked by his inability to control his body's reaction. It wasn't as if there was anything he could do about it now, damn it! He tried to think of her as someone who was sick, someone he was performing a kindness for, but he was acutely aware of her body softly curving against his. Frantically he searched for a distracting topic of conversation.

"Jessie?"

"Hmm?"

"Did you realize you let me keep my side of the bed?"

"Oh, well, I decided since most men are right-handed I'd better get used to sleeping on this side. I wouldn't want to handicap the next man I sleep with by making him lie on his proficient hand."

Tony felt a brief flash of anger at the idea of her sharing a bed with another man. "Is that true?"

Jessie giggled. "Actually, I was trying to be considerate. I didn't want you accidently choking yourself to death by having to make any more of those disgusting snorts you tried to pass off as snores."

His rich chuckle joined hers. "When did you figure out I wasn't really asleep?"

"The next night when you looked so smug coming to bed and crawling into your side."

They lay in silence for a while, listening to the night sounds of the prairie—the occasional screech of a hawk, the incessant chirping of crickets, the wind whispering in the long grass. Each of them tried to ignore how good it felt to be curled up together. Jessie had trouble shaking off his mesmerizing closeness, the intimacy of his palm stroking her belly.

"Tony, what are you going to do in California?" she asked, wondering if he would answer her this time.

His hand paused in mid-circle for a moment before it resumed its motion.

"I have to see someone."

Jessie waited for him to elaborate. When he didn't, she prompted, "And then?"

"Then I go back to Kentucky and start my own horse farm."

Surprised, Jessie rolled onto her back, looking up at his face in the deepening twilight. "You don't want to go back to Winchester Meadows? When you speak of it you seem to love it so."

"I do love it," he answered, enjoying the intriguing shadows drifting across the planes of her face. "But I want to build something of my own. I want to be able to look around me and know I've succeeded because of my own talent and work, not simply because I'm Edward Winchester's son."

"Won't your father be upset that you don't want to take over his business? Daddy was furious with J.J. when he wanted to go prospecting instead of studying law and joining his practice."

"Father was a little upset at first, but he made his own way in the world, and I think he understands why I need to do the same. Besides, if he has half as much sense as everybody seems to think he does, he'll let Angelina take over Winchester Meadows."

"Angelina—that's your little sister, right?"

"If there's anybody who has more of a touch with horses than I do it's Angie. She should; she's been following me around since she could toddle. She loves Meadows and wants more than anything to be allowed to run it someday, but she drives our father to distraction. My two older sisters are born flirts and are now married and busily producing grandchildren for him. But Angelina would much rather wear pants and muck around in the stables than dress up and dance with young men. She says she hasn't met an "idiot in breeches," as she terms us, who is nearly as interesting to spend time with as Lancelot."

"Lancelot?"

"He's one of General's colts. I gave him to her for her sixteenth birthday."

"She named him Lancelot? She must have a romantic nature."

Tony laughed. "Angie's the least romantic woman I've ever met. Actually, she said he's the only knight in shining armor she would ever need—except for me, of course."

"Of course." Jessie smiled up at him and pushed aside the thought that Tony was more handsome and intriguing than any knight who had ever populated her childhood dreams. "Actually, the two of you sound much like J.J. and me. I trailed after him continuously when we were young. I made a complete pest of myself; he said I was harder to shake than a flea off a dog. Of course, if anyone else even tried to tease me he instantly became my protector. He claimed he was the only one who had the right to call me obnoxious names, and even if I was a royal pain I was *his* royal pain. When he left I missed him terribly, but now I realize what an annoyance it must have been to David and him to have a gawky child following them around

when they fancied themselves quite the dashing young
men."

Tony frowned. David? He'd never heard her mention that name before. "Who's David?"

"He's J.J.'s best friend, although I've never really
figured out why, since the two of them are nothing
alike. They even went to California together. I used to
have the worst crush on him you could imagine. It
must have embarrassed him terribly, but he's so sweet
I never knew. I positively mooned over him. When
they left, David kissed me good-bye and I didn't wash
my cheek for three days."

"And since he left how many young men have you
fallen in love with?"

"None."

Tony would have preferred that the answer had
been dozens. For some reason he didn't like the idea
of Jessie pining away for years over this David fellow.

"Oh, come now, I find that hard to believe. I'm
sure the boys were falling over each other to get to
you."

"I was sort of a late bloomer. At fifteen, none of the
boys looked at me twice, and then Daddy got sick and
I didn't have time to worry about it."

Tony felt a queer pain in his chest. Fifteen. No
mother, a brother she idolized gone to find his fortune, and she left to take on the responsibilities of an
adult, to run a house, to care for an ailing father, and
to watch him die. He was inexplicably angry that she
had had to deal with so much, so young, so alone.

"Why didn't your brother come back to help when
your father took ill?"

It was a long time before she answered him.

"He never knew. My father was very angry at J.J.
when he first left, and then, later, Daddy didn't want
me to tell him. He wanted J.J. to have his chance, to
not give up his dream and come home just because his
father was sick. Besides, I don't think Daddy ever be-

lieved he was really going to . . . to die. By the time he knew, it was too late. There was no point in writing to J.J. then; he would never have made it back in time. He never knew about the illness until I wrote him about Daddy's death."

Tony searched her blank face in the dim light, feeling all the pain she wasn't showing. At least her brother hadn't done it to her purposely, but her father! What had he been thinking, asking so much of such a young woman? Whatever his reasons, he had asked too much.

"Tell me about your father."

Jessie rolled back to her side, facing away from Tony. She could feel the painful lump clogging the back of her throat, and she swallowed, shutting her eyes tightly. She wouldn't do it, she would not cry over his death. She had done so much weeping during those last, endless months of her father's life, it would have to be enough. She could feel Tony moving even more closely behind her, his hand still gliding in slow, circular patterns on her stomach. Pressing back against him, she accepted the silent comfort he offered and sought to change the subject.

"What does it feel like to be in love?"

What a forthright little thing she was. He found it oddly appealing. He'd always hated it when people asked questions, when they wanted to poke and prod into corners of a person that were best left alone. Yet, he found, he liked her asking, her interest in everything. In him. "Why would you ask me a thing like that?"

Jessie shrugged. "Curiosity. Who knows when I'll get a chance to ask such an expert again?"

He chuckled. "What makes you think I'm such an authority on love?"

Jessie glanced over her shoulder at Tony, her eyes showing her surprise. "Why, you did, of course."

Tony shook his head slowly. "I know next to nothing about love, *cara.* My area of expertise is making love. Do you still want the benefit of my experience?"

"They should be the same thing."

Maybe they should, but he had never thought that they would. Not until lately, that is. He discarded the notion that he had begun to reconsider his views on the subject around the time he had met Jessie.

"I've never been in love, Jessie."

"Never?" She was astonished.

"No. I'm sure I'm quite incapable of it." His voice sounded heavy with regret, or sadness, Jessie wasn't sure which.

"What makes you think that?"

She searched his eyes, black and fathomless in the dim light. It seemed impossible that Tony—handsome, gentle, strong, with charm to spare, who clearly cared very deeply about his family—believed he was unable to love. His voice was low when he finally answered her. "I've known a lot of women, Jessie. Many of them were beautiful, intelligent, everything a man could want, but I've never managed to fall in love with any of them. If I could, it should have happened by now. There was a woman, once, who loved me and deserved to be loved back. I tried. *Dio,* I tried. I couldn't do it. She's . . . I hurt her terribly in the process. I swore I'd never make that mistake again."

"I don't think love is something you can make happen, Tony. It seems that the harder you look for it, the less likely you are to find it. Besides, it probably all worked out for the best in the long run. I'll bet she's happily married with a batch of little kids by now, isn't she?"

Jessie felt his body tense abruptly.

"She's dead." His tone made it perfectly clear the subject was closed.

She tried not to ask, she really did.

"But what happened—"

"Hush." He pulled her closer and resumed the soothing, circular strokes of his hand. "Go to sleep."

Lulled by his closeness, the worst of her pain dissipated, she was able to sleep.

For Tony, haunted by images of the past he was not entirely successful in suppressing, it took longer. Finally, he allowed Jessie's presence—her scent, her gentle heat, her softness—to push away the dark thoughts.

It was a first for each of them. For Jessie, it was the first time she felt the warmth, the utter contentment, of sleeping wrapped in another's arms. For Tony, it was the first time he held a woman all night long after nothing more than a conversation.

7

Jessie carefully dipped a slotted spoon into the pale liquid, fishing out the last bits of butter. Making butter, she decided, was the only chore easier on a wagon train than at home. Since there was no time in the morning to churn, she simply put Wilhelmina's cream in a covered pail, hung it on a hook in the wagon, and let the bumping, jostling, and shaking along the trail do the rest.

Wrapping the collected butter in damp cheesecloth, Jessie patted it into a ball. Since Wilhelmina gave more milk than she and Tony could possibly use, she gave most of it away. It was the way of the trail. Those who had good luck hunting or fishing shared with those who came back empty-handed; and families who brought along chickens traded eggs for the milk produced by other's milch cows.

Jessie picked her way across the crowded camp. The small patch of ground enclosed by the circled wagons was littered with cook-fires, pots, brush piles, and those necessities that were unpacked and repacked nightly. She nearly tripped over Dragon, the tiny black and white dog belonging to the Walker twins, before she reached the wagon of the two clergy-men who were planning to start a new church in the Sacramento Valley.

"Jessie! How is it, little one, that you get prettier every time I see you?"

She smiled at the elderly man who bore the unlikely name of Reverend Parson, hurrying forward to greet her. Although he looked frail, Jedediah Parson's faded brown eyes held a wealth of quiet strength and gentle humor. In the late afternoon sun, his bald pate beamed as brightly as his broad smile.

"We had some extra butter. I thought perhaps you could take it off my hands before it spoils," Jessie said, offering him the cloth-wrapped bundle.

The minister thanked her gratefully and slowly set the package in the shade, his restrained motions be-traying the arthritis he suffered from.

"Are your joints acting up again, Reverend?" Jessie asked. "You shouldn't try to do so much. I would be more than happy to do your wash and cooking when I do ours. In fact, I find it very difficult to prepare meals for only two people. It's no fun at all. I'm only happy if I can cook for a crowd. Won't you please do me a favor and come eat with us?"

"No, child, I feel better when I keep busy. I think it's the Lord's way of telling me to keep going. Now, do you have time to stay and talk for a bit?"

Despite her fondness for the minister, Jessie looked around apprehensively before nodding her assent.

Reverend Parson noted her hesitation and chuck-led. "You don't have to worry, Jessie. Silas went off to read his Bible, and I don't expect him back for some time."

"Then I can stay, provided you let me get the cof-fee."

When Jessie returned with two mugs of hot coffee,

Reverend Parson had creakily lowered himself onto an upturned crate. She seated herself on an empty box nearby.

"Silas is a dedicated man, Jessie. He can't help it if he's a little, ah, overenthusiastic sometimes."

Overbearing was more like it. The Reverend Silas Donner was a spare man with a booming voice and a beaklike nose that seemed perfectly made for looking down, something he did with frequency. Reverend Parson saw only the best in everyone, but Jessie was unable to agree with his opinion of his colleague. She inhaled the fragrant steam rising from her cup and changed the subject.

"The men went out after antelope. I hear they're fairly difficult to bag, but everyone thought we should have something special tonight to celebrate reaching Fort Kearney."

It had taken more than two weeks of steady travel to get this far. Although there were no plans to cross over to the Fort on the south side of the Platte, since supplies were holding up well, the entire party was happy that the first stage of the trip was completed successfully. It would only get more difficult from here.

"If I know that husband of yours, he'll manage to bring home plenty of meat. Tony's a right good shot as well as a fine young man."

Jessie's eyes sparkled mischievously. "I'll tell you a secret. It's not because Tony is such a great shot, it's that horse of his. General is smarter than half the men out hunting, much less the animals they're chasing."

Jessie felt a surge of mingled guilt and inappropriate pride at the minister's praise of Tony. The pride was inappropriate because she had no right to feel any where Tony was concerned; she had no claims on him at all. She felt guilty because, despite the necessity, she was not comfortable deceiving a man of the cloth, especially one who had such clear vision about others that she had great doubts about her continued ability to fool him. His steady gaze was too astute, and she looked away quickly, glancing back along the trail.

There appeared to be a small pile of sticks more than a hundred yards back. Jessie could barely make them out, but she knew what they were: six rough boards hammered clumsily together into three crooked crosses, listing away from the wind, bearing carved words long faded into illegibility.

"Reverend," she asked, her voice low, "do you suppose we'll ever get used to the graves?"

They had started to pass the graves only the second day out of Council Bluffs. Some days there were six or eight; other days the number reached into the dozens. They were crude wooden crosses, rock markers, or just bleached animal bones, each bearing a name, date, and cause of death. Cholera. Gunshot. Dysentery. Snakebite. Fever. And at every river crossing, there were markers testifying to the lives swept away in the relentless rushing water, leaving families with no corpse to mourn and nothing to grieve over but a hastily erected memorial. Even these empty graves were less haunting than the ones that had clearly been disturbed, their sanctity invaded by wild animals or human robbers. To the passing travelers there seemed an endless parade of graves marching west, bearing mute testimony that the journey they embarked on was a difficult one. For some, the price they would pay might be the highest one of all.

When Reverend Parson answered, his voice was deep with empathy. He was staring off into the distance, and Jessie knew he was not seeing the immense muddy Platte or the seemingly infinite fields of verdant grass, but some mental image only he could see. "Yes, child, I am very much afraid we will become inured to the graves. And that, I think, is the saddest thing of all."

A breeze blew a small gray cloud across the sun,

obscuring it and blotting out the friendly rays. Jessie tried to shake off the gloom that seemed to descend.

"The trip has gone exceptionally well so far, don't you think?"

The Reverend chuckled again. "Especially since I didn't think we were going to get across Shell Creek on the second day."

Shell Creek was a small stream just west of Council Bluffs that should have provided no barrier. However, Pawnee Indians charged a toll to cross, and some train members had balked at paying to ford a brook that could be easily traversed without assistance. Walt Morrison and his gold-hungry companions had threatened to leave the train, travel several miles upstream, and cross there, but Buffalo had explained that increasing hordes of overland immigrants had depleted the Pawnees' hunting and fishing grounds, threatening their way of life, and that they were well within their rights to charge a fee for the use of their lands. Finally, the entire train had paid the fifty-cents-per-wagon toll, and the crossing had been made without incident.

"We have certainly been lucky so far," Jessie said. "There has been plenty of fresh water, fuel, and forage, the hunting has been good, and every good-sized river has had a ferry or bridge. I'm beginning to think tales of the difficulty of the California trail are exaggerated."

The old minister shook his head almost imperceptibly. "Jessie, my girl, I wouldn't count on the rest of the trip being this easy."

And that night, the rain began.

Jessie awoke, disoriented, to velvety, impenetrable blackness, unsure of what had awakened her. She was wrapped in Tony's arms, her head pillowed on his shoulder, her body pressed tightly to his side. She had been waking up to find herself in this position disconcertingly often in the last few days. Although she and Tony fell asleep back to back, his warmth was a magnet that seemed unfailingly to draw her close during the night.

She knew she should move away, but she lingered for a moment longer, listening to the thud of his heart and enjoying the powerful feeling of safety that always crept over her when he held her close. Sounds began to penetrate her consciousness: the rhythmic drum of raindrops on the taut oiled canvas overhead and the unmistakable trickling of rivulets of water.

A slight quickening of his breathing warned Jessie that Tony, too, was no longer sleeping. His deep voice rumbled beneath her ear, and she felt as much as heard his words.

"I always loved the sound of rain when I was a child, wrapped snug in my bed. Somehow it's not quite as appealing when you have to contemplate sleeping outside in it."

Holding her wasn't a good idea; he knew he should let her go. But she wasn't moving, and he wanted to keep her in his arms for just a little longer. Separated by the rain from the rest of the world, reality seemed very far away, and he couldn't quite remember why it seemed so important to stay away from her.

"I'm glad I already had watch tonight," he went on. "I certainly wouldn't want to go back outside."

"Mmm." She had to leave his arms; this was completely improper. It was bad enough that she slept this way; she shouldn't stay close when she was awake. But he felt so good. She was glad she had a mattress in the wagon and they didn't have to sleep outside like so many of the others. Jessie sat up suddenly as a thought struck her.

"Tony, Samuel and Susannah sleep under their wagon. They must be getting soaked."

"I'm sure Stuart brought them into the wagon."

"The four of them are going to be awfully crowded."

Tony groaned, resigned. He'd be going out in the rain after all. "I'll go get one of the kids to spend the night here." He groped for the wide-mouthed jar, which held matches, and lit the small lantern hooked on the highest point of the wagon's arched ribs.

An apricot-colored glow filled the small space. Jessie blinked at the sudden, dim light, and watched the interesting shadows playing across Tony's muscular back as he searched for his India rubber poncho. Tugging it from one of his cloth packs, he threw it over his shoulders before slipping out into the night.

What a shame. He looked better without the poncho. Sleepily, Jessie snuggled back into her warm bed. She was glad she didn't have to go outside. Husbands were actually rather useful creatures, on occasion.

Only a brief time passed before Tony returned, carrying Susannah Walker wrapped tightly in his poncho against the driving rain. Jessie handed Tony a linen towel while she unwrapped Susannah and tucked the surprisingly bright-eyed child under the blankets.

Tony tossed the towel back and turned to go outside again. "They're digging trenches around the Bolton tents, trying to get the water to run off away from camp. I'm going back to help. Take care of my little bunny." He blew a kiss at Susannah before the flap closed behind him.

Jessie turned her attention to Susannah. "Aren't you sleepy, punkin?"

The little girl shook her head. "Can I really sleep over with you tonight? I wanna stay up and play games and tell stories and you can teach me to braid hair like you promised and—"

"Whoa, honey!" Jessie laughed at Susannah's excitement. "If this rain keeps up, tomorrow will be tough going, and even if you don't need much rest, I do."

"I know. Mama says you're a muddlehead in the morning."

"Oh, she does, does she?" Jessie reminded herself not to say anything in front of the children she didn't want repeated. "Well, I am."

"Are you sure we can't stay up?"

"Yes, I'm sure."

Susannah screwed up her face in disappointment. "One story? About California?"

"One story," Jessie agreed and gathered the child close. She softly recited the old folk tale of a two-hundred-and-fifty-year-old California resident who was tired of living but had to leave the healthy climate in order to die. When his body was shipped back to California for burial, he came back to life.

Jessie stroked Susannah's hair. The strands were soft and light as they slid through her fingers.

"That's the way it's going to be for us, Suze. We're all going to be happy and healthy, and no one we love is ever going to leave us."

She smiled fondly at the child who struggled but failed to keep her eyes open. Jessie was still smiling when sleep overtook her, too, moments later.

Exhausted, Tony dried himself quickly and slid into bed on the other side of Susannah. Tired as he was, he stayed awake long enough to admire the picture the two of them made. They looked like angels, or maybe an angel and her apprentice. The dim light brought a peachy glow to their smooth skin and illuminated their fine, delicate features.

This was what it would be like if he had a family.

But he already had a family. Maybe not a family of his own, but certainly all the family he was ever going to get. He'd make a lousy husband, anyway.

Just look at what had happened with Liza. He hadn't loved her. He hadn't known how, and he damn sure hadn't learned how since. God knew he'd proven that much.

But he'd been young. Maybe he'd changed since then.

He knew one woman would never be enough for him. After all, it never had been before.

Jessie might be, a nagging voice inside him told him.

Tony stretched to extinguish the lantern. A conscience was a hell of a thing to have when you were trying to get a good night's sleep.

The next day was what Jessie figured hell to be like, if hell was filled with water instead of fire. She decided that fire might be preferable after all.

The gray sky streamed unending torrents of rain. After the travelers downed a cold breakfast the wagon train reluctantly turned westward into the gusting wind, which blew sheets of warm spring rain into their faces. Sodden boots and heavy, wet clothing made each single step more tiring than ten on any other day. On the hills, water collected in the ruts made by the multitudes of wagons that had used this trail before, forming miniature rivers that rushed downward as the travelers struggled to climb up.

Jessie trudged on, sometimes sinking into mud up past her ankles, forcing each step as the earth seemed reluctant to relinquish her feet. She dared not ride in the wagon. Any additional weight increased the chance that it would become imbedded too deeply in muck for the oxen to pull it free.

It was inevitable that some wagons would become bogged down. Oxen strained from the front while people pushed from behind. Women and young children gathered armfuls of long grass to lay on the trail in front of the train, providing better footing for the teams. Occasionally, the wagons were so solidly stuck that an extra yoke or two of oxen had to be hooked up to drag them forward.

Jessie struggled to keep her oxen moving at a steady pace, hoping that constant motion would keep them from becoming mired in the mud. Her team, however, wanted nothing more than to quit for the day. In an effort to prevent that, Jessie found herself becoming increasingly strident, her voice rising until she was fairly screeching.

"Stupid, idiotic cows. Beauregard, you get your as . . . *rear* moving or I'll turn it into rump roast! Can't you see I don't like this anymore than you do?" Jessie cracked her whip over the oxen's heads when they tried to pause before plodding up a small hill. "Shi . . . oot! Giddap now!"

Jessie heard Tony's muffled laughter as he walked up to her. "Lecturing the cattle again, are you, *mia poco incendio?* You should take lessons from Harriet; her language is a bit more emphatic."

Through the sheets of water dripping off her poncho hood, Jessie peered at Tony. What a sight he made! The rain slicked down the thick black waves of his hair, emphasizing the strong bones of his face. Long ago he had given up his battle against getting wet and stripped off his poncho and shirt, leaving only his tight black breeches, so unlike the baggy panta-loons favored by the other men. She supposed it was indecent of him to run around half-naked, but he looked so glorious, who cared? The water made his muscular, tanned torso look sleek and oiled. Admiring him, she felt a strange tingle through her body. How odd!

"What does that mean, that *poco* thing you call me?" Jessie asked, trying to keep her gaze above his neck.

"It means 'my little fire.' Your eyes are blue fire, your hair gold fire, and your temper, well . . ."

"A temper? Me?" Jessie's face was the image of injured innocence before she ruined it by breaking out in laughter. "If I'm a fire, I'm a thoroughly doused one right now. Why don't you ever seem to get angry?"

It was true; throughout the day, while the other men were shouting loud enough to be heard back in Iowa, their faces turning the color of ripe August tomatoes, the only signs of agitation Tony ever showed were the two vertical lines that sometimes appeared between his eyebrows.

"What good would it do? At our house, between my mother and my sisters, there wasn't much room for anybody else to have a temper. Someone blowing up is an hourly occurrence at home. It wouldn't attract much attention."

"Don't you ever get so furious you just can't hold it in anymore?"

His brows drew together as he stared off into the distance. "I've been really angry a few times. Doesn't seem that yelling does much good to fix it, though."

"It makes you feel better. Sort of cleans out the emotional system, you know, so you can start over fresh."

"Maybe." His face grew stony. "I think I'd rather put my energy into fixing whatever upset me in the first place."

Jessie wondered what things made him angry, what things he had to work so hard to fix. It seemed that there was so much about him she didn't know, and so many things she wanted to know, but she knew it wouldn't do any good to ask. If he didn't want to tell her something, she wasn't going to find out. She'd learned that much about him so far. Flicking her whip above her team's heads, she tried to urge them forward.

"So, you don't think my language is strong enough

to get these stupid animals moving, huh? My father drilled it into me when I was younger that I was most definitely not to use the words I kept learning from my brother. I guess it's a hard habit to break." She pondered her lack of vocabulary for a moment. "I know! You can teach me to swear in Italian."

"What?" Tony looked into her eyes. They were gray today, like a reflection of the stormy sky, but they were shining with mischief.

"Please, Tony, I know I could swear in Italian without feeling guilty."

"Why would you want to?"

She forced her face into serious lines. "It would be ever so cleansing for my emotional system."

"I think your emotional system gets cleansed regularly enough—usually on me."

"You have to be good for something." She smiled beguilingly, looking up at him through her lashes.

When had she learned that flirtatious look? Tony wondered. Wherever it came from, he found he couldn't resist it. He searched his limited vocabulary for a relatively harmless word and wished he'd paid more attention when his mother had tried to teach him Italian. "All right. How about *merda*?"

"Merda." Jessie rolled the word experimentally off her tongue. *"Merda.* I like it. What does it mean?"

"It means . . . ah, how should I put this? Manure."

Jessie waved her black whip in the air and shouted triumphantly, "Let's go, you idiotic, *merda* cows!"

Tony rolled his eyes. There was no hope for the woman. "I'm going up front to see if anyone needs help. I'll be back in an hour to spell you."

Jessie watched him saunter away, enjoying the way the wet cloth clung to his buttocks. She supposed it was most improper of her to watch his body as much as she did, but it was rather like enjoying one of nature's wonders, wasn't it? If people could admire a beautiful flower or gorgeous landscape, why couldn't she do the same with Tony? He certainly was one of the more interesting sights she'd ever seen.

Unfortunately, she wasn't the only one who thought so. Jessie bristled as Delia Bolton, Tom's daughter, grabbed Tony's arm to stop him as he passed. Delia was seventeen, redheaded like all the Bolton children, with a round, childish, freckled face and an anything-but-childish bosom. As far as Jessie was concerned, Delia had one major flaw: she practically drooled every time Tony got within twenty feet of her.

Delia didn't even have the sense to leave another woman's husband alone, Jessie fumed, before remembering that Tony was, in fact, unwed. Double *merda*!

When the train finally halted for the evening, it had taken them all day to cover the ground they usually traveled in one hour. Determined to prepare a hot supper for her brood, Harriet Bolton stood over her cook-fire with an umbrella for nearly two hours.

An hour later, the rain stopped.

8

Slowly, relentlessly, the wagons moved west. May passed and then the beginning of June. The abundant emerald grass began to fade to a lusterless greenish tan. There was no more wood to burn as fuel, so the travelers turned to the dried buffalo chips littering the plain. Women and children carried baskets as they walked along, collecting as they went. It took at least three basketfuls to cook a meal.

They passed the landmark Chimney Rock, a massive mound of red-brown clay topped with a spear that thrust skyward like a monstrous, accusing finger pointed toward heaven. Its towering spire, across the river on the south side, was in view for more than a day.

The travelers supplemented their diet with wild lamb's tongue and berries, grouse, an occasional antelope, and catfish from prairie streams. Of buffalo, the animal they wanted most to find, there were none.

In the evenings, women mended and gossiped while the men played rousing games of euchre or old sledge. Sometimes they gathered around the flickering flames of the camp fires and, accompanied by guitar and harmonica, sang "Home, Sweet Home," "The Girl I Left Behind Me," or, Tony's favorite, "My Old Kentucky Home." Unfailingly, they ended with the anthem of all overlanders:

"Come along, come along, don't be alarmed; Uncle Sam is rich enough to give us all a farm."

One day Tony took Jessie and the Walker twins to explore a prairie-dog town. There were hundreds of small mounds stretching over the plains. The small animals sat on their hind legs just outside their burrows, eyeing the strange intruders and then quickly turning tail and disappearing down the nearest hole if one of the humans ventured too close. The children laughed over the antics of the burrowing owls, which lived interspersed with the prairie dogs in abandoned burrows. These small, sand-colored birds with disproportionately long, thin legs bobbed up and down like corks on a wavy lake, emitting cackling alarm calls if startled.

For Jessie, only two things disturbed the pleasant rhythm of these endless, satisfying days.

One was Walt Morrison. It seemed that every time she turned around he was there, watching her, his pale eyes glittering as his tongue repeatedly flicked out to wet his thin lips. His bony frame with its incongruously round belly reminded her of a snake after it had just gorged itself on its monthly meal. Since he never made an improper move toward her—in fact, he rarely spoke to her—Jessie could not explain why his presence made her so uneasy.

The other blot on her days—and nights—was Tony, or rather, her growing feelings for him. She found herself looking for him eagerly during the day, just as she had awaited her father's return from work as a small child. Increasingly, she thought of him as her Tony, and the rush of jealously she felt every time he spoke to Delia Bolton confirmed that. Her long-cherished image of David Marin was rapidly fading, replaced by Tony's rugged, handsome face. Warmth swept through her every time he called her *cara* in the deep, resonant voice he seemed to reserve for her alone. Her besotted bride act was becoming only too real.

Unfortunately, she had no reason to believe that Tony felt anything for her. He turned his lazy charm on every woman in the train. He was an inveterate ladies' man for whom flirting was as instinctive as breathing. She tried to discount her feelings as only natural. Tony was a handsome, compelling, blatantly sexual man, and any woman who was forced to spend as much time with him as she was would likely fall under his spell. It was simply that she had never met a man like him before. Caring for her father had left little time for a social life, and the enforced proximity of the wagon train was exacerbating the problem.

It would be better when she reached San Francisco, she told herself. Undoubtedly she would meet lots of men as intriguing as Tony. Why, then, was the end of the trip beginning to sound decidedly unappealing?

Tony bent under the wagon, squatting down to brush the wheels with grease, carefully checking for signs of wear on the rig. The last thing he wanted was for something to break at a crucial moment on a steep hill. Damn! There was a crack in the front axle. He would have to unpack half the wagon to get at the spare. He shoved the brush in the grease pail and hooked it on its place at the back of the wagon between the two rear wheels.

It was hot and he was sweating by the time he had unloaded enough supplies to allow him to pry up the false floor of the wagon. The extra parts were in the storage space underneath. He pawed through a collection of seldom-used tools, winter clothing, and surplus ammunition. Where were the axles? Ah, there they were. He moved a box of leather straps and pieces and a heavy folio tied securely with twine, tossing them out of his way to the ground.

Having retrieved the part he needed, he slumped down against the rough wood side of the wagon and mopped his damp forehead with his forearm. The weather was beginning to heat up, and he was glad they would be climbing to higher altitudes before the peak of summer really hit.

The folio lay on the grass where he had dropped it. He wondered what was in it. Jessie had told him very clearly at the beginning of their agreement what things of hers were private and off-limits, and she had never mentioned this. Curious, and willing to use any excuse to postpone returning to his labors, Tony opened the folio.

After wiping his dirty fingers on his shirt, he removed the thick sheaf of papers inside. He sifted through them, holding them carefully by the edges. Any lingering doubts he had about nosing in Jessie's things soon evaporated; he was too captivated by what he found to worry about the appropriateness of his actions.

There were dozens of drawings; pastel sketches of a stormy Lake Michigan and a large brick house with glorious, tangled, colorful gardens; pencil studies of hands, eyes, and a large, sleepy cat. Tony was stunned. The pictures were magnificent and full of life, charm, and humor. On the bottom of each, there was a flowing signature: *Jessamyn.* She had never given him a hint that she had such an extraordinary talent. He could not remember her so much as picking up a pencil since they met.

Near the bottom of the stack were portraits. There were several pictures of a stunningly handsome young man with golden hair and deep blue eyes, anything but typical, stilted portraits. In one he was standing in the rain, soaking wet and laughing. In another he was sprawled across a thoroughly mussed bed, sleeping peacefully. In a third he was angry, both fists upraised, his rage emanating from the paper.

Was he her brother? Tony wondered. Why hadn't she told him she could do this? Why didn't she draw now? They'd passed lots of things that would have made intriguing pictures. He wouldn't have thought any artist could resist trying to capture just a bit of the land they'd traveled.

Next was a single sketch of a lovely, ethereal young woman in old-fashioned clothes and a dated hairstyle. Her pure, fragile bones reminded him of Jessie. Perhaps it was her mother, copied from an old daguerreotype.

Second to last was a full-length portrait of a large, imposing man with a full beard and piercing eyes. He wore a dignified, tailored suit, his hand in the pocket with a large, gold watch fob. The picture glowed with love. It had to be her father.

Tony flipped to the last drawing and stared at it for a long time while his grin faded. It was her father again, but he was barely recognizable. There was no color, and the stark black lines depicted a shrunken shell of a man lying listlessly in an oversized bed. His eyes were dull and his cheekbones stuck out prominently. Looking at the picture, Tony could almost smell the sickroom, an odor of pain, wasted bodies, and lost hopes.

Oh, Jessie! What had it cost her to watch him die, day by day? Carefully replacing her work in the folio and retying the string, Tony's chest constricted, and his heart ached for what she must have suffered.

*　　*　　*

That night Tony returned late from watch duty, expecting to find Jessie in bed. Instead, she was curled into a ball, seated on the front bench of the wagon, her arms wrapped around her knees, her face lifted to the night sky. Tony swung up beside her.

"I know you're a creature of the night, *cara*, but isn't this a little late even for you? You're going to pay for it in the morning. I'll have to make sure Beau is kept far from Wilhelmina or you'll injure his male pride again."

Jessie remained still, gazing up. "I don't like the prairie during the day. It's too empty, too desolate, too lonely. But at night . . . Tony, at night it's like thousands of candles are lit just for me, scattered across an endless bolt of black velvet. It makes me feel like I'm part of it all."

Tony barely glanced at the stunning night sky. He was more entranced by the view right next to him. The moonlight was bright enough to enable him to see Jessie's delicate profile clearly. Her eyes shone silver in the light, and her hair was loose, tumbling in soft, heavy waves down her back. She was as lovely and unique as the art she had created.

Would she be annoyed with him if she knew he had found her work? Suddenly, he wouldn't really mind if she was. It seemed more important to find out why she wasn't working now.

"Jessie." She started at his voice. Although soft, it held a note she had never heard before and couldn't identify. "Jessie . . . I found your drawings."

She didn't move. "They're not important. I don't draw anymore."

"Why not? They're beautiful, spectacular. I don't even know how to tell you how good they are."

A small glimmer sparked in her eyes. "You really liked them?"

"I loved them. You have such a gift. How can you just stop?"

It took her a long time to answer. "I just can't do it anymore. There's nothing left . . . inside me. Nothing left for art, anyway."

"I saw the . . ." He cleared his throat, unsure how to broach the subject. He had never lost anyone he loved, and he could scarcely imagine how it had hurt her. But he believed she couldn't continue to keep it all inside, letting the pain fester until it ate away her soul. "I saw the one of your father. Was that the last picture you did, Jessie? Was that the reason you quit?"

Tears begin to trace silent silver paths down her cheeks. She didn't sob, didn't attempt to brush the tears away, didn't even seem aware that she was crying. She just stared, unblinking, at the blanket of stars overhead. Finally she whispered, so softly that he could barely hear, "I just can't talk about this."

He grasped her upper arms and turned her, forcing her to face him. "You have to talk about it, don't you see? You have to let it out. Tell me about your father, Jessie. Tell me about your father."

"I can't," she repeated, her voice hoarse.

"Yes, you can. It's just me. Talk to me, Jessie. You can tell me about your dad. What was he like?"

Once she began to speak it was as if a dam broke. The words came out, tumbling over one another, as fast as Jessie could talk. "I told you I never knew my mother. After J.J. left, it was just Daddy and me. He was a great, big bear of a man, and could he roar! He had such . . . *presence.* He commanded every room he was in. When he was in court, it was like he dared the jury to find his client guilty. I thought he was invincible."

She paused, struggling for control. "Then he got sick. Oh, Tony . . . do you know what it's like to see that, to hurt inside, knowing there isn't anything you can do that will make it any better? The consumption . . . it was like it rotted him from the inside out, leaving nothing but a weak, empty body and a bloody handkerchief. And the coughing—God, sometimes I thought he was going to force his lungs out his throat. He was gone long before he actually died, and there was nothing left . . ."

She lurched toward Tony, and he enfolded her tightly in his arms. He knew no words that would help, so he held her close, smoothing the heavy silk of her hair, his throat aching, hoping that somehow his strength would flow into her and comfort her.

Her voice was raw, broken. "Goddammit, Daddy, why did *you* have to leave me too?" She wept against his chest, her tears dampening it, soaking through the thin fabric of his shirt. He didn't notice. They sat there for a long time, all the emotions she had held in for so long escaping in a rush.

When she finally quieted, he imprisoned her head in his large hands and tipped her face up to look at him. With his thumbs he wiped the last remnants of tears off her cheeks. "It's time to let it go, Jessie. You know that."

Their gazes locked, and Jessie forgot everything but the mesmerizing black eyes above her. She could feel him breathing as soft, warm puffs of air reached her skin. He dropped one hand, sliding the other to the side of her neck, lightly resting four fingers there while his thumb traced the curve of her jaw from ear to chin. Slowly, he moved his thumb down the curve of her neck to the hollow of her throat where he paused to rub it gently.

He barely touched her, like the brush of a butterfly wing, but she could feel it, piercingly acute, as if each nerve in her neck had become exquisitely sensitive and was waiting, reaching out for his touch.

He lowered his head, brushing his mouth softly against hers, once, twice, then slipping his tongue out to lingeringly trace the delicate curve of her lips before he reluctantly lifted his head. He didn't want to stop, but he knew he had to do it now or he wouldn't be able to stop at all.

Jessie sat frozen, stunned. How could such a small kiss—barely a kiss at all—have unleashed such a torrent of feelings? The sensations tumbled through her body like a mountain stream swollen from the spring thaw.

Tony rose to go into the wagon, but he paused, holding the canvas flap in one hand. As if he needed to touch her just once more, he stroked his forefinger lightly down her profile, tracing a warm line from her forehead to her chin, pausing just the slightest moment on her lips. Some of her shock must have shown on her face, for a rueful smile dented his left cheek.

"Don't look so stricken, Jess. It was just a kiss."

But it wasn't just a kiss, and as Jessie sat, wrapped in the welcoming, magical darkness, she knew it.

It was a beginning.

9

It was supper time. Tony settled back comfortably upon the folded blanket padding the wagon wheel he leaned against. One long, muscular leg was stretched out before him, the other propped up. He spooned another large bite of dessert into his mouth and let the flavors slide over his tongue. Jessie had cooked up a sauce of dried strawberries, sweetened and spiced with just a hint of cinnamon. The rich, ruby-colored sauce was poured over snowy, freshly cooked dumplings and slicked with a splash of Wilhelmina's heavy cream. It was delicious. If Tony's original intention had been to find himself a cook, he figured he had done mighty well. So why did food seem unimportant compared to the sheer pleasure of having Jessie around?

He let his gaze drift over camp. The air smelled of fresh grass being cropped by grazing animals, roasting meat, and cook-fires. The buffalo-chip fires did not have the same wonderful tang as wood smoke, but the slight odor was not offensive.

Women bustled around, scouring pots or starting preparations for the morning's breakfast. Men lazed in clumps of two or three, dissecting the day's events while smoking pipes and hand-rolled cigarettes. Even the children were slightly subdued, tired from the day's exertions. They played with the few homemade toys they had been able to bring along, raced about in disorganized games of tag, and generally got in their mothers' ways as much as possible.

It many ways it was little different from an evening at home. Tony marveled at how, in a month on the trail, this motley collection of humans had melded into a community. They were like a tiny village, each person occupying a niche, contributing his or her own skills and quirks. Like any other group, there were some people he liked and some he didn't. His gaze found Jessie delivering to the two clergyman the extra dessert she had "mistakenly" made. She laughed with Reverend Parson over some jest, the old man's face lit with pleasure and the love he obviously felt for Jessie. There was one person, Tony mused, who he liked far too much.

After their kiss, he had stayed away from her as much as possible. It was becoming clear his control was not as strong as he'd always believed, and he wasn't taking any chances on something getting away from them before they could stop and think.

But he couldn't help remembering how her lips felt under his; fresh, clean, sweet, the kind of lips he'd long ago given up his right to. And he couldn't help but wonder what she thought of him now. On the surface she treated him the same as always, but she never seemed to quite meet his eyes, and he wondered if she'd dismissed it so easily.

A low rumble intruded on his thoughts. Thunder? He searched the sky for clouds; there were only a few unthreatening wisps gliding across the sky, washed with the rose-gold color of approaching dusk. He pushed himself to his feet, feeling an almost imperceptible tremor through the soles of his boots.

It seemed to be coming from the north. Over the rim of a small ridge he saw a dark, ragged cloud of dust, as if agitated by some isolated but powerful wind.

The sound intensified. Throughout the camp, one by one, heads lifted. The ground began to tremble, faintly and then with increasing vigor. There was uncertainty, fear, and finally a dawning understanding.

Buffalo!

People began to run, at first hesitantly, then, as caution and restraint were overtaken by anticipation, with increasing excitement. A few men had enough presence of mind to grab their rifles before joining their families, all heading for the hump of land some two hundred yards north of camp. Young men pelted hell-for-leather, mothers were slowed by the children grasping their hands, fathers shouldered toddlers, and the elderly straggled behind, struggling in an attempt to override their ancient legs. But they all stopped, awestruck, as they reached the top of the rise and beheld the panorama spread out on the plains.

There were bison filling the otherwise empty reaches of land to the horizon, a seething, churning, overwhelming mass of the majestic animals, thundering east as if chased by some unseen force. Each member of the party felt the exhilaration of the moment. It was impossible not to feel alive, touched by, and a part of the wonder that was nature, vast and untamed.

For a brief, suspended instant of time, no one thought of shooting one of the magnificent beasts. But the travelers needed meat, and so, with an abrupt crack of his gun, Buffalo Bolton felled one of his namesakes. Tony, to the west of the main party, shouldered his rifle and picked out a young bull. He squeezed the trigger and watched, wondering if perhaps he had missed after all, as the buffalo continued to run. Its front legs abruptly buckled, and it fell heavily to the ground. The herd parted and ran, unchecked, around the body. Tony was sighting another target when he suddenly froze.

Was that a scream he heard? It was difficult to hear anything above the stampeding buffalo. His ears strained. He swept his gaze around, searching, and saw Mary Ellen Walker, awkward in her advancing pregnancy, laboring up the hill. Her eyes were wide and terrified, and she was waving her arms frantically, motioning northwest.

It was Samuel. He lay on his side on the ground, both small hands wrapped around his right ankle. Tears streamed down his dirt-streaked face, but his eyes never left the huge bull not more than twenty feet away.

The massive animal was separated from the rest of the herd. His thick, shaggy, deep brown coat was dusted with the gray dirt stirred up by the rampaging animals. The outsized hump behind his large head marked him as a dominant male. He was pawing at the ground, tossing his head while keeping a wild eye upon the small creature curled on the ground before him, apparently trying to decide if Samuel constituted a threat.

Tony cursed and set off at a dead run, dropping his empty, now useless rifle. He hadn't thought to grab any extra ammunition before he ran out of camp and, in any case, he doubted he had time to reload. It took him only seconds to reach the little boy's side. Sam had tripped in a buffalo path, the foot-deep trail that generations of buffalo had worn down in traveling to their water supply.

The boy was sobbing, frightened, as Tony bent to lift him. Sam wrapped both arms tightly around his neck. "Tony! I just wanted to see the buffaloes, but I fell an' my ankle hurts an' I couldn't get up or nothin'.

An' you know what, Tony? I don't think that big one likes me."

Tony tried to loosen the arms that were threatening to cut off his air supply. "Easy, there, short stuff. You're darn near strangling me. Everything's going to be O.K. now." Slowly, with his gaze never wavering from the animal, Tony began to back away.

Until the buffalo decided to charge.

He swiftly placed Samuel on the ground behind him. Then he unsheathed the bowie knife strapped to his thigh. His heart was pounding as heavily as the hoofs of the approaching buffalo, his fingers reflexively loosening and tightening on the handle of his knife, but his eyes never left the animal bearing down on him like a runaway locomotive.

Tony waited until the buffalo was nearly upon him and then, in a motion as clean and sharp as his blade, reached out and slashed him across the muzzle. The buffalo swerved abruptly, shaking his head violently as if he could rid his nose of some painful enemy riding it. Tony kept his gaze steady, feeling droplets of sweat trickle down his temples, wondering what the hell he should do if it decided to attack again, and praying that it wouldn't. Finally, with a toss of his mammoth head, the bewildered animal lumbered off to rejoin his herd, leaving a bloody trail in the dust.

Relieved, breathing heavily, Tony dropped to the ground beside Samuel and gathered him tightly to him. It was only when a thankful, weeping Mary Ellen arrived to hug her son and he released Sam did Tony realize he was still clutching the blood-covered knife. He tossed it aside, wiping his dark-red-stained fingers on his pants.

"Mama, Mama, did you see it? It was the giganticest buffalo I ever sawed and it was gonna get me but Tony saved me. He cut it with his knife and it ran off like a scared puppy and, oh Mama, wasn't it great?"

Tony laughed weakly and flopped backward,

throwing a forearm over his eyes. He was scared to death, his heart still felt as if it were going to burst, and the kid thought it was great?

Mary Ellen gave her son one last squeeze before giving him a much-deserved scolding. "Samuel Stuart Walker, I love you and I'm very glad you are all right, but if you *ever* disobey and run away from me like that again, you will not be alive to see your fifth birthday, and it won't be because a buffalo got you, you hear me?"

"Yes, Mama," Samuel said, momentarily chastened. Then, under his breath, he added, "But I still think it was great."

Tony removed his arm to glare at Sam. "Now listen here, short stuff. It wasn't great. You scared your mom, and you scared me. You could have been badly hurt, and how would those of us who love you feel? For that matter, how would you have felt if I'd gotten hurt trying to help you?" Tony knew his lecture would have more impact if he delivered it standing up, but he couldn't quite drag himself to his feet. Somehow it wouldn't be as impressive if his legs collapsed underneath him.

Sam was incredulous, having never heard Tony speak to him in that tone of voice before. "No dumb old animal coulda hurt you, Tony."

"That big bull could have snapped me in two like I was a dry twig."

Sam's big blue eyes began to shimmer with welling moisture. "I don' want ya to get hurt, Tony." His lower lip quivered. "Are ya really mad at me, Tony? Ain't ya my friend anymore?"

As all his nieces and nephews could attest to, Tony was a sucker for a child's tears.

"Ah, no, Sam, of course I am. I didn't mean to yell at you. It's just, your mom and dad give you rules, not to spoil your fun, but because there are lots of dangerous things out here if you're just a kid, or even a grown-up if he's not prepared. So promise me, you'll listen to your parents. I don't want to end up battling a bear next time."

"A bear? Ooh, I'd love to see a bear!" A red-faced, panting Stuart, with Susannah slung on his bony hip, had arrived just in time to catch the end of the conversation, and Susannah was clearly entranced. "Do you really think we could find a bear, Tony?"

Feeling beleaguered, Tony moaned. "Stuart, could you please explain to your daughter that under no circumstances am I going to find her a bear?"

"Be glad to." Stuart lowered Susannah to the ground. "Right after I thank you. I was clear the other side of the hill with Susannah. If you hadn't been here . . ." Stuart stopped, his voice breaking.

Tony gave a careless wave. "Was nothin'."

"It was everything. If there is ever anything I can do for you . . . well, you know the rest." He surveyed Tony, still sprawled on the ground, and smiled. "Could you use a hand up?"

"No, thanks. I think I'll just lay here until I'm fully recovered. A year or two should be about right."

"Tony?"

Jessie dropped to her knees beside him, and he turned his head to look at her. The sun behind her lightened her hair, falling loosely from its bedraggled knot, to a halo of gold.

"Tony, I . . ." The words stuck in her throat. She wanted to tell him how wonderful she thought he had been, how brave, but she couldn't seem to get past the stark terror that had seized her when she saw the buffalo pounding toward him. Her mind kept conjuring images of him being crushed to a pulp beneath its hooves.

Suddenly it didn't seem to matter anymore that he'd ignored her ever since the night he'd kissed her. Nothing seemed to matter, except that he was safe. She groped for his hand and gripped it in both of her smaller ones, pressing them tightly to her chest, silently thanking God.

When the stampede was over, the party had killed three buffalo. They roasted large haunches of meat for supper, feasting lavishly before bedtime and storing the rest for cold lunches. The next morning they fried huge steaks for breakfast but still barely dented the bulk of the meat harvested from the huge beasts. They could not afford to stop for the two days it would take to preserve the meat, but they were unwilling to waste so much food. Instead, the men cut long, thin strips of meat and the women hung them from strings running along the sides of the wagon tops. When the travelers left the next morning, all the wagons looked like they were decorated with buckskin fringes. The sun did the rest of the work, and within two days they had a generous supply of dried, jerked buffalo.

10

The last wisps of an early morning fog were just beginning to burn off. The sun slipped in and out of clouds, and patchy, dark shadows danced over the long brown grass.

Feeling energetic in the refreshingly cool morning, Tony sprang to his feet from the spot on the damp grass where he'd been savoring the last bites of his breakfast. Rolling his coffee mug between his palms, he wandered around the camp fire to the crate where Jessie half sat, half slumped.

Her head sagged to her chest. A tender breeze lifted the loose tendrils of her red-gold hair, waving them around her face. He couldn't help smiling; despite the delicate snores issuing from her mouth, she looked as gentle and soft as the shifting fog.

He bent to her ear. "Jesssieee," he called softly.

"Hmm?" Her eyelids cracked open slightly. "Is it time to get up already?"

"You are up, *cara.* In a manner of speaking, anyway."

"Oh?" She arched her back, circling her head loosely on her neck.

"Do you want me to pack up the cookware? Maybe I should whip up a batch of biscuits for lunch first?"

She sat bolt upright, wide awake at last. "Don't you go near my kitchen, Tony Winchester!"

Laughing, he looked at the packed earth, dying fire, and haphazard arrangement of boxes and barrels.

"I haven't seen a kitchen since we left Council Bluffs."

"It's enough of a kitchen so you should be kept far, far away."

"Jessie," he said in an injured tone, "one would think you didn't like my cooking."

"I love your cooking. It's eating it I can't handle." Taking his cup, she backhanded the few remaining swallows of coffee to the ground. "I'd better get this put away. Is it time to go already?"

Buffalo Bolton swung around the corner of the wagon. "It's time, all right. 'Cept we won't be goin' anywhere just yet. A wheel on the preachers' wagon snapped a spoke as it was pullin' in line this mornin'. Gonna take a couple of hours ta fix it."

"Need any help?" Tony was already turning for his box of tools.

"Naw. Me 'n my boys'll take care of it. Just stopped by ta tell ya we ain't leavin' yet, an' if you decide to spend the time huntin', bag a coupla rabbits for us, would ya?"

"Buffalo, we have pounds and pounds of jerked meat and you want me to go shoot some scrawny little rabbits?"

Buffalo stroked his beard. "If we keep eating that jerky I'm not gonna have any teeth left by the time we git to California. Damn stuff keeps gettin' stuck." He ran his tongue over his teeth as if he could still feel strands of meat embedded there. His expression grew solemn. "Best we use fresh meat while we can an' save the dried stuff for when we need it."

Tony slung an empty game sack over one shoulder and a bag of spare ammunition over the other. He bent to Jessie, whose eyes were drifting shut again.

"Do you mind if I go hunting? Or do you have something here you're planning to do that you need me to help with?"

She leaned toward him, her hair falling over her flushed face, and whispered, "I'm planning on regarding this morning as an unexpected gift from above, and I'm putting it to the best possible use. I'm going back to bed."

He grinned. "I don't suppose you'd like my help with that, huh?"

She crooked her finger at him, bringing him closer until his face was inches from hers. "No."

He gave an exaggerated sigh. "I didn't think so. You're a wicked woman, you know, raising a man's hopes like that only to stomp them into the ground."

He kissed her hard, quick, and easily, as if it were his right, as if it were an ordinary event, leaving Jessie, surprised, blinking after his disappearing figure.

With his rifle resting loosely in the crook of his elbow, its barrel pointing at the ground, Tony strolled along with the small hunting party. Away from the river, the vegetation had thinned, and the spindly grass was interspersed with patches of bare ground and low clumps of scrub bushes. Despite the apparent barrenness, the land supported plenty of grouse, jack-rabbits, and other game.

He had picked up Stuart and Andrew on the way out of camp, knowing that the three of them could bag enough game to fill everyone's stewpots for one day. They had chosen to leave their horses behind for a

change, concentrating on small game, and Tony anticipated a long, tranquil hike.

At the last minute Walt Morrison asked if he could
join them. Tony had been reluctant; he was looking
forward to relaxing with his friends, and he wasn't
sure he liked Morrison. But Tony let Walt come along
because he had been raised on Kentucky manners, and
he couldn't put his finger on exactly what it was about
Morrison that rubbed him the wrong way.

Now he knew.

Tony kicked at a small clump of dirt, watching it
break into a shower of brown dust as it struck a bedraggled stand of grass, startling a cloud of bugs up
out of the vegetation. He wondered if he could somehow urge the insects in Morrison's direction. Maybe
they would get him to shut up.

He was getting damn tired of listening to Walt
claim his prowess with his gun and with women. Walt
obviously thought the only way to prove his manhood
was the number of animals he killed and women he
screwed.

Morrison wasn't actually a half-bad shot. Unfortunately, he fired at everything that moved. He had
picked off three or four prairie dogs, shouting gleefully as he watched the tiny bodies tumble over, before
Tony rather forcefully suggested that Walt not shoot
anything he didn't plan on eating.

Walt had gone into a sullen silence, like a little boy
whose favorite toy had been taken away.

Unfortunately, it hadn't lasted long.

Tony was secretly satisfied that his game bag had
three more animals than Walt's, but darned if he was
going to start telling him about his conquests, even if
he'd love to wipe that arrogant grin off Morrison's
face.

He glanced at Andrew, who was walking beside
him shaking his head in disgust, and Stuart, who was

ignoring Walt, studiously searching the brush he passed.

Tony closed his ears to Walt, concentrating on the landscape. One or two more rabbits, and he could go home. Home to Jessie.

There he went again, thinking about her. He had to stop it; he knew he had no business in her life. No good business, anyway. But he couldn't seem to help it; it felt so damn right when he touched her, when she touched him.

His head snapped up. Who the hell was Morrison talking about now?

". . . yes, she was a mighty tasty piece. Nicest tits I ever saw. Now, then, that Delia Bolton has ones almost as nice. Can't wait to get me some of that."

Tony gave Walt an even look, one filled with a quiet warning, that Walt was too obtuse to notice.

"I'd keep my hands off Delia Bolton if I were you."

Walt was painfully aware of all the longing looks Delia threw Tony's way. She followed him around like a starving puppy waiting for the crumbs from his table. Why couldn't she ever look at him like that? Winchester already had a woman of his own, a woman Walt would dearly love to get a shot at. Why'd Tony have to get all the other ones so stirred up they wouldn't even look at the other men?

Walt puffed out his chest.

"Yeah? Who's gonna make me? You?"

Tony bent down to pick up a long blade of grass and place it between his lips. "I won't have to." He chewed the stalk meditatively and squinted against the glaring sun. "Buffalo will break you in half if you so much as lay a finger on his daughter."

"He ain't never gonna find out. I'll keep her so happy she'll keep quiet just ta keep gettin' it."

Tony cocked an eyebrow. "Think so?"

Smirking, Walt reached down and readjusted his

crotch. "Oh, yeah, I got plenty ta keep any woman moanin' an' wigglin' all night."

Tossing the stalk of grass over his shoulder, Tony smiled with false joviality. "Let me tell you a secret." His smile disappeared and his eyes turned black and icy. "Whatever you've got doesn't do any good if you don't know how to use it."

Walt's courage was bolstered by pride and anger. "An' I suppose you do?"

Tony's satisfied grin was all the answer anyone needed.

"Wish somebody'd tell me how to use it," Andrew mumbled under his breath.

"Problems, Andy?"

Andrew's face bleached white, then flooded with hot color. "I didn't mean for you to hear me."

"I have excellent senses."

Andrew shook his head violently, his pale hair flying in all directions. "I didn't mean . . . it's just . . ." He screwed up his face and expelled a great mouthful of air. "If I could just get Ginnie to stop talkin' the entire time maybe . . ."

Tony threw his arm around Andrew's shoulders and bent to whisper in his ear. His explanation was long and punctuated occasionally with undecipherable hand gestures. Andrew's mouth dropped open.

"Noooooo," Andrew said. "I couldn't."

"Yes."

Stuart watched the proceedings with amusement. "Newlyweds," he muttered.

Walt clenched his fists, longing to unleash them on Tony, but he wasn't fool enough to attempt it while the bastard was surrounded by his friends. Damn Winchester thought he knew everything about everything. Well, they'd just have to see about that.

"Hey, Winchester," he called. "Better worry about your own woman first. That's a right nice piece of tail you got there."

Tony's voice was perfectly controlled, and perfectly deadly. "I better not have heard you right, Morrison."

Walt leered. "Oh, you heard me fine."

"Jessie's not anybody's piece of anything, Morrison. She's my wife."

"Still . . ." Walt shrugged. "Man's gotta take advantage of opportunities as they arise . . ."

Tony deliberately lifted his rifle to his shoulder and fired.

He strolled over to where Walt was cowering on the ground with his arms wrapped over his head.

"Jackrabbit."

With studied nonchalance, Tony scooped up the carcass resting not more than three feet behind Walt and deposited it in his game bag.

"I'd say we have enough meat, wouldn't you, fellas?" he asked.

Andrew and Stuart struggled to keep their amusement under wraps. Andrew, not trusting himself to speak, merely nodded his agreement.

Stuart clapped Tony on the back. "Mighty fine shot there, Tony."

"Thank you." He checked the loading of his rifle. "What do you say we go home to our wives?"

The three walked several yards before Tony paused and turned to Walt who, whitefaced with shock, was slowly rising from the ground, clearly not quite sure he was still in one piece.

"Well? Are you coming? It's really not terribly . . . safe out here alone. Wouldn't want you to stumble into an unfortunate . . . accident." Tony's expression made it perfectly clear he'd like nothing better. Not waiting for an answer, he spun on his heel and left.

Through the red haze of anger clouding his vision, Walt watched Tony saunter away. Damn superior bastard. Walt's hands shook with the temptation to pick up his weapon and fire at his swaggering back. Only the possibility that one of Winchester's friends would shoot back before he'd have a chance to down them all kept him from doing it.

Patience, patience, he told himself. He'd get him someday. Just you wait, Winchester. Someday.

11

Jessie spilled the basin of dirty wash water on the ground and watched the parched earth suck it up in seconds. Lord, they could use some rain.

But not too much! she thought, glancing skyward. Just a nice, soft, gentle shower. He didn't have to drown them again.

She walked slowly toward her wagon, thinking how nice it was to have a morning when she didn't have to rush to get going. Tony wasn't back from his hunting trip with Andrew and Stuart yet, despite her nap and the leisurely pace at which she had performed her chores. The breakfast dishes were washed, lunch was started, she had washed out her underthings, and she still had free time. What luxury!

Passing the Wrightman wagon, she thought she heard a soft sob. Was somebody crying?

It couldn't be Ginnie; she was relentlessly cheerful. But who else would be in their wagon?

Jessie knew how to mind her own business, but

Ginnie was her friend, and she knew Andrew was off with Tony. What if someone was ill?

She set her pan on the ground and squared her shoulders. She'd just peek in, and if she wasn't needed she'd skedaddle away.

Brushing aside one of the end flaps, she peered in. The Wrightmans' wagon was larger than hers, but who could tell? It was stuffed with crates of china, bundles of delicately embroidered linen, bolts of cloth, several tools that Jessie could only assume were some sort of farm implements, and a massive oak headboard and matching chest of drawers. She wondered how Ginnie and Andrew managed to find a corner to sleep in.

She heard the muffled sobs again. Boosting herself into the wagon, she crawled over the chests and barrels toward the source of the noise.

It was Ginnie after all. The mattress was spread on top of a platform of crates, and Ginnie was on it, curled up tight into a ball, although whether from choice or necessity Jessie couldn't tell, for more supplies crowded the bed from all directions, leaving only a tiny section of the bed bare.

"Ginnie?"

Her only answer was a renewed torrent of louder wails.

Climbing over the chest of drawers to the bed, Jessie felt as if she were creeping into a cave, for the shirts and pots that hung from the overhead hooks only cleared the mattress by a couple of feet.

Not by nearly enough, apparently, Jessie thought, banging her temple against a heavy kettle, setting off a clanging reaction among the cookware that momentarily drowned out Ginnie's cries.

Jessie winced at the noise and collapsed on the bed. "How does Andrew ever get in here?"

Evidently that was the wrong thing to say, for Ginnie's weeping increased markedly in intensity.

"Ginnie? Is something wrong with Andrew?"

Ginnie shook her head, the brown curls bobbing wildly.

"Are you ill, then? I could go get Harriet—"

"Noooooo! It's worse than that!" Ginnie wailed.

Worse than being sick? Jessie lay a hand on Ginnie's shoulders. What if something was seriously wrong? "Ginnie, I . . . is there anything I could do for you? Please . . . I'd really like to help."

Ginnie lifted her head from her arms. Her face was red and blotchy, her eyes puffy, and tears still streamed down her cheeks.

"I'm not pregnant!"

"Is that all?"

"All?" Ginnie screeched, tears pouring anew from her big eyes, making them look like melted chocolate.

Obviously this was a greater disaster than Jessie realized. She would have considered it a blessing. Who wanted to be pregnant out in the middle of nowhere?

Jessie tried again. "Ginnie, I'm sure you and Andrew will have lots of babies."

"But we've already been married two and half months!"

"Gee, as long as all that. I had no idea."

Ginnie gave a snort of laughter through her tears that nearly choked her. "Don't you dare laugh at me, Jessamyn Winchester."

"I wouldn't dream of it. Not when you're in the midst of a disaster of epic proportions," Jessie said, her face sober but her eyes dancing.

Lifting the hem of her dress, Ginnie dabbed at her cheeks, smiling wryly. "Oh, all right, maybe I did overreact . . . just a bit, mind you. Only . . . I want to give him a child so badly."

"You will."

"Think so?" Ginnie sniffed. "Doesn't it bother you? I mean, you're not expectin' already, are you?"

"Are you out of your . . ." Realizing what she was

about to say, Jessie bit her tongue just in time. "Well
. . . no."

"Are you sure?"

"Damn right, I'm sure!"

Ginnie jumped at Jessie's outburst. "Well, you
don't have to be so snappish about it. I, of all people,
certainly understand how you feel."

"I'm not snappish!" Jessie took a deep breath to
calm herself. "We're not trying . . . exactly. Tony
. . . well, he thought it'd be better to wait until we
get settled."

Ginnie gave an empathetic sob. "I understand how
upset you must be about that. But at least you know
it's not . . . oh, Jessie . . . it's . . . it's my fault, I
know it. I think we just don't . . . don't *do* it often
enough to make a baby. Maybe he doesn't want me
enough."

"Ginnie, Andrew loves you. I can see it every time
he looks at you."

"You think so?" Ginnie flipped up onto her knees,
a hint of eagerness lighting her eyes. "How often do
you and Tony do it?"

Jessie resisted the urge to cover her hot cheeks with
her hands. Somehow she was going to have to bluff
her way through this.

"Ummm . . . pretty often."

"How often is that? 'Cause Andy 'n me, we don't
do it more'n once a week or so. I thought at first it was
'cause we were stayin' with his folks, but now . . .
well, there's no reason not to, 'n we still don't."

Jessie fussily tucked a few strands of hair back into
the knot at the base of her neck. "I'm sure he's just
tired after working all day."

"Tired, humph. What's tired got to do with it when
we're trying to make a baby? He's got enough energy
to complain about my talkin', says I distract him too
much."

"You even talk then?"

Ginnie looked concerned. "Don't you?"

Jessie crinkled her nose, trying to imagine it. Did people talk when they were . . . ? How was she supposed to know? "Not . . . always."

"It's not as if it lasts all that long, anyway."

"If it doesn't last that long, maybe you could be quiet?"

Ginnie's eyes grew watery. "You think I should shut up, too?"

"Ah . . . if it bothers him, maybe you should try it his way."

"See, I knew it was my fault!" She started sobbing again, her shoulders shaking violently.

Jessie patted Ginnie on the back. "Listen to me, Ginnie. Stop that and listen. My mother and father were married for three years before they had J.J. I'm sure it's not anybody's fault. It's simply the stress of you just getting married, then packing up, and now the trip. As soon as you get to the coast and get settled in, I'm sure you'll be expecting in no time."

Ginnie's tears stopped. "Are you sure, Jessie?"

Jessie mentally begged God for his tolerance of her lies. "Of course I'm sure. I'm a married woman, aren't I?"

Ginnie glanced up from her mending as Andrew entered, wiggling his solid form through the small opening.

"Oh, Andrew, I'm so glad you're back. I've got so much to tell you about. I spent the afternoon with Jessie, and I feel so much better. Before I was really upset because . . . how was the hunting? I was feeling bad because we haven't—"

"The hunting was good. Interesting. Informative," he broke in. He was staring at her oddly, and Ginnie wondered if something had happened while he'd been gone.

"Informative? How can hunting be informative? Did you find a new kind of animal or something? Now, what did you get? I waited to plan supper 'til you got home, because I'd knew you'd bring some fresh meat, and . . ."

Andrew watched her babble on, saw her delectable little red mouth move and her brown eyes shine happily. She sure was pretty. Sometimes he had a hard time believing she was really his, all that bubbly energy. It still astonished him that he had the right to touch her soft, curvy, generous body. He always got excited just at the thought.

But he'd always worried it wasn't the same for her. That he was too fast, or too rough, or too strong, or too . . . something. It had gotten so he was almost afraid to touch her. He didn't want to bother her, didn't want to be too demanding. He knew he was lucky just to have her at all.

All those things Tony had told him today . . . Andrew wasn't sure he could ever do some of them. But others, well, they sounded pretty interesting. Now if he could just work up the guts to try them . . .

There was no time like the present. He was a determined man. If there was a way to make his wife happy, Andrew Wrightman was going to find it.

He reached for a cloth, dunked it in the small bucket of water hanging over his head on a hook, and began to scrub the trail dirt from his skin.

"Andrew, I'm sorry, honey. Here I've been chattering on about my day and you haven't had a chance to get a word in edgewise. I've been promising myself I'm going to be a better listener. It's just all these words keep piling up inside me and sometimes I swear it's like I'm gonna burst if I don't get them out. Andrew . . . what are you doing?"

"I'm taking off my clothes, Ginnie," he said calmly, steadily unbuttoning his shirt.

"Oh. But, Andrew, it's still daylight. It suppose you

got dirty out hunting, but, honey, you know I don't mind. You don't have to gussy yourself up for me. We're not courting anymore. Still, if you really want to . . ."

Ginnie looked down at the ripped shirt in her lap and tried to concentrate on her stitches. She couldn't help it, her gaze kept sneaking up to Andrew. His shirt was gone, and now he was stripping off his boots and socks.

She wasn't used to seeing him undress in daylight. Nighttime was kind of dark and romantic, but you really couldn't see much.

The canvas top of the wagon wasn't thick enough to block out light completely. Inside, the light was diffuse, mellow, homey. The air was still and warm, and suddenly very difficult to get into her lungs.

He was taking off his britches now. Andrew wasn't tall, but he was sturdy and broad and solid. She liked that about him. He didn't look like a man who would blow over in a stiff wind like some of those skinny fellas. He looked like a man you could lean on.

Finally naked, Andrew glanced up to find her watching him. She averted her gaze quickly.

"Uh, Andrew, don't you think maybe you should put some clothes back on? You might catch a chill, or something, or . . ."

Andrew flushed brick red, then a look of dogged determination spread over his face.

"I'm not cold. Don't you like the way I look?"

"Well, uh, yeah, I . . ." She couldn't think of anything to say, for the first time in her entire life.

He dropped to his knees next to her. He was very close. Their wagon was very small. She should have known they needed more room.

He picked up her mending and set on top of her heirloom dresser shoved against one wall.

"What are you doing? I was working on that."

"I like the way you look."

He reached for the top button on her blue gingham dress and slipped it through its hole.

"Andrew!"

He undid another one.

"Andrew!"

He lifted his gaze and met her uncertain one. His pale blue eyes were light, intent, resolute.

"Let me, Ginnie."

"Oh, Andrew," she cried, "are we going to make a baby?"

"Nope," he said, returning to his task.

"We're not?" Her shoulders drooped in disappointment.

"Nope. We're leavin' the babymakin' up to the Lord. From now on, it's his department. What we're doing, Virginia Wrightman, is makin' love."

"But, Andrew, what if we can't—"

"Hush." And he shut her up the only way he could —with a kiss.

It was quiet in the Wrightman wagon for a very long time. It was only later, much later, that Ginnie softly said, "Oh, Andrew."

And, not much later, a surprised: "Again, Andrew?"

"Again, Ginnie."

12

Jessie thought she had never been so happy to see any place as she was to set eyes on Fort Laramie. As June aged, the heat had increased to unbearable levels, baking the lush green prairie grass brittle and dry. The movement of the train stirred up clouds of choking dust. Women pinched the wings of their sunbonnets shut, and men tied dampened bandanas around their lower faces. Still, everyone coughed continuously in an attempt to clear their lungs. Coughing conjured up too many unpleasant memories for Jessie, memories of her father and the months before his death, and so the days become an endless trial. The continual daily grind shortened everyone's temper as people were forced to spend day after day in close proximity, and minor quirks became more and more annoying.

Finally, they reached Fort Laramie. There they would rest, restock, gaze on the first new faces they had seen in far too long, and, most importantly, celebrate the completion of the first sizable stage of their journey. They had covered over six hundred miles, nearly a third of the distance to California.

They took the soldiers' ferry—a dollar a wagon—across to the south side of the Platte. Tom Bolton scornfully claimed the river to be "a mile wide, a foot deep, too thick to drink and too thin to plow."

The Fort consisted of a motley collection of some two dozen buildings, all surrounded by an adobe wall. Some of the buildings were stone, some tumbledown brick. A few, like Old Bedlam, the bachelor officers' quarters, were built of wood. Old Bedlam itself was a large, two-story building, painted spanking white with trim black shutters and porches that ran the full length of both floors.

Surrounding the Fort, a large tribe of Sioux Indians were camped. A young lieutenant, resplendent in his brass-buttoned, dark blue uniform, informed Jessie that the Sioux spent every summer there, trading with the passing travelers.

Jessie eagerly took advantage of the opportunity to replace depleted supplies. She had used up all her eggs weeks ago, so she bought several dozen, burying them deeply in the flour barrel to protect them from breakage as the wagon bounced over the trail.

There was going to be a party that night in honor of arriving at the Fort. Excited at the prospect of some fun after all the hard work, Jessie quickly made up several dried apple pies, her contribution to the feast. She scurried around, rolling the dough on the flat wooden seat of the wagon, filling the crusts with sweetened, spiced fruit, pinching the pies into half-moon shapes, and frying them in hot fat.

Slipping up slowly behind her, Tony grinned at the picture she made, flitting around like a nervous hummingbird. Several strands of red-gold hair had escaped from her topknot and drifted down around her neck and temples. The knot itself had slid askew and settled over her left ear. Her golden brown dress was dusted with flour, reminding him of the confectioner's sugar coating on his mother's fresh doughnuts. She looked just as delicious.

"Did you get any flour in the dough or is it all on you?"

She whirled to find him close—too close—behind her. One hand flew to the mess of her hair, the other to smooth her skirt before she realized it was hopeless and let her arms fall to her sides. What was she primping for, anyway? He had seen her at less than her best after a long day of travel, and he surely would again. She had more important things to think about than what Tony thought of her looks.

He, on the other hand, looked splendid. His pristine white cotton shirt set off the deep tan of his face and the darkness of his black hair, including the whorls of dark hair peeking out of the unbuttoned neck of his shirt. He was smiling widely, his eyes gleaming with barely suppressed excitement, and both hands were hidden behind his back. He was definitely up to something.

"What are you hiding, Tony?" she asked, suspicious.

"Oh, I don't know. Perhaps a present."

"A present? For who?" Her curiosity piqued, she rose on her toes, craning her neck to try to peek behind him.

"Uh-uh. Not so fast, my little snoop." Tony took a couple of quick steps backward. "It's for a certain lovely young woman of my acquaintance."

Miffed, Jessie folded her arms across her chest. "Oh? And who might that be?" There was no way she was going to let him give presents to other women. It was not that she was jealous, oh, no, of course not. It was just that it would be embarrassing if it appeared her husband was giving gifts to females like that obvious little—well, all right, not so little—Delia Bolton.

Tony suppressed a chuckle. Why, she was jealous!

For some reason, the thought pleased him very much. And she looked adorable with her lower lip thrust out, all rose-pink and puffy.

"Actually, it's for you." He thrust toward her a bulky, medium-sized package wrapped in plain brown paper and tied clumsily with twine.

"For me?" She touched her chest briefly, just over her heart, before reaching out trembling hands to take the bundle. Her fingers seemed unable to work the ties free until Tony, impatient, sliced the strings with one swift sweep of his knife.

Jessie tore off the paper and uncovered a pair of moccasins. Her fingers caressed the soft, fine, cara-mel-colored suede while she admired the intricate beading. Tiny, jewel-toned beads were worked into complex floral and geometric patterns, looking like miniature rubies, sapphires, and emeralds.

"Tony, they're so beautiful."

"I hope they fit."

"Let's find out." She plopped unceremoniously on the ground, jerked off her sturdy black boots, tugged on the moccasins, and laced them up quickly before jumping to her feet again.

"They fit perfectly! And they feel wonderful! But why did you get them for me?"

He shrugged. "I saw them in the Sioux camp and liked them. I know your feet sometimes hurt after walking all day in your boots, and the Indian who made them was amenable to a trade."

It was only a small part of the truth. In fact, he wanted in some small way to make up for the empti-ness the past few years of her life must have been. Why it mattered to him so much was something he didn't dwell on. She deserved some joy, some frivolity, and he intended to see that she got it.

"But what did you trade for them? You didn't have much along."

"Didn't anyone ever tell you it's not polite to ask

the price of a gift?'' He tapped the tip of her nose with his long, brown forefinger. "If you must know, I let General cover one of the Sioux's mares."

Jessie could feel herself flushing. Why was the mere thought of mating causing her embarrassment? She wasn't usually so squeamish, and they were talking about horses, not people, for pity's sake.

"Tony, it's too much. General is such a valuable stallion, his usual fee must be—"

Tony cut her off with a quick wave of his hand. "Not another word, Jessie, or I'll think you're not grateful. General hasn't been getting any . . . ah . . . exercise on this trip anyway." Much like his owner, Tony thought with more than a little regret. "Now, tell me the truth. Do you like them?"

She looked up, gray mists swirling in the blue depths of her eyes, before throwing her arms around him and hugging him tightly. "They're absolutely beautiful, Tony, and I love them. It's been so long since anyone's given me a present, I . . . I don't know how to thank you."

Tony wrapped his arms around her slender waist, resting a cheek on her soft hair, and closed his eyes, steeling himself against a physical reaction to her nearness. Don't get excited, Tony, he told himself. It was only a hug of gratitude.

It was too late. He was already excited. Fully, completely, and royally excited. So aroused that it hurt. It had been too long since he'd had a woman.

But the hitch was, he didn't want a woman, any woman. He wanted *this* woman.

And he couldn't have her.

He cleared his throat, placed his hands on her upper arms, and pushed her away.

"I guess we'd better get ready for the party. I'm going to wash up." He walked away, slowly and awkwardly. He hoped to God that the creek was cold.

Very cold.

*   *   *

Jessie pulled the brush one last time through the length of her hair and then returned it to one of the many small pockets sewn to the inside of the wagon cover to hold various personal items. Just for tonight, she decided, she was going to wear her hair down. She pulled the tresses at her crown straight back from her face and tied them with a peach ribbon that matched her dress. It was her best dress, the one she had packed carefully away in Chicago and never expected to have a chance to wear until she reached San Francisco. It had a full skirt, tied snugly at her waist with a wide sash, and broad bands of cobwebby, hand-crocheted ivory lace around the hem, neckline, and cuffs. It was far too fancy for trail wear, but tonight . . . tonight there was something special in the air.

"Pssst, Jessie. Are you ready yet?"

Jessie poked her head out through the flaps. "Ginnie? Is that you?"

Ginnie grabbed Jessie by one wrist, hauled her out of the wagon, and dragged her around the back where Mary Ellen was waiting.

"What's going on?" Jessie asked.

"Shhhh." Ginnie clapped a hand over Jessie's mouth before continuing in a whisper. "We have to be quiet. If Andrew finds out I'll never hear the end of it."

Jessie nodded and pulled Ginnie's hand away from her face. "Give over, Ginnie. What are you plotting?"

Mary Ellen passed out three tin mugs while Ginnie produced a small earthenware jug from her voluminous skirts. She uncorked the jug and filled each cup with amber liquid.

Jessie sniffed her cup. "Ginnie, what *is* this?"

"It's my mother's secret recipe for peach brandy. Made her famous back home. Go on, taste it."

Jessie cast her a dubious glance. "I'm not used to spirits, Ginnie. I'm not at all sure I should."

"Oh, fiddle. The men will be swilling corn whiskey all night. We have every right to have a little fun, too. Besides, it's fate. It's peach brandy. It matches your dress."

"Mary Ellen, are you in on this, too?"

The calm, sensible, reserved Mary Ellen giggled. "Absolutely. Look at me, swelled up like an October pumpkin." She patted her belly affectionately. "I have to grab my opportunities for fun while I can."

"All right, here we go." Jessie held her cup at arms length, and her two companions clinked it with their own mugs. "To California."

"To California," Mary Ellen and Ginnie chorused.

Jessie took a tentative sip of her drink. The liquid felt warm going down, tasting slightly spicy, slightly sweet. She took a larger gulp. A glow started in her belly, heating her from the inside out. It was an odd sensation. Odd, but nice. Yes, definitely nice.

The unmistakable sound of a fiddle tuning up floated over the camp, calling them.

"Drink up, ladies," Ginnie cried. "Tonight, we dance!"

Jessie drained her cup. They hid their mugs and the jug behind the wagon's wheel. Clasping hands like children, the three ran toward the celebration.

And dance Jessie did. Flying from arm to arm, she felt young and free, as she hadn't felt in nearly four years. She danced with Tony, with Stuart and Andrew, with the gold miners, the blacksmith, a couple of Indiana farmers, a handsome young officer from the Fort, and with Tony again. She dragged Reverend Parson out for a waltz and giggled helplessly when he kicked up his heels to "Turkey in the Straw." She even tried to cheer up Reverend Donner by inviting him out for a turn.

"It's a lovely evening, isn't it, Reverend Donner?" Jessie ventured, at a loss for a topic to discuss with the intimidating clergyman.

"Disgraceful, if you ask me. All this frivolity when there is so much wickedness in the world."

"I don't think the Lord would begrudge us a little joy and celebration over the success of our trip thus far."

He sniffed and looked down his long nose with an air of disdain. "Mrs. Winchester, is it possible you have been indulging in alcoholic beverages?"

Oh, Lord. She should have known that honker of his would pick up the slightest scent. "Well, I may have had just a sip. Merely to be polite, of course. To join in the celebration."

"Shameful!" the Reverend Silas Donner pronounced, disapproval oozing from every pore.

Jessie gave up her attempts to brighten his disposition. The minister was clearly beyond hope. She didn't utter another word the remainder of the dance.

After the fiasco of her dance with Reverend Donner, Jessie decided she was in need of fortification and slipped to the back of her wagon. She knelt down to forage behind the wheel and pulled out the jug and a cup.

"Might as well pull out the other two cups too, dearie." Jessie jumped at the unexpected voice behind her, crashing her head into the wooden underside of the wagon.

"Ouch!" She cradled her head in both hands and then looked up to find Mary Ellen and Ginnie sinking to the ground, holding their sides in convulsive laughter.

"You weren't planning to sneak all the brandy for yourself, were you Jessie? Didn't your parents ever teach you to share?" Ginnie managed to get out between giggles.

"Fine friends you two are. I'm in extreme pain, and you think it's hilarious," Jessie said while retrieving the jug of brandy and refilling all three cups.

The liquor soon worked its magic, however, and her head began to feel better. It felt just fine, in fact, although her lips felt slightly numb and her cheeks began to tingle.

Mary Ellen's and Ginnie's mirth proved contagious. Jessie found herself swept up in their gaiety and soon had them both helpless with laughter, tears streaming down their faces while she gave a credible imitation of Reverend Donner's stiff-necked dancing style, complete with nasal snorts in time with the music.

"Stop, Jessie, stop. I'm laughin' so hard it hurts," Ginnie forced out, clutching her stomach. "Besides, I have to ask you a very serious question."

"A very serious question? You?" Mary Ellen and Jessie struggled valiantly to compose their faces into sober lines, but one look at each other and they both dissolved into peals of giggles.

"Come now, you two. This is important to me." Ginnie drew herself up and smoothed her burgundy cotton gown. "Oh, Lord, how do I say this? I'm not sure I have the words."

"Out with it, Ginnie. When have you ever not had the words for anything?" Mary Ellen prodded.

Jessie was curious. Ginnie had been acting strangely lately. The morning after finding her crying in her wagon, Jessie had gone to check on Ginnie and found her with a vacant grin on her face. Her vague and very brief answer to Jessie's concerned question was uninformative, and since then Ginnie had been uncharacteristically quiet and inattentive, wandering around in a dreamy-eyed daze.

"Jessie . . . um . . . do you really like it when Tony kisses you . . . you know . . . *there*?"

"Where?"

"Ahh . . . you know." Amazingly, the unflappable Ginnie appeared embarrassed. Finally, she managed to spew out the words. "Between your legs."

"What!" Jessie bit her tongue in a fruitless effort to keep from blushing as red as a slice of ripe watermelon. "I know you're boshing me now, Ginnie. Whatever possessed you to ask me a thing like that?"

"Jessie, I know perfectly well Andrew picked up the notion from Tony. Now he wants to try it, and, much as I loved all the other things, there's no way I'm letting him try *that* experiment on me before I asked you what it was like."

Jessie stared at Ginnie, her mouth agape. People didn't actually do that, did they? She'd never heard of such a thing in her life, but she couldn't very well tell Ginnie that, could she?

"Actually," Mary Ellen put in, "it's really quite wonderful."

"You?" Jessie and Ginnie choked out together, shocked.

Mary Ellen nodded before all three of them lost control and fell back against the ground, shrieking in helpless laughter.

Jessie was weak by the time she returned to the dance and her head was spinning. How wonderful it felt to have fun, to be free of responsibilities. How long had it been since she had had friends she felt free to be silly with? How long had it been since she had felt this exuberant, this carefree? Too long.

"May I have this dance?" Tony's voice was deep, sending a thrill through her that reached clear to her toes.

As they moved into the group of dancers, Jessie was aware that, although they must have danced a half-dozen times already tonight, this dance was different.

This time, she was unable to concentrate on anything but Tony's mouth. Her conversation with Ginnie and Mary Ellen swirled through her head. She kept conjuring up images of him touching her . . . *there,* with his lips and his tongue. She was fascinated by his white teeth as he smiled and glimpses of his tongue as he talked. She knew he was speaking to her, but she couldn't seem to grasp the words.

Tony wondered what was the matter with Jessie. Oh, she was dancing with him, rhythmically moving in his embrace, but she wouldn't look him in the eye, and she didn't seem to be paying attention to anything he was saying. For some reason she kept staring at his mouth. Maybe there was a remnant of supper stuck on his teeth. He ran his tongue over them quickly to check.

Jessie was mesmerized as his tongue glided over his teeth, leaving them wet and gleaming. She opened her mouth to take in breath and stumbled against Tony when her knees suddenly gave out.

"Oops. Easy there," Tony said, tightening his arms quickly to keep her upright. "Are you sure you're feeling all right?"

"Hmm? Oh . . . I feel wonderful."

She didn't look like she felt wonderful. She looked like she'd had a little too much to drink. She'd been having so much fun trying to sneak around he hadn't said anything to her, but he'd kept a close eye on her. He didn't really think she'd had that much, but maybe it had affected her more than he'd thought.

He racked his brain, trying to remember if he had done something that could have possibly offended her, but nothing occurred to him. He gave up and decided to simply enjoy the view instead.

She was a melange of autumn colors. Her delicate cheeks bloomed with rose, her hair glowed red-gold, her dress was a soft peach, all gilded with the apricot rays of the setting sun.

"You look beautiful tonight."

"Do I?" she murmured.

Tony grasped her chin and tilted her head up, forcing her to look him in the eye.

"Yes," he said. "You do."

Jessie forgot to breathe. There was a disturbing intensity in those dark eyes, gleaming like chips of polished onyx. He was looking at her as if there were no other women in the world for him, and she was strongly tempted to pretend that it was true. Ginnie and Mary Ellen had given her glimpses of the physical side of a relationship, and Jessie was beginning to wonder what she was missing. It was all she could do not to press her body as tightly against him as she could.

"Jessie?" His voice was low, intimate.

"Hmm?"

"The music's stopped."

"Oh!" Flustered, Jessie stepped back, fluttering her hands in the air before resting them on her flaming cheeks. "I . . . I need to go fix my hair." She whirled and flew toward her wagon as if there were coyotes nipping at her heels, fleeing Tony and the feelings he aroused in her.

13

"*I've been looking* for you, handsome."

Tony glanced at the woman approaching him. "Hello, Delia," he said absently before again fixing his gaze on his wagon. The night was close and dark around him, and Jessie was still in there. What the hell had he done this time? It was tough to fix things when you didn't know what was wrong.

He ran his hand through his hair. Should he go after her or not? He didn't like making decisions without all the information. It seemed like people tended to make even more stupid mistakes that way. But his patience was getting a little frayed around the edges.

Delia wasn't used to being ignored, not by men, at any rate. But Tony never seemed to notice anybody else when that flat-chested little twit of a wife of his was around.

O.K., maybe she wasn't completely flat chested, but she sure didn't have what Delia had, and Delia pushed her assets a bit farther forward.

Delia understood about men and women. She was

a farm girl, after all, and her mother and father were a bit more blunt than most of her friends' parents. Delia had gone along many times when her mother had delivered babies.

But that was nothing compared to what she'd learned when she'd met Matt McConnelly. He was the wildest man in three counties, and the most handsome. Delia had taken one look at him and decided he had to be hers, and he hadn't had too work too hard to sweet talk her into doing something she knew her father wouldn't approve of.

Delia had thought she'd had it all arranged properly when her father caught them in the barn with her dress loosened. Matt would have to marry her then. But Matt had skipped town before the preacher had arrived, and Delia knew half the reason the Bolton family was going to California now was to get her out of town, too.

She didn't really mind. With Matt the rat gone, there was no reason to stay. Besides, there were all kinds of men in California, rich miners. She'd forget all about Matt.

What she couldn't seem to forget was the way he made her feel. She'd almost given up hope that any man would ever make her feel that way again—until she'd laid eyes on Tony Winchester.

She sighed in longing. Tony had caused her no end of trouble, making her chase him around, pretending like he wasn't interested, all the while grinning at her with that smile that would make any woman weak at the knees.

It was annoying as hell, but he was going to be worth it. She could feel it. And she'd make him happy, too, she knew. Matt had taught her well.

Oh, she knew Tony was married. If her Daddy found out, she'd get whupped but good for breaking one of the commandments. But Delia figured if God meant people to keep the one about adultery, He would have made enough men like Tony to go around.

As it was, his wife was just gonna have to learn to share.

He was still staring at that stupid wagon. Snuggling up against him, she twirled a fingertip in the dark curl of hair exposed by the neck of his shirt, gaining his attention at last.

"You don't want to be doing that, Delia."

She smiled up at him coyly. "You got that right, sugar. I wanna be doing a whole lot more."

He captured her hand and took a step back. "It's not that I'm not flattered, Delia. It's just, I respect your father too much too hurt his little girl."

She leaned forward, squeezing the sides of her breasts with her arms, making sure her cleavage was well displayed. "I'm plenty grown-up, Tony."

Damn, she didn't give up easily. He had an innate distaste for insulting women. When you got right down to it, turning them down was always insulting, and he tried to do it as gently as possible. But he was getting tired of being diplomatic with this one; she just wasn't giving up. He didn't relish the idea of her hanging on him the rest of the trip, but he couldn't bring himself to tell her flat-out that she didn't appeal to him.

It sure wasn't doing any good to stand around in the dark with her. Maybe if he got her back to the crowd he could brush her off more easily.

"You want to dance?" he asked, not noticing the light of anticipation that flared in her eyes as he shot one last regretful glance toward the wagon.

Jessie returned to the celebration some time later, after splashing cold water on her face and rebrushing her hair. It had taken her longer than she expected to regain control; perhaps escaping to the wagon had not been her best choice. Her gaze had kept returning to the bed where Tony stretched out beside her each night. But now, her composure firmly in place, she braved the party.

It took all of fifteen seconds for her hard-won calm to evaporate into the night air. Within that time she located Tony, gaily dipping and twirling Delia Bolton around the packed-earth dance floor. Delia bent forward at the waist, her overripe bosom in indecently cut green challis nearly touching Tony's chest. It was amazing that she managed to dance like that without tipping over. Jessie's temper, always easily aroused, kicked in as swift and fast as a cantankerous mule. Well, it certainly hadn't taken him long to find another woman to entertain. The man passed out cheap thrills as easily as a barkeep served cheap whiskey.

Her outraged anger caused her to do something she would never have done otherwise—agree to dance with Walt Morrison.

Walt grabbed her by the waist with both hands and tried to pull her close while Jessie fought to maintain a respectable distance between them—as much for the sake of her nose as propriety. The stench emanating from Walt reminded Jessie of sour milk. She swallowed heavily and tried not to breathe.

Walt leered down at her. "You look right purty tonight, Miss Jessie."

"Oh . . . thank you," Jessie muttered, trying to peer over his shoulder clad in dirty, sweat-streaked chambray, searching out Tony and his little dance partner. She was nearly as angry at herself as she was at Tony. What had she expected? He'd told her what he was like. Still, she'd thought—and hoped—that he'd felt . . . something for her. "But it's not Miss, it's Mrs.—Mrs. Winchester."

"Sorry." He grinned, showing coffee-stained teeth and releasing a gust of onion-scented breath. "I just don't like to think of you being married to someone else, I guess. Not when I know we could be so good together." His arms tightened, and his pelvis brushed her belly with each step. Trying to keep away, Jessie sucked in her stomach as far as she could.

"Mr. Morrison!" she returned, appalled. She tried to jerk away, but his grip held her fast. "I'm sure it's not proper to suggest such things to a happily married woman."

"I reckon not, but then, bein' proper never seemed like a whole lot of fun to me. 'Sides this is a long trip. Lots of women bury husbands. Happens all the time."

"I'm sure Tony will outlive all of us."

Much as Walt hated the idea, Winchester was one of the lucky ones in this world. Still, sometimes luck ran out, or changed. Maybe, just maybe, if the right opportunity came up, Walt could make sure Winchester's luck changed, and, in the process, he could change a little bit of his own. He tried to tug Jessie a little closer.

Politeness was well and good, Jessie thought, but sometimes pain was a bit more effective. Treading heavily on his toes, she stepped down with as much weight as she could manage without falling on her nose—or worse, into Walt's arms.

"Oh, I'm terribly sorry. How clumsy of me. If you'd rather dance with someone who didn't stomp all over you, I'd certainly understand."

"Naw. A little bit of a thing like you couldn't hurt me."

Too bad. Looking around at the ground, she searched for a convenient hole to steer him into, wondering if he'd be accommodating enough to sprain his ankle in the process. Oh, Lord, what had she gotten herself into? Jessie didn't want to create a scene, but neither did she want to continue this dance, and it seemed that Walt had no intention of letting her go gracefully. There was something about the way his pale, flat eyes glittered at her that made her blood run cold and her stomach tighten.

She braced both forearms against his chest, trying to force a reasonable space between them. She was just going to have to bear the remainder of this dance, but she certainly didn't have to make it easy on him. Slamming her heel down on his instep again, she decided this was one mistake she wasn't going to repeat. She wouldn't let Walt Morrison within spitting distance ever again.

Across the dance floor Tony tried to make polite conversation with Delia, still wondering why Jessie had scurried off as if she was frightened of him. Him, who had never frightened a woman in his life. A few of their fathers and brothers, maybe, but never a woman. What could account for such a reaction in Jessie?

Delia's chattering was beginning to get on his nerves. He nodded when she seemed to expect some response to one of her comments. She was pretty enough, but Tony had no intention of encouraging the crush she showed every sign of developing. His taste ran to women, not girls.

A bit of peach caught his eye as it whirled by. Ah, there was Jessie. What the hell was she doing dancing with Walt Morrison? Two horizontal lines appeared between Tony's eyebrows. He didn't trust Morrison for a second. It was not so much that Walt spent an inordinate amount of time staring at Jessie—most men had trouble keeping their eyes off her. But Tony was still steamed about the things Walt had said on the hunting trip. Although Tony avoided violence whenever possible, on the principle that there were plenty of other ways to solve problems, he still wasn't convinced that, in this particular case, stronger measures wouldn't be immensely satisfying.

Tony's patience passed its limit when Walt took advantage of a quick turn in the dance to pull Jessie off-balance toward him, pressing her breasts against his chest. Her eyes met Tony's for a brief instant in a silent plea. Abruptly, Tony stopped dancing.

"Delia, you're going to have to excuse me. There's something I must attend to." He turned and strode away, leaving Delia staring at his back.

A brief word to the fiddler stopped the music, and Tony clapped his hands to gain everyone's attention. "All right, y'all, time for the sing-along." He retrieved his guitar from the wagon while the other dancers, exhausted, plopped themselves on the ground in a circle.

Tony sat down, cross-legged, with his guitar on his lap. He strummed a few discordant notes while tuning it, then looked up. He glanced around at the gathered crowd; four or five dozen people, give or take a few, all dressed in their homespun best, simple rough clothes that were clean and well mended. He couldn't keep track of the number of people on the train.

One family had elected to leave the train at Fort Kearney, a couple of babies were born, and somebody's elderly mother-in-law had died. Tonight there were a few off-duty soldiers mixed in, their snappy uniforms and unfamiliar faces making them stand out like shiny new pennies amongst a bunch of tarnished, but still valuable, coins. He found Jessie near the back of the group, Walt still close by her side, hanging onto her arm. He didn't know if she was there by choice or not, but there was no way he was letting it continue.

"Jessie? Where are you, darlin'? I need inspiration. Come here and sit by me."

There was a round of chuckles as Jessie pulled away from Walt and moved forward to join Tony. She was unsure as to whether she should be grateful to him for saving her from Walt or remain miffed that he could look at her with his soul in his eyes one minute and have a gay old time dancing with Delia the next. Oh, fiddle, he probably just decided he felt like singing and didn't stop the dancing in order to rescue her at all.

"O.K., let's try 'Our Goodman,' and feel free to join in if you know the words. 'Course, you have to understand that this song's not inspired by *my* wife." There was a loud burst of laughter. Tony flashed an impish grin at Jessie before swinging into the rousing tale of a drunken husband who staggers home to find another man's hat, gun, and horse. When he sees a head on his pillow next to his wife, she tries to convince him it is only a cabbage head and only his inebriated state makes him believe he sees a mustache.

By the end of the song the men were in such good spirits they immediately jumped into "The Farmer's Curst Wife," relishing the old tune which told of a farmer so beset by his "bitch" of a wife he bargains with the devil to take her away, but she causes so much trouble in hell the devil eventually returns her. They were nearly laughing too hard to finish the song: "That goes to show what a woman can do. She's worse than the devil and she's worse than you!"

Ginnie jumped to her feet in mock outrage. "Ladies? Are we going to let them get away with that?"

"No!" The answering chorus came from all sides.

Tony smiled a challenge at Jessie. "Jess? How about you? What would you like to sing?"

Jessie shook her head vigorously. "Oh, no, I can't sing. I'm perpetually flat."

Unable to stop himself, his gaze dropped to her bodice. Oh, no she wasn't.

"I'll sing." To the surprise of the rest of the party, most of whom had never heard her speak three words, Mary Ellen waddled over to Tony and whispered in his ear.

"You're sure?" Tony seemed amused.

Mary Ellen smiled and nodded. "I'm sure."

Tony began to strum his guitar and Mary Ellen's clear soprano rang out:

Come all you fair and tender ladies.
Be careful how you court your man.
They're like a star in a summer morning.
First appear and then they're gone.
They'll tell to you some loving story,
They'll tell to you some far-flung lie.
And then they'll go and court another
And for that other one pass you by.

"Unfair, Mary Ellen!" Stuart called, acting in-sulted. "I'm wounded to the core. You know I'm faith-ful as a dog."

"Yes, darling," she said soothingly, patting him on the head like he was a favored pet as she returned to his side.

Yes, but Tony wasn't an old dog, he was a tomcat, Jessie thought. He had told her more than once that faithfulness was not one of his nobler qualities.

The evening degenerated into one of general hilar-ity as the warm, velvety night deepened. The travelers felt safe here, so close to the Fort. The welcome ab-sence of responsibilities freed them, seducing them as surely as the mesmerizing prairie sky. As night fell, a half moon like a giant pearl sliced cleanly in half ap-peared, casting a luminescent glow on their faces. Gradually, the party became more subdued, entranced by the magical night.

Jessie let a deep sigh slip out. She couldn't remem-ber feeling this relaxed since before her father had fallen ill. She sipped the last of the peach brandy. By now all the men—with the exception of Reverend Donner, who, thankfully, had retired over an hour ago —were too far gone to notice, or, if they noticed, to care what she was drinking. Feeling warm and tingly all over, she let herself relax against Tony's side.

Plucking a soft melody on his guitar, Tony began to sing. His deep baritone filled the air, casting a spell on

her as potent as the bewitching constellations overhead.

> When I was a young man
> Far places called to me.
> Wanted to see the wilderness
> I needed to be free.
>
> And so I left my family
> I left behind my love
> Went off to find those new sights
> That I'd been dreaming of.
>
> I wandered fifteen years or so
> From mountains to the sea.
> Saw all those far-flung places
> But my heart was still lonely.
>
> I yearned for those who loved me
> Someone to say she cared.
> I longed for all I left behind
> And all that we had shared.
>
> No matter where you travel
> Or how far you roam
> The only trip worth takin'
> Is a journey home.

Jessie was still, with her head thrown back and her
eyes closed, drinking in the song and the moment.
Tony slipped an arm around her shoulders and whispered, "Come, *cara*. Let's go to bed."

14

Jessie fumbled with the light blue ribbon at the high neck of her nightgown, once again tangling the ties into a knot. She forced her shaking fingers to slow down, working the knot free as Tony's words burned through her mind again.

Come, cara. *Let's go to bed.*

They were innocent enough, on the face of it. After all, she and Tony had been sharing a bed for the past month and a half. What made her think that tonight he meant something more? Did she *want* him to mean something more?

Finally managing to tie a lopsided bow, Jessie dove for bed, yanking the covers up to her chin. She felt safer under the blankets, albeit hot. She didn't know whether to credit her excessive warmth to too much brandy, her uncharacteristically nervous mood, or both.

Tony slipped into the wagon and flopped down on his back beside her. He remained on top of the bed-clothes, with his hands linked behind his head and his legs crossed at the ankles, and stared at the wagon cover. It could have been any other night, except that he didn't acknowledge Jessie's presence.

Tony *always* said good night.

She rolled to her side, facing him. He didn't look at her. It was dark in the wagon. She could barely make out his features, but her memory filled in the rest—the sharp planes and angles of his face, the strong bones, the intriguing hollows, the boyish dimples.

"Tony? Is something wrong?"

Finally, Tony rolled his head to meet her gaze. His perpetually laughing eyes were serious now, burning with some emotion she couldn't identify. His answer was curt, abrupt.

"No." Only that he wanted her too much. Only that he didn't know how he'd survive another night, aching, knowing she was beside him, but knowing, too, that to touch her would be wrong.

Time hung suspended. Jessie's body responded to Tony's nearness, to the look in his eyes. It ceased to matter to her that there had been other women in Tony's life before her, and that there would be more after. What mattered was that no one had ever made her feel this way, and she knew no one would again. In some deep corner of her soul she was sure that a man like Tony came along only once in a lifetime. Was it so wrong to seize the opportunity when it was here? To learn what she was sure he could teach her? To enjoy the moment and forget the future? Men—men like her brother and Tony—took whatever pleasure life offered. Why couldn't she do the same?

The night and the brandy emboldened Jessie, silencing her conscience. Deliberately, slowly, she pushed the blankets off her body and down the bed. She moved her body to press tightly against his, where it longed to be, and hesitantly lifted her mouth to his.

For a long, tense minute he didn't move. Silently Jessie willed him to respond, knowing her pride could not stand his rejection. It had taken all her courage to make this first move—but it would have been even harder to do nothing.

Finally, with a groan, he slipped one hand behind her head, cradling it in his palm. His other hand slid around her back, exerting gentle pressure, urging her to move closer yet. He lifted himself slightly on one elbow, tilted his head, and took control of the kiss.

His tongue moved into her mouth, tracing the insides of her lips, exploring the edges of her teeth, before gliding deeper, finding her tongue, stroking and coiling. Jessie reveled in the unfamiliar sensations, loving the sleek wetness, the slightly abrasive texture. A low sound, halfway between a purr and a growl, came from deep in her throat.

At that, the kiss changed, becoming more demanding. Tony tightened his embrace and crushed her against him, his tongue now plunging and swirling in an ancient, intoxicating rhythm. He broke off suddenly and took several deep, gulping breaths. Haltingly, he lifted his hands to the ties of her gown, giving her time to stop him if she wished.

Jessie could no more have stopped him than stopped breathing. The edges of her consciousness were blurred, indistinct, obscured by the mists of desire. Her skin felt hungry, hungry to be touched by his skin. She couldn't seem to get close enough to him. She writhed, trying to ease the ache coming from somewhere deep within her body.

He untied her ribbons, letting one strand slide between his fingers. With infinite slowness he slipped the tiny pearl buttons through their holes. One . . . two . . . three. His lips moved to delicately trace the line of her cheekbone, her jaw. He trailed his tongue around her ear and down the side of her neck, gently nipping the curve where it joined her shoulder, sending shivers rushing through her body. Tony slipped his hand inside the soft cotton of her gown, curving his fingers around the underside of her breast while his thumb teased the hard nipple, brushing back and forth, back and forth.

Jessie was mindless, floating. She could no longer think; she could only feel. She was unaware of Tony brushing aside the top of her nightdress, exposing her breast, until his head lowered and his mouth claimed one aching peak. He swirled his tongue around her nipple, then drew back slightly. Jessie moaned and threaded her fingers through his thick, soft hair, clasping him tightly to her chest. He drew her breast into his mouth and sucked before easing his way to her other lonely nipple.

"Jessie," he murmured again and again. "Oh, my God. Jessie."

He glided his hands across her body, down her rib cage, over her flat stomach, past her thighs, leaving fiery trails in their wake, long, easy strokes that savored, tantalized, ignited. He lifted the hem of her gown, sliding it seductively up her skin, his fingers searching.

Ah, the feelings . . . the smooth sweep of her back. The sweet taste of her lips as he nibbled on the corners. The tempting curl of her tongue when he sucked it tenderly. The silken column of her throat. The satin texture of her hair. The incredible softness and warmth of her skin. So new, so fresh, so intoxicating.

So Jessie.

He teased her, his fingers tracing patterns on her upper thighs, combing through the triangle of springy curls between them. She arched into his touch, calling his name, and he knew she felt it, too, the astonishing passion that flowed between them. Unable to wait any longer, he slid his middle finger into her softness, finding her so hot and moist that he nearly lost all control. Carefully, he eased his finger into her body. God, she was so small, so tight. His throat constricted; he didn't want to hurt her. He had only taken one other virgin in his life, all those years ago, and it . . . it had ended in tragedy.

It had ended in death.

The memory brought him up sharply. He sat bolt upright, rubbing his face with both palms. Oh, *Dio,* his hand smelled like her, and the musky, sweet scent nearly shattered the last shards of his control. He half turned, intending to take her in his arms again, before he caught himself and froze. He wouldn't do that to her. He couldn't do that to Jessie. He must not take what she had to offer when he had nothing to give in return. She deserved better than that. She deserved better than him.

"Tony?" Jessie mumbled, her voice husky, confused. She reached out and stroked his back. He jerked away from her touch. He had to get out of there. If he stayed, he would take her anyway, his one brief moment of nobility be damned. Tony tore out of the wagon without one word of explanation.

It was his turn to escape.

Jessie was stunned, still dazed with passion, unsure what to do. Her emotions vacillated wildly between frustration, confusion, and anger. What had gone wrong? Why had he left? Damn him! Damn him for making her want him and leaving her in this state, bewildered and aching. She was hit with a tidal wave of embarrassment.

She had thrown herself at a man who clearly didn't want her—a man who, if his version of his past could be believed, had never shown much discrimination before. She felt unattractive and ignorant, rejected by the only man to whom she had ever offered herself. Worst of all, she knew if he climbed back through the flaps right now her traitorous body would welcome him back.

Damn Antonio Winchester to eternal, celibate hell!

*　　*　　*

Tony raced full speed, mindlessly, across the prairie, his destination anywhere but where Jessie was. His arousal made his usually fluid strides awkward and painful, but he welcomed the hurt, hoping it would drive the raging desire from his body. Finally, lungs burning, unable to run any longer, he collapsed backward to the ground, arms outspread. His legs burned and he gasped for air. He ripped up clumps of dry, brown grass and angrily hurled them skyward.

It was no use. He still wanted her. Swearing, he jerked open the buttons of his breeches and took himself in hand. With hard, swift strokes he sought a relief he had not needed since adolescence. A shudder overtook him as his release came and he spilled himself on the dusty ground.

He dug the heels of his hands into his closed eyes, heart beating with ragged syncopation. It had been the only way he knew to keep himself from pouncing on Jessie the next time he saw her, but it left him feeling empty, wasted.

It was a familiar feeling. The last few years he had, more often than not, felt more alone after lying with a woman than before, the space inside him a yawning, echoing cavern. How was it, then, that Jessie seemed to shrink the space so easily? One beaming, joyous smile from her and the emptiness began to fill.

Her responses to his lovemaking had been so sweet and genuine, a wealth of fiery passion lying untapped just beneath her surface. At the memory, his body grew hard and heavy again. The recent release had done him no good at all. How would he ever be able to stay away from her, now that he knew Jessie wanted him too?

*　　*　　*

"Ohhh."

It took Jessie a minute to realize that the awful groaning noises were coming from her own throat. She was lying down—that much she could tell, despite the pounding pain in her head—but why was she being shaken and jostled like dice in a gambler's hand? Cautiously, she opened one eyelid, then slammed it shut against the intrusion of a piercing, incredibly bright ray of light. During the brief peek she had been able to register white canvas; evidently she was in a wagon. She let out another loud moan as first one side of the wagon, then the other, dropped several inches, banging her body uncomfortably in the process. A moving wagon, obviously.

Clearly, she was ill. Jessie based her deduction on her pounding head and unsettled stomach, as well as the fact that she was still sleeping when the sun was high enough in the sky to produce that awful light. She set herself to discovering precisely where she was and what was wrong with her.

With extreme care she allowed small slits to open between her lids, veiling her eyes from the assaulting light with her lashes. Well, at least it was her own wagon, Jessie thought with relief, finding herself surrounded by familiar objects. And she was still alive, although the way she felt, she wasn't entirely sure she wanted to be.

Jessie slowly pushed herself to a sitting position. The world swirled for a minute, and she placed both palms on her cheeks, steadying her wobbly head. God, what was the matter with her. Fever? Cholera? Some other truly awful disease she'd never heard of?

After a time she decided her head just might stay attached to her neck, after all. She crawled to the front of the wagon and peered out between the cloth flaps.

Fighting against the glare, she was able to make out the shiny brown rumps of her oxen, plodding along as usual. The sun was behind her—thank heaven for small favors. From its position in the sky, she guessed it must be near ten o'clock. At home in Chicago it was not unheard of for Jessie to stay in bed 'til mid-morning, but on a wagon train where Buffalo awoke everyone with a gunshot at four A.M., it was positively scandalous.

"Finally decided to get up?"

Jessie squeezed her eyes shut against the loud, intruding voice, though what protection her eyelids furnished against sound was anyone's guess.

"Could you talk a little more softly, please, Tony?" she managed to croak out. Her mouth and throat felt incredibly parched.

Tony muffled his laughter as he strolled alongside the oxen.

"Believe it or not, *cara,* I am talking softly. Feeling a bit under the weather, are we?"

"We? Is this the royal we? You appear to be perfectly fine, but I certainly appreciate your touching concern. I, on the other hand, am in complete and total misery. How long have I been ill?"

"You're not sick, Jessie."

"I'm not sick? How can you say such I thing? I'm in utter agony. Do you think I'm faking it?" Jessie pressed the back of one hand to her forehead as her outburst brought on a fresh rush of pain. "How long do I have to live?"

"Jess, I assure you, you're not dying. You're suffering the aftereffects of indulging in a wee bit too much of the grape last night—or, rather, several cups too many of that brandy you managed to polish off."

"Last night?" At Tony's answering nod, Jessie tried to recall exactly what happened last night. The memories were foggy, but she managed to grasp one or two.

"Fort Laramie? The party?"

"Yep." Tony watched her carefully, trying to guess how much of last night she remembered. Perhaps it was better if she forgot most of it. It could be embarrassing if she was overly effusive in her gratitude, as she was bound to feel grateful to him for protecting her virtue. He wondered if she realized the extent of his sacrifice. Probably not. It was just as well. He wasn't particularly humble, but if her thanks were too lavish they would probably be right back in the situation that got them into that mess.

Maybe she would kiss him.

His body heated as he imagined Jessie, in payment for his gentlemanly behavior, wrapping her arms around his neck and pressing her warm lips against his. He was so lost in his daydreams it took him a moment to realize that walking was becoming decidedly uncomfortable. Damn! He couldn't remember the last time he had a reaction like this just from thinking about kissing a woman, for Christ's sake. Hell, she better not thank him after all; damned if he could be that noble twice.

Tony was brought out of his reverie by the solid *thunk* of a pottery mug hitting the side of his head.

15

"Ouch!"

Tony instinctively threw both arms over his head and crouched down for protection while he tried to find the source of the attack.

To his surprise, there were no Indians or bandits. There was just Jessie, this time sailing a flat tin plate toward his neck with a quick flick of her wrist. He barely had time to deflect the plate with his palm before she struggled to lift a small, obviously full water cask.

One swift, agile motion had Tony in the wagon and Jessie wrapped securely in his arms before she had a chance to continue her attack.

"What did you do that for?"

Tony's voice boomed in her ear, and Jessie flinched involuntarily at the loud sound splintering in her head. Righteous anger had dimmed her agony, but now her pain returned in full force. She hadn't realized he would get to her so quickly. She was so used to his habitual lazy saunter, she had forgotten he could move with catlike speed when the occasion called for it.

"You're right, Tony. I should never have wasted water on that thick skull of yours. You're not worth it. I should have used fresh cow *merda* instead."

He stared at her in shock. What had gotten her so riled? Tony was not accustomed to women being mad at him, and on the rare occasions they were he usually knew what he had done to cause it. Besides, women never stayed angry with him for long.

"Would you care to tell me what this is about?"

Jessie gaped at him, astonished. How could he not know? She had practically thrown herself at him, and he had turned her down. Turned her, Jessamyn Johnston, down, when he had probably slept with every marginally appealing woman east of the Mississippi. And now he was going to San Francisco to get started on the west side! What's more, he didn't even have enough consideration to turn her away right at the start. Oh, no, he had to wait until she got all hot and bothered so he could just leave her hanging there. Must have fed his monumental ego to have her know exactly what she was missing.

Fueled by a renewed spurt of anger, Jessie heaved hard against his chest, breaking his hold. She smiled in satisfaction as he took two rapid, unbalanced steps backward until the side of the wagon came up against the backs of his knees. His arms cartwheeled wildly in the air as he fought to regain equilibrium.

The battle was decided when Jessie deliberately reached out and gave his chest a tiny but decisive shove. There was nothing he could do, no handholds to grab. Tony toppled backward over the side of the slow-moving wagon.

He landed with a thud and a cloud of dust. Jessie laughed. The look of utter disbelief and helplessness on his face the instant before he had gone over had been priceless. Amazing what a balm it was to her wounded to pride to put that calm, competent man flat on his back in the dirt. She whisked her hands together, as if brushing off dust after a job well done.

Tony lay on the ground, unmoving, too stunned to be angry. One by one, he gingerly tested each part of his bruised body, deciding the damage was minimal. The damage to his body, anyway. One look at the amused faces on the passing wagons proved that his pride was considerably more wounded.

The woman tried to muffle their laughter behind their hands, but their eyes danced. Most of the men were not so diplomatic. Their hooting and hollering was accompanied by a variety of delighted comments.

"Nice of you to check out the ground so thoroughly, Winchester, but we're not ready to make camp yet."

"Right neighborly of you to show us how to handle our wives, Tony."

"Interesting way of getting out of a wagon, son, but it seems like it might rightly be a bit painful. I think I'll stick with the usual way, but I sure appreciate yer testin' it out."

Smiling wryly, Tony lifted his hand with one finger upraised in an age-old gesture.

Pushing himself to his feet, Tony missed Walt's interested and distinctly satisfied stare as his wagon rolled passed. "Well, well," Walt muttered under his breath. Maybe the perfect husband wasn't quite as perfect as he appeared. If he wasn't, Walt had plenty of ideas on how to console Tony's heartbroken wife.

When Tony caught up with his wagon a few minutes later the oxen were plodding along unattended. Jessie had evidently disappeared back inside. Deciding upon discretion as the better part of valor, he was inclined to let her be. She was probably feeling a bit surly from the aftereffects of the brandy. Jessie's temper was like a flash fire. It ran quick and hot, but it always burned out rapidly, too. He'd give her a few hours to cool off before he tried to talk to her again. She'd undoubtedly be more reasonable later.

"Tony, old boy, you're losing your touch."

Tony shut his mouth with a snap when he realized he had been reduced to talking to himself. He was obviously losing whatever mind he had previously possessed.

No, not losing it. He knew exactly where it went. Jessie was stealing it, bit by bit.

It had been four days since the wagon train had left Fort Laramie. Four long, grueling, disheartening days. The land had become progressively more varied, the hills so unlike the flat prairie they had been crossing. Passing through the southernmost tip of the Black Hills, the pungent stands of pine and fir scented the air and provided a welcome contrast to the endless, dry, grass-covered plains. The hot days were tempered by nights that had become increasingly cool, signaling the steadily rising elevation.

Tony glanced around the familiar camp. It was funny how, no matter what the land surrounding it, camp always looked the same. He noted the weariness in his fellow travelers as they gathered for the evening meal.

Today had been difficult. They had reached the crossing of the North Fork of the Platte River. Unfortunately, this part of the river was too deep to ford, and for the first time on this trip there was no ferry or bridge to aid them. The train had been forced to improvise, removing the wheels from each wagon and sealing all the cracks with tar and candle wax before floating the wagons across. It was demanding work, trying to keep the wagons from being swept downstream, tipping over, or sinking. The adolescent boys were forced to do the work of men, tying casks around the livestock and helping the animals cross safely.

Despite being physically exhausted, it was not the work that was depressing him. It was Jessie. How wrong he had been when he thought she would cool off in a few hours. She was not simply cool, she was positively frigid, allowing a rare crack to form in the ice that surrounded her only long enough to lob an occasional insult his way.

It was obvious that ignoring the problem was not going to make it go away. It was time to talk it out, once and for all. Unfortunately, that required getting Jessie alone, something that she had made impossible over the last few days. She had even taken to coming to their wagon at night long after he, disgusted at waiting for her arrival, had given up and fallen asleep. He didn't have the heart to wake her in the morning. Besides, he doubted he would be able to accomplish anything by trying to talk to Jessie before sunrise.

His decision made, Tony wasted no time. He put aside his supper plate, which Jessie had served him silently before scurrying off to eat with Reverend Parson. He ambled across the camp, nodding greetings to all he passed but declining offers to join friends and sit for a spell.

Reverend Parson greeted him warmly, inviting Tony to join Jessie, Reverend Donner, and himself in a cup of coffee and a bite of dessert. Tony automatically mumbled his agreement and dropped to sit cross-legged on the ground, but his eyes lingered on Jessie as she wordlessly handed him a tin mug of hot coffee steaming in the cool evening air.

He had never met a woman the mere sight of whom gave him so much pleasure, nor one who held his attention with so little effort. He had always been attracted to women who worked at emphasizing their femininity, dressed up in silks, women who wore ribbons and bows, their hair elaborately curled and their faces artfully painted. But Jessie's classic simplicity intrigued him as none of those sophisticated women ever had.

She wore an ordinary long-sleeved cotton dress, buttoned from the high neck all the way down to her serviceable black boots. The dress was a fresh green, like new spring leaves, and the color somehow brought out the blue in her eyes and the glint of red in her hair, which she wore in one long, gleaming, braided rope down the back of her head. The pure, basic lines of the snug bodice and full skirt emphasized her trim curves, and it took little imagination for him to envision himself unfastening it, button by button, exposing her creamy skin for his eyes and lips.

"Tony?"

The name finally registered as Tony realized Reverend Parson had been speaking to him for some time. He must really be in bad shape, fantasizing about Jessie in the presence of not one but two ministers. With an effort he turned his eyes and his attention to the elderly man at his left.

"I'm sorry, Reverend, I was woolgathering and didn't catch what you said."

Tony had never seen a man of the cloth who looked so much like a mischievous elf. A conspiratorial twinkle in his pale brown eyes, the minister repeated his suggestion. "I was just saying Jessie works much too hard. Perhaps she would enjoy a stroll. It's going to be an absolutely lovely evening."

Tony jumped on the opening the Reverend provided. "Yes, that's a great idea. Jess, come for a walk with me."

Her eyes took on a frosty gray hue as Jessie answered. "I can't. I promised Mary Ellen I'd . . . help her with the twins' lessons tonight."

She was gone before Tony could stop her. She obviously wasn't going to give him a chance to make it right between them. She wasn't even going to tell him what was wrong so he could try to resolve it.

"Well, Tony, perhaps you would accompany me on a short constitutional. I'm not as charming a companion as your lovely wife, but there is something I would like to discuss with you."

Tony suppressed a groan. The last thing he needed was more advice. It had been obvious to the entire party that the young Winchester couple was having some marital troubles, and in the days since Fort Laramie he had been nearly buried under an avalanche of unsolicited but well-meaning suggestions.

A giggling Ginnie Wrightman told Tony to romance his own wife, while Andrew thought it would be better if Tony waited until it all blew over. Mary Ellen had quietly offered to provide an ear if he needed someone to talk to; Stuart had expressed his bewildered sympathy; and Susannah wondered why Jessie wouldn't play with Tony anymore. Delia Bolton said she would be happy to console him—Tony had a pretty good idea what Delia's consolation would consist of—while Harriet offered to brew up her special nerve-calming tonic. Tom Bolton had bluntly suggested Tony drag Jessie off to bed and keep her occupied there until neither she nor Tony could remember what had caused the rift in the first place. Heaven only knew how much Tony would like to follow that advice.

On the other hand, Jessie was very close to Reverend Parson, and he seemed to have a clear understanding of human relationships and their intricacies. If anyone could help Tony, it would be the minister.

Walking slowly, in deference to Jedediah's arthritic legs, it took the pair quite some time to get a few hundred yards from the wagon camp. The light breeze was refreshing, the evening was gentle, and the wagons were hidden from sight behind a hill, although sporadic shouts and other reminders of the camp's proximity occasionally floated to them.

Jedediah chatted congenially of the day's labors and

tomorrow's plans, and Tony's impatience grew. He had nearly decided to throw Jessie over his shoulder, carry her off, and force her to tell him what was wrong, when the minister brought up the subject that was on both of their minds.

"You know, Antonio, you just need to tell her how much you love her."

"Love?" The single, choked syllable was all Tony was able to force past his suddenly tight throat.

"Yes, love." Reverend Parson looked amused. "Don't tell me you're one of those young men who thinks it is unmanly to admit his feelings. I thought you had more self-assurance. It's hardly a secret, anyway. One need only see the expression in your eyes when you look at Jessie."

"No, I . . ." Tony was unsure how to continue. He could hardly deny that he cared for the woman who was supposed to be his wife without arousing suspicions. It would not bode well for their charade if he admitted the light in his eyes when Jessie was near was not love, but pure, unadulterated lust.

"I know you two have not known each other long."

"Oh?" Tony eyed the Reverend speculatively, wondering if the man had guessed more about the Winchester "marriage" than they wanted anyone to know, but Jedediah merely nodded in response. There seemed to be no suspicion or accusation in his eyes, only warmth and concern.

"Jessie is unsure of herself around you. I don't think she is confident of your feelings for her. She was jealous when you were dancing with Delia at the party in Fort Laramie."

"Jealous? Really?" A queer stab of something that felt suspiciously like pleasure rushed through Tony at the thought.

"You needn't look so pleased." Reverend Parson shook his head, the remnants of daylight glancing off his bald dome while he chuckled under his breath. "I

guess Jessie's not the only one feeling a bit insecure."
He paused, as if considering his next words. "Talk to
her, Tony. Tell her how you feel."

Tony grimly nodded his assent. Oh, yes, Reverend,
he silently agreed. He'd talk to her. But what Jessie
was going to hear was not what the Reverend thought.

Tony's opportunity came sooner than he had
hoped. A distinct chill swept in that night, bringing
with it dark clouds that unleashed an assault of wal-
nut-sized balls of ice. The hailstorm continued into the
next day, and venturing out of the shelter of the wagons was akin to being continuously pelted with small
rocks. All plans for the day's journey were forgotten,
and the men dared the elements only long enough to
check on the livestock huddling together in the lee of
the wagons, trying to find whatever scant protection
they could. The entire party was sentenced to the wagons for the duration, eating cold fare and trying to
repair the tears ripped into the wagon covers by the
driving projectiles.

Tony and Jessie were thus trapped together in their
wagon.

Jessie tried to ignore him, concentrating on mending their hard-used clothing, but he was always there.
He lounged on the mattress, playing desultory games
of solitaire. His long legs were in the way when she
reached across the wagon for the extra buttons in her
sewing box. She was uncomfortably aware of his gaze
frequently resting on her. In the closeness of the
wagon, she was sure she could smell him, his warm,
musky scent calling up too many memories. Damn,
did he have to keep lying on the bed, reminding her of
what had passed between them? If she closed her
eyes, she could almost feel the stroke of his hands on
her breasts, the . . .

"Something wrong, Jess?"

Abruptly recalled to her senses, Jessie snapped her eyelids open.

"No."

"Would you like to play with me?"

"No!"

"I meant cards, Jess."

"No."

"Well, then, how about I play the guitar for you while you work?"

"No."

"Are you ever going to speak with me in words of more than one syllable again?"

"No."

Tony's temper, already frayed to a fine edge by her recent behavior and by having to stay in the enclosed wagon with her and not being able to touch her, finally snapped. He grabbed a handful of cards, hurled them across the wagon, and pounded his fist against the rough wood of the wagon side.

"Damn it, Jess, I don't know what the hell you want from me!"

Jessie started at his uncharacteristic outburst, sinking the sharp tip of her mending needle deeply into her forefinger. She thrust the wounded finger into her mouth before lifting her gaze to Tony. She was too surprised to respond with her usual quick tongue. She had never before seen him truly angry.

He was magnificent.

His black eyes snapped, fiery and intense. His rage sharpened his features, throwing his strong bones into relief as the black wings of his brows drew together. A muscle pulsed in his clenched jaw, the cords of his neck standing out tautly.

How she would love to paint him. The thought surprised her almost as much as his temper, for it had been so long since she had felt the old urge to capture beauty on paper.

Slow down, Tony, slow down, he urged himself.

Anger had never gotten him anywhere. He felt his tense muscles slowly relax, and he rolled his shoulders to loosen them. He hoped his outburst hadn't made her even madder, or worse, frightened her. When he looked at Jessie he was surprised at her expression. She was staring at him, yes, but she didn't look angry or scared. She looked catatonic.

"Why are you looking at me like that?"

Jessie shut her eyes and shook her head, trying to clear her mind of his mesmerizing image. When she opened her lids she found him kneeling in front of her, only a handsbreadth away, his eyes boring into hers intently as if to read her innermost thoughts.

His voice was husky, compelling, drawing her in before she realized the words he was saying.

"Jessie, I know you probably don't remember much of what happened that night in Fort Laramie. The only thing I can think of that would make you so upset is if you thought something happened that didn't. I promise you, Jessie, I didn't touch you."

Her temper finally blazed to her rescue. "You touched me!"

Tony winced. "Well, all right, I touched you, but I didn't *touch* you, if you know what I mean."

"Oh, I know very well what you mean. I know more than you think. I remember everything that happened in Fort Laramie."

"You do? Then what exactly are you so upset about?"

"What am I upset about? How about your falling all over Delia Bolton?"

Delia again. So she was jealous. The thought was unexpectedly gratifying.

"Delia has nothing to with this. This is between us."

"She has everything to do with this. It's embarrassing for me if everyone knows that your wife pleases you so little you have to seek out other women just months after we were married!"

"But, Jessie, you aren't my wife."

Did he always have to be so calm and reasonable about everything? It was extremely annoying. "I know that, but no one else does!"

A loud thump on the bottom of the wagon interrupted them. Ears straining, they made no sound, but heard nothing further.

"I'm going to check that out. And you—" Tony waved a finger under Jessie's nose—"are not going to move so much as a muscle. We'll finish this when I get back."

Tony clamped his shabby, wide-brimmed black hat on his head and swung out of the wagon into the pounding hail. Grimacing against the painful hits, he dived under the wagon.

The space was empty.

But the grass was flattened, as if something heavy had rested there. He frowned as his gaze swept the area, finding nothing else amiss. He didn't see the small opening between the still-swaying flaps of a nearby wagon, nor the pale eyes that peered out.

Tony took a moment to compose himself before returning to the wagon and Jessie. He shouldn't have gotten so angry, but *Dio,* the woman confused him. He didn't like being confused, and he hadn't a clue how to handle her. He couldn't remember ever meeting a woman whom he couldn't charm out of her anger in four minutes, much less four days. Nor could he recall ever knowing a woman who tied his insides up in knots the way Jessie did.

He took a few deep breaths, steeling himself for the confrontation to come. One way or the other, this would be settled before the day was over.

* * *

Walt dropped his wagon flap, cackling in glee, and fell back against the splintery wall. He'd been annoyed when his pals had kicked him out in the hail to answer the call of nature, but what he'd heard when he'd been creeping back under the protection of the wagons made it all worth it. He blessed the urge that had made him stop underneath Winchester's wagon, dreaming what it would be like if he was in there with Jessie instead, and planning ways to make that happen.

His luck was finally changing.

He laughed again, a sound that was hollow, satisfied, oddly disturbing.

His wagonmates looked at him strangely, but they didn't ask. Morrison was an odd bird, and they'd long been sorry they'd hooked up with him in Iowa. They knew better than to ask what was on his convoluted mind this time.

Tony returned to the wagon to find Jessie sitting on the mattress, her head bent over the socks she was darning. Her hair was loose, forming a silk curtain that hid her face. He dropped to his knees in front of her.

"Look at me, Jessamyn. Please."

She lifted her face, and he was lost in the swirling blue mists of her eyes. He could see so many emotions there, anger and fear and heartbreaking vulnerability, all blurring together until one flowed seamlessly into the next. He reached out, intending to stroke her cheek, before catching himself and letting his hand fall to his lap.

"We can't keep this up, trying to ignore each other all the way to San Francisco. Can't we be friends again?"

"Friends!" Jessie snorted. "I'm good enough to be a friend, but nothing else, is that it?"

"What is that supposed to mean?"

Jessie debated, chewing on her bottom lip. She had to know. It would be embarrassing, but what was a bit more mortification on top of what she had already experienced?

Her voice was soft, tentative. Tony had to strain to catch her words. "That night after the dance . . . tell me, did you enjoy proving that you could make me want you before you left me, or did you just find me so . . . unappealing you couldn't continue?"

There was a stunned silence before his chest began to shake with rueful laughter.

Jessie bristled. "I'm glad you find it so amusing!"

"No, *cara,* it's not . . . it's just . . . I never considered . . ." He moved closer to her, rustling the crisp muslin bedsheets, and cupped her face in his palms. "I never found you unappealing." He gently smoothed the loose wisps of hair from her forehead. "Far from it. I want you so much it hurts every time I see you. But I don't take advantage of young women who have indulged in a bit of an experiment with peach brandy."

"Are you saying I'm not mature enough to know what I'm doing?" she asked, indignant.

His head fell back in frustration. "I seem fated to say the wrong things to you." He looked her in the eye, willing her to understand. "No. I think you're very . . . mature. But how would you have felt the next morning? I can't promise tomorrows, Jessie."

She paused, adjusting her perceptions. He wanted her? "What if I said I don't care about tomorrow?"

He shook his head before placing a light kiss on the tip of her nose. "A woman like you deserves tomorrows, *cara.*" And, for the first time, he wished he were a man who could give them.

"Oh. Well, that's that, then. Friends again?" Jessie said with false brightness.

"Friends," he affirmed, taking her slender hand in

his large rough ones for a brief moment before turning to collect the scattered playing cards.

"Oh, and Tony?"

"Hmm?" He was relieved to see the sparkle back in her eyes.

She flashed him an impish grin. "It really hurts, huh? That's . . . interesting. I'll have to remember that."

16

The great gray mass of rock rose from the plains like the hump of a huge beached whale. The wagon train halted just after noon, and the travelers were somewhat amazed that they had, indeed, reached Independence Rock on July Fourth.

It had taken three hard, punishing days of travel since the North Fork crossing to do so. A canyon had forced them away from the river. For the first time since beginning their trip, scarce and poor-quality water had been a problem. The midsummer heat had parched people and cattle equally, and many of the pools they passed were so alkaline that drinking from them could cause the livestock severe cases of the scours at best, death at worst.

But that was behind them now. They were within easy distance of fresh water, although they were, as always, camped at least three hundred yards from the river, and a ridge of land stood as a barrier between the water supply and the wagons. It was common knowledge that bodies of water produced disease-causing, noxious vapors that were carried on air currents.

Rapidly unpacking cooking utensils from the grub box, Jessie's spirits rose in anticipation of the evening's feast, for of course they had to celebrate the birth of the nation they were helping to expand. Harriet Bolton had spent the last few days feverishly sewing an American flag from donated bits of red, white, and blue cloth. All the women had been digging through their limited wardrobes to unearth appropriate patriotic attire.

Jessie rummaged through her supplies, debating over her contribution to tonight's spread. She wanted to make something special and festive, but it was difficult to be creative with the ordinary foodstuffs she stocked. She crossed her arms over her chest, tapping her foot impatiently. If only she had some fresh fruit, or perhaps—

"You shouldn't frown so, *cara*. Wilhelmina will give curdled milk if she sees you."

Jessie's heartbeat speeded up as Tony's deep voice resonated through every corner of her body. She took a moment to compose herself before turning to him, finding his eyes shining warmly at her.

"Then I'd imagine tonight you'd just have to have sour cream instead of butter on your potatoes."

He chuckled softly. "I was just going to explore the Rock. Would you care to accompany me?" He made a formal bow and offered his elbow.

It was tempting, but, regretfully, she had to refuse. "I really have too much work to do before this evening. I can't."

"Oh, come on. How many times in your life will you have a chance to climb the famous Independence Rock?" He grinned, his teeth flashing white against his dark skin and his dimples deepening.

She wanted to go. They had been tentative with each other these past few days, trying to reestablish their friendship while they struggled to resist the underlying tension between them. The opportunity to spend a few hours alone with him was simply too tempting to resist.

Picking up her skirt in both hands, she took off at a dead run, her musical peal of laughter trailing behind her.

"Come on, slowpoke! Let's go conquer a rock!"

Independence Rock was often aptly termed "The Register of the Plains," as generations of passing travelers had carved their names into the soft gray rock, the only record of their journey. Jessie clambered over the lower reaches, delightedly looking for J.J.'s or David's name, only vaguely disappointed when she failed to find them. It was too beautiful a day to ruin.

She watched as Tony paused on the upward trek to etch their names in the stone. Seeing "Jessamyn and Antonio Winchester, 1853" indelibly carved into the rock gave Jessie a queer thrill. It seemed so solid, so real. So permanent.

She buried the tempting thought where it belonged —under as big a pile of mental garbage as she could muster. Nothing in life was permanent.

Especially nothing that she wanted this much.

She dropped to her knees, lightly tracing the outlines of the letters with her fingertip. "What did you do this for?" she asked, trying to subdue the tiny, persistent spark of hope flaring in her heart.

"Our names?" He shrugged. "What else would I write?"

"Even if it's not the truth?"

He paused, his eyes dark and unreadable. "Especially since it's not the truth."

She turned away, not wanting him to see any vestiges of hurt in her face, and resumed her trek up the hill.

Her climbing abilities were hampered by her full skirts. Jessie was puffing by the time she reached the

.

top of the mound, complaining good-naturedly between gasps for breath.

"Whose idiotic idea was this, anyway?"

"Shhh." Tony took her hand, pulling her up the last
few feet to stand beside him at the summit. "Look."

At first Jessie was too aware of the man beside her,
of the warmth of her hand in his, to notice the panorama spread out before her, but once she did she
sighed in pleasure.

They were five hundred and fifty feet above the
plains, giving them a sweeping view of the prairie they
had so recently traversed. The afternoon sun burnished the grass to a mellow gold, bisected by the tiny,
meandering Sweetwater River. Here and there other
lumps of rock, gray or tan and much smaller than the
one on which they were standing, thrust out of the
soil. A large group of dark brown dots in the distance
were buffalo, while a nearer, smaller gathering of yel-
low-tan spots were antelope. The white patches that
were alkaline flats shone crystalline in the warm rays.
They would be salt lakes in the rainy season.

Tony and Jessie turned to the west, shading their
eyes to see the mountains they would soon reach. The
peaks were high and sharp, forbidding yet utterly
beautiful, gleaming blue, purple, and white in the distance. It seemed impossible to haul the wagons over
such intimidating barriers, yet they knew they would
find a way.

A sense of rightness grew, flowing in the air and
between Jessie and Tony. It was as if there had to be
this time, this place, these people. Neither spoke, for
neither needed to. The connection between them was
simply there, like the land and the sky and their beating hearts.

Tony groaned aloud, patting his overstuffed stomach in satisfaction. The feast had been truly that, and

he had enjoyed every bite. There had been roasted buffalo, sage hens, and jackrabbits, as well as the antelope he had contributed, so much juicier and more tender than venison. The women had prepared not only potatoes but beans and rice as well. Treasured jars of pickles and preserves, carefully protected since the journey's start, had been added, but the crowning achievement had been dessert. The ladies seemed to delight in competing with each other to produce the most delectable sweets, turning out cakes, pies, dumplings, and dried-fruit compotes, as well as contributing precious hoarded chocolate.

"It really wasn't necessary to try *every* dish," Jessie said, glancing at him out of the corner of her eye.

"Of course it was. I couldn't hurt any of the ladies' feelings after they worked so hard, could I? Besides, I've never felt better," Tony responded, knowing the sense of well-being suffusing him had less to do with the tasty food than with the woman who had been at his side throughout the meal. "I need to put a little meat on my bones, anyway."

Unable to help herself, Jessie's gaze swept Tony from head to toe. His bones looked simply wonderful to her. Decked out in tight navy britches; a loose, flowing, snowy-white shirt which set off his deeply tanned complexion; and a red bandana carelessly knotted around his neck; he was breathtaking. The artist in her appreciated the classic handsomeness of his face, but the woman in her responded to the strength and undeniable masculinity he radiated.

A warmth grew within her, spreading out through the farthest reaches of her body. Why did he have to be the one man who could make her feel this way? He had made it perfectly clear that he was not the man for her. Why, then, did her heart simply refuse to listen? She knew it was already too late for her to have a simple, uncomplicated relationship with him. Any further step they took toward each other was a step

toward her heart being broken. She knew it, and yet
she couldn't seem to stop it.

To distract herself, she tried to draw him into their
usual teasing banter. "If you keep eating like that
you're not only going to get meat on your bones,
you're going to get fat. You'll lose your touch with the
ladies."

"Darlin', I'll never lose my touch with the ladies."
He should have left it at that; he had no right to give
either one of them hope. But he said it anyway. "Besides, there's only one lady I want to touch."

The heat in his gaze made it perfectly clear who
that one lady was. Jessie could feel herself responding,
melting and weakening, even as she knew the words
flowed as easily from him as wine from a bottle.

"Excuse me." Jessie jumped up to leave, but Tony
caught her wrist. His long, lean fingers could feel the
leaping pulse beating there.

"Where are you going?"

"I . . . I just to need a bit of privacy to, um . . .
you know," Jessie stammered, feeling a flush creep up
her neck to heat her cheeks.

"Oh." Tony released her wrist. "I thought maybe
you were running away from me again. Don't be gone
long."

"I won't." Just long enough to get her wayward
heart back in line, she hoped.

Jessie wouldn't be gone long, huh? Delia thought
grimly. Well, she'd have to see if she could do something about that.

Delia was behind Tony, so all she could see were
those wide, wide shoulders and his softly gleaming
hair. She knew that if she could have one more good
chance at him she could get him interested in her. She
just knew it.

Her eyes narrowed in speculation as she looked

around the camp. She needed help—someone to keep Jessie occupied, away from Tony. There was no one to help, no one except—

There. Walt Morrison watched Jessie leave the gathering, his pale eyes filled with naked longing and wistfulness. When she had passed out of sight, his gaze turned to Tony. In his eyes Delia could see anger and bitterness and, above all, jealousy.

Delia wasn't a particularly smart woman, but she was clever. Clever enough to understand men's emotions. Clever enough to know that jealousy was an extremely useful one.

Walt would be an easy man to manipulate. He was too eager, too ruled by what was in his pants. Delia was always aware of how a man looked at her, and she certainly knew that Walt wanted her.

It had amused her at first. It certainly wasn't anything she'd ever given much thought to before. He definitely didn't appeal to her at all, and if she thought of him in that way it was always with a vague sense of distaste. But if he was going to be useful, she could certainly put aside that distaste—for a while.

She patted her red hair, hair of a color she was sure was a symbol of her passionate nature. She settled her ice-blue dress around her curves and sashayed over to Walt.

"Hello, Walt."

He gulped in surprise. "Hello, Delia."

"How are you doing?"

"I'm doing well." He knew his luck had changed. Delia, who hadn't blinked at him the whole trip, had come over to talk to him. He leaned closer. "You sure are lookin' good today."

She forced herself not to lean away. "How come you're sittin' here by yourself?"

His eyes glittered. "I'm not alone now, am I?"

"Well, no, you're not. But I thought you'd be headin' out after Jessie."

"After Jessie?"

Delia shrugged and nodded toward the direction she'd seen Jessie leave camp. "Yeah, she wandered off that way. I'da thought you'd be following her."

Walt frowned. "Why would you think a thing like that?"

She smiled coyly. "Well, I've seen the way she's been watching you."

"Watchin' me?"

"Well, of course, watchin' you."

"How's she been watchin' me?"

No doubt about it, the man was a little slow on the uptake. "Oh, you know, Walt. I'm sure women watch you like that all the time. Kinda friendly-like. You know, admiring."

"Jessie?"

"Of course. I noticed it right off."

"Yeah? Oh, well, of course she has."

"Sure. That's why I haven't set my cap for you. I figured you were spoken for already."

He leered at her, his gaze firmly fixed on her chest. "Oh, honey, I got no problem with handling two of ya."

Delia almost pulled away but caught herself in time. "Walt, I could never handle sharing a man like you. Makes me powerful jealous. 'Sides, if she saw ya first, she gets ya. I never poach on another woman's territory."

"That's a shame."

"Isn't it, though?" She smiled brightly. "Still, if you're gonna catch her, you better go now."

Walt glanced uneasily at where Tony still sat chatting amiably with Ginnie Wrightman. "How do I know Tony isn't gonna come after her?"

"Shoot! You ain't afraid o' him, are you?"

"'Course not!" Walt puffed up his sunken chest. "I jes' wanna pick my time, that's all. Take care o' him on my own terms."

"Walt, you gotta take your opportunities when you got them. 'Sides, you don't have to worry about Tony. He's going to be occupied."

"Occupied?"

Delia smiled. "Yeah. Occupied."

She barely waited until Walt charged out of camp before she headed for Tony. "Ginnie, Andrew's lookin' for you."

Ginnie glared at Delia. This was the last person she'd leave alone with her best friend's husband. "What did he want?"

"How should I know?" Delia replied. "He told me to come get you. He needed you for something. You'd better go."

"I don't know . . ." She glanced reluctantly at Tony.

"It's O.K., Ginnie," he said.

"Still . . ."

"I'm a big boy, Ginnie." His eyes gleamed with amusement. "I can take care of myself."

"Well, you'd just better if you know what's good for you."

He lifted one hand in promise. "Absolutely."

Delia plopped quickly into the space Ginnie vacated.

"Hello, Tony."

"That seat's taken, Delia. I'm waitin' on Jessie."

"Oh, I'm sure she wouldn't mind if I rest here for a little bit."

"Yes, she would."

Delia bit her lip and inched closer. What was it with this man? He had more willpower than any man should have a right to. It had never occurred to her that he really was completely uninterested.

"I'm sure we've got time for a little chat," she said.

"No, we don't."

"Well, that was rude."

"It was meant to be."

"You might as well settle in, Tony. We've got plenty of time. Jessie's not going to be back for a while yet."

His eyes narrowed. "How would you know?"

She rested a palm against her cheek, pursing her lips innocently. "Just a feelin'. I get lots of feelin's."

"What the hell is going on?"

He made her nervous when he looked at her like that. Somehow he'd be less scary if he yelled. It was his soft, calm voice that seemed really dangerous.

"Nothing," she squeaked.

He grabbed her wrist. His grip was just shy of painful, and his voice harsh. "Delia, you are going to tell me where Jessie is."

Delia thought quickly. It was time for an alternate plan. If she couldn't distract him, maybe she could at least turn his anger in a more useful direction.

"I promised."

"Delia . . ."

"All right, all right. Only because I feel bad she's treatin' you so shabbily. She went off to meet Walt. I heard 'em plannin' it."

Tony's fingers tightened around her wrist, sending tiny, sharp slivers of pain shooting down her arm.

"Why, you lying little bitch. You are going to tell me where they are right now, Delia. And this time, you're going to tell me the truth."

After attending to her needs a good distance from camp, Jessie strolled back slowly. It was the softest time of the day, the time when evening sighed gently into night. Lost in reflection, she paid no attention to the beauty of the encroaching darkness nor the distant camp fires which beckoned with gaiety and laughter.

Her mind had room for only one thought: Tony. It seemed increasingly impossible they would be able to deny the emotion between them for the next three months. If she accepted that, what were her alternatives? It didn't seem likely that she could handle a temporary relationship with no regrets, but would she regret more not exploring the feelings that pulsed so strongly in her? Was there any hope that Tony would change his views on love? She couldn't answer that without knowing what had caused his disillusionment in the first place.

She wasn't even sure she wanted to answer it. Loving meant losing; sometimes quickly, sometimes slowly, but, inevitably losing. She had sworn never to make herself vulnerable to that kind of pain again, but she had a terrifying suspicion that it was already too late.

She was going to hurt, no matter what.

So inattentive was she to her surroundings that she did not see the shadowy figure waiting to the left of the path until a voice rasped out of the night.

"Hello, Miss Jessie."

Jessie gasped and turned abruptly, her heart suddenly thudding in her breast. His back was to the faint remaining light, but Jessie did not need to see his features to know who it was. The fact that it was Walt Morrison detaining her did nothing to subdue her sudden nervousness. Her unease, persistent if unexplained, tightened her chest. It didn't matter that he had done nothing to threaten her; it was instinct, as prey feels the presence of predator.

"Walt—" Her voice cracked, and Jessie swallowed, trying to sound normal. "I was just on my way back to camp. Would you care to join me?" She sidled away, easing toward the safety of the wagons.

He wet his lips with one quick swipe of his slender tongue. "Oh, yes, I would most certainly like to join you."

There was no mistaking his meaning. She quickened her steps, realizing with relief that she had reached the first two vehicles—relief that evaporated quickly when he stepped in front of her, blocking her path through the wagons.

"Get out of my way!"

He didn't bother to acknowledge her command, but ran his hand over her shoulder. She flinched. His touch was not casual or friendly. Light as it was, somehow it felt repulsive.

"Don't you ever touch me again."

Stepping back, she felt the comforting, rough wood bulk of the wagon against her shoulder blades. She could see his eyes glittering above her. When he spoke, it was soft, sounding genuinely perplexed. "Now, honey, I don't see what's your problem. I just want to have a little fun. I know what you are."

What she was? Jessie didn't understand, but, debating the best way around him, she dismissed his comment.

She couldn't dismiss what he did next. His hands shot out and grabbed her waist, tugging her to him.

She was too incredulous to react immediately. Could he really be that stupid? To try something with her when camp, and Tony, were only a few steps away?

She twisted her arms free of his grip and jumped away.

"I told you to keep your filthy hands off me!"

"Filthy?" He held up his hands and looked at them, as if he couldn't believe she was talking about him. "Perhaps you're a bit mistaken about just who's dirty and who's clean."

His eyes narrowed, and Jessie felt the first edge of true fear. Something was definitely not right here.

She was getting out.

She tried a quick move around him, but he was faster than he looked. He slammed one arm into the side of the wagon in front of her, the other behind, caging her in.

Screaming for help was beginning to look like her only option.

One minute he was there. The next he was gone.

She saw a large, familiar form holding Walt by the throat. His feet were dangling a full four inches from the ground while he swung his fists wildly, ineffectually.

Relief swept through her at the sound of Tony's voice, low and deadly calm.

"I should kill you."

"What's the big deal?" Walt managed to squeak out. "She's just a whore."

The blow was so swift that Jessie didn't see it, but she heard the crack of bone against bone as Walt's head snapped back.

Twisting his fist in the back of his shirt, Tony dragged a groggy Walt toward the camp fire. A relieved but somewhat bewildered Jessie trailed in their wake. When they reached the circle of firelight he heaved Walt to the ground and stood over him, impassive, while a crowd gathered.

Walt lay in the dust, dazed, bleeding heavily from his mouth, while the others pressed forward, all staring at Walt. Jessie couldn't seem to look away from Tony, for he wore an expression she had never thought to see on his face. His eyes were cold, his features set, and there was no doubt in her mind— here was a man who could kill. She had never dreamed that easygoing Tony was capable of ruthless violence. It frightened her, but it was also undeniably exciting.

"Now see here, Tony, what's going on?" Buffalo Bolton hurried over, booming the question all were thinking.

"Mr. Morrison is leaving the train."

"You can't—" Walt mumbled through swollen lips. He paused to spit out a stream of blood, spittle, and one decayed tooth before continuing. "You can't kick me off the train out here in the middle of nowhere!"

"Watch me."

Buffalo tried to gain control of the situation. "Tony, you know we can't force someone to leave the train without a damn good reason. Tell me what's goin' on."

"That bastard attacked my wife."

Amazingly, Morrison grinned widely, showing a black gap where his front tooth had been.

"But that's just it, Bolton. She ain't his wife."

17

A *stunned hush* fell over the crowd for a long instant, and then murmurs of speculation raced through like wildfire. Jessie clamped one hand over her mouth, as though she could somehow draw in Walt's words before they did any damage. Her eyes, wide and uncertain, met Tony's. He shrugged once before lowering his gaze on Morrison, who was struggling unsuccessfully to get to his feet.

"What the hell is that supposed to mean?" Tony asked in a harsh voice.

"I overheard the two of you talking—well, arguing really," Walt continued eagerly. "I know she ain't your wife. She ain't nothin' more than your own private piece o' ass."

Tony moved toward Morrison again, his fists balled, ready to attack. Buffalo stopped him by throwing his massive arms around Tony from behind.

"Is what he says true, Winchester?"

Tony's face was impassive except for the muscle twitching in his jaw. "What does it matter? He attacked her, and I want him thrown off the train." He shook off Bolton's hold.

"But you can't do that! It's dangerous out there!" Walt shouted. He paused, his reptilian eyes growing cunning. "Besides, I didn't attack her. She's been sendin' out invitations ever since we left Council Bluffs. I finally decided to take her up on it. Can I help it if you ain't enough man for her, Winchester?"

This time Buffalo anticipated Tony's reaction and knocked the knife from his hand just as he drew it from its sheath.

His fury concentrated on Walt, Tony was oblivious to his fellow travelers, but Jessie was keenly aware of the looks being directed her way. She heard the whispered questions, saw the eyes that gleamed in excitement over the potential bloodletting, felt the doubt and scandalized surprise. Delia Bolton smirked with smug satisfaction. Ginnie and Mary Ellen watched her with confusion and sympathy, while a number of men grinned at her with barely concealed leers.

It had all seemed so simple and logical in Council Bluffs, when she and Tony had agreed to this charade. How had she gotten into this mess?

"All right, now, you people just settle down. I'm calling a meetin', and we'll get everybody's side of the story before we make any decisions." Buffalo's voice held a ring of authority that had an effect on everyone but Tony.

"I want him out of here in ten minutes."

"Now, Tony, be reasonable. We can't very well get rid of the man if she really did, um . . . if she . . ." Buffalo reddened, "enticed him."

In her outrage, Jessie couldn't seem to find the words to defend herself. She didn't even know where to start—with Walt's absurd, insulting charges, or the all-too-true ones concerning her marriage.

"Oh, for heaven's sake, Tom," Harriet Bolton put in, exasperated. "Now you're being ridiculous. Don't you have eyes? How could any woman with a man like Tony in her bed even look at a worm like that!"

The last shreds of Tony's patience deserted him. He reached Morrison in two long strides and hauled him roughly to his feet before giving him a hard shake. His eyes were narrowed, intensely serious as his gaze bored into Walt's. "I've had enough of this bullshit. I don't care what Bolton, the council, or anybody else says. You have a choice to make, and it's a real simple one. You leave this train, or you die."

Like any animal, Morrison knew death when he smelled it. Quivering in pain and fear, Walt took one look at Tony and knew he spoke the truth. In that moment fear turned to hatred, but Walt knew he had no time for anger now.

"I'll go."

Tony instantly released him, and Walt fell heavily to the ground. He pushed himself to his feet and muttered, "I'll just collect my stuff and I'm gone." He slunk away into the darkness.

Oblivious to the questions being tossed his way, Tony's only concern was Jessie. He made his way to her side, sweeping her into his arms in a tight hug that said everything he couldn't say before pulling back and searching her face.

"Are you sure you're O.K.?"

Jessie managed a tremulous nod before turning to their immediate problem. "What are we going to do now?"

"I'm not sure. Maybe we won't have to do anything." He stroked her cheek gently in reassurance. "But whatever happens, you're going to be fine. I'll make sure of it."

The tight ball of trepidation in her stomach eased. Everything would be fine, Tony said so. She felt safe with him, safe in a way that she couldn't remember feeling since her father fell ill.

"Am I to understand that you two aren't married?"

an imperious voice demanded. Jessie and Tony groaned in unison before turning to face Silas Donner.

"I don't believe my relationship with Jessie is anyone's business but our own," Tony said, squeezing Jessie's hand.

"It most certainly is, if the two of you are living in sin." Reverend Donner raised his prominent nose even higher in the air. "There are impressionable children in this community. We simply cannot harbor an influence such as this in our midst."

Jessie felt Tony stiffen. "What precisely are you suggesting?" he asked.

"She must return to Fort Laramie immediately."

Jessie's panic returned in a rush. Her free hand clenched her skirt tightly, bunching the fabric. "But you don't understand—"

"Young *lady*—and I use that term extremely loosely —I understand only too well."

"Silas, she deserves an opportunity to speak. You can give her that much." Reverend Parson's voice was calm, without a hint of accusation, and Jessie took strength from it.

"Tony and I aren't . . . I mean, we're not . . ." Jessie flushed, but forced herself to continue. "We're not intimate. It was simply a business arrangement. I needed to join the train and he—" Jessie glared at Buffalo Bolton, "wouldn't let me. Tony was simply helping me."

A male voice hooted behind her. "And we all know what he got in payment, don't we, boys?"

Jessie felt Tony move toward the unknown man, and she grabbed his arm tightly with both hands. "No, Tony, don't make it any worse." He froze for a moment, clearly debating, before she felt the hard muscles under her fingers relax.

"I'm afraid Reverend Donner is right. We can't have an unmarried couple livin' together on the train," Buffalo said.

Tony raked a hand through his hair and rubbed the back of his neck. "Look, I'll just move out of her wagon."

Buffalo shook his head. "No, we've got rules about single women on the train. I made that perfectly clear from the start."

"But I'll take care of her, damn it!" Tony shouted, his frustration clearly evident.

"No." Buffalo was as stubborn and immovable as his namesake. "She's just going to have to leave. Sorry, but we all signed an agreement before we left Iowa. Rules are rules."

Jessie was breathing heavily while thoughts whirled through her head, incoherent and fragmented. What to do? How could she go back and what would she do at the Fort? She couldn't just move into another wagon; everybody thought she was a fallen woman. She thought of San Francisco and J.J. She had to get to California.

"What if we got married?" Jessie looked around frantically, sure that the words had come from some other mouth than hers. From the expression of shock on Tony's face, the idea was certainly her own. She could blame it on temporary insanity, perhaps, but not on someone else.

"That would be acceptable," Reverend Donner said, looking to Buffalo Bolton for agreement.

Buffalo pulled a hand down the length of his beard, cocking an inquiring eyebrow at Tony. Finally, almost reluctantly, he nodded his assent.

"Uh, fellas, I don't . . ." Jessie clamped her hand over Tony's mouth before he could say anything else. She flashed a forced smile at Bolton and the Reverend Donner.

"I think Tony and I need a moment alone." She grabbed Tony's arm and began to drag him away from the crowd.

Tony trailed along behind her, unprotesting. He

waited for the cloying sense of entrapment and imprisonment that always enveloped him whenever the word marriage was mentioned in connection with him.

Strangely, it never came. So she wanted to marry him, eh? He felt flattered. A little bit intrigued. And decidedly excited. She could drag him off any time she wanted.

He decided he'd better put up a token protest, however, so that when he hurt her—and he almost inevitably would—he could at least say he warned her.

Jessie stopped when they were behind a wagon on the far side of camp. She released her viselike grip on his arm and turned to face him but was unable to meet his eyes. Wiping her damp palms on her full skirt, she debated over the best way to phrase her proposal.

"I have to tell you, *cara,* maybe you should think about this a bit. Not that I wouldn't try to make you happy, of course, but I've never had much luck being faithful. If you don't think you can handle that—"

"Oh, for heaven's sake, Tony!" Jessie cut him off abruptly. "I don't expect you to stay married to me forever. We can get an annulment as soon as we get to San Francisco. If the marriage is not"—she bit her lower lip, hoping that the moonlight was dim enough to hide the blush she knew was heating her cheeks—"consummated, there shouldn't be any problem."

She didn't want to marry him after all. What a relief! Only a fool would be disappointed. Except he had the feeling that he was one hell of a fool. He ignored it, gathering the tattered remains of his male pride.

"I guess it's not much different than the arrangement we already have. Sure, Jessie, let's get married." Tony turned on his heel and strode back to camp, leaving her staring at his rapidly retreating figure and wondering at the faint note of derision in his voice.

*   *   *

"Here. Every bride should have a bouquet, shouldn't she? Even one who doesn't want to get married."

Jessie grasped the bundle of stalks that Tony thrust in her hands. He had gathered a bunch of blazing star, their feathery, purple-pink tufts appearing dark in the wavering firelight. Wondering how he had managed to find the flowers in the dark during the brief time before he returned to camp for the ceremony, she mumbled her thanks while trying to force down a wave of panic. It was all happening so fast!

"Are you ready, my children?"

The stalks quaking in her trembling hands, Jessie turned to face Reverend Parson. She had refused to have Reverend Donner perform the ceremony, and now she found herself comforted by Reverend Parson's gentle presence. The elderly minister took her hand in both of his, stroking the back of it with his papery-skinned palms.

"Jessie, I want you to think about this very carefully. It is not absolutely necessary for you to go through with this marriage. There are other possibilities," Reverend Parson said.

Jessie lifted her chin. "I have thought about it, Reverend. This is the only solution."

"Then let us begin." Jedediah opened his tattered, black-bound Bible, cleared his throat, and began to read a scripture.

Jessie smoothed her sky-blue skirt and adjusted the wide, red sash of the outfit she had chosen especially to celebrate her country's independence. It was odd how today, of all days, she was losing her own freedom, at least for a while. The high lace collar of her white shirtwaist seemed chokingly tight, and she ran a forefinger underneath it.

The minister's voice faded to a faint drone as Jessie, unable to concentrate on the words, chanced a peek at Tony out of the corner of her eye. He was standing to her right, stiff and very tall, his feet spread wide and his hands clasped behind him, an unreadable expression on his face. The firelight threw his features into shadows, lightly gilded with a touch of gold. She was suddenly incredibly proud that she could claim this man for her own, if only for a brief time.

She was so lost in thought that she was startled when Tony began to speak, repeating his vows in a deep voice that seemed to vibrate through her. When it was her turn to speak, he half turned to her, lowering his gaze to her face for the first time since the ceremony began. Her voice quavered as she saw his eyes. They were completely empty.

He had looked at her with amusement, annoyance, laughter, or passion, but never had she looked into those black orbs and seen absolutely nothing. As Jessie vowed to obey him, his left cheek indented briefly, and then, just as quickly, his face was wiped clean of expression again.

"You may kiss the bride." At the Reverend's pronouncement Jessie dropped her gaze to Tony's mouth. His lips were well shaped, almost unfairly sensual, and she remembered with startling clarity how they had felt, warm and seeking, against her own. She drew a sharp, anticipatory breath as he lowered his head.

It wasn't the same at all. His lips were cool as they touched her mouth for only the briefest instant before retreating. Her stomach dropped in—what? Relief? Or disappointment?

Tony bit his tongue, hoping that the pain in his mouth would distract him from the pain further down his body. Once again, the rapidity and strength of his response shocked him. He had only touched her lightly, on her soft lips and her hands, but his imagination had filled in the rest—parts of her that were tender, pink, and ivory and extraordinarily responsive to his slightest touch.

How the hell was he going to stay away from her now that she was legally his?

Jessie rubbed her eyes with the heels of her hands. It felt as if grit was permanently embedded behind her lids. She was drained, and the events of the day had swept away her mental anchors, leaving her adrift. She was now Mrs. Antonio Winchester, but, somehow, it seemed even less real than when she had just been playing the part.

Tony had disappeared from camp almost immediately after the ceremony. Shortly thereafter Jessie had thought she heard a horse's hooves pounding into the darkness, but she couldn't be sure, for she was surrounded by well-wishers. The men wore sly, knowing grins, and the women were flustered, looking for the right words; but no one condemned her. Even Reverend Donner had congratulated her without censure, as if her supposed sins were suddenly erased by her marriage.

Mary Ellen and Ginnie soon whisked her away to prepare her for her wedding night. Jessie tried to explain her deception to her friends, that her relationship with Tony was not what it appeared, but simply a business agreement.

It was important to Jessie that her friends believe and trust her. The demands of caring for her father had left little time for personal relationships, and having close friends was a luxury she hadn't been able to indulge in. Now, on the trip, she felt less alone than she had felt in years, and she needed to know that Ginnie and Mary Ellen still liked and respected her.

Mary Ellen accepted her explanation without a word, and seemingly without a question. Ginnie said, "Lord, honey, you don't have to defend yourself to us, no matter what you did. Goodness knows if Tony flashed those dimples at me I'da probably done any-thin' he asked, too."

Jessie protested again that it was all a mistake, it was just a practical arrangement.

She couldn't help smiling at Ginnie's answer: "Sweetheart, if you ask me you'd be makin' a mistake if you *don't* sleep with that man, married or not."

After they left, Jessie fell backwards onto the mattress. Absently, she plucked at the ribbons that tied the neck of her nightgown. Ginnie had declared that it was not nearly bridal enough and offered to lend her something more seductive, but Jessie certainly didn't feel like a bride, so why should she dress like one?

She rolled to her side and settled in, rubbing her cheek against her pillow, enjoying the coolness of the sheets after the heat of the day. She let her mind drift, floating in that semiconsciousness between awareness and sleep.

Her husband. She tugged Tony's pillow close and wrapped her arms around it, snuggling in, wishing he was there to cuddle, missing the security she always felt when he was near.

When Tony entered the wagon he found her like that, sleeping curled up on her side and holding his pillow as she would a lover, with a relaxed smile on her face. She had tied back the front flaps, probably to catch the night breeze, and moonlight flooded the small space. The silver rays made her look like a white marble sculpture, created by a gifted artist as the embodiment of womanly beauty. He ground his teeth against an overwhelming urge to take her in his arms and caress her until cool stone turned to warm living flesh.

He swore vehemently under his breath. He had ridden General hard and long, hoping to exhaust his mind as well as his body. Before returning to camp he had stopped at the river to bathe the sweat from his skin, but now he was as hot as if the chilly water had never touched him. The night was unusually warm, but Tony knew that the fires came as much from within as without.

He sat on the end of the mattress and pulled off his boots, grunting when they finally gave way. He yanked off his socks, balled them up, and tossed them into the far corner of the wagon. He didn't feel like being neat tonight. He hadn't put his shirt back on after washing; it was still flipped over his shoulder, so he flung it off into the darkness at the back of the wagon, too.

He eased his pillow away from Jessie. She clutched at it briefly before giving it up, mumbling something unintelligible as she rolled to her back. Tony punched the pillow twice before settling down to sleep.

Twenty minutes later he was still tossing and turning, unsettled and uncomfortable. He was too warm. He propped himself up on his left elbow and cast a disgruntled glance toward the woman slumbering so peacefully by his side. Even if she had rejected a real marriage with him without a second thought, he was going to claim at least one of his husbandly privileges, starting now.

He hated sleeping in clothes, anyway. They were constricting and always seemed too warm. He stripped off his pants and drawers in one rapid motion and expelled a contented breath as he leaned back against his pillow.

He hoped to hell no bandits picked tonight to attack.

18

Jessie came awake slowly, struggling to leave her dreams and reach awareness. It was very bright; was it morning already? If so, why hadn't someone woken her? The entire camp was usually up before sunrise. She blinked, trying to clear the sleep from her eyes.

It was only moonlight, thank God. She could go back to sleep. She closed her lids gratefully, but before she fell asleep she became aware of the deep, even breathing next to her. So, Tony was back, finally. Carefully, trying not to wake him, she rolled to her side, her gaze sweeping over him to assure herself of his comforting presence.

He was stark naked.

Her hand reflexively flew up to cover her eyes. What was he trying to pull? Her curiosity got the better of her, and she spread her fingers slightly so she could peek between them. She couldn't see much through the tiny opening, just one lean length of well-sculpted muscle highlighted by the moon. Tony was sprawled comfortably on his back, one arm flung over his head while his other arm lay loosely across his waist.

Traitorous thoughts prodded her. She would never have an opportunity like this again. After all, she was an artist. It was perfectly acceptable—even necessary —for her to study anatomy.

And what an anatomy it was.

She lowered her hand from her face, first checking carefully to make sure that Tony was still deeply asleep. As if she were trying to memorize his appearance, her gaze lingered on the strong bones of his face before slipping to his torso. She had seen his chest before but had never felt the freedom to look as long and thoroughly as she wished, so she was going to make the most of the chance to do so now.

His shoulders were impossibly wide, his arms and his chest heavily muscled before tapering abruptly. The light was too dim to see the nipples hidden by the curls of dark hair, and Jessie leaned closer to assuage her sudden, strong urge to find them. His abdomen was ridged like a washboard and Jessie unconsciously brushed her hand over her own stomach, marveling at the difference.

Her gaze skipped over the part of him she was most curious about, as if she was not willing to admit— even to herself—what it was she really wanted to see. His legs were long, the lower portions disappearing into the darkness, and the strong, horseman's thighs were lightly sprinkled with black hair.

Jessie halted her scrutiny at the tops of his thighs. Lord, did she dare? Oh, go ahead, her curiosity urged. He was her husband, wasn't he?

A bright shaft of moonlight illuminated the lower portion of his torso. She was no longer frightened or embarrassed, but intrigued.

Oh, God, something was happening to him! He was . . . changing. . . .

She suddenly looked up at his face . . . and found herself looking straight into his dark, intense gaze.

"Oh, no," Jessie moaned, shamed to the marrow of her bones at being caught peeping at him. She rolled over and curled into a tight ball, her back to Tony and her arms covering her face while hot tears of embarrassment streaked down her cheeks.

"No, Jessie, please—" Tony sat up swiftly, slipped one arm under her legs and another around her back, and lifted her onto his lap. "Hush, *cara,* don't cry. I didn't mean to frighten you, but I couldn't help it. It's not that awful, is it?"

Tony could feel her soft hair brush against his chest as she shook her head. Her voice was muffled. "I wasn't frightened. I'm mortified and humiliated. You caught me looking at you while you were sleeping like I was some kind of perverted—"

"Hush. Don't say another word." Tony wound his fingers into her hair and tipped her head back. Her eyes were closed. "Look at me, Jessie." When she didn't obey his voice became more forceful. "Look at me!"

Reluctantly she opened her lids a tiny crack. She steeled herself for a look of anger or disgust but found neither. Her eyes opened wider in surprise. He looked sort of amused, almost happy.

With gentle fingers he brushed back the tendrils of hair that clung to her tear-dampened cheeks. "I don't ever want to hear you use that word in relation to yourself again. It's not perverted; it's natural. And there's no reason to be embarrassed. If I had a chance to see you in the buff, you could bet I'd jump at it."

"Really?"

"Really," he affirmed in a voice that left no room for doubt, and he pressed his lips against her forehead for an instant. "It would take our entire ox team to drag me away. Besides, it was pretty obvious I was enjoying it, too."

"You were?"

Tony barely managed to smother his chuckle before it escaped. He doubted she would appreciate his amusement, but, *Dio,* she really didn't know!

"Jess, you saw what happened to me, right? When I . . . changed?"

Her gaze slid away from his, and she gave a brief, almost imperceptible nod.

"That's what happens to a man when he gets excited. Knowing you were looking at me aroused me, and that's what happens when I want you. And, *Dio,* Jessie, I do want you!"

He touched her cheek, and Jessie was mesmerized, enthralled by the heat in his dark eyes and the hoarseness of his voice. He seemed to be fighting some almost uncontrollable urge.

Awareness rushed through Jessie with lightning speed. How could she have not noticed before the intimacy of their position, and, separated from her by only a thin layer of fabric, the hardness of his manhood beneath her buttocks? She squirmed slightly, pressing herself against him, trying to ease the ache building between her thighs.

"Jessie, no!" His hands clamped around her waist, forcing her to remain still. His head fell back, and she could hear the hissing intake of air through his clenched teeth. "I'm hanging on by a thread here, *cara,* but you're going to have to give me some help."

Jessie looked at the agony on his face, so closely mirroring her own longing, and in that moment her decision was made. She wanted him. No matter where the trail led them from there, she knew, deep down and unequivocally, that there would never be another man for her.

"Then let me help you," she whispered, pulling his head down to meet hers.

The instant before their lips touched, he stopped. She could feel the muscles in his shoulders bunch.

"Be very sure, Jessie, because I haven't got the strength to leave you again. Are you absolutely certain?" he asked, searching her eyes.

"Yes."

"God, Jessie!" He kissed her once, hard, pressing his mouth on hers before he wrapped her tightly in his arms, holding her close against his chest for a time, letting the fires grow.

"Tony, I can't breathe."

He gave a short bark of laughter. "Sorry." He lifted her and half turned, laying her out across the mattress before settling his big frame next to her. He bent his left arm at the elbow to prop up his head. With one strong finger he traced her profile, forehead to nose to chin.

"Ah, Jessie, you're so—" He stopped and shook his head, a rueful grin lifting one corner of his mouth. "I was going to say beautiful, but that doesn't begin to describe you. There are many beautiful women in the world, but few who are like you. You're . . ." He traced the graceful curve of her throat where her pulse was beating lightly, rapidly. "Radiant."

His finger continued on its path, sweeping a line down the center of her body to brush briefly against the feminine mound between her legs, causing Jessie to curl up instinctively. When she saw the look in his eyes, she relaxed again. There was so much emotion there, such intensity of tenderness and longing, that Jessie began to tremble.

"You're shaking, *cara*. Are you afraid?" His hand slid over her shoulder and down her arm, finding her hand and bringing it up to his lips. He kissed each knuckle before turning her hand over and tracing intricate designs on her palm with his tongue. "Don't be afraid."

"I'm not." How could anyone be afraid? she wondered, lost in an anticipation she had never imagined. "I'm just not sure what to do."

"Only what you want, whatever you want."

He kissed her, his lips drifting over hers. His mouth was open, and she fit hers to his, waiting impatiently for the touch of his tongue. When it didn't come, she slipped her own into his mouth, searching.

Perhaps that was the signal he was waiting for, because when her tongue reached his he growled low in his throat and quickly, suddenly, the kiss transformed. It was still gentle, but there was a new hunger as he stroked and teased and aroused her. He explored the smoothness of her inner cheeks, the sharpness of her teeth, and Jessie could only follow mindlessly where he led.

He lowered his mouth to her breast, drawing it in strongly, tonguing her through the flimsy cotton of her gown. The slight abrasion caused ripples of sensation to start deep within her, spreading outward to her furthest extremities.

He stopped, turning his head to the side and pressing his cheek to her chest, breathing heavily.

"Could we take off your gown? I want to see you, like you saw me."

She would have denied him nothing now—nothing, as long as, this time, he didn't leave her. She rose to her knees and began to lift the hem of her nightdress, but he was quicker, sweeping the garment over her head and tossing it toward the darkened back corner of the wagon where it floated down into a pale puddle of cloth, echoing the color of the moonlight.

Tony knelt in front of her, sinking his hands into her hair and tilting her head for his kiss. He had not yet touched her anywhere except her face, her lips, and, briefly through her gown, her breasts. Still, her body tingled all over. He rolled to one hip, bringing her down with him in a fluid move which left them lying side by side. Never breaking the kiss, he moved closer, pressing their skin together, letting them learn the fit and the warmth of their bodies.

His hand slipped down her back, around her waist and up her ribs, finally cupping her breast. Jessie gasped against his mouth as he moved his work-roughened palm in slow, seductive circles over her tight nipple. Almost regretfully he tore his mouth from hers, gliding his tongue down the side of her neck and pausing to taste the skin of one creamy shoulder. Closing his lips over her breast, he circled one nipple with his tongue while using his fingers to mimic the motion on the other.

Jessie was unaware of anything but the sensations flowing through her body: ripples of joy, the purest physical pleasure, and an intense, tangible connection between her and this man. How could she not have known, not have dreamed? It seemed so elemental, so necessary. She made a feline sound, almost a purr.

At her sensuous groan Tony nearly lost all control. He had wanted her for so long and so fiercely, had fantasized about this moment too often, and he didn't want to wait any longer. He wanted to plunge between her thighs and lose himself in her warmth. But he needed to make this good for her. Her first time would only happen once, and if it was in his power he intended it to be extraordinary, a private memory that would make her smile when she was a cute, feisty, little seventy-year-old.

He pulled back a bit, caressing her in every place he longed to, watching in pleasure as his hand skimmed over her hip, her thigh, her belly. When she giggled, he lifted his gaze to meet her eyes, shining silver in the moonlight.

"You were right. You do have proficient hands."

He grinned. "You can do this, too," he said, his teeth flashing seductively.

He closed his eyes at the intense pleasure when she touched him. Curving her fingers against his chest, she searched for and found his small, pebble-hard nipples. She teased them lightly with her fingertips before her hands moved to test the muscles at the sides of his waist.

Jessie reveled in her investigation. She loved the bulging muscles of his arms, the flat planes of his back. She caressed his thigh, marveling that flesh could be so hard. She reached to explore his abdomen and accidentally brushed his manhood. He jerked back, and she immediately curled her fingers and withdrew her fist.

"Tony, I'm sorry, I didn't mean to hurt you, I—"

He chuckled, although the sound seemed hoarse and strained.

"No, it didn't hurt—at least not the way you mean. It's O.K., you can touch me." He groped for her hand and urged it forward.

She hesitated. "I don't know, Tony, I—"

"Please."

Reassured, her trepidations overwhelmed by her strong need to feel, to know, she reached out and pressed her palm lightly against the shaft jutting from his body.

"Ohhh," she breathed, fascinated. It wasn't what she had expected. The skin was incredibly smooth, soft, like hot silk stretched over carved, polished oak. Circling him with her fingers, she tested the slight curve. She slid her fingers upward and over the blunt tip, surprised to find a small drop of moisture clinging there.

"Jessie!" Tony hissed through clenched teeth. He rolled over, sweeping her beneath him and pressing her deeply into the mattress. He brought his mouth down on hers, hard this time, his tongue plunging and retreating in an intoxicating cadence that soon had her writhing beneath him. He drew her tongue deeply into his mouth and then sank his teeth lightly into her lower lip, tugging on it. He rolled slightly to one side, lifting himself on one elbow, watching her face intently as his hand slid down, over her collarbone, through the valley between her breasts, into the hollow of her waist, dipping one finger into her navel before he glided his fingers into the curls between her legs.

Finding her soft and wet, he slid his middle finger into her body. He watched her intently, so entranced by the expressions fleeing across her face—confusion, raw passion, ecstasy—he could almost ignore his own biting need. Her head was thrown back, her throat curved, her eyes shut tightly. With his thumb, Tony found and stroked her exquisitely sensitive bit of flesh, and her eyes flew open in shock and intense pleasure. He kissed her again, deeply, distracting her as he carefully inserted another finger and spread them, stretching her gently, trying to make their eventual joining as easy for her as he could. With the pad of his thumb he continued to tease, to entice, pushing her closer to the edge, waiting until he could feel her muscles begin to tighten, knowing that he wanted her too much and too desperately to make it last as long as he wished.

Jessie was only dimly aware when Tony spread her thighs wider and moved over her, bracing himself on his forearms. She was lost in her own riotous, thundering desire. "Oh, Tony, I—" She broke off, unable to express the feelings that shimmered just beyond her reach. There were no words, she didn't have the language to express it.

"I know, Jessie. Me, too." He pressed a soft, lingering kiss to her warm lips before whispering again. "Me, too." He flexed his hips, and in one clean, powerful stroke, she was filled. Filled in her body, filled in her heart, and filled in her soul.

Her senses were aroused, almost unbearably acute. She could feel the texture of the wiry hair on his thighs against the soft flesh of hers, the friction of his furred chest on her breasts, the pulse in his abdomen, pressed so tightly to hers, and the unfamiliar, extraordinary pressure deep in the most secret reaches of her body.

Burying her nose in the hollow of his neck where his scent was strongest, she inhaled deeply. She loved the way he smelled: heat, skin, and man.

He began to move, and the world faded away, like deep fog rolling in and blurring the edges of reality, obscuring all things unimportant. She was conscious only of waves of elemental sensation, rising in her higher and higher. She wrapped her arms around him, sliding her hands down his back, which was slick with moisture, to his tight buttocks. She dug her nails into muscle, her palms flat against the indentations on the sides of his hips, and tried to bring him closer, deeper —anything to satisfy the driving need.

Suddenly the dam broke, and pleasure flooded through her in pounding waves, seeping into the furthest recesses of her body. She cried out, unaware, a primitive sound, releasing emotions that had no other outlet.

Tony felt Jessie convulse beneath him. Where they were joined her body tightened around his in rhythmic contractions, pushing him to his own completion. He shuddered above her in a blinding, turbulent rush of pleasure, clutching her tightly as if he could absorb her into him and keep a part of her with him for always.

One by one, his tense muscles relaxed. He dropped his forehead to hers, taking in great gulps of breath, cooling his mind and his body. Reluctantly, he slipped out of her, falling to one side but keeping her near in his embrace. He couldn't let her go, not yet. His hands, toughened by years of working with horses, smoothed her tangled hair, sometimes snagging on the soft threads.

Unwilling to mar the moment, he said nothing, finding no words worth speaking. Her breath stirred the hair on his chest, and it was some time before he realized that her breathing was steady and deep.

She was asleep. He laughed softly and threw one leg over hers, pulling her even closer. He was exhausted from the continuous struggle of the last two months, the sleepless nights when he had wanted the woman he couldn't have. With his body finally sated, he knew that he, too, would soon find the haven of slumber, and he wanted to keep her with him while he slept.

But despite his fatigue, his mind couldn't find the peace his body needed. A vague unease crept into his contentment. The exceptional satisfaction he had found with Jessie was unmatched, and, much as he wanted to attribute his overwhelming reaction to his recent celibacy, he could not.

He had never before dissected his pleasure after being with a woman, but he found himself doing precisely that. There was something different about making love with Jessie, something that made it decidedly unique. He thought he knew what it was, and it scared the hell out of him.

He had been with dozens of women in his life, but there was always a piece of himself that had never been involved in his lovemaking, a piece he had held back: his heart. He was honest enough with himself to admit that perhaps the parade of women that passed through his arms was his way of preventing any one from coming too close.

But now one had.

19

Tony was gone, as usual, when Jessie woke, grumbling and blinking, trying to shut out the inevitable dawn as long as possible. The feeling of well-being and contentment that suffused her lasted all of perhaps two minutes before the uncertainties hit.

What had she done? She remembered each touch, each caress, each feeling, with a sharp clarity that, even now, tightened her nipples and sent a surge of excitement through her lower regions. She couldn't really regret last night—not when it had been so truly beautiful. It had opened her up to a brilliant, sensual world, changing her forever.

No, what concerned her was Tony's reaction. She had given herself to him only a few scarce hours after she had sworn that their marriage would be in name only. He must think that she had lied—that she had wed him under false pretenses, then seduced him, trapping him into a marriage he had never intended.

Jessie scrambled to get dressed, her typical morning lethargy replaced with urgency. She threw a plain,

checked gingham dress over her head, refastening it
twice before getting the buttons in their proper holes.
She finger-combed her hair, freeing only the worst of
the tangles before tying the mass at the base of her
neck with a white strip of cloth. She slipped on the
soft moccasins Tony had given her, not bothering with
stockings in her rush to leave the wagon and find him.

In one night, he had given her more beauty and
pleasure than she'd had in her entire life up to now. In
return, she would give him the only thing she could.

His freedom.

Tony tossed the dregs of cold coffee on the ground
and refilled his cup from the pot simmering on the
small fire. He took a careful sip, not wanting to burn
his lips on the metal rim heated by the fresh coffee. He
stretched his legs, cramped and stiff from sitting
cross-legged on the cold ground for so long, and
twisted, trying to ease the tightness in his lower back.

He had been there for hours, sitting and thinking.
The massive bulk of Independence Rock had still been
inky black when he had arrived, its outline only barely
discernible in the dim light provided by the setting
moon, muted by the thin veil of clouds that had blown
in overnight. The rock had slowly, almost imperceptibly, lightened to a gray that matched the predawn sky.
Now it was gilded with a wash of red-gold, heralding
the dawn, and still he had no answers. The western
reaches of the Rock remained lost in purple shadows,
contrasting with the rays lighting the eastern slopes.
The sky was a pure, shining gold that reminded him of
Jessie's hair.

Jessie. His wife. It seemed unreal, unimaginable. He
had trapped himself in the one thing he had spent the
last eight years running from—a promise, a commit-
ment. He prided himself on being a man of his word.
In all areas of his life but this one, he always had been.

He had broken a promise only once. Liza's image floated at the edges of his consciousness, and he found he could no longer see her face clearly. He had hurt her in every way possible. Even though he hadn't meant to, he had taken everything from her, and his own actions still made him sick to his stomach, neither blunted nor dissipated by time.

He was a man incapable of being faithful, of being a good husband. Much as he despised that trait in himself, he would not delude himself. So what was he going to do about Jessie?

He lifted his mug for another fortifying gulp of the strong coffee. His hand paused, mid-motion. She was there. He didn't know how he knew. Did he hear her, smell her, *sense* her? He took a large, scalding mouthful of coffee, forcing the swallow past the lump in his throat, steeling himself before turning to face her—the woman whom he desperately didn't want to hurt.

He knew he almost certainly would.

Jessie was startled when Tony suddenly swung his head toward her, spearing her with a cold, remote look. She had crept up on him silently, hoping not to disturb him until she found the proper words. With his sharp, handsome profile backlit by the rising sun, he had seemed distant and troubled, and Jessie had nearly decided to slip away and confront him later. When he turned toward her, she wished she had escaped. His eyes were dark, the brows drawn together sharply, and Jessie could read a hint of pain and some emotion she couldn't define and instinctively knew she didn't want to.

Squaring her shoulders, she continued to walk to him, stopping when she was more than an arm's length away. She tried a tentative opening, probing carefully. "Tony, I . . . about last night, I—"

His voice was sharp, like the cracking of an ox whip. "Last night is over. We need to concentrate on the future now. We're stuck with each other, so—"

"Stuck with each other?" Jessie's voice rose in volume and pitch. *"Stuck* with each other!" She welcomed the anger, for it swept away her hesitation and embarrassment. "I'm not stuck with anything, much less an overgrown adolescent who wouldn't know a good thing if it hit him in the face. I'm getting an annulment the instant we get to San Francisco, and it can't be too soon for me!"

Tony groaned. He hadn't meant for it to come out like that. Didn't she know how much he wished he could be what she needed? Logic would win over emotion any day, so he retreated to the safe refuge of reason. "We can't get an annulment now. Our marriage has been consummated—rather thoroughly, too."

"Well, I hardly think they'll check, will they!" Jessie said, her cheeks stained brightly with anger and mortification. "If I say I'm still untouched, who's going to be able to say otherwise?"

I will. Tony clamped down on the words before he said them out loud, the muscles of his jaw bulging as his molars ground together. It hurt, *Dio*, it hurt, knowing she would commit perjury rather than remain married to him. Even though his rational mind knew it was for the best, the rest of him wanted—and needed—to believe last night had meant something to her.

Why had she given herself to him? Now there was a question. It obviously wasn't because she cared for him, or she wouldn't be so quick to end their marriage. Pure feminine curiosity, then? A curiosity she now felt free to indulge with the blessings of church and society?

He didn't want to be anyone's damn experiment.

"I'm riding General this morning. You've got first shift with the wagon," he said, and was gone before Jessie could say another word.

*   *   *

The night was black. It was spooky how it absorbed light. Even a bright fire's glow seemed to lose its potency only a few yards away.

Walt Morrison crawled a little further, pushing his way slowly through the tall, dry grass, lifting his head just enough to see the tiny encampment a few hundred yards ahead. His eyes strained, and he wished it was just a little brighter. Enough so he could see exactly what he was up against.

He still wasn't sure exactly what he was going to do. He only knew that the past five days he'd spent wandering behind the wagon train he'd been kicked off of had been worthless. He'd stayed a day behind them, far enough so they'd never know he was there, but close enough so he could get there quickly if there was trouble. If there was one thing he knew, it wasn't safe out here alone.

He glanced nervously over his shoulder. It was said that those Indians could creep up on a man, wound him enough to kill him, and slip away before the man ever knew he'd been hit. Walt had spent half of the last few days sure that this was just exactly what was going to happen to him.

He had to do something. His stomach gurgled, and Walt rubbed it as if he could silence its demands. He was hungry. All he'd had to eat lately was a few dried biscuits and a couple of small animals he'd managed to kill and char over the fire.

He wanted real food. He wanted whiskey. He wanted to be able to sleep without worrying he was going to lose his scalp in the process.

And so, Walt Morrison was going to turn outlaw.

He'd gotten the idea when he'd been trying to catch up to the wagon train. He'd figured that maybe he could talk them into letting him come back. If he couldn't rejoin the train, how was he ever going to stay close enough to Winchester to give him the lesson Walt knew the bastard was just ripe for? If they wouldn't let him stay, at least his partners could slip him a few more supplies. Maybe they could do it on a regular basis, meet him every couple of days or so.

But then he'd seen the little fire. A camp that tiny was bound to be relatively unprotected. And on a night this dark, no one would ever see him. He could steal what he needed. He'd had enough of trying to work for things; he knew now that it was never going to work out for him. From now on, Walt was just taking what he deserved.

He crept closer to the camp. There were just two men, a skinny one and a short, fat one. Couldn't be too tough to take them. There were two expensive-looking horses. Fellas who had horses like that probably had a few valuables sitting around.

And they had food. He could catch a whiff of beans and salt pork and biscuits, and Walt felt the saliva moisten his mouth.

It was time. His palm was damp as he gripped the handle of his gun, but he was steady. He jumped to his feet and aimed at the tall one.

"Don't move!"

The fat one continued to shovel beans into his mouth. The tall one calmly looked up from his plate and squinted into the darkness. "What's going on out there?"

Walt sidled closer to the light, close enough so the man could see him.

"You're being robbed, that's what's going on."

"Shit." The skinny man shook his head. "Son, you don't want to be doing that."

"Yes, I do. I'm an outlaw."

The tubby one giggled around a mouthful of food. "Well, what do you think we are?"

Walt gaped at him. "You are?"

He shouldn't have looked away from the thin one,

who moved like lightning, sharp and quick. Walt's arms were wrenched behind his back and the barrel of his own gun pointed at temple before he even saw the flash of motion.

"First rule of outlawing, son," the skinny one said. "Always make sure the odds are in your favor before you move."

"Look, I'm sorry." Walt was very conscious of the cold metal against his forehead. "I was hungry, that's all. I smelt your food, and—"

"Aw, Stitch, don't kill him," the fat one said between bites.

"He held a gun on me."

"Well, you weren't none too good at it the first time, neither."

"Shit, Pudge, I was thirteen years old!"

"You heard him, Stitch. He said he was hungry."

"Yeah," Walt said. "I said I was sorry. I just smelled your food."

"Still . . ." Stitch's thumb caressed the hammer of the pistol.

"Look," Walt said. "I can show you where a good wagon train is, one worth stealing."

Speculation lightened Stitch's dark eyes. "We know where it is."

"Yeah, but I came from that train. I know where all the good stuff is, and the best ways to go in."

"See?" Pudge started filling another plate with food. "Let him go, Stitch. He'll be useful."

After considering for a moment, Stitch gave a brief nod and released Walt.

Walt scrambled away gratefully. He held out his hand. "Hey, what about my gun?"

Stitch shook his head and gestured with the gun toward the fire. "Not now. You eat first. We'll talk later."

Walt stumbled down by the fire, grabbed the plate, and stuffed a biscuit into his mouth. Later he'd worry about the close escape he had. Now there was real food.

He chewed in overwhelming appreciation. It was the best biscuit he'd ever had in his life—light, savory, and buttery.

"Oh, Pudge," he mumbled with his mouth full. "This is wonderful. You're one hell of a cook."

Pudge laughed. "I didn't make it, boy. I can't cook worth a damn. Stitch made it."

Walt settled down to fill his empty belly.

This outlawing business was going to be great.

"Jessie! It's real ice! Take me to see the ice!" Samuel Walker called in the excited voice belonging only to small, happy children.

With a large stick Jessie heaved the last heavy, sopping petticoat out of the boiling wash water. She twisted the cloth, wringing it out, the hot liquid nearly burning her hands. She flipped the fabric over the line strung tightly between the Walkers' wagon and hers. With the back of her wrist she wiped off the sweat and steam that mingled on her forehead before answering Sam.

"Sam, sweetheart, I've got lots of work to do. Can't you find someone else to take you?"

He thrust out his lower lip in a pout that somehow only made him look more cherubic. "Daddy's out hunting and Mama says she's too big to walk that far. You're no fun anymore, Jessie. How come?"

Jessie sighed, knowing he was right. Having never before set foot out of Illinois, she had spent much of her youth longing to see the exotic sights she had only read about. Now, as they passed new wonders almost daily, she could find no heart for it. The colors seemed faded and dull; all the magic had gone out of the journey for her. The oddity of Split Rock had not moved her, nor had the spectacular, sheer gorge of Devil's

Gate sent her running for her sketchbook. But there was no reason to impose her lack of enthusiasm on Sam.

Seemingly aware of her weakening, Samuel added one last prod. "What if I never getta chance to see ice in the middle of summer again? If I don't have a story to tell my grandkids, it'll be all your fault!"

Unable to resist his smile, Jessie scooped up the child for a quick hug. "All right, I'll take you. How does your mother ever resist you? If you have this much charm when you grow up, the girls will be falling at your feet." Just like Tony, she thought.

Samuel's face took on the expression he wore when his mother made him eat his beets. Evidently the idea of girls falling all over him held no appeal. "If that means girls are going to bother me all the time like Delia Bolton does Tony, I don't wanna have any charm at all."

Jessie's throat tightened as her smile froze. There had never been any hint that Tony had encouraged Delia even in the slightest way. But she might as well get used to it. She had no claims on the man, no claims at all. She'd given him his freedom. So why was she having such a hard time remembering that?

It did little good to dwell on it. Reluctantly, she set Samuel down. "Yes, you will. You'll love to have all those girls bothering you all the time." She brushed a stray curl of near-white hair from his forehead. "Now, where's this ice supposed to be?"

By the time they reached their destination, Samuel's infectious chatter had cheered Jessie, and she felt better than she had at any time during the past week. The Ice Slough looked like an ordinary swamp, but when they fell to their knees and scraped away the grass, Samuel digging ineffectually but energetically with his hands and Jessie more carefully with a large knife, they discovered a thick layer of dirty ice, insulated from the summer heat by the heavy vegetation.

Jessie produced a canvas sack. "Here, Sam, hold this for me, please. We'll bring some of the ice back to camp with us. If we mix a little citric acid with sugar and water, then pack the jug with ice, we'll surprise your mother with cold lemonade just like I used to make for my Daddy on hot summer days back home in Chicago."

They worked industriously, Jessie chipping away at the ice with her knife while Sam collected the pieces and placed them in the bag. The sack was nearly two-thirds full when Sam dropped it and sprinted away.

"Look, Jessie! It's Tony and Susannah! Tony! We're over here!" He catapulted himself at Tony, who grasped him under the arms and tossed him high in the air. Sam shrieked when he pretended to drop him.

"Tickle attack!" Susannah shouted. The twins jumped on Tony as he fell to the ground, pretending to be helpless against their assault. Tony collapsed on his back, each arm encircling a breathless, giggling child.

"Jessie 'n me are gettin' ice. We're gonna make lemonade," Sam informed him when they paused to catch their breath.

"Better save some for me, short stuff. A man gets mighty thirsty tangling with a couple of tough guys like you two." He rolled easily to his feet, hauling the children up with him. He spared a quick glance for Jessie, the light in his eyes dying as his gaze fell on her. Then he snatched up the ice bag and slung it over his shoulder. "I'll carry this back."

Jessie trailed behind the trio, her pleasure in the day evaporating as quickly as it had come. It hurt to have him look at her as if she was a stranger, a stranger who was both unwelcome and immediately dismissed. He was clearly the reason for her recent depression.

She missed him.

Since their wedding night he had been cool, aloof. He made sure their time together was minimal, and when they were forced into each other's company he treated her with a polite indifference she wouldn't have believed him capable of.

Since they had met he had teased, annoyed, and comforted her. He had flirted with her, and at times frustrated her, but he had never ignored her . . . until now. She hadn't realized how dependent she had become on his companionship until it was taken away. His perpetual good humor, his easy appreciation of what life had to offer, was what had made the wrenching monotony and tedious labor of the trip bearable, even enjoyable. Jessie felt his absence keenly, even as she failed to understand it.

Perhaps she shouldn't have called him an overgrown adolescent, but she had called him far worse before, and it had always seemed to amuse him, not anger him. She had only wanted to return to him the options fate had taken away, to keep him from being saddled with a wife he hadn't chosen, a woman whose inexperience had caused her to lose her head thoroughly in bed, making it impossible for her to return the pleasure he had given to her effortlessly.

Repeatedly, Jessie relived that night and morning, examining her actions and the reasons behind them. It all made perfect sense to her, but Tony's obvious anger indicated that she had missed something somewhere. What could it be?

Several yards ahead, Tony's thoughts traveled the same path. He had seen the pain in Jessie's eyes, and it had been all he could do not to give in to the instinct to take her in his arms and comfort her. Damn it, he had known he was going to hurt her sooner or later, anyway; it might as well be now.

Samuel tugged hard on his sleeve, but Tony was unable to concentrate on the child's excited conversation. Why was he so angry with Jessie? He told himself it was because, for the first time in years, he had made love with a woman who meant something to him, only to discover that he didn't mean anything to her. But if she didn't care, then how could he have hurt her so much?

No, she had feelings for him, too. The truth was painfully obvious to Tony: He was upset because she had given him a way out of their marriage. He had allowed himself to dream of the life they could have together, of the family and home they could build. But when the wedding had been forced upon them by the dictates of others and the whims of fate, some of the responsibility was lifted from his shoulders. If he failed at being a husband, at least it wouldn't be entirely his fault if he was unable to keep promises he had made against his will, nor if he broke a covenant made without his full cooperation.

Now, if he wanted a future with Jessie, the decision was his and no one else's. If he made her a promise, it would be without any extenuating circumstances, and he would be obligated to keep it. He wouldn't be much of a man if he couldn't. The problem was that he wasn't sure that love, honor, and fidelity *forever* were ideals he could achieve.

He didn't feel like much of a man. A man would have enough guts to give a woman like Jessie what she deserved.

The Continental Divide was strangely disappointing.

South Pass should have been breathtaking, a soaring peak to commemorate the halfway point of their journey, an uplifting view to celebrate over two months and a thousand miles of travel.

What they got instead was a broad, grassy plain, indistinguishable from hundreds of others. The only indications of altitude were the below-freezing nights and the vista of the snowcapped Wind River Mountains to the north. The train made camp near the first westward-flowing stream they found, and quickly settled in for the night, following the routines that were now automatic.

A tiny shard of new moon glowed in the sky, its dim light barely penetrating the inky night. From a vantage point in a small grove of trees a few hundred yards back from the circle of vehicles, only the pale shapes of the wagon tops were visible.

In the little grove a tall, bony man surveyed the train speculatively and then spat out a long stream of tobacco juice before turning to his two companions who were well hidden by the accommodating night. "I don't know, Pudge. Ain't much of a train. Hardly looks worth the trouble. Whaddya think?"

"'Course it's worth it, Stitch," Walt whispered. "It's the easiest job you'll ever pull. 'Sides, that horse I told you about is worth it all by himself."

"I don't recall that I was asking you, boy," Stitch said. He chomped twice on his tobacco plug before continuing. "Ya wouldn't be lettin' your personal feelin's interfere with business, now wouldja? Can't have that."

Pudge rubbed the huge, round bulge of his belly and tilted his head way back to speak up to his much taller partner. "Aw, come on, Stitch. We're already here, might as well do it. Things been pretty dull lately, anyways."

Stitch readjusted the large chaw in his cheek with his tongue. He had the brains in the bunch and he knew it, so the final decision was his. "Shit. Let's go." As his two cohorts turned to leave, he whipped out his arm and caught Walt by the back of his collar, snapping him back sharply. "It's your job to get ridda those friends of yours at lookout. And jes' remember, boy, to stick to the plan. If ya make things difficult 'cause you're runnin' around on your own, you're gonna answer to me."

Walt snorted in agreement. "Meetcha back at camp."

20

Jessie's body was slammed onto the hard ground, but she already ached so much that she hardly noticed the additional pain. She had no concept of how much time passed while she was slung belly down over the back of a horse, her stomach pounding unmercifully with each jarring step the animal took. Her head throbbed with the blood that rushed into it as she hung upside down, while her chest ached with the effort it took to draw each musty breath against the coarse wool blanket that imprisoned her.

That blanket had been thrown over her, abruptly and without warning, after she had slipped from the sleeping camp to rid her body of the three cups of coffee she'd indulged in before bedtime. Despite her furious struggling, she had been trussed up tightly as a Christmas goose. It had been unforgivably stupid of her to leave camp unprotected, but the journey thus far had been so safe that she had grown careless. Throughout the long, painful ride Jessie had berated herself and her unknown captor fiercely. Somehow, the anger was easier to deal with than the fear she barely managed to keep at bay.

Jessie felt her bindings jerk, then she was rolled, over and over, as someone tugged at the cord, unwrapping her. She was shoved roughly into a sitting position, and the blanket was pulled away. Gulping several lungfuls of cold night air, she pushed her tangled hair from her face, focusing her eyes on the man towering above her.

Her jaw dropped as she recognized him. "You!" she said in a violent rush of rage that nearly choked her. Until that instant she had cherished a faint hope that this was another one of Tony's "lessons," like the attack back at the creek, even as she knew he would never go this far. But now her last hope was snuffed out.

"Yes, me." Walt Morrison's eyes glinted, smug and triumphant, in the wan light.

"Tony will kill you for sure this time—if I don't get to you first."

Walt's smile wavered for the barest instant. "You can't touch me now—either of you. I have friends this time."

"No one would be stupid enough to be friends with the likes of you."

Jessie became aware of the pounding hoofbeats that signaled approaching horses. Were they indeed friends of Walt's, or friends of hers? Walt, too, seemed unsure, for he rushed to grab a rifle that was leaning against his pack several feet away.

Jessie took the opportunity to take a quick inventory of her surroundings. The camp was small and primitive, consisting only of a few bundles and bedrolls and a tiny, smokeless fire all crowded into a little clearing. If Walt did have some companions, there couldn't be many. She felt a small, precious spark of hope. Perhaps she would have a chance to escape. But the camp was surrounded on all sides by a thick, deep growth of forest. She had no way to gauge her location.

But she couldn't think of that now—first things first, and her first priority was to get free. She'd worry about finding her way home later. When Walt peered off into the darkness, searching for the incoming riders, his back was to Jessie. Quietly, she rose to a crouch and crept closer to him. She had no intention of waiting to be rescued. She'd grab any opportunity she could.

She was almost near enough now. With any luck, if she hit him from behind, he'd try to break his fall with his hands and drop his rifle in the process. Jessie figured she had as good a chance to get to it first as he did. He had longer arms, but she had desperation and surprise on her side.

Jessie braced herself to spring and hurl her body at the small of his back. Her legs must have been still numb from the tight bindings, however, and in the fraction of an instant it took her to move, Walt spun, catching her across the face with the back of his hand. Jessie sprawled face down in the dirt from the force of the blow and lay still, giving herself time to think before she moved, unwilling to give up yet. She pushed herself up and used the hem of her skirt to dab at the blood spilling from her split lip.

"Don't you ever try that again!" Jessie flinched at the voice shouting in her ear. "I don't want to hurt ya, but I will if I have to. One way or the other, I'm going to get what ya owe me."

"What in the goddamn hell is going on around here?" Neither Jessie nor Walt had noticed that the other horses had arrived, and Jessie was gratified to see the fear which showed briefly on Walt's face.

Two men had joined them, she realized. The one who had spoken was tall, almost gaunt, but he carried himself with an air of arrogance. The other man was short and round and at present was fully occupied in trying to dismount. It took him three attempts before he was able to swing one tubby leg over the back of the horse, and he held on to the saddle horn for dear life as he slid down the side of his mount to the ground.

"Stitch! Pudge!" Walt greeted the arrivals in a jovial voice. "Glad you're back. Well, was I right? Was it worth it? Did you get much of a haul?"

"We got shit!" Stitch yelled. "All we got was a few supplies an' a couple horses. If there was anythin' in that train worth takin'—an' I ain't sure there was—it was packed away so we couldn't get to it without shakin' up the whole camp."

"But you at least got the horse, didn't ya?"

"Oh we got him, all right," Pudge said, his jowls quivering as he spoke. "But gettin' him here was somethin' else entirely. Damn horse wouldn't move, jes' dug in his heels and leaned back. Wouldn't follow our horses for nuthin'. Finally got him here by Stitch pullin' from the front an' me proddin' him from behind with my knife. Even then, he made the trip as hard as possible, swingin' from side to side as far as the rope would allow and kickin' up his heels every few steps. Damn near kicked me more 'n once. Swear the thing knew what he was doin'."

No, it couldn't be! There was only one horse she knew of that could be capable of such behavior. Jessie clasped her hands tightly over her stomach as a hard, icy ball of fear congealed in her gut. She searched the darkness behind the men with frantic eyes. Oh, no, it was General! What could it mean? What had happened to the rest of camp? Tony would never have let anything happen to General if he could have prevented it. God, please let Tony be all right, she prayed. She didn't know if she could bear to lose him, too.

"Enough about that damn horse!" Stitch roared, dismounting swiftly and striding over to Walt. Stitch planted his fists on his skinny hips and glared. "What the hell is a woman doing here?"

Unable to meet Stitch's gaze, Walt gave a small, nervous laugh. "As I was leaving, she wandered away from camp, sweet as you please, so I snatched her. Figured it was high time we all had a bit of fun."

"You stupid idiot! I told you to stick to the plan! If all we'd taken was some stuff and a little livestock, the train would have gone on their way without anybody worrying about it, figuring they got off lucky. But you took one of their *people.* You don't think they're gonna come lookin' for her?"

"Well, she's here now, and I need a woman. I'll use her 'til I'm wrung out, then I'll get rid of her. How about you, Pudge?" Walt turned to the chubby man. "Bet you could use a bit of fun, huh?"

Pudge drew himself up to his full height, smoothing his stained linen shirt over his immense belly. "A man who has to force a woman isn't much of a man in my book, Walt. Besides, the reason we've been in business so long is we never mix business with pleasure. Isn't that right, Stitch?"

"She's gonna have to go back, boy." Stitch gave his decision with the confidence of a man accustomed to having his orders followed.

"I'm not lettin' her go back unless she's in more 'n one piece!" Walt's eyes bulged with fury. "She's nothing but a two-bit slut, and I had to watch her twitch her tail through camp for the last two months. She's the reason I got kicked off the train, and I'm gonna take what she owes me out of her skinny ass!"

Stitch's voice was frighteningly quiet. "When you joined up with us I told you to never, and I mean *never,* let business get personal, or it was all over." He swung his fist hard, catching Walt in the gut. Clutching his stomach in both hands, Walt doubled over. "Boy, next time ya decide not to follow orders I'll kill ya. Pudge 'n I gotta go back an' see if they noticed

she's gone. If you're lucky, the whole place will still be
sleeping an' we can slip her back in without anybody
bein' the wiser. We'll be long gone before they realize
what happened."

"Aw, Stitch, do I hafta go with ya? Ya know I hate
ridin'." Pudge's round face bore an expression of
comic dismay.

"Yes, ya hafta go with me," Stitch said, mimicking
Pudge's whine. "I need ya to be lookout while I creep
closer to camp to check things out."

Stitch walked to the back of his horse, untying
General. Jessie bolted forward and clutched his arm.
With grim satisfaction, she'd watched him hit Walt.
He was an outlaw, true, but one without any of Walt's
frightening malice. She'd follow him and Pudge in the
dark, if she had to, but she wasn't staying here with
Walt.

"Take me back with you. I won't be any trouble, I
promise. Just take me anywhere close to camp and I'll
walk back the rest of the way myself. I won't say anything about you, I swear it."

Stitch gently pried her stiff fingers off his biceps
and led the now-compliant General to a tall, bare pine
tree where another horse was tethered. He looped a
rope around the trunk and tied General's head close to
the ground.

"Can't do that—I stayed alive this long 'cause I
don't leave nothin' to chance. Naw, ya gotta stay while
Pudge 'n me scout around. We'll find a good spot to
leave ya so's the train'll be sure ta come across ya
tomorrow."

She shot a quick glance at Walt, whose strangely
pale eyes were alight with hollow anticipation and the
promise of retribution.

Jessie's voice grew shrill with hysteria. "You can't
leave me here with him!"

Stitch spewed another glob of tobacco juice. "I'm
truly sorry, miss, about this whole thing. I'm a thief,

an' I killed more'n a few men in my time, but the one thing I never done was hurt a woman. My mama taught me better'n that." His eyes narrowed and focused on Walt. "He's not gonna touch you while we're gone, 'cause I'm ordering him not to, an' he knows this here's his last chance." He returned to his horse and mounted it.

"Ah . . . Stitch." Pudge gave two tiny, one-legged hops in an attempt to pull his bulk back atop his mount. "I'm gonna need a bit o' help here."

Stitch swore loudly before swinging off his horse again. He braced one shoulder under Pudge's round rump and gave an upward heave. Pudge wavered for a moment before spreading himself crosswise over the saddle with a grunt. He grabbed the saddle horn and pulled himself forward, flashing a triumphant grin when he reached a sitting position. His grin faded as he stared across the camp. "Ah . . . Stitch?"

"What is it now?" Stitch asked, clearly exasperated.

"Look!" Stitch and Walt's eyes followed the chubby finger to where Jessie was just slipping into the shadows at the edge of the clearing, disappearing into the forest beyond the reach of the firelight.

"Shit, shit, and double shit! Walt, you're supposed ta be watchin' her."

Jessie broke into a frantic run, but Stitch's much longer legs ate up the distance rapidly. He hauled her in and threw her over his shoulder, unbothered by her fists pounding his back. He crossed the clearing and deposited her in Walt's arms.

"Shit. Come on, Pudge, let's get outta here before anythin' else goes wrong." He mounted his horse, then turned back for one final warning. "Remember, Morrison. Hands off the lady, or ya answer ta me."

Jessie listened to the hoofbeats fading away, muffled by the dense vegetation. The trees seemed sud-

denly larger and darker, closing in suffocatingly. She
was alone with Walt—utterly and completely alone.

"You can let me go now."

He chuckled malevolently. "Oh, no, I can't do
that." He dropped one arm, letting her slip down
against him, but holding her solidly to him. She could
feel his sharp bones poking through his rough clothes.
Jessie gasped at the hatred, pure and palpable, written
clearly on his face. She struggled against his hold, but
his grip tightened painfully, twisting the skin on her
arms.

"Stitch said you couldn't touch me."

His mouth turned up in a cold smile. "Yeah, he did,
didn't he?" Walt freed one hand and ran it down her
side. His touch was somehow both impersonal and
terrifyingly threatening. "But he didn't say you
couldn't touch me."

Walt unsheathed the knife strapped to his thigh and
pressed the sharp metal to the curve of her neck. He
dropped his other arm, freeing her. "Kneel down," he
ordered.

Jessie tensed, preparing to run, but she felt the
point of the blade just pierce her skin, and she gave in
to the pressure, sinking to her knees before the knife
could slide in deeper.

"Stitch said he would kill you."

Walt snorted. "That old man? He's going to have to
catch me first."

That old man? Walt wasn't much older than she
was, and Stitch couldn't be more than fifteen years
older than him. She knew Stitch would have no trouble at all catching Walt . . . but that did her little
good now.

"Why?" she rasped. "Why are you doing this? You
can't want me enough to risk everything."

"Want you?" Walt reached out to test the drops of
blood around the knife, smearing the red liquid
against the soft skin of her neck. "This has nothing to

do with wanting you. It has everything to do with collecting what's owed me—both from you and that bastard lover of yours. For now, we'll work on settling your debts. I'll take care of him later."

Still holding the knife against her throat, he withdrew his other hand, moving it to his waist and jerking open the buttons of his pants.

"No, don't!" Jessie closed her eyes in panic. She began to shake, trying desperately to find some escape.

"Take me into your mouth."

"I can't!" She tried to shake her head but the knife pressed harder against her, stilling her movements.

"Don't give me that—I'm sure Winchester taught you lots of interesting tricks."

"Oh, God!" Jessie fought the temptation to give in to hysteria, knowing it would do no good. There had to be a way out of this, there just *had* to be.

She remembered the way she had escaped Tony by the creek. It was true he hadn't wanted to hurt her, but the principle was the same: she needed to outthink Walt, to catch him off guard. She didn't know if it would work, but she had to try. The alternative was intolerable.

She knew he was still fumbling one-handed with his clothes. He wasn't touching her; the only thing holding her in place was the awful pressure of the knife on the left side of her neck. The only question now was who was quicker. If she was faster, she had a chance. If Walt was faster, she was dead.

She had no choice. This might be her only chance.

She dove to the right, toward the fire, falling and rolling away. Grabbing a fiery log, she thrust it at him, aiming the glowing end somewhere toward his face. She didn't even take the time to see if she'd connected. All she hoped was that it would buy her just a little bit of time. Enough time.

Jessie only dimly heard his outraged howl of pain,

for her entire consciousness was concentrated on only one thing: escape. She scrambled toward General, tripping once in her haste. She tugged frantically on the rope that tied the horse. Her fingers just wouldn't work the way she wanted. She swore fiercely, thinking irrelevantly that Tony would have been proud of her vocabulary, and the knot suddenly tore free. Not chancing even a brief glance behind her, she wrapped her fists in General's mane and tried to pull herself up on his back. She jumped as high as she could, but the effort was futile. The horse was just too big.

Sagging against the side of the horse, she pressed her face against his neck. "Please," she begged, "oh please, God, let me get on this horse." Incredibly, it seemed that General heard her, for he bent his front legs, lowering his shoulders enough for her to swing onto his back.

A hand clamped heavily on her calf. "No!" Jessie screamed. She was so close! She couldn't let him catch her now. She kicked hard, trying to shake Walt off her leg, but General had a better idea. The stallion swung sharply aside and kicked out with one strong rear leg. Jessie heard a muffled thud and they were off, flying through the dark forest.

Clinging tightly to General's back, Jessie wrapped her arms around the neck of the horse, not even bothering to attempt to guide him. "Find Tony," she whispered, and let him fly.

Leading the horse he had borrowed from Stuart Walker, Tony carefully picked his way through the deep woods. It was too dark to do any tracking from horseback, and it had taken quite some time for his eyes to become accustomed enough to the moonlight for him to follow the trail on foot. He really should wait for morning, he knew, but there was no way he could sit around and force himself to twiddle his thumbs until sunrise. He could only hope he was following the right path.

When Tony had woken up to find Jessie gone, it felt as if someone had kicked him in the gut—hard. His stomach was still tight, and it didn't seem odd to him that only a couple months ago the worst thing he could have imagined was someone making off with General. General was gone now too, but all he thought about was Jessie. He could picture her so clearly in his mind, imagining her face twisted in terror and pain, and the back of his eyes burned. *Dio,* what an idiot he had been! She was his wife, his responsibility, and she was gone.

Why hadn't he watched her more closely, protected her more carefully? He knew why. He'd been moping around, spending as little time with her as possible, because he was hurt that she had dismissed their marriage so easily. It didn't matter how many times he told himself it was for the best, he couldn't deny that he wanted her to at least *want* to stay married to him. But what did it matter now? She was out there somewhere, alone with God knew who, and he had to find her. He just had to.

Was that a sound up ahead? Tony raised his arm, halting the group of men who were following behind, trailing their own horses. His ears strained to catch the slightest sound, but at first he couldn't hear anything over the pounding of his own heart. *Thump-thump, thump-thump.* It wasn't his heart, but the steady, rhythmic drumming of hooves. Only one horse, far as he could tell. Who would be fool enough to ride at such a pace at night through a forest filled with unknown obstacles? Tony silently reached behind for his rifle, checked the loading, and raised it to his shoulder in preparation, aiming down the barely visible trail.

As soon as he began to make out the dim outlines

of the huge bulk thundering toward him, the animal stopped abruptly and gave a soft, familiar nicker.

He lowered the rifle an inch. "General?" The horse closed the distance between them rapidly, then nuzzled him on the shoulder. Tony stroked the soft coat of his neck and spoke softly. "So you got away, did you, you clever monster." His breathing quickened in anticipation. If General was here, Jessie couldn't be far away now.

She was closer than he dared hope. He heard one weak, tremulous "Tony?" and dropped the gun, rounded the horse in one quick stride, and swept her off General's back and into his embrace. He held her tightly to his chest, thinking that if he could just get her close enough, she would become part of him and never be away from him again.

They stayed that way for a time, unmoving, Jessie weak with fatigue and relief and Tony hardly daring to believe she was here, alive and safe. He said nothing, for words seemed inadequate. He let his arms tell her what he could not until he felt a large hand on his shoulder.

"I know how you feel, son," Buffalo Bolton said. "But we need to talk with your lady. Gotta find out what happened."

"Huh?" Tony lifted his head. He had completely forgotten about the men who had accompanied him on the search. "Oh . . . oh yeah, of course." His fingers brushed her cheek tenderly. "Jessie, honey, do you think you could tell us about it? If you don't feel up to it, we can—" A cloud shifted away from the moon, and Tony broke off with a quick oath as he saw her face clearly for the first time.

Her hair was a wild tangle, her face was smeared with dark blotches—blood or dirt, he couldn't tell in the faint light—and her lower lip was swollen. But what really frightened him was her expression.

Her features were set into rigid lines, and her eyes

were huge, dark, and hollow. She looked like someone who had just watched an act too horrible to comprehend.

"Dio, Jessie, they hurt you!" Jessie felt him stiffen as he tenderly rubbed her split lower lip and the knife prick on the side of her neck. "Are you all right, *cara?"*

"I'm . . . fine," she whispered, grateful for the strong arms holding her up.

"Did they touch you, *cara*?" His jaw tightened and his brows drew together until they looked like one. "If they touched you—"

"No." Jessie straightened, praying her knees would hold her sagging body. Her voice grew stronger. "No, I really am fine."

"Fine? What's 'fine' mean?" He looked intently into her eyes. "You would tell me if they had . . . you would tell me, wouldn't you?"

She nodded. "He never had a chance to, Tony." She closed her eyes against the terrible memories. "Walt tried, but I—"

"Walt!"

At the startled exclamations around her, Jessie, who had been aware only of Tony's presence, looked around. Tom Bolton was there, along with Andrew Wrightman and Stuart Walker, and, to Jessie's surprise, Jedediah Parson.

"Reverend Parson," she said. "What are you doing out here? The cold night air isn't good for your joints."

He reached out to pat her hand. "Never you mind, my dear. I had to know you were safe." He gave her a small smile that seemed forced. "Besides, you don't think I'm going to let these young ones have all the fun, do you?" His fingers tightened around hers, and he looked at her with concerned and knowing eyes. "You're a strong woman, Jessie. You don't need a man to lean on, and these old shoulders aren't much good for it, anyway, but my ears and my heart still work fine. If you need to talk, I would be honored if you would allow me to listen."

How could he know? She didn't want to go into it, not with him, not with anyone, but she should have realized that he would see through her attempts to make light of the matter. But just thinking about it made her gag. She never wanted to think about it again. "Reverend . . . there's nothing to listen to."

He nodded sadly. "I have lived a long time, little one. There is little you could tell me I have not heard before. Just remember, if you have need . . . I am here."

"I'll remember."

"Jessie," Buffalo said impatiently, "are you going to tell us what Walt had to do with this or not?"

Tony's arms tightened around her protectively. "Jess, if you don't feel up to talking now, I want you to say so."

"No, it's all right." She leaned her head against his chest. He made her feel so safe, she wasn't sure she ever wanted to leave the comfort of his warm embrace. "I'm not sure of everything. I know Walt took me away from camp, and he's evidently joined up with a couple of outlaws since he left the train, but they didn't seem too happy to be involved in a kidnapping. They were going to make him give me back, I think, but when they left camp to scout around, he . . . well, I took the chance to get away."

"Damn it!" A muscle in Tony's jaw ticked, but he seemed unable to tear his eyes from Jessie, as if she might disappear again if he so much as blinked. "I knew I should have killed him when I had the chance."

"Now, Tony," Buffalo said, "ain't much we can do about that now."

"Oh yes there is," Tony said, a thread of steel running through his voice. "I'm going after him. How far is it to their camp, Jessie?"

"I . . . I don't really know. It didn't seem like far, but I was upset and—" Her voice broke. "Please don't leave me, Tony."

He didn't want to. Lord knew, he didn't want to. He wished he could tear himself in two so there'd be one part to hunt down Walt and another to stay with Jessie. Hell, he felt like he was being ripped in half, anyway. But much as he wanted to stay, he felt compelled to make sure Walt could never touch her again.

"I have to, Jessie." He smoothed a tangled strand of hair from her cheek. "I have to make sure he can't ever get near you again. I won't be gone long, I promise." He crushed her to him briefly, then released her and stepped back. "The Reverend and Andrew can see you safely back to camp. Will you be O.K. now?"

Jessie drew a breath and stiffened her spine. She'd always been fine on her own. Surely nothing had changed. "Yes."

Tony knew she would be fine. She had more inner strength than almost anyone he knew. Still, the thought of leaving her even for a moment, even for the best of reasons, was painful. He wanted her by his side, always, but he knew that was impossible. He bent to retrieve his rifle and jumped onto General's back in one easy motion.

"Come on, fella, you and I've got work to do." He applied light pressure with his leg, and General wheeled, his muscles bunching in anticipation of the hunt, but Tony held him still. From his seat on the horse Jessie seemed small and distant, and Tony couldn't bring himself to look away.

"Jessie? How did you manage to escape?"

"Remember what I did to you the day you snuck up on me by the stream?"

"You did that to Walt?"

She gave a small, satisfied smile, a smile that chilled rather than warmed. "Not quite."

His eyebrows lifted slightly. "I hope it was painful."

"Oh, yes. Definitely painful."

His teeth flashed white in the dark night. "That's my woman."

And with a light tap of Tony's heels against his side, General went racing into the night.

21

She could see nothing.

Jessie blinked and turned her head. She moved slowly, as if underwater. She had no perception of light, shadow, or depth—just unending, monochromatic gray, not shiny or silvery but a dull, dead gray, as if all color were removed—or had never been there at all. She wasn't frightened, though, for she wasn't alone.

Someone was holding her hand.

Still floating, Jessie turned her head again, and there she was, a figure of luminescent, brilliant color in a boundless sea of nothing. Jessie saw the familiar red-gold hair, the delicate features, the old-fashioned dress.

"Mother?"

The figure smiled—beautifully gentle, heartbreakingly sad. She dropped Jessie's hand and was gone.

A single tear slipped down Jessie's cheek. She had known the figure wouldn't be able to stay. She had never been able to stay.

"Hiya, brat."

Jessie stuck out her tongue at her brother before she grinned. He was handsome as always, a man of sunshine and exuberant life.

"Oh, J.J., I'm so glad you're back, I—"

"I've gotta go, Jess."

"Take me with you."

He shook his head regretfully. "Not this time, kid. Things to do, you know. Maybe when you're all grown up."

"I'm grown up now. I can help you, I know it."

"Later, kid." He smiled, his blindingly beautiful smile, took two jaunty strides, and disappeared.

"J.J.!" Jessie lifted her skirts to follow, but her feet wouldn't budge. How odd. The first prickle of unease skittered down her spine. "J.J.!"

"Everything will be fine, muffin."

"Daddy!" He looked just as Jessie remembered him, a hulking, intimidating bear of a man whose eyes softened perceptibly each time he looked at her.

"It's not going to be fine," Jessie said, squaring her shoulders and lifting her chin. "Everyone keeps leaving me and they won't let me come along. I *want* to go. Please, Daddy, you'll stay with me, won't you?"

"You know I can't do that, muffin. Your place is here." An aching sadness glazed his eyes. "I love you," he said softly. His features began to change, and he withered into the grotesque facade of a man he had been in the days before his death.

"No!" she screamed. Tears streamed down her face as she desperately tried to grasp the elusive gray mists swirling around her. It was futile; her father was gone. Her fear was a living creature now, shortening her breath and quickening her heartbeat. She began to kick, trying to free her feet, but the shifting fog obscured her lower legs and she couldn't see what was holding her down.

A warm hand caressed the back of her neck, and

she stilled. She knew that hand, comforting and unbearably exciting at the same time.

"Trust me, *cara*. Why do you struggle so? I won't leave you."

She wanted to believe him—oh, how she wanted to believe him—but she couldn't. He would leave her. Everyone always left her. Jessie had a brief glimpse of Tony's face, eyes glowing with amusement and temptation, before he, too, was gone.

The creeping mist was around her waist now, and somehow Jessie knew that if it closed over her she would disappear, too. She began to fight in earnest, sobbing, twisting, lashing out, but it was useless. The terror slipped ever higher.

"Wake up, Jessie. Wake up!" Tony's voice penetrated her fog-shrouded brain, and Jessie abruptly crashed into consciousness. She threw her arms around his neck in a tight stranglehold and pulled him down to her. Her face was wet against his neck, and her shoulders still shook violently.

He moved his hands over her back in soothing strokes. "Shhh, *cara*, shhh. It was just a dream. Just a dream."

"Don't leave me Tony!" she cried. "Please don't leave me!"

He leaned back to see her face, barely discernible in the dim light. Her eyes were wide, holding remnants of fear, and he wiped the tears off her cheeks with his palm. He ached with the need to give her the reassurance she wanted, but he could not. Honesty was all he had to give her, but at least he could give her that much.

"I won't leave you tonight, *cara*."

A deep sigh escaped Jessie. His words were oddly comforting. Perhaps if he had promised her he would never leave her she wouldn't have believed him. *I won't leave you tonight*—those were words she could hold on to, words she could trust, for now.

Her tight muscles suddenly relaxed, and she snuggled closer to Tony's warmth.

"I'm sorry I didn't get back before you fell asleep."

"That's all right," she said. "Harriet doused me with one of her sleeping concoctions and tucked me in." She hesitated, debating if she really wanted to know the answer to her question. "Did you find Walt?"

"Yes."

She waited, but when he didn't elaborate she prompted him. "And?"

"And he'll never bother you again."

"You . . . killed him?"

"Didn't have to. He was dead when we found him."

"Oh, God, I never meant to—"

"You didn't." He tucked her head firmly under his chin, enjoying the feel of her body nestling softly against him again. It had been too long. "General did. Good thing, too, or I would have."

"Oh." Her eyes drifted shut. She was safe . . . so safe. "Did you find the other two—Stitch and Pudge?"

"No. They seem to be long gone, and it didn't seem much use to try tracking them in the dark."

"Good," Jessie mumbled, and slipped into soft, blessedly dreamless sleep.

It took a month of monotonous travel to reach Fort Hall, the trading post owned by the Hudson's Bay Company on the Snake River. Only the forty-five miles between the Big Sandy and Green River were difficult, for both water and forage were scarce there. The travelers were forced to cut, load, and carry the necessary grass and depend on stored water. Fortunately there was a ferry over the Green River, for it had been an unusually rainy year, and the river was too high to ford.

It was a hard month for Jessie. At first she had nightmares nearly every time she fell asleep. Fragments of her past mixed with those terrifying moments with Walt, and she would wake clutched in fear, her heart pounding, her skin clammy and cold. But Tony was always there, a comforting body on the other side of the bed, his presence making the horrors recede. During the day, she spent much time with Reverend Parson, and his humorous and loving perspective on life never failed to enchant her. Gradually, the residual terror abated.

Fort Hall was a welcome respite, and the entire party enjoyed the chance to rest, restock depleted provisions, and see new faces. The train often seemed a world unto itself, and the Fort reminded them there was a whole world out there, filled with other people, other places, and other goals than crossing the next fifteen miles.

Pleasant as the rest was, Buffalo allowed them only a brief stop before pushing on. The Fort was yet another marker of just how far they had traveled, and he was anxious to get started on the last leg of their journey. There was little argument, for no one relished the thought of being caught in the mountains ahead when the snow started.

Only a few days out of Fort Hall, Tony approached Jessie as she foraged around in their supplies, trying to decide what to prepare for supper.

"Don't bother cooking tonight, *cara*. Pack some food and come with me. I have something to show you."

Jessie's heart expanded a bit, as it did each time he called her *cara* in that warm, seductive tone of voice. He did so frequently now. Whatever had disturbed him after their wedding seemed to have evaporated after the incident with Walt. She didn't know why, but no matter what the cause, Jessie was grateful for the change.

A spark of anticipation gleamed in his eyes, and his dimples looked deep and boyishly charming. All the chores she had intended to finish ran through her mind briefly before she dismissed them. Tony was impossible to refuse when he was in this mood—moreover, she didn't *want* to refuse.

Tony barely had time to register her consent before she thrust an empty sack into his hands. In it she dumped leftover biscuits, some cheese purchased at Fort Hall, some jerked buffalo, and a few raisin-filled griddle cakes. She was halfway out of camp when she whirled to face the bemused Tony and flashed a broad smile.

"Well? Are you coming or not?"

He chuckled and shouldered the bag. "Try and show a little enthusiasm, would ya, Jess?"

It was wonderful just to walk with him. He never rushed, but he ambled along with an easy, graceful saunter that afforded her plenty of time to appreciate the trip as well as the destination. There was no reason to talk, no reason to do anything, it seemed, but enjoy the warm sun on her face, the light breeze against her skin, and the presence of the man by her side.

Jessie was surprised when Tony grasped her elbow to help her pick her way over a rough patch of ground. Over the past few weeks, they had managed in many ways to rebuild some semblance of their past friendship, but this was not one of them. They took pains not to touch each other in even the most casual of ways, neither daring to test their resolve. Even this light contact was unexpected and unsettling.

The sound of rushing water grew increasingly loud. Reaching the edge of the Snake River, they halted. Jessie's jaw dropped in awe. The river flowed through a canyon with dark, gleaming, sharply perpendicular walls before spilling over a rock barrier into a spectacular waterfall.

"I can't believe you don't have any comment," Tony teased, less interested in the magnificent scenery than the rapt expression on Jessie's face.

"There aren't any words," she said, absorbing the beauty as if imprinting it on her memory.

"Then perhaps you should use your pencil."

Deep within Jessie a spark of an interest long dead flared to life. She hadn't sketched in such a long time; did she dare try? "Maybe."

They bickered good-naturedly over the best spot to eat, finally settling, as Tony had intended all along, on Jessie's original suggestion.

Jessie spread a bright red-checked cloth over a small patch of grass which was still green, even in August, with the nourishment of the nearby river. She scurried around, setting out food and smoothing the cloth, then lifted her eyes to find Tony watching her. He often looked at her like that. She would be doing the most mundane tasks and would look up to find his eyes filled with such tenderness and longing that an answering warmth would sizzle through her body. It was as if deep within each of them glowed an ember, ignited by their one night together, awaiting the slightest breeze to burst back into flames.

Instinctively, Jessie took a step toward him, then stopped. She couldn't go to him again, she just couldn't. The wound from the last time was still too fresh, too raw. She fought the urge to rush into his arms, to wrap herself around him and never let go. Images danced through her head, flashes of Tony, naked, moving over her in the dark, bringing her a pleasure greater than any she had ever imagined.

God, she could remember it all clearly—could still taste the flavor of his skin, smell their mingled scents, feel the delicious fullness when he pressed deep within her. She clenched her thighs together, trying to ease the ache.

She remembered. He could see it in the way her breathing quickened, see it in the way her eyes glazed as she stared at him. He closed his eyes. Maybe if he couldn't see her, he wouldn't want her so much.

Every thought in his mind was blotted out but one: the feel of her skin. Soft, so incredibly soft, finer than any silk he'd ever touched. Like slipping into fresh water heated to the exact temperature of his body.

Dio, was it really so wrong? So what if he didn't know what kind of a future he could offer her; who did, really? What difference did it make if there were a few things in his past she didn't know about?

He opened his eyes. What he could see couldn't be any worse than what he could imagine. She was still standing there, absolutely still, eyes fixed on him. She was more tempting, fully clothed out in the middle of nowhere, than any other woman was, naked in bed.

Why was he fighting it so hard? Maybe, just maybe this time he could make it work. He was damn sure he couldn't go on like this much longer, walking around day after day a hairbreadth from sweeping her into his arms and making her promises he swore he'd never make.

It had been a month. One long, torturous month, when he hadn't let himself reach for her. Four weeks of trying to be her friend, when even being her lover somehow didn't seem like enough.

Relief flowed through him, relaxing the tight muscles of his chest. If his head wasn't completely sure of his actions, his body sure as hell was. He lifted one arm toward her, palm up as if in invitation.

"Jessie," he said, his voice low and hoarse.

She shivered slightly. All he had said was her name. Was she reading too much into it? No. She could feel it, calling to her heart and her body.

He was waiting for her.

She lifted her skirts in both hands, preparing to walk straight into his arms.

"Tony! Jessie!"

A frantic shout shattered the moment. Jessie squinted, trying to make out the approaching horse and rider, smiling at the oaths Tony was muttering under his breath.

The rider pulled his horse to a stop and vaulted his gangly adolescent frame from the saddle. Tom Bolton, Jr., removed his dusty hat, exposing his wild, fiery thatch of hair.

"Tony. Ma'am." He turned the hat round and round in his large, bony hands. His Adam's apple bobbing, his gaze flitted from Jessie to Tony and back again.

"Well?" Tony prompted, anxious to rid himself of this interruption as quickly as possible. He really wasn't in the mood to stand around jawing with some adolescent pip-squeak.

"I'm sorry, sir, it's just . . . ah . . ." his voice broke, and he cleared his throat before continuing. "It's Reverend Parson, ma'am. He's come down sick, and Ma thought you'd probably want ta know."

Jessie grabbed his forearm so abruptly that Tommy dropped his hat to the ground. "How bad is he?"

"I don't rightly know, ma'am. You'd hafta talk ta Ma about that. She just told me ta find ya an' let ya know."

"I have to go back," Jessie said.

"Ya can use my horse."

Tony wasted no time on words. He swung smoothly to the horse's back and lifted Jessie in front of him, wrapping his left arm securely around her waist. He tried to ignore the feel of her buttocks nestled between his thighs. There was no time for that now.

Chewing on her lower lip, Jessie glanced at their supper, still spread out near the river. "But . . . our things . . ."

"Don't worry about it, ma'am. I'll pack everything up and lug it back for ya."

Tony leaned forward, pulled Jessie tightly against his chest, and headed the horse toward camp.

"How is he?"

Harriet Bolton, kneeling beside the mattress, didn't look up but merely pursed her lips slightly and gave a small shake of her head.

Jessie dropped to her knees on the other side of the bed and took Reverend Parson's hand between both of hers. His skin was delicate, thin, and stretched tightly over his bones.

It was uncomfortably warm in the wagon, and bright sunlight leaked through the white canvas, but still he shivered. The air smelled of sickness—a scent Jessie had sworn, after she'd left her father's sickroom for the last time, that she'd never smell again—and she choked down the nausea it provoked. For Reverend Parson, she'd tolerate almost anything.

"Reverend?" she said softly. "It's me, Jessie."

His eyelids fluttered open, exposing eyes that were sunken and dull, his usual elfin twinkle absent. He curved his cracked lips into a weak smile.

"Jessie, my dear, I—"

Placing her fingers softly over his mouth, Jessie hushed him. "Don't use up your strength chattering at me. I want you to use all of it to get well as quickly as possible."

"But I—"

"Hush! Close your eyes and go back to sleep. I'll be here when you're stronger. You can talk all you want to then."

He blinked once, twice, and then his eyes stayed closed. His breathing slowed and deepened.

"Harriet," Jessie whispered. "What—"

Harriet pressed a finger to her lips, quieting Jessie,

and jerked her head toward the entrance to the wagon. They crawled out, one at a time.

Tony lifted both women down and then slipped a supporting arm around Jessie's waist. She leaned against him, worrying her lower lip with her teeth.

"It's not . . . cholera, is it?" It was an ugly and efficient killer completely capable of wiping out an entire train of people.

"No, dysentery." Jessie's sigh of relief was interrupted when Harriet continued. "But that's not all that much better—at least not for him." She tucked a strand of graying red hair back into its bun. "He's an old man, Jessie, and weak. We can try to get as much fluid into him as possible, but—I don't know, Jessie. I just don't know."

Jessie sagged against Tony. He pulled her to him, his big hand holding her head securely against his chest. His heart thudded near her ear.

Her throat hurt when she spoke.

"I don't think I can do this again, Tony."

He rubbed his chin softly against her temple. "You won't be alone this time, Jess. I swear it, you won't be alone."

"It's time, Jessie."

The words called softly from outside her wagon were not a surprise. Despite the late hour, she was awake, half expecting the summons.

The train had not traveled for a day after the Reverend fell ill, but when he hadn't improved they were compelled to continue their journey. It had been a hellish few days for Jessie, forced to nurse Reverend Parson as he was jostled painfully in a moving wagon. Harriet administered small dosages of opium, giving him some relief from the pain, but he grew steadily weaker, despite Jessie's best care.

Passing through the eerie City of Rocks, even the

landscape echoed her mood. The reddish brown spires
and peaks seemed to rise from nowhere, belonging to
another land, another world.

She wondered what world Reverend Parson would
soon belong to.

"Coming," she answered, pulling on a dress right
over her nightgown.

"I'll go with you," Tony said, yanking on his shirt.

"You don't have to."

He slid the last button through its hole and laid his
palm against her cheek. "Yes. I do. I'll wait outside,
but I'm coming with you."

They hurried through the warm night to the softly
lit wagon where the Reverend lay.

"My dear," Jedediah said in a throaty voice. "I told
them not to wake you up in the middle of the night."

"Wake me up? I'm a night owl. You know that."

"But—"

She lifted her fingers, intending to place them on
his lips to silence him, but he raised a shaky hand and
took her own.

"Stop shushing me, my dear. A bit of conversation
will make no difference now." He rolled his head to
the other side. "Silas, will you leave us for a bit?"

Reverend Donner closed the Bible and stood. "Of
course, Jedediah. But you must not overexert yourself."

Jessie watched him leave. Her opinions of The Reverend Donner—she would always think of him as *The*
Reverend Donner—had risen significantly since Reverend Parson fell ill. The Reverend Donner had cared
for his colleague, alternating with Jessie and Harriet,
with surprising gentleness and grace. Dysentery was a
degrading sickness, messy, smelly, and embarrassing,
but he had never shown even a hint of revulsion. He
seemed to hold a genuine respect and affection for his

fellow minister, and it had done much to redeem him in Jessie's eyes.

Her gaze fell again to Reverend Parson. He was so still. She brushed her free hand across his hairless—or, as Jedediah himself termed it, hairfree—dome.

"Now, my dear, when I'm gone—"

"No! I won't allow you to speak that way!"

"Jessie." He gave her a slight smile. "I have had a wonderful life, filled with people I loved and important work I enjoyed. If it is my time, I have no regrets."

"Please—"

"Let me finish. I wanted to talk to you because I know you have already lost much, and I don't want you to mourn me, too."

Her eyes stung, and she didn't dare blink, knowing that if she did the tears would fall. "It's so hard."

"Do you wish you hadn't known me?"

His question caught her by surprise. She thought of the evenings they had spent laughing over coffee, his childlike wonder at each new sight, his deep understanding and love, his extraordinary joy in life, his gentle wisdom. She swallowed the painful lump in her throat.

"I will always be grateful for knowing you. I . . . I love you."

"I love you, too, and that is precisely the point, my child. Love is always worth it. No matter the pain, no matter the difficulty, love is always worth it."

She tightened her fingers around his limp hand, wishing that somehow she could send some of her strength into him. "I don't want to be left alone again."

His voice grew weaker, and she knew it was taking all the energy he had to speak. "You will never be alone. When you've loved . . . you are never alone, for those you loved live on in you . . . in the ways you've grown and changed by their presence in your life. It makes me very proud . . . to know . . . there will always be . . . a part of . . . me . . . in you."

Her nose filled and her chest ached, making it difficult to speak.

"But it hurts so much!"

"If it didn't hurt . . . it wouldn't be love." His eyelids fluttered before drifting shut one last time. Her vision blurred as she watched his chest grow still.

Love is always worth it.

22

Reverend Donner's quavery voice droned on, ending the eulogy and beginning to read a passage of scripture, but Tony scarcely noticed. He was too preoccupied with Jessie, rigid and white-faced beside him. He took her hand in his. Her fingers were ice-cold, and he rubbed them between his palms, trying to warm them. He knew it was useless, for her chill came from within, but he was helpless to do anything else, and he needed to do something.

When Jessie had tumbled out of the ministers' wagon last night, shaking and pale, he had known immediately that the Reverend was gone. He hadn't given her time to speak but lifted her in his arms, carried her to their own wagon, tucked her into bed, and promised he would take care of everything. He knew she considered the arrangements her responsibility, but there was no way he was letting her carry this burden alone—not now, not ever again.

Jessie curved her fingers around Tony's now, gripping them tightly. He felt solid, real. Nothing else did.

Her gaze drifted across the rough, dry plain. The landscape was dull, gray and brown, littered with sagebrush, prickly pear, scrub grass, and little else, whipped by a gusty, hot wind. It looked empty, desolate . . . dead.

She tried to focus on the small group of mourners gathered around a small cross of two boards pried from a wagon bed and hammered together. The marker, listing to the north, was simply a memorial. There was no body buried beneath.

Her dreams last night had been terrifying, and she had woken up sobbing, seeing over and over Reverend Parson's mutilated body dragged from its grave. It happened often. She had seen too many disturbed graves along the trail to delude herself into believing otherwise. But Tony had promised he would take care of this, too, and he had.

The Reverend's body was buried far from his cross —far enough away that no human grave robber would be able to find it. The animal scavengers were harder to confuse. The grave had been dug deep beneath the trail itself. Wagons would roll over it and oxen would tread upon it, packing the earth hard, obliterating any sign or scent of the body buried there. It was undignified, but necessary. Jessie was only grateful the grave would not be invaded.

Mary Ellen began to sing, one of the spirituals favored by Reverend Parson. Jessie closed her eyes, letting the purity of Mary Ellen's voice wash through her. The powerful words of hope buoyed her spirits. It seemed that the song was speaking to her, telling her to put aside her own pain and remember the Reverend's life, not his death.

Mary Ellen finished the song with an odd, off-key note. Jessie opened her eyes to find Mary Ellen rubbing her swollen abdomen and flashing Stuart a smile.

"The baby's coming."

*   *   *

Jessie dipped a cloth in a small bowl of water, wringing it out thoroughly before wiping the sweat from Mary Ellen's flushed face. The heat was vicious, and the small wagon crowded. Mary Ellen was surrounded by women—Jessie and Ginnie on either side while Harriet worked between Mary Ellen's widespread knees.

Harriet had insisted that Jessie and Ginnie shouldn't be there. Since neither had any experience in childbirth, they couldn't possibly be of any help. But Mary Ellen had been implacable; she needed her friends. Ginnie spent the afternoon chattering nonstop, entertaining them all with wildly improbable childbirth stories—all absolutely true, she swore—of her assorted aunts and cousins, causing Mary Ellen to burst into laughter between contractions. Jessie did what she could to keep Mary Ellen comfortable, sponging down her damp skin, holding her hand, and giving her tiny sips of water from a jug that she had wrapped in wet cloths, hoping that evaporation would cool the water fractionally.

Pressing one hand to the small of her back, Jessie leaned back, easing the persistent ache. It seemed that Mary Ellen had been in labor for days, although Jessie knew it had only been a matter of a few hours.

". . . and it's all the truth, Mary Ellen, I swear it on my Andrew's manhood—oh, dear, you probably don't want to hear anything about *that* right now, do you? Anyway, my third—or was she my second, once removed?—cousin, Adna—wouldn't you just hate to be named *Adna,* it sounds like you have a head cold— well, she birthed her son and two days later was back runnin' the house like a major general, only she couldn't figure why her belly wasn't flattenin' out. It was a full week later when she went into labor again, and this time she—"

"Oh, hush, Ginnie. It's time to push, Mary Ellen."
Harriet shifted on her haunches and lifted the sheet
spread over Mary Ellen's legs.

"Already?"

Jessie gaped at Mary Ellen. *Already?* Mary Ellen's
serene acceptance of her labor pain was one thing, but
it was supposed to go on longer? Oh, Lord, whose
stupid idea was this childbirth business, anyway? Jessie's swift prayer of apology to her maker was interrupted when Mary Ellen grabbed her hand in a grip
tight enough to break bones.

Three pushes later Harriet triumphantly held up a
red, wrinkled, squawking, and absolutely beautiful
baby boy. Jessie hastily handed a blanket to Harriet,
who efficiently wrapped up the baby and handed the
entire bundle back to Jessie.

"Here, honey, you clean him up while I see to Mary
Ellen."

"No, I couldn't, I've never . . . oh, Mary Ellen,
he's so sweet."

Jessie looked across the wagon and saw that Ginnie's brown eyes were sheened with tears. She'd almost forgotten how hard it must be for Ginnie to be
here, wanting a baby of her own so badly, but she had
shown nothing but cheerful support and much-appre-
ciated good humor the entire time. Jessie hoped Ginnie could see her silent admiration.

She carefully sponged the blood off the baby. She
had never been close to a newborn before, and she
was entranced. It seemed unbelievable that anything
could be so small and so completely perfect. Watching
the tiny hands curl into fists, she smoothed the sparse
tufts of pale hair over his delicate scalp, where his
rapid pulse beat just beneath the tender skin.

After cleaning the baby she swaddled him in the
softest blanket she could find and cuddled him close
to her body. He was light in her arms, a faint, sweet
scent drifting from his skin, and she couldn't resist

pressing a light kiss to his forehead. He was so incredibly soft.

"Jessie?"

Jessie blinked to clear her eyes and looked over at Mary Ellen.

"Jessie, Stuart and I talked about this before the funeral this morning. His name is Jedediah Parson Walker."

The large rock warmed her back as Jessie leaned against it. It was past supper time, she knew, but she didn't want to return to camp just yet. The isolated clump of boulders, out of site of camp, formed a rough circle around her and gave her the privacy she needed as she struggled to come to terms with the shock of confronting both birth and death in a span of less than twenty-four hours.

She had never felt more alive in her life. She had had plenty of experience with the end of life, but none with the beginning, and she found it made all the difference.

She could accept Reverend Parson's death now. She would always miss him, but she could cherish the time she had had with him, knowing that he regretted nothing and that a precious new life carried on his name. Life was always renewed, and it was meant to be lived, not endured.

She brushed her fingers over the pad of paper in her lap, savoring the feel of the pristine white sheet. Lifting a vibrant burgundy stick of pastel, she rolled it between her fingers, admiring the deep, almost jewel-like color. She had missed it—how she had missed it!

She lowered the pastel to the paper but stopped, unable to still the tremble of her hand. What if she still couldn't do it? Her work had always been an expression of her joy in life. When the joy had left, so had her talent.

Remembering the Reverend's warm smile and the feel of a tiny, brand-new baby in her arms, Jessie drew a bold streak of rich, wine-red color across the blank paper.

Tapping his hand lightly against his thigh, Tony stared at the clump of rocks as if he could see through the solid stone that hid Jessie from his view. Uncomfortable with the isolation of the spot she had chosen, he had managed to keep the boulders in his sight most of the day, and always in earshot. What was she doing in there all this time, anyway? He respected her desire to be alone, but she'd been in there such a damn long time. What if it all had been too much for her?

The sun would be going down soon. He had to see if she was all right.

Jessie didn't even notice Tony's arrival when he eased between the two largest rocks. Her head was bent, and she was engrossed in something propped up in her lap. He would have been annoyed that she had kept him worrying all this time for nothing, but he was too enchanted with the sight she made, her tongue caught between her teeth and her brows puckered in concentration. Her bare toes peeped out from under the hem of her dress. She brushed a stray lock of hair from her cheek and left behind a large, dark smudge.

She was sketching. She hadn't touched her art supplies in all the months he had known her. He had always regretted the waste of her obvious talent and regretted even more the pain he suspected was behind it. But for some reason, now, she had decided to work again.

She was singing as she drew, the song so badly mangled it was unrecognizable. He winced when she attempted a high note and failed miserably. The woman could not sing. The amazing thing was that he found such a flaw endearing.

"What are you up to, Rembrandt?"

She lifted her hand and flashed him the brilliant smile he hadn't seen since before the Reverend had fallen ill. God, he had missed that smile.

"Want to see?" He didn't even have time to answer before she sprang to her feet and tossed the sketchpad to him. He turned the paper right side up, holding it carefully by the edges.

It took no effort to identify the empty plain where Reverend Parson was buried, but the drab, desolate spot was transformed into something compelling and appealing by the sunset she had drawn over it. The sky was a swirl of intense, pulsing color in every shade from a purple just this side of black to an impossible variety of reds and the purest, sheerest gold.

There was something not quite right about it. His brows drew together as he tilted the picture from side to side, unable to put his finger on just what was missing. Something was not in the right place, something not . . .

It wasn't a sunset at all, he suddenly realized.

It was a sunrise. A joyous, triumphant sunrise.

He lifted his gaze to Jessie's beaming face. She was more gorgeous, somehow more alive than he had ever seen her.

"You understand it, too, don't you, Tony? It's not all about leaving and losing and dying. It's about living and loving and being grateful for every wonderful second you're given and the people you get to share them with."

He knew she wasn't just talking about the picture; she was talking about life, too. Unable to resist, he ran his forefinger down the curve of her cheek.

"Yes. I understand."

At his touch, her smile faded, and her eyes darkened to smoky gray. She slipped the picture from his grasp and placed it near the edge of the clearing. Then she darted back and very deliberately placed her hand squarely in the middle of his chest, spreading her fingers wide as if to touch as much of him as possible.

"Touch me, Tony."

His body reacted immediately, hardening with an abruptness that nearly buckled his knees. But he didn't want this to be simply because she needed something of life to block out the death. He had to be certain, for he'd never be able to give her up after one isolated night again. It had nearly killed him the last time.

He stepped closer, still not touching her, but close enough so he could feel the heat from her body. He looked deeply into her eyes, trying to read the truth.

"Jessie . . ." He swallowed, trying to clear the hoarseness from his throat. "You'd better be damn sure. If I touch you now, there is no way I'm ever going to stop."

She removed her hand from his chest but didn't step back. Instead, she reached for her neckline and slipped the pearly button through the matching hole in the apple-green fabric. There were dozens of tiny buttons, running all the way down the front of her dress, and she undid each, one by one, while Tony's nostrils flared and his breathing quickened. She had to bend at the waist to reach the final buttons. Finally sliding the dress from her shoulders, she straightened, and the garment dropped to the ground. Then she gave him a sweetly sensual smile that sent desire simmering through his veins.

His laces were already loose, and he ripped his shirt over his head. Jessie's breath caught at the sight: bronze skin, black hair, and rugged muscles. With shaking hands, she crossed her arms at her waist, grasped the hem of her camisole, and lifted it off, tossing it carelessly over her shoulder.

She should have been embarrassed, standing there

in the still-strong evening light, her breasts bare. Perhaps, in some dim corner of her mind, she was. But she had imagined their lovemaking so many times in such precise and frustratingly clear detail that she felt she knew each cranny of his body intimately, and he, hers.

His gaze never wavered from her as he yanked off his boots and socks. Her shoulders gleamed in the light, and he knew exactly how soft the skin over her ribs was. He wanted to touch her, badly, but the breathless yearning was too sweet to end quickly.

She dropped her petticoats, and their movements slowed, each savoring the anticipation. Tony bent and slid off his pants and undergarments in one fluid motion. Her fingers tingling with the need to touch him, she lowered her simple white cotton drawers, the last remaining piece of clothing.

Neither knew how long they stood there, not touching, just looking and wanting and needing.

"Do you know often I've thought of you, dreamed of you, wanted you?" He wanted to show her. Her gaze followed his hand as he dropped it to his hard shaft and stroked himself once, tip to base and, slowly, back to the head.

Her eyes widened but she did not look away. "I dreamed of you, too." Her cheeks pinkened as she lifted one trembling hand to her throat, trailing her fingers over one white breast and beaded nipple. "I imagined you touching me . . . like this." She cupped her breast in her fingers, squeezing the hard tip between her thumb and the side of her palm.

They could stay apart no longer. Moving together, they wrapped their arms tightly around each other, pressing hungry skin to hungry skin.

And then he kissed her, a soft, gentle kiss which quickly heated out of control.

"Dio!" Breathing hard, he glanced around frantically. Grabbing the blanket Jessie had been sitting on

earlier, he spread it out with a quick snap, not bothering to smooth out the wrinkles.

"Hurry up, Tony."

He gave her a wry look. "I am not going to lay you on that damn prickly, dried-out grass."

She laughed, and he swept her into his arms. The grass rustling and crackling beneath them, he placed her gently on the blanket and stretched out beside her. Tony pressed his mouth to hers, and her amusement evaporated abruptly. His lips were firm and warm, his tongue was soft and even warmer, and it had been too long. He passed his hands over her skin, sweeping strokes that moved from neck to thigh and back again.

This was the way it was meant to be, she thought. The movements, the feelings, the intensity. Above it all, the knowledge that it was Tony who touched her, who tasted her, who caressed her. It was Tony, who made her feel this way.

She mumbled a protest when he rolled her to her stomach.

"Shhh." He brushed the heavy fall of hair from her neck. "You walk around all day with your hair up in that damn knot, and all I want to do is taste you right here." He kissed the nape of her neck, and she shivered. His tongue was hot as he circled the small mole on the back of her neck and drew swirling designs on her shoulder blades, then slid his mouth down her spine. He paused to flick each vertebra before he slipped his tongue down the cleft between her buttocks. It was slightly shocking and completely arousing.

"Tony!"

Lightly, he bit one soft mound. "What?" he asked with a smile in his voice.

Jessie rolled onto her back. It was too much, and she wasn't sure how much more she could take. "Come here," she whispered, trying to pull him to her.

"Soon, *cara.*" He kissed her gently, soothingly, his tongue caressing hers lightly before he moved to her cheek. She closed her eyes, awash in the sensations he evoked.

Tony dragged his mouth down her throat and over her body, teasing her breasts, nipping her waist, dipping into her navel. How had he managed it? he wondered. How had he kept himself from touching her for so long, when he knew this was how it was between them? When it felt as if he needed her more than food, more than air, more than life?

He spread her thighs wide and moved between them. Jessie arched, anticipating his thrust.

It did not come. Confused, she lifted herself up on her elbows and opened her eyes to find him kneeling between her legs, staring at her intimate flesh with eyes that were intensely black. Embarrassed, she sucked in her breath.

His gaze met hers. "Jessie, do you trust me?"

"Yes."

"Then believe that you are so beautiful to me. All of you."

Extremely sensitive, she jerked when he touched her. He moved his fingers slowly, in a way that somehow managed to be both soothing and exciting. She bit her lip hard when his fingers dipped into her, giving her just a taste of the fullness she craved.

Then he leaned forward slightly to annoint the peaks of her breasts. He watched her nipples darken from pink to a deep, beckoning rose and blood thrummed in his temples. He took her breast in his mouth, licking, sucking softly, and Jessie gave a small moan. "You taste so sweet," he said, his voice muffled against her skin.

She knew what he was going to do when he lowered his head further, but she couldn't look away. The contrast of his gleaming black hair against her white belly was unbearably erotic.

He kissed her in the valley between her right leg and her torso, and she curled up a bit, for it tickled. He shifted slightly, then slipped his tongue out to taste her, tracing and swirling and dipping. Jessie could watch no longer. Her head fell back and she was lost in pleasure so acute it was nearly unbearable.

Concentrating on her most sensitive spot with his tongue, Tony pushed two fingers deeply inside her. The sensation sent her to the edge of fulfillment, and she groaned in disappointment when he moved away.

"No, don't go!"

"I'm right here, Jessie . . . right here."

He entered her in one swift motion. They were still for a moment, savoring the feeling of being one. Tony began to move, thrusting deep and hard with a steady, drugging rhythm that drove them both to the edge of sanity and beyond.

It was passion. It was youth and love and joy.

It was life.

23

Waiting for his pounding heartbeat to slow to a normal rate, Tony tightened his arms to bring Jessie even closer. God, she felt good. An incredible languor seeped through his body, and it seemed to require tremendous effort for him to open his eyes. Sometime while he and Jessie were lost in each other the sun had dropped to the horizon, and the resulting twilight was soft and dim.

He looked at her, peaceful and satisfied in his arms, and he knew. He *knew*.

He wanted her in his life.

It didn't matter that he still had no answers to why or how or when. He simply had no choice anymore. He was hers, and she was his.

Jessie shivered slightly and opened her sleepy eyes.

"Cold?" he asked.

"I'm never cold with you around."

Tony flipped a corner of the blanket over her anyway, tucking her in snugly and throwing his large, warm thigh across her legs.

"Better?"

"Mmm." Rubbing her cheek against his chest, she toyed with a curl of dark chest hair with her fingertip. "I wish we could stay here forever."

God, so did he. What the hell was in California, anyway?

Only Benjamin, his conscience whispered. Only Benjamin and his dreams and his past.

Damn it, he had to tell her. She had a right to know who and what he was before he asked her to stay with him.

He ground his teeth together until his jaw hurt. He couldn't stand the thought of the revulsion on her face when he told her of the pain his callousness and lust had caused. What an idiot he had been! Somehow he would find a way to convince her that he was no longer the same man—rather, no longer the boy he had been, back when Ben and Liza and he had gotten their lives tangled together in such a stupid snarl.

Jessie was smiling at him, her beautiful eyes shimmering with emotions he wasn't sure he had the right to accept. Unable to watch her expression change, Tony looked away, focusing on the large gray rock behind her. It looked like a donkey sitting on its rump, and he wondered why that seemed to matter.

"Jessie . . ." How was he going to find the right words? "We have to talk."

She yawned. "Not now. Tomorrow."

"Yes. Now," he said.

Suddenly alert, Jessie tightened her fingers on his chest.

He softened his tone slightly. "There are some things you need to know. When we get to California, I have to—"

"No!" Jessie sat up quickly. "I don't want to talk about this."

"Yes, Jessie, you have a right to know about—"

"I said no!" Jessie grasped his face in both hands,

turning his head so he was forced to look at her. "I'm tired of bemoaning the past and worrying over the future. What good has it ever done me? All I want to think about is you and me, together. I'm not going to ruin this time with things that might never happen. Whatever comes up when we get to California, we'll decide about it then. Now the only thing I'm going to think about is this."

Throwing her arms around his neck, Jessie gently pushed Tony back to the blanket and kissed him with all the passion and skill he had taught her.

Oh, what the hell. He'd settle things with Ben before he told her. He'd be able to put his past behind him, once and for all. That was his last conscious thought before he rolled her beneath him.

"Darn it, Beauregard, you're the most useless hunk of beef I've ever had the misfortune to come across."

Jessie braced herself against the ox's massive haunch. Reaching down and grasping his hoof firmly, she heaved with all her might. A large, dirty tail whipped sharply across her face, and she stumbled back.

"You really are the biggest piece of *merda*."

Jessie wiped the sweat off her forehead with her sleeve, noting in distaste that her dress was already so stained and dirty that the additional moisture wasn't even noticeable. It was so damn hot. As the train had followed the valley of the Humbolt River for the last few weeks, the air had grown increasingly hot, the water increasingly salty, and the trip increasingly interminable. Now that they had reached the Humbolt Sink, where the river dissolved into a maze of sloughs, swamps, marshy meadows, and salt lakes, they were faced with the most difficult and dangerous part of their journey.

From their grumblings and mumblings, Jessie knew

that her companions were also sick of traveling and weary of the continuous, oppressive labor. The land they recently traveled was gray and dusty, the only vegetation sagebrush and an occasional prickly pear, and the only game jackrabbit. Now they were faced with over fifty miles of desert, as dry and dusty as fireplace ashes. Many in the group were beginning to believe that the trip would never end.

Jessie could only pray it wouldn't.

Her time with Tony was too precious. His presence made the day's drudgery tolerable, but the nights—oh, the nights surpassed her wildest dreams. She was far from ready to give him up, even though she knew she soon would have no choice.

"Looks like you could use a bit of help."

Tony came up behind her and slipped his arms around her waist. Jessie leaned against his solid, familiar bulk. This was what she liked best, the physical affection he bestowed so naturally. He didn't even seem aware of how often he rubbed her neck, held her hand, walked beside her, their thighs brushing with each step, but she certainly was. She hadn't been aware before of how desperately she craved simple human touch.

"Beau's got a sore hoof. I've been trying to get this moccasin on him, but as usual he's not cooperating."

"Let me help."

He released Jessie, then slid his hand soothingly down Beauregard's neck. The animal responded to Tony as readily as Jessie did. Tony dropped to one knee, lifting Beauregard's lower leg, and resting the hoof on his thigh.

Jessie was so busy admiring the way his pose stretched the fabric of his pants tightly over his muscular legs that she nearly forgot to slip the circle of soft leather over Beauregard's injured hoof. She tightened the thongs that gathered the leather and tied it securely.

"There. That should do it."

Tony dropped the ox's leg and stood up, his lean, powerful muscles unrolling with smooth grace.

"I think I've finally figured out why animals always behave for you. They all know you think the same way they do." Jessie said, a little miffed that Tony handled her livestock so much more easily than she did.

Tony grinned. "It's all in the touch, sweetheart. Animals are excellent judges of character."

Jessie stuck her tongue out at his conceit. Without warning, Tony pulled her abruptly against him.

"I can show you much better things to do with your tongue."

He kissed her, more roughly and desperately than he normally did. The fine edge of his passion excited her, sending her heart into a rapid, uneven rhythm. She pressed closer, barely able to feel the hard ridge of his arousal through the layers of clothing separating them, frustrated by the distance between them.

"Criminy, Tony, seems like all you two do these days is trade spit."

"Hmmm?" The words finally penetrated Jessie's consciousness. She pulled away, fanning her face to cool her heated cheeks. "Oh, Samuel, where'd you hear a term like trading spit?"

"Delia Bolton. I heard her talkin' ta Charlie Belshaw behind his wagon, an'—"

"Never mind," Jessie said quickly, deciding that the less said on that subject, the better. Let his parents deal with it.

Tony hunkered down to bring his face level with Sam's. "Something we can do for you, short stuff?"

Sam nodded vigorously. "Daddy tol' me to come ask ya if you're ready to go."

"Just about. Tell him I'll be there in a minute, O.K.?"

"Going somewhere?" Jessie asked, trying to keep

her tone normal, as if the mere thought of his leaving didn't make her stomach tighten with trepidation.

"Yes." Tony put his hand on the back of her neck and rubbed the little mole with the pad of his thumb. "We've filled every available container with water, but I'm afraid it's not going to be enough. There's supposed to be a hot spring part-way through the desert. If I can ride ahead and dam up part of the water, maybe it'll cool off enough by the time the train gets there, so at least the cattle can drink it."

Jessie moved closer to him and leaned her head against his chest. It was strange how the action, which not long ago she would have considered completely forward, seemed utterly natural now.

"When will you be back?"

"With any luck, sometime tomorrow." He hugged her tightly. "Jess, is there something wrong? If you really don't want me to go—"

Jessie pushed him away and squared her shoulders. "No. I'm fine." She watched her foot as she traced circles in the dust, knowing that if she looked him in the eye he would see her lie. She was being ridiculous, she knew. People left all the time, and they always came back.

All except the people she loved.

Oh, God, I didn't mean that. I don't love him. I don't. I don't, she repeated in her head, and wondered if the words sounded as false to God as they did to her.

She glanced up to find Tony still standing there, one hand on his hip, massaging the back of his neck in indecision.

"What are you still doing here? Shoo, now. Go on."

He grinned, dimples denting his cheeks, and blew her a kiss as he trotted off, while Jessie tried to force her unruly heart back in line.

I swear I don't love him.

* * *

Oh, damn it, she did love him. For only the man she loved would offer to bury a dead ox in the middle of fifty-five miles of desert.

The train had left the Truckee sink shortly after Tony and Stuart had, crossing fifteen miles as dry as the dust under her brother's bed before reaching a small pond of brackish water. Tony and Stuart were waiting there, and the party spent a short, restless night before pushing on.

The desert was a place of deep sand, choking dust, and overpowering heat. It was hard on people and even harder on the animals, forced to pull wagons heavily loaded with water through dragging, sucking sand. There were no grasses to fuel the livestock. They were fed only loaves of bread the women had baked in preparation for the crossing.

Jessie ached for her animals, watching them grow exhausted and weak, but there was nothing she could do. Nothing anyone could do except keep grinding forward, step after step, hoping that the desert would give out before their strength did.

There was no reason to stop for the night. Any time wasted would only further deplete their water stores. So they kept walking, trudging over sand turned white and surreal in the moonlight. Empty. Pure. Deadly.

The train reached the hot springs a few hours after midnight. Jessie, struggling along beside her wagon, could hear the springs hissing and gurgling before she reached them. She could smell them, too, the unmistakable rotting-egg odor of sulfur. Finally, as she clambered over a small rise, sand shifting beneath her feet, she could see the springs. Some were smooth and silver, others bubbled and spat water a few feet into the air.

"Watch out, he's going down!" Tony's shout rang in her ears as he shoved her aside.

Beauregard sank slowly to the sand, and Tony scrambled to loosen the leather traces before Beau dragged the other oxen down with him.

The sand was hot beneath her knees as Jessie knelt beside Beau. The moon glinted off his horns as she stroked his velvet muzzle.

"Come on," she urged. "You don't think I'm going to let you give up now, you big, stubborn piece of *merda*! Not after putting up with you this long!"

She felt Tony's hand on her shoulder and looked up. His face was grave, and his eyes, sympathetic.

Her throat felt suddenly raw. "There's nothing we can do?"

"No. He's gone as far as he can, and we can't afford to wait for him to recover. We'd all be in danger then. There's just not enough water, and we have to get out of this desert as soon as possible." His knife flashed as he squatted beside her. "Damn, I'm sorry, Jess, but I swear it's better this way. He won't suffer."

Tony shifted his weight, moving closer and cupping her head with the back of his hand. "You shouldn't see this."

Jessie blinked and felt moisture slide down her cheeks and evaporate into the thirsty air. "No. I want to be here."

She kept her gaze on Beau's dark, absurdly long-lashed eyes when Tony moved to Beauregard's neck. She didn't look, knowing she couldn't stand the sight of the animal's blood spilling out, darkening the pale sand. The ox jerked once, and Jessie murmured to him softly, soothingly, as his eyes closed.

Tony knelt behind Jessie, pulling her back against his body. "It's over, sweetheart."

She shuddered and sagged against his familiar warmth. "What happens to him now? I couldn't eat him, Tony . . . no matter what, I can't do it."

"You won't have to. We can't take the chance if it was more than exhaustion. The last thing we need

now is for everyone to get sick from tainted meat."
Stalling, Tony kissed her on the soft skin beneath her
ear. How could he tell her that they had to just leave
him there? How could he remind her about beetles
and vultures, flies and coyotes? "Do you want me to
bury him for you?"

She gave an unladylike snort of laughter. It was too
absurd, the idea that Tony would stop in this dangerous, desolate place to bury her ox. She could only
imagine what Buffalo Bolton would have to say about
that sort of foolishness. She turned in his arms, smiling up at him through her tears.

"You're crazy, you know that?"

Linking his arms behind her back, he sat back on
his heels, pulling her flush against his body. He regarded her seriously. "I would do it for you."

Who could not love him?

"This place is so . . . dead. If Beau can provide
some sustenance for other life, it's better than rotting
away under the sand. We'll just leave him where he
is."

And so, after the remaining animals had drunken
their fill of water cooled to the temperature of a hot
bath, the wagons moved on, leaving insects and small
animals already feasting on an unexpected bonanza of
fresh meat.

Jessie took a step forward and sank knee-deep in
sand. Sand hot enough to scald her calves. There was
sand in her shoes, sand in her socks, sand in her hair,
and, from the feel of things, sand in her drawers.

She was getting really sick of sand.

"Jessie, just wait a minute and I'll be down to help
you." She shaded her eyes against the blinding sun to
look up at Tony. He had already helped haul their
wagon to the top of the ridge—by far the largest they
had encountered—that she was still struggling to

climb. Now he came skidding toward her, half stepping, half sliding down the slope of the hill.

Reaching her, he grasped her arms and tugged. His
footing was unstable, and when Jessie was pulled free,
Tony went flying backward.

"Ooof." Jessie landed hard on his stomach.

She giggled, then stopped to spit the grit from her
mouth. "Lord, Tony, lot of help you are. I've already
got sand in crannies I never knew I had."

His eyes gleamed as he gave her an exaggerated
leer. "If we had a little privacy I'm sure I could think
of some way to help you clean them out."

He licked her lightly under her chin, and heat siz-
zled down her body—heat, when she was already hot
enough to melt into a puddle of sweat.

Smiling down at him innocently, she scooped up a
handful of sand. She rolled off him, but not before
shoving the sand down the front of his pants.

Her laughter mingled with his outraged squawk.
Crawling on her stomach seemed to be the easiest way
to move. When her foot had pulled free of the sand,
her boot had stayed behind.

"Now I'm really looking forward to you helping me
get this stuff off," Tony said, standing and jumping
around in an effort to shake loose some of the sand.

"Not if you don't help me find my boot."

He flopped down next to her, giving a grunt as he
hit the ground. His big hands shoved the sand aside,
and he soon hit a piece of tan suede.

"Aha!" he shouted triumphantly, holding his prize
high.

"Give me that." Jessie snatched the boot from his
hand and turned it upside down, shaking out a small
river of sand before deciding it was pointless. There
was sand everywhere else, anyway. Shrugging, she
bent over to yank her boot back on.

Tony rolled to one side, propped his chin on his
hand, and watched her, smiling.

He was happy. In the middle of the desert from hell, where it was so hot that the fat in the bacon had melted, ruining their entire store. He was crotch-deep in sand, everything he had worked for in the past eight years was still in Ben's hands; and, still, he was happy.

Damn, he had it bad.

He reached for Jessie's hand and gave her a sharp tug. She landed against his chest, struggling a minute in surprise, but when he cupped the back of her head and pulled her lips down to his, she forgot their location and everything else and wrapped her arms around his neck.

"I know you two are still honeymooners, but don't you think you could find a bit more comfortable place to kiss your wife, Tony?" Stuart Walker's amused voice brought them abruptly back to reality.

Tony loosened Jessie and chuckled. "By now you should know that anyplace is comfortable. After all, you're the one with three children."

Jessie scampered to her feet, knowing that the flush in her cheeks wasn't just from the sun. Jedediah was wrapped in some sort of cloth contraption that held him tightly against his father's chest, leaving Stuart's hands free to help the twins. A twin was clinging tightly to each arm, and in their father's drawn, exhausted face Jessie could see the effort it took to drag them along. Mary Ellen was trailing behind, pale and gasping for air.

Tony took one look at the family and acted. He tossed Samuel on his back, where the boy clung like a tiny monkey. He scooped Susannah up. "I always wondered what it felt like to be the stuffing in a sandwich," he said, sending Susannah into peals of giggles as he pretended to eat some of the "bread."

Jessie hurried to take one of Mary Ellen's arms, and Stuart, the other. Together, they pushed their way to the top of the rise.

Jessie blinked twice, not believing her eyes. Before her was one long, gradual, downhill slope.

And on the other side was green. Green, as in plants. Green, as in the end of the desert, Green, as in the cottonwoods that signaled the Truckee River.

Green, as in no more sand.

24

Thrilled as the travelers were to see the Truckee River, they soon learned to curse it, for during the next week they were forced to cross it several times. The river, formed by Sierra snow melt, was swift, deep, difficult to ford, and numbingly cold.

They followed the river up the eastern slope of the Sierras, seventy miles of hoisting wagons over boulders and up steep passes on a narrow trail littered with furniture and other treasures, discarded from earlier overlanders who found it impossible to haul the heavy pieces over the mountains.

Passing enough furniture to appoint even the largest of mansions, Jessie often wondered about its former owners. Was the battered oak rocking chair used to calm an entire family of restless children? Was the shiny, polished dresser part of a young bride's bedroom set? She could easily imagine a large, boisterous family sitting down to Sunday dinner around the massive, round dining table. How sad it must be, to carry these pieces of home so far, only to be forced to abandon them so close to the end of the journey.

There was no denying that the land was breathtaking. Tall, spindly pines gave off a distinctive, pungent smell. Small lakes, like pieces of the sky dropped to earth, reflected gleaming, craggy peaks. The air was so pure you could feel it going down, like drinking ice water. But when Jessie tried to capture the landscape on paper she felt not peace but an undeniable tension.

The trail through the mountains was twisting and tortuous, holding more potential for sudden, violent death than any they had followed previously. Going uphill, a broken chain could send a wagon and all in it hurtling backward over a precipice. Downhill, the men dragged pine trees behind the wagons as additional brakes, for a runaway wagon would only be stopped by smashing into the rocky face of a mountain.

It was cold. The men wore heavy, knitted wamassuses most of the time, and some women dressed in a double layer of gowns. It seemed odd, so soon after the baking heat of the desert, but it made Jessie all too aware that they were traveling through Donner Pass.

Every California-bound traveler knew the story, how the Donner party, eighty-seven strong, had set out for California in the spring of 1846. Things went wrong almost from the start, and after five deaths in the desert, the party was trapped by snow in the Sierra Nevada mountains. A horrific winter of starvation, robbery, murder, and cannibalism followed, and only thirty-seven travelers reached Fort Sutter the next spring.

Jessie's muscles hurt from being constantly tight, and her stomach quivered so with nerves that food lost its appeal. She tried to pass her tension off to the work and the atmosphere, but she knew, deep in her heart, what the matter was: When they started down the western slope toward Sacramento, her time with Tony was nearly over.

There'd been too many good-byes in Jessie's life, and far too many that were permanent and forever. She didn't want to do it anymore. But here she was, trying, once more, to get through the good-byes.

Words and tears poured out of Ginnie Wrightman in abundance, and Jessie hugged her tighter. She hadn't known how hard it would be to say good-bye. She had no sisters, and her responsibilities to her father had taken up all her free time when other girls her age had giggled and shopped together. She hadn't known until now how much having friends like Ginnie and Mary Ellen meant.

Mary Ellen, her eyes shiny and damp in her placid face, slipped an arm around each woman's waist, joining in their embrace. Over Mary Ellen's shoulder Jessie could see the adobe walls of Sutter's fort, the outlines blurred by her tears, and the California hills, just beginning to turn green from the early October rains. How odd it seemed to be in a place where the vegetation turned green in the fall instead of the spring.

"Well." Jessie stepped back reluctantly, wiping her cheeks with her palms. She knew the women had already said their farewells to Tony and the rest of the train; she was the only one left. "I'm keeping you two from your families." Her lips trembled a bit as she forced a smile. "I'm so glad you will be homesteading near each other."

"Oh, fooh." Ginnie's lower lip thrust out. "I don't understand why you and Tony don't come settle by us, too."

Jessie sniffed sadly. How could she explain that she and Tony wouldn't be settling anywhere together? "I'll try to come visit you both."

"That's not the same," Ginnie said.

"Oh, stop pouting, Ginnie. You look like Susannah after Sam's stolen her dessert." Mary Ellen reached out and gave Jessie's hands one more squeeze. "You do know, Jessie, if you ever need anything, if anything ever changes, you can always come to us."

Touched, Jessie could only nod silently. "Could I . . . could I hold Jedediah one more time?"

Mary Ellen retrieved the baby from her patiently waiting husband and deposited the child in Jessie's arms. Jessie cuddled Jed close, trying to memorize his warmth, his lightness, his sweet baby smell. Closing her eyes, she rubbed her cheek against his infinitely soft one, smiling at his gurgling noises.

Maybe someday she'd have a baby just as sweet as this one, only with dark hair and dark eyes, just like . . .

She had to stop torturing herself, wishing for things that would never happen.

Jessie abruptly returned Jed to his mother, gave the twins smacking good-bye kisses, and rushed off to her own wagon.

She didn't watch the Wrightmans and Walkers leave. She couldn't.

Jessie gave a sharp tug on the last of the leather straps, hitching her team securely to her wagon. She gave Wilhelmina a fond pat, whispering a few words of praise to the gentle cow who had never blinked an eye at being forced into taking Beauregard's spot in the yoke.

Jessie wished she could be so accepting of her fate.

"Going somewhere?"

Jessie jerked up. She hadn't known that Tony was near. He was leaning casually against the wagon, looking tempting and dangerous dressed in skin-hugging black, and the glint in his eyes belied his relaxed pose.

The man was not happy.

Jessie fiddled with the traces, checking and rechecking her rig. "San Francisco. You know that."

"By yourself?"

Jessie straightened, twisting her hands together so tightly that the skin burned. "We're in California now. I know you have . . . business to attend to. I don't want to hold you up any longer."

He strolled over to her, not stopping until her nose was only inches from his chest. "Were you planning on telling me you were leaving?"

Jessie tried to focus on his shirt button, but he was too close, and her eyes crossed. "Of course." Her voice sounded too high, even to her.

Gently grasping her chin in his big, rough palm, he forced her to look up at him. "Were you?"

"Yes." Licking her dry lips, she tried to gather her scattered thoughts. How could she think straight when she knew she only had to slide a bit forward and she could be pressed against the warm, hard body she now knew so well? "I know we have . . . things to settle between us. I was going to find you before I left."

"You are not taking two goddamn steps without me," Tony said, his voice both calm and completely implacable.

Jessie stiffened. Half of her was angry at his high-handed assumption that he could give her orders. The other half was completely, undeniably tempted by the idea of having even a few more days with him. But she had been prepared to let him go now; could she go through it again? All she needed was enough will-power to walk away.

Tony watched her carefully, waiting for the eruption. He knew he shouldn't have challenged her like that. Nothing got Jessie's back up so quickly as threatening her independence, but damn it, did she really think he was just going to let her walk out of his life?

Jessie tilted forward, slid her arms around his waist,

and laid her cheek against his chest. She sighed in contentment as he shifted to bring her closer, wrapping his arms around her.

Willpower, she decided, was a highly overrated trait.

"But Tony, this can't be the right place!" Bewildered, she glanced around at the ramshackle, slapdash buildings that clung to the San Francisco hills, looking like they'd be washed down into the bay with the first good rainstorm. The muddy streets were clogged with the most exotic, bewildering collection of people and vehicles she had ever imagined.

"Why don't you check the address again?"

Jessie dug through her small, ivory handbag, finally unearthing a crumpled letter. J.J. had written her not long after he and David had arrived in California to tell her that they had given up prospecting for the more reliable and profitable business of outfitting other miners. Jessie tried to smooth the paper against her thigh before scanning it for the address J.J. had given her.

"147 Hillside," she read aloud, and then compared it with the shiny brass numbers over the door of one of the finest buildings they'd passed. The address matched, but where she was expecting "Johnston and Marin, Suppliers" were large, bold letters proclaiming "The Naked Rose."

Tony took her hand and laced his fingers with hers. "Well? What now, *cara*?"

"We go in there and ask them what the hell they did with my brother's store."

Tony smiled, his dimple peeking out of his left cheek. "Ah . . . Jess . . . um, don't you think it'd be better if I went in there by myself?"

"What's the matter, Winchester, afraid I'll cramp your style with all those saloon girls?" Jessie frowned in a mock threat. "Not a chance, Tony. We've come this far together, haven't we? You had your chance at Sutter's fort. You're stuck with me now."

His amusement vanished, and he looked down at her with a gaze that was suddenly warm and intent. "God, I hope so, *cara,*" he whispered just before covering her mouth with his.

As always when he kissed her, Jessie forgot everything but Tony, until the catcalls and cheers of passing pedestrians interrupted them.

"Attaboy!"

"Way to go, sonny."

"That's right, show that girlie what you got!"

Jessie gave Tony a small shove, then pressed her palms to her heated cheeks. A small group of disheveled, disreputable-looking men clustered around them on the uneven boardwalk. Their dirt and whiskers made it difficult to guess their age, but she could see that they were all smiling gleefully.

"Oh Tony, what do you think you're doing to me?"

His eyes gleamed wickedly as he leaned down so only she could hear, "I know what I'd like to be doing to you."

"Tony!"

"It's a little late to start getting proper on me, Jess, but if that's the way you want it." He tugged down an imaginary vest and gallantly offered his elbow. "Mrs. Winchester, may I have the honor of escorting you into this exceedingly improper establishment?"

Jessie smiled, shook the dust off the skirt of her best peach dress, and slipped her hand through his arm. "You may, indeed, Mr. Winchester."

"Oh, my God." With her eyes wide and her jaw slack, Jessie stared around the room she and Tony had just entered. It was large and airy, the ceiling two stories high and hung with a huge, glittering crystal chan-

delier that cast rainbows of light onto the highly polished wood floor. The flocked wallpaper was cream
and old gold, the same colors as the plush banquettes
scattered around the room. The gaming tables were
burnished oak, as was the long, gleaming bar that
stretched across the back of the room, above which
hung a huge painting of a very blond, very curvy, and
very naked woman—naked, that is, except for one
strategically placed, exceedingly red rose that didn't
quite manage to cover all of her curly golden pubic
hair.

"Oh, my God," Jessie repeated as Tony waved a
hand in front of her unblinking eyes. The room appeared washed in gold. Rich, voluptuous, and decadent, it somehow managed, despite the painting, to
stay just this side of garish.

"Jessie, do you want to leave?"

"Huh? Oh . . . oh! No, of course not." There
were people here, Jessie realized. Three men who
looked as disreputable as those outside the building
were seated at one of the tables, playing cards with a
man dressed in an expensive-looking gray suit. Draped
over his shoulder was a striking redhead in a skimpy,
emerald-green dress that left bare many parts of her
body Jessie was sure she herself would never expose in
public. Two more men, leaned against the bar with
their backs to the door, each resting a bent leg on a
shiny brass rail. They didn't even glance at the new-
comers. Their attention was completely caught by
their companions, two dark-haired women as beautiful and shockingly dressed as the woman at the card
table.

Behind the bar, with one hand swirling a crystal
snifter of some amber liquid and the other arm draped
loosely over the shoulders of a stunning blond in deep
rose satin, was a handsome golden-haired man
dressed in flawless white.

"J.J.!" Jessie shouted and dashed across the room.

The man looked up, his forehead wrinkled in confusion. Then his face cleared, registering first recognition, then shock, then joy. Not bothering to walk around the bar, he vaulted over it in one smooth, quick leap, meeting Jessie halfway. Jessie leaped at him, and J.J. caught her in midair, twirling her around three times as their exultant laughter echoed off the high ceilings.

"Hey, kid, let me look at you." J.J. set Jessie down and held her at arm's length, giving her a thorough perusal. He whistled through his teeth. "Wow! You're gorgeous. What happened to my scrawny, pesky little sister?"

Jessie blushed. "I grew up."

"Did you ever! Come 'ere." He tugged her back into his embrace.

Tony hung back, unwilling to interrupt their reunion. Seeing them together, their relationship was obvious. It was odd how the same features, the same clean lines, generous mouth, and tilted nose that were so endearingly feminine on Jessie could be blatantly masculine on her brother. His jaw was heavier, solid instead of delicate, and their coloring was slightly different. J.J.'s hair was pure gold, with none of Jessie's coppery highlights, and his eyes were more intensely blue, the color of fine turquoise.

Remembering the sketches Jessie had made of her brother, Tony tried to define the differences between the portraits and the man before him. Jessie's brother still had the same exuberance and lively enthusiasm, but he had aged, not so much in his face but in his eyes. Some of the mischief had been replaced by assurance, and there was a barely perceptible edge of hardness.

The blond woman from behind the bar sauntered over, bringing with her an overpowering scent of roses. She leaned against Tony, pressing her generous breasts against his arm, and smiled.

"Honey, if she's your woman, I'd get her away from J.J. before she suffers permanent damage."

Tony cocked an eyebrow. "From you or from him?"

"From either one of us." Her eyes narrowed as she gave him an assessing look. "Then again, you might be the only man I've seen in years who could give J.J. a run for his money."

Tony acknowledged the compliment with a slight bow. "I'll keep that in mind, but I don't think either one of us has anything to worry about. She's his sister."

"His sister?" The woman brightened. "Well, well." Her hips swayed in a naturally provocative rhythm as she walked to stand by J.J., laying one perfectly manicured hand on his arm. "J.J. honey, aren't you going to introduce me to your family?"

Laughing, J.J. slung a casual arm around Rose's shoulders, drawing her up against his side. "Jessie, this is my co-worker and friend, Rose. Rose, this is my baby sister, Jessamyn."

Jessie opened her mouth to protest the "baby," then shut it again with a snap. The woman was beautiful, pale, blond, and generously curved. She was also familiar.

Jessie's stunned gaze flashed to the painting over the bar, then back to the woman.

"You're the . . . uh . . . you're *that* Rose, aren't you?"

Rose laughed heartily. "Actually, that Rose is me. I'm the hostess here at my namesake, and I'm so pleased to meet you. J.J. has missed you terribly, I know."

"Aw, Rosie, don't tell her that. She'll start thinking I'll let her get away with anything if she knows I might be slightly fond of her." His face darkened when a tall, handsome man came up and placed his hands on Jessie's shoulders. "Excuse me, buddy, but I don't believe we've met."

"We haven't." Tony gave an easy smile but refused to move his hands. "I'm Tony Winchester. I'm Jessie's—"

"Friend," Jessie broke in. She felt Tony's hands tighten on her shoulders, but she ignored the brief twinge of discomfort and continued. "That's right, he's my friend. We happened to be on the same wagon train, and he just happened to be coming to San Francisco from Fort Sutter, too, so he sort of . . . escorted me."

Tony felt the breath exit his chest. After all that had been between them, she introduced him as a *friend*? He thought they had left that simple relationship behind weeks ago.

"Jessie," he said softly.

"We'll talk about it later, Tony, please." She gave her brother a forced smile.

He didn't smile back. "Jessie, what exactly is going on here?"

"J.J., put away your big-brother instincts and stop glowering at me. Nothing is going on here."

"I am not putting away any instincts. I *am* your goddamn big brother, and it's my goddamn *job* to glower at you." His color and voice rose. "I was so happy to see you I didn't stop to ask any questions. I'm asking them now. Just what the hell are you doing here with this man unchaperoned, and how the *hell* did you manage to get halfway across the country by yourself?" he bellowed.

"Now listen here, brother," Jessie said, emphasizing each word with a forefinger poked into her brother's chest. "As long as we're asking questions, you mind telling me what the hell happened to Johnston and Marin, Suppliers?"

J.J. winced and gave her an abashed smile. "Ah . . . when did you start swearing, anyway?"

"When I grew up," Jessie snapped. "About the same time I stopped answering to you. But I tell you what, you answer my questions and I'll answer yours."

"Well . . ." J.J. rubbed the back of his neck. "We are suppliers. I just wasn't precisely accurate about what we supplied. We don't sell tents and pick axes, but we do supply relaxation and comaradarie to hard-working miners, good will, and—"

Jessie snorted. "I can see perfectly well what you supply."

"Now, now, I can see you all have a lot of catching up to do. Why don't we all sit down and get comfortable," Rose suggested. In minutes she had them all seated around one of the highly polished wood tables. She fetched Jessie a cup of tea and poured three small shot glasses of very good whiskey for herself and the men.

Tony snatched a deck of cards from the nearest table and slouched in his chair. He began to shuffle desultorily, still somewhat disgruntled at being relegated to the status of friend. Amazing how accustomed to the term husband he had become.

He balanced a card on two others, patiently building a two-story structure while he listened to Jessie describe her decision to come west and give her brother a highly edited version of the trip.

"So that's really all it was then?" J.J. leaned toward Tony. "You two became acquainted on the westward journey and, when you found she was coming to San Francisco too, merely offered to accompany her? Purely out of your gentlemanly instincts, of course."

Tony flicked one of the bottom cards, sending several of the others sliding across the table.

"Of course." Tony leveled his gaze on J.J. "I certainly couldn't leave a young woman alone and unprotected. I would have done no less for my own sisters."

J.J.'s eyes clouded, and he knocked back his glass of whiskey in one gulp.

"God, Jessie, I'm sorry." He took one of her hands, playing lightly with her fingers. "I didn't really give you much choice, did I? If I had known Dad was sick, I would have come back."

"I know you would have. That's exactly why we didn't tell you. After the way things were between you and Dad when you left . . . he felt terrible about it, J.J. He wanted to make sure you had your chance."

"But it wasn't fair to you. I should have come back as soon as I heard, anyway."

"Does it really matter now?" Jessie asked softly. "I'm here, safe and sound. Even if you had left as soon as possible when you found out about Dad's death, you wouldn't have made it back in time. We probably would have passed each other on the trail."

"You're right. You're here now, and that's all that matters." J.J. returned his attention to Tony. "So, Winchester, what exactly is it you do for a living?"

"I raise and train horses."

"Horses?"

"Yes, horses. You know, big four-legged animals people like to ride."

"Horses?" J.J. repeated in a tone of utter disgust.

"What's the matter with horses?"

"They're stupid and smelly, they step on your feet, and they shit in the street."

"Not my horses. Perhaps you've been the problem, not your horses." Tony said indignantly. *Nobody* insulted his horses.

"Ah, geez, Jess, I thought you had better taste in friends than a horse-lover."

"J.J.!" Jessie said in a warning tone. She flashed Tony an apologetic smile. "You have to make allowances. J.J. has a little trouble with animals in general and horses in particular. I'm sure not even General could change his mind."

"Jessie? Is that really you?"

Jessie whirled to the source of the voice. "David!" She launched herself at the man entering from the back of the saloon. Laughing, he hugged her tight, planting a kiss on each cheek.

"Squirrel! I can't believe you're actually here! J.J. never let on that you might be coming."

Squirrel? Tony thought sourly. What kind of a name was that for a beautiful woman like Jessie? This was the man Jessie had worshiped for years?

"He didn't know I was coming." Her eyes sparkling happily, Jessie tugged David toward Tony. "I'll explain all that later. First, there's someone I want you to meet."

When Jessie introduced them, Tony rose to shake David's hand, studying her old friend carefully. The man had touched her, had put his arms around her and held her. Tony had seen Jessie held by her brother and Reverend Parson, hugged by Stuart, Buffalo, and Andrew. It had never bothered him even the slightest bit, but now he wanted, violently, to dislike David.

He couldn't. David's hazel eyes were open and friendly, with a gentle and accepting wisdom that reminded Tony of Reverend Parson.

Jealousy was a bitch. Liking your rival was even worse. How was he supposed to leave Jessie here with David while he went off to find Ben?

25

Tony was brooding.

He was sprawled, stark naked, on the rose satin comforter that covered the bed in the room he'd been given. His powerful legs were stretched out and crossed at the ankles. One hand was behind his head, propping him up against the pillows, and the other balanced a glass on his ridged abdomen.

He wasn't good at brooding. He had always considered it a waste of time, so he hadn't had much practice.

But the whiskey helped.

He swirled the glass and took a sip. It burned satisfyingly going down.

Oh, yes, the whiskey helped.

He had to leave. There was no point in putting it off. The sooner he settled his past, the sooner he could get on with his life. But it bothered him that Jessie hadn't informed her brother of their marriage. It bothered him even more that Jessie was spending the night in a spare room down the hall, and he was spending it here, alone.

The room he'd been assigned was obviously Rose's. The brass bed was massive, the walls were covered in a shimmering silk that matched the bedspread, and the lamps were shaded in deep pink glass.

It didn't take much deduction to figure out where Rose was spending her night. Tony wondered how Jessie felt about her beloved older brother having a mistress.

He wondered how Jessie felt about everything.

The door to his room eased open a crack. He didn't even bother to grab for something to cover himself. It was bad manners, but right now he didn't particularly care. He figured whoever barged in without knocking deserved an eyeful.

Jessie slipped in, wearing a white, airy nightgown.

"Tony—" She stopped abruptly at the sight of him. Her breath caught, and her heartbeat quickened.

She would have thought she'd be used to his body by now, but her intimate knowledge of him only multiplied her reactions. Her response to him seemed as inevitable as the sunrise.

"Well? Come on in."

Jessie clambered onto the bed and knelt next to Tony. She didn't touch him. She knew that if she did she would forget what she had come to say.

Unfortunately she couldn't seem to get the words out anyway, so she sat there, silent, her tender gaze on his face.

Her hair was tumbled down, glowing with pink highlights from the lamps. Her eyes were wide, uncertain. She looked utterly young and vulnerable, and he felt a fresh surge of never wanting to leave her.

"Well?" he repeated.

Couldn't he see it in her eyes? Did she have to spell it out?

"It isn't what you think . . . the reason I didn't tell J.J. about us."

"What you choose to tell your brother is your business."

"I did it for you."

"How the hell do you figure that?" He tossed back the rest of the whiskey, then looked around for more.

"Tony." She took his glass and set it on the small, silk-covered table by the bed. She brushed her fingers gently over the lines between his eyebrows, smoothing them out. "Right from the beginning you've never had much choice in any of this. I know you never had any intention of getting married. You certainly didn't *want* to get married. But you did it for me, and you made the best of it.

"I know you feel a responsibility to me. I know you think we could make this work. But we've been thrown together the entire time. There were no other women around. There weren't any other . . . options for you."

She sighed and then continued. "I know my brother. If he finds out we are married, that's it. There will never be an annulment. But Tony, what if you leave and discover the way you feel about me is simply based on proximity, or honor, or circumstances? I want to leave you a way out. I *need* to leave you a way out."

He reached out, pulling her toward him, holding her tightly against his chest where she could hear his heartbeat.

"We are not getting an annulment."

She believed that, right now, he meant it. What she wasn't so sure of was if he would still mean it when his life was back to normal, free of the pressures and the isolation of the train. When she tried to protest he tugged on her hair, tilting her head back so she could look in his fiercely serious eyes.

"We are *not*."

Her heart warmed and expanded. Maybe, just for tonight, she'd allow herself to believe it, allow herself to dream. Snuggling closer to him, she drew her knee up over his thighs, tracing languid patterns on his chest with her fingertips.

"When are you leaving?"

She felt his muscles tighten.

"Tomorrow."

Her fingers stilled.

"Will you tell me where you are going?"

He had left his confession for too late, he found. He couldn't leave her here with David and the knowledge of Tony's sins, without his presence to show her that he had changed and was no longer the same man who had carelessly made a mess of three lives.

He looked deeply into her eyes, hoping that she would see and believe his intentions.

"I am coming back for you."

"Of course you are," she said, but he could sense her disbelief.

"Damn it, Jessie," he said, his voice quiet and desperate. "Why can't you trust me enough to believe it when I tell you I'm coming back?"

"Why can't you trust me enough to tell me where you're going?"

Their gazes held, each seeing in the other uncertainty and hope. But neither could take that final leap of faith.

Her eyes darkened to a stormy gray, filled with regret and sadness. "I love you, you know."

"Oh, Jessie." Tony combed his fingers through the long, soft, length of her hair. "I lo—"

"No!" The single word exploded from Jessie as she scrambled to her knees. "I don't want you to say it."

Her hair tumbled over her shoulders, and Tony wound a single lock around his fingers. "Why not?" he asked gently.

"I don't want you to say anything that you will construe as a promise you'll feel obligated to keep." She bit her lower lip. "Besides, if you choose not to come back, it will be harder for me if I believe you love me."

"But—"

"No buts. And no regrets, either. Just you and me and this."

Stripping her nightgown over her head, she left herself bare for his gaze and sent her hands gliding over his body.

He sat up, intending to take her into his arms, but Jessie smiled and shook her head, pressing him back against the pillows.

"Lie back down." She stroked his cheekbones, eyebrows, the curve of his ear, the sweep of his jaw. "I want . . . to show you what you mean to me, what these last months have meant to me. I want to give back some of the pleasure you've shown me."

"You don't have to do this." He studied her intently. Hadn't he made himself clear? Could she honestly not realize? "I get immense pleasure every time I touch you."

"Well, then." She let her hands drift down his chest, finding his nipples and circling them lightly with her fingertips. "Maybe I just want to do this."

He grinned widely and leaned back, relaxing. "Never let it be said I kept you from doing something you *wanted* to do . . ."

She explored his body, caressing his arms, his smooth sides, his flat belly, his solid thighs. She teasingly touched him everywhere but the part of him that grew and stretched for her touch.

He watched her, her pleasure and curiosity, her hands as they skimmed over him. She was smiling some womanly secret smile that held hints of promises and knowledge and feminine power. She was sexy as hell, and he had to touch her. He lifted his arm, reaching for her breast that swayed tantalizingly out of his reach, but she caught his arm and pressed it over his head.

"No, Tony, not yet. If you touch me, I'll get distracted."

"That's the general idea, Jess. You're supposed to get distracted when I touch you."

"Not yet . . . there are things I want to do first. Things I've dreamed about." Her eyes gleamed with temptation and excitement.

"You dreamed about me?"

"Always."

That did it. He flipped his other arm up to join the first. He'd do what she asked. It damn well might kill him, but he'd do what she asked.

Jessie pulled her hair over her shoulder and leaned forward, letting the long strands pool on his chest. She moved back and forth, sweeping his body with the smooth silk. Her hair was warm and soft, and Tony felt the individual strands curl around him, touching, tickling, seducing.

Pulling her hair back, she leaned lower, pressing her breasts against his chest. She stroked him with the soft peaks, brushing them tantalizingly over his lips and moving away before he could taste her, then sliding down his legs. Her flesh was soft, her nipples hard, and the contrast was incredibly arousing. Finally, she caressed him with one beaded nipple, slowly burning a trail up the full length of his manhood.

"Jessie!" He could only resist touching her by twisting his fingers into the coverlet until his knuckles turned white.

"Shh," she whispered, moving up to kiss him. Was this how he always felt? she wondered, feeling his muscles clench, his skin grow taut and slick with perspiration. Was there always this luxurious, sensuous joy in giving pleasure to another? She felt erotic, feminine, powerful.

She delved into his mouth thoroughly before dropping a kiss on each eyelid, then tested the rough texture of his beard-shadowed jaw with her tongue. She bit his chin, sucking on it lightly, then drew her mouth down the slope of his throat and over the hill of his Adam's apple.

His nipples responded readily to her touch, and she tasted him everywhere she had ever dreamed of—every place he had ever tasted her—licking, nipping, sucking. She sank her teeth gently into his thigh, and he jumped when she swirled her tongue around his big toe.

"That tickles!"

"Does it?" She giggled, then, suddenly serious, crawled up to kneel next to his hip. She regarded him intently, watching him swell yet bigger. Loving her effect on him, she leaned over.

At the first touch of her mouth Tony threw back his head and closed his eyes, his hands desperately gripping the brass headboard. "Ahhh . . ." She was so gentle, so sweet, so hot.

Jessie licked him experimentally, tracing the vein on the underside of his member, feeling it pulse against her tongue. She inhaled deeply. His essence was concentrated here, and the scent was powerful and heady, undeniably Tony. With delicate strokes of her tongue she made slow, sensuous circles.

He groaned when she pulled away.

"Sorry." She laughed and plucked something from her tongue. "Hair." She gave him a mischievous glance from the corner of her eye. "Do you have that problem, too?"

His voice was hoarse. "Could we talk about this later, please?"

Then she took him into her mouth, first tentatively, then with more confidence, gauging her rhythm from his moans of pleasure.

He couldn't take it anymore; he had to touch her. Opening his eyes, he released the rails and ran his hand down the slope of her back and over the sweet, tempting curve of her buttock, searching for her center.

Finding it, he slid his middle finger into her body, matching his strokes to hers.

"Come to me now, Jessie. Please, now."

She pushed herself up, swinging a knee over his hip to straddle him. But she didn't take him into her body yet. Instead, she teased him with her softness, her curly hair tickling his abdomen and upper thighs, leaving damp trails that cooled as they dried.

Finally, she stroked his hardness with her warm center, one long smooth stroke that made him suck in his breath and clench his teeth.

"Tony!" she cried, trembling. She grasped him in one hand and then sank down on him fully. God, it felt so full, so deep, so incredible. "You can touch me now. *Please*, touch me now."

He slipped his hands up her ribs to cup her breasts as she slid up and down, seeking maximum sensation and fulfillment. She experimented with rhythms, with depths, wondering how he had so easily found the ones that brought her the most pleasure, hoping she could do the same for him. The intensity built, and she could wonder no more, could only slide faster, harder, further. She shuddered, her internal muscles contracting around him rhythmically.

When it came, it came to both of them, sweeping them into a swirling maelstrom of sensation that stunned them both, even after all the pleasure they had shared before.

In the aftermath, they lay entwined, spent and silent, traces of tears drying on Jessie's cheeks.

Was that the last time she would ever touch him? Was it the last time in her whole life she would ever feel that . . . ever feel love? She couldn't imagine ever letting another man touch her. The thought was repulsive, but she couldn't stand the idea that she would never feel so alive again.

A deep pain welled through her, the pain she'd been fighting to keep at bay for weeks. Sadness twisted her, seeping so deeply into her heart she wasn't sure it would ever leave.

She had known the hurt would come, and yet she had chosen this path. Had it been worth it? Worth this pain?

The answer was swift and absolute.

Yes.

Tony absently stroked her back, listening to Jessie's breathing deepen, unwilling to waste any time in sleep. He tried to imprint her feel, her scent, her taste in his mind so he could pull it out when they were apart and remember her like this.

He waited until he was sure she was sleeping, hoping her unconscious mind would accept what she, awake, could not.

"I am coming back, *cara*. I swear to you, I *am* coming back."

26

When she awoke, he was gone.

She felt as if a piece of her soul had been sliced away. The pain was not a clean, merciful cut from a keen, edged blade. Oh no, this wound was made from a weapon that was nicked and dull, and she could feel each jagged tear where the edge had caught and pulled.

But time dulls pain, and in the days and weeks that followed it became, if not faded, at least muted enough to be bearable.

The routine of the saloon suited Jessie's natural rhythm. She stayed awake into the wee hours and slept until the sun was high. She still couldn't quite believe her brother and David owned such an establishment, but if there was one thing she had learned in the past months and years, it was that judgment was best left to God.

Jessie sat at a small table tucked into a corner of the main saloon, drawing aimless curls and lines on her sketchpad.

She spent most of her evenings here. At first, an occasional man had been overenthusiastic in attempting to make her acquaintance, but J.J. and David had made it clear that she was strictly off-limits. Now the men either ignored her entirely or treated her with the deference most had believed they had left back east.

When a grizzled old miner had presented her with a small, exquisite dragon figurine from the Chinese district, Jessie had quickly sketched a small portrait in thanks. The flattered miner flashed the picture around the saloon, and others clamored for portraits to send back to the sweethearts and families they'd left behind. It had evolved into a small but profitable business, and it kept her hands busy even if it was not entirely successful in keeping her thoughts from Tony.

David dragged a chair over from a nearby table and spun it around. He straddled it and sat down, his arms resting on the chair back.

"What's the matter, Marin? Business so slow you have to come bother me?" Jessie teased.

"Rose is tending bar. She'll be able to struggle along without me for at least a little while." He studied her face. She was pale, with faint violet shadows under her eyes. "Are you all right?"

"Don't I look all right?"

"No."

Expecting denials, his blunt answer caught her off guard. She bopped his head lightly with her sketchpad and laughed.

"Serves me right for fishing for compliments."

"Haven't you been sleeping well?"

"Well enough." In truth, although she was so exhausted she often nodded off during the day at inopportune moments, she was sleeping poorly at night. Her bed was simply too big, too cold, and too empty.

David smiled boyishly. "Maybe you need more pillows."

Just after Tony left, Jessie had tried to go back to

sleeping on the right side of the bed. After several restless nights, she had given up and returned to the left side, trying to fill Tony's empty spot with pillows. J.J. and David never passed up an opportunity to tease her about what, exactly, one person needed eight pillows for. She was only grateful that they had never figured it out.

"Maybe I need more sympathetic friends." She flipped to a fresh sheet of paper, moving her pencil rapidly over the page.

"You haven't been eating enough."

"Would you stop?" She frowned at her drawing, trying to capture the face just right. "I've gotten along without a mother all these years, David. You don't need to take on the job now."

"I'm going to the kitchen to get you something to eat."

"No." Perhaps she hadn't been eating properly lately, but so often food made her nauseous. She rolled her eyes at him. "Look, it's probably just delayed stress from the journey, and I'll be fine once I get rested up. If I promise to take better care of myself, will you back off?"

He ruffled her hair affectionately. "I worry about you, Squirrel."

She smiled. He was such a good friend. "I know." After giving the sketch one last stroke, she handed it to him. "What do you think?"

The picture was of one of the saloon girls going upstairs with a customer. The middle-aged merchant had a belly that strained the buttons of his tailored vest. Hair from just above one ear was combed all the way over the top of his head, failing to camouflage his bald pate, and his face was flushed and eager.

The pretty young girl clutched his arm tightly, her face schooled professionally into an expression of lusty welcome. But she couldn't hide the look in her eyes—old, cold, and empty. Dead.

David sighed. "Ah, Jessie. What have we done to you? You shouldn't have to see this. You don't belong here."

"And you do?"

He lifted his shoulders, then let them fall. "The money is good. So's the friendship. And I have nothing else I want to do."

"I understand about the saloon and the gambling, I really do. But how can you have those . . . women here?"

"They're good for business."

"David!" she exclaimed, shocked.

"God. Maybe I have been here too long." He rubbed his hair, leaving the sandy curls even more disheveled. "They're better off here than anyplace else, Jessie. In the brothels, they have no control over their customers, and the madames keep all their earnings, giving them only a tiny percentage. Here, we charge them only a small, fixed rent for their rooms. They see who they want to, when they want to, and any money they make is theirs to keep."

"David, do you—" She broke off at his startled look. "Forget I asked that. It's none of my business."

"No, it's O.K." He met her gaze steadily. "I don't. If love is bought instead of freely given, it means nothing. It feels like the expression you drew in that girl's eyes."

"Then I'm glad you don't."

"What are you two looking so serious about?" J.J. sank into a nearby chair, placing his drink on the table. "We can't have it! This place is supposed to be fun. You're spoiling the atmosphere with your gloomy faces."

Jessie appraised her brother. His brilliant smile revealed gleaming, perfect teeth. Although the room was overheated, steaming from the press of too many people determined to have fun or get heatstroke in the attempt, there was no sheen of perspiration on his tanned skin. How did he stay tan in San Francisco in November, anyway, when every day was overcast and foggy? Not a single golden hair was out of place, and his white attire was as pristine as when it came from the laundry.

His perfect appearance was depressing.

"Go away."

J.J. frowned at Jessie. "Are you all right?"

Jessie groaned. "Oh, no, not again. I am fine. Tell David I am fine, tell Rose I am fine, tell every damn customer in the place I am fine, and the next person who asks me if I am all right is going to get a demonstration of just how healthy I am!"

"Excuse me!" Looking affronted, J.J. smoothed his already wrinkle-free shirt front. "Excuse me for worrying about my baby sister."

Jessie leveled a determined gaze on her brother. "I am not your 'baby' anything. If I were, would you let me in here?"

"There is absolutely nothing wrong with my establishment." He tried to look insulted, but his blue eyes were sparkling too much to pull it off.

"Oh, really? Then why the hell did it take me two damn weeks to persuade you to let me downstairs after supper?"

"Lord. Such language. That's precisely why I didn't want you down here. I knew you'd corrupt us."

Jessie batted her eyes. "Brother, you ain't seen nothing yet."

His amusement vanished. "Jessie!"

David chuckled. "You might as well give it up, J.J. The little girl who trailed us around with worship in her eyes is long gone."

J.J. sighed dramatically. "And she was such a sweet child, too. How could she turn out like this?"

Laughing, Jessie tossed a pencil at her brother. He caught it in midair, placed it on the table, and flicked it lightly with his finger, sending it rolling back to her. "Lose something?"

Jessie smiled fondly. Laughing and teasing with J.J. and David always made her feel better. It was almost enough.

Almost.

It was strange how for so long her greatest wish was to be with the two of them again. Now, here she was, and she wanted to be somewhere else. Anywhere else, as long as it was with Tony.

She remembered the way he laughed and his boyish, mischievous smile. She remembered his caring and tenderness, and the hints of sadness and danger he kept so well hidden.

And, dear God, how she remembered the way he touched her. His strength, his hardness, his gentle hands, his intoxicating kisses.

She remembered far too well.

J.J. watched the happiness fade from his sister's face. Her expression was wistful, yearning, a little sad. It was obvious that she was happy to see him, but sometimes she seemed very far away.

He knew that a lot had happened to her the last few years. First their father's illness and death, then the long journey west on her own. He was proud and a little in awe of her strength and determination. But it wasn't just that she'd grown up; there was acceptance in her eyes, as if she understood the rewards of life and their costs. There had to be more to it than the brief recital of the last few years she'd given him.

Hell, he didn't know. He'd never been much good at digging beneath the surface, figuring out what other people were thinking and feeling deep down. He'd always assumed that if they wanted him to know, they'd tell him.

But now, for his sister, he wished he was one of those people who could look through the facades, straight to the center. He wanted to erase at least a bit of the pain he saw in her eyes, but he didn't have the slightest clue as to where to start.

"Whew, it's hot in here." Fanning her face, Rose plopped into J.J.'s lap, winding one arm around his neck.

Jessie smiled at her brother's mistress. It had ceased to surprise her that she wasn't shocked by J.J.'s affair. She knew that she would have been Tony's lover back in Fort Laramie, long before they'd been married, if Tony hadn't had that annoying attack of nobility. She was in no position to make judgments. Besides, Rose was clearly madly in love with her brother. Jessie couldn't figure out why J.J. seemed completely oblivious to it. Maybe he didn't want to know.

"Shouldn't at least one of you three be working?"

Rose reached for J.J.'s drink and took a large gulp. "Honey, if you think I'm going to work while these two are lazing around chatting with you, you've got another think coming. That's what we hire people for."

"I wouldn't think you'd hire someone for anything you could do yourself," Jessie said. Rose's tightness with a penny was legendary, and Jessie knew her close watch of the books was a good part of reason the saloon was so successful.

"True." Rose readjusted the curly pink plume in her pale curls. "But I couldn't leave you alone for these two to pick on. I decided to even the odds."

"Hmph," J.J. said, all the while conscious of Rose's soft bottom wiggling in his lap. "She didn't need any help."

Rose giggled, reminding Jessie that, despite her worldliness, Rose was really a young woman. "Honey, I sure am glad I was around when you showed up. I didn't think I'd ever see the day when someone got the better of J.J."

J.J. scowled. "I have to take it easy on her. She's my sister."

"Um-hm." Rose gave Jessie a closer look. "Honey, you look kinda pale. You sure you're all right?"

The scream was loud and piercing in its intensity.

The room fell dead silent. The laughing stopped, the piano player's hands went still on the keys, no cards were shuffled, and even the constant clink of glassware stopped.

Scooping up her sketchpad and pencil, Jessie rose and swept up the stairs, giving her brother a triumphant smile over her shoulder.

J.J. dug his forefinger in his ear. Across the table, David was rubbing his ear gingerly. Their gazes met, and they burst out laughing.

Their laughter broke the silence, and soon all the normal, noisy activity in the saloon resumed. Rose glanced from J.J. to David and back again with a perplexed frown on her face.

"Was it something I said?"

Jessie shoved her door shut and leaned against it, finally letting the giggles escape. She'd had to bite her lip all the way up the stairs to keep a straight face, but it was worth it. The looks on their faces!

Tony would have loved it.

Her elation disappeared, leaving in its place the exhaustion that plagued her so frequently now. Pushing herself away from the door, she tossed her sketchpad on the bed, noticing that one of the maids had thoughtfully left a small lamp burning on the bedside table. She stripped off her simple lavender cotton dress, so different from the flashy outfits the saloon girls wore. She stood out among them in the bar as prominently as they would in church.

She let her dress and undergarments lay where they fell. She would pick them up tomorrow, after she had some sleep.

Naked, she sprawled out on the spring-green satin

cover of the bed. She loved this room. Decorated in peach and green, silk and brass, it was luxurious and just a bit decadent, a far cry from the frilly pink and white room she had had in Chicago. This, she thought with satisfaction, was the room of a woman.

A woman. She glided her hands across the smooth skin of her stomach and ribs. Is this what Tony felt when he touched her? Soft, sleek, warm? Not long ago she would have pulled on a nightgown as quickly as she had stripped, uncomfortable at being naked even when she was alone. It was amazing how differently she felt about her body now.

She slipped her hands up to cup her breasts. Tony's hands were so much bigger. She imagined his hands, large, dark, and rough-textured, contrasting with her pale breasts. She groaned, unprepared for the sudden rush of desire heating her body.

How could just the thought of him excite her so much when he was so far away, when she didn't know when or if he would be back? She didn't even know if he really *was* far away. She'd assumed he was, but all she actually knew was that he wasn't with her.

She sat up on the bed, plumping the silk-covered pillows behind her back, and reached for paper and pencil. As soon as she looked for her portfolio and the rest of her supplies she realized that they weren't there.

Damn. She must have left her stuff downstairs. She briefly considered going back down to get it, but she didn't want to spoil her grand exit. Besides, she didn't really want to get dressed again. She'd retrieve them in the morning.

She stroked the nub of a pencil that she'd managed to find across the paper in languid, curving, sensuous strokes. She visualized Tony the way he looked just before they made love: intense, tender, powerful, magnificently naked. Her pulse beat in time with the movement of her hand.

The noise from downstairs in the saloon stopped long before she finished, but Jessie, lost in her work and her memories, never noticed.

She smiled sadly at the completed portrait. Tony's eyes were filled with fire, his body finely sculpted and muscular, his strength clearly evident. It was a passionate piece, probably the best work she'd ever done.

It was a shame that no one could ever see it.

Rolling to the side of the bed, she lifted the peach glass chimney off the lamp and touched a corner of the paper to the wick. She watched the flames flicker across the paper, waiting until the fire almost singed her fingers before she dropped the remaining bit into a delicate flowered china dish.

She turned down the wick, cloaking the room in darkness. Sliding into bed, she curled on her side, pulling a pillow to her chest. She had smuggled the pillow from Tony's room after the night she had gone to him. She always slept with the pillow cuddled against her. For days it had carried his scent, and she could pretend he was sleeping beside her.

She knew it was probably her imagination, for his smell was certainly long gone by now, but it seemed as if she could still catch whiffs of him, musky and warm.

And for a few moments before she fell asleep, she allowed herself to dream that maybe, just maybe, the words he had said might be true:

I am coming back to you, Jessie. I swear. I'm coming back to you.

J.J. stroked a soft cloth once more down the length of the gleaming bar. His bar, he thought with satisfaction, and since it was his he made sure it was spotless, shining, the best and cleanest bar in San Francisco. It'd been cleaned once already, of course, after the customers all left, but J.J. cleaned it again. It wasn't that he didn't trust his cleaning lady to do the job right. It was simply that it was *his* bar.

The sky was already beginning to lighten from black to charcoal, the first hint of the approaching dawn. He could see it through the double front doors, which were thrown open to the air. He wanted to rid the room of the inevitable odor left by a night of entertainment.

The room smelled like lust, he thought. Lust for liquor, lust for money, lust for women, it didn't matter much which. Unfortunately, the air outside didn't smell fresh, either. It carried the stench of the harbor: salt air, rotting fish, and spoiling cargo.

But at least it didn't smell like lust.

He shuffled the bottles stretched on the shelf behind the bar, aligning them carefully until they were as straight and even as a regiment of soldiers. He fastidiously polished the bottles of excellent liquor, the best whiskey and brandy, rum and scotch available, admiring the colors as light spilled through the golden liquids.

It hadn't always been like this. He shuddered, remembering the mud and dirt, the pervasive cold and exhausting labor of his year spent prospecting. Not to mention the damn stubborn mule he could never get to follow directions.

Yes, this was a much better life. He got a slice of every lucky strike in the territory, and every booming business and profitable farm in the area. For they all came to The Naked Rose eventually.

He lifted his gaze to the painting over the bar. It was the perfect symbol of his saloon: tempting and provocative, somehow managing to be both elegant and earthy.

Rose crept up behind him and slid her arms around his waist. "Honey, how come you waste time looking at a picture when you can see the real thing any time you want?"

J.J. smiled down at Rose. She was his friend, one of the best he'd ever had, generous both in and out of bed. He dropped an affectionate kiss on her forehead.

"Did you get the money counted?"

She yawned widely. "Mmm-hmm."

"It was a good night?"

"As always."

"Why don't you go on to bed?"

She snuggled closer. God, she loved him so much. She had struggled so hard the past few years to keep that fact from him. She knew that if he ever caught even a whiff of how deep her feelings really ran, it would be over. He'd end it gently, tenderly, maybe even regretfully, but end it he would.

"Why don't you come with me?"

"Soon."

She pouted and ran her hand over his chest. "Are you sure?"

"Yes." J.J. kissed her deeply but pulled back when she tried to tug him closer. "God, you're tempting, but I'm not quite finished yet. I'll be there soon, I promise."

Rose traced his lips with her fingertips. "I'll be waiting."

His eyes glowed as he watched her sashay up the stairs, her sweet, full rump swaying. He wondered if perhaps he should join her now after all. But no, business came first.

He locked the doors and windows securely and then wandered around the room, straightening chairs, brushing his fingers over the tops of picture frames to check for dust, peering behind brass spittoons. Everything was perfect, as always.

He shoved the last chair into its place by the corner table. Jessie's leather folio was still leaning against the wall. She must have forgotten it when she made her grand exit. He'd give it to her in the morning.

He weighed it meditatively. She'd shown him only

a small portion of her work and had hardly spoken at all of her trip. Much as she tried to deny it, something was clearly bothering her. There were traces of sadness in her eyes, even when she was laughing. As her brother, wasn't it his responsibility to know what was going on in his sister's life? Perhaps through her pictures he could get a better idea of what had happened to her.

He kicked out a chair and sat down, opening the packet. He flipped through the stack of papers, smiling. Jessie was even better than he remembered. There were dozens of landscapes, portraits of people he didn't know, and humorous sketches of animals. All were rich, vivid, and mature. His sister's talent had grown to be even greater than her early promise had indicated.

He came across a portrait of a familiar face. It was that man who'd brought Jessie here . . . Winchester, that was it.

He still didn't like it. The man was too damn goodlooking for his own good, and he didn't like the idea of him sniffing around Jessie, pretty little thing she'd turned into. The picture was a flattering one, and the man looked cocky, mischievous, full of life. It looked like a picture drawn by a woman completely enamored of her model.

He frowned up the stairs toward Jessie's room.

Damn, was that what was the matter with her? If Winchester had hurt her, J.J. would make sure he paid for it.

27

Sleet stung his face, and Tony turned up the collar of his sheepskin jacket against the frigid wind. General shifted and stamped restlessly beneath him, and Tony stroked the horse's neck soothingly.

"Easy there, fella. You'll be warm soon."

He tugged his shabby felt hat lower on his forehead, shielding his eyes from the icy precipitation, and stared at the tiny cabin, the welcoming yellow light glowing through two small windows. It seemed unreal in the dark, damp night, like something his battered imagination had conjured up.

It was Christmas Eve, and Tony was empty, cold, and hurting. Emptier than when Liza had died. Colder than when Benjamin had betrayed him. Hurting more than when he found out why.

He'd been cold ever since he left Jessie more than two months ago, a bone-deep chill that had nothing to do with the weather. Where were the fires of revenge that were to fuel him? They had dwindled to nothing, it seemed, compared to how much he missed her.

There had been so many times in the past months, as he searched fruitlessly for Ben as one lead after another evaporated, when he had been tempted to forget it all and rush back to her. But what did he have to give her? If he didn't find Ben, he had no money and no horses . . . no future. It would take years to rebuild what he had lost. How could he ask her to live like that? He could go back to Winchester Meadows—his father would be happy to let him run the place—but his pride demanded that he offer Jessie a life of their own.

Business aside, there was a more crucial reason to find Ben. Tony wanted to go to Jessie a free man, his past settled and laid to rest, his future a clean canvas they could paint together. He would be able to give her at least that much, or he wouldn't go back at all.

But, *Dio,* it was hard. Especially today, this holiday he had always spent with his family, a nephew clinging to each leg, a niece attached to his back, his stomach stuffed with his mother's cooking, and gifts spilling out of each pocket. He couldn't stand the idea of spending the holidays alone, so when his search had led to the foothills of the mountains, he couldn't resist stopping in this small valley first.

He dismounted and led General to the rough shelter behind the cabin. The two horses already stabled there nickered softly in welcome as Tony unsaddled his horse and rubbed him down thoroughly. Leaving General with a Christmas Eve feast of hay and grain, Tony turned toward the house.

He paused before the door. Maybe this was a mistake. They weren't expecting him, and they were bound to ask questions about Jessie, questions he had no answers to. But he couldn't stand the thought of going back out into the cold alone.

He rapped hard on the door—too hard, as the unsanded wood scraped his knuckles raw. Surprised, he looked down at his damaged hand, then stuck the knuckle of his forefinger into his mouth, nursing it. The door opened, spilling the soft light out into the darkness.

He lifted his head and pushed up the brim of his hat.

"Hi," he said. "Got room for a visitor?"

Stuart Walker's eyebrows shot up when he saw who was standing on his stoop, but his surprise was quickly replaced by pleasure.

"Tony! Of course, of course." He stepped aside. "Come on in. It's cold out there." He peered behind Tony. "Isn't Jessie with you?"

Tony stepped in, removing his hat and turning it around and around in his hands. "Uh . . . no, she's not. She's visiting her brother."

"Oh." Stuart's face was impassive. If he thought Jessie's absence was odd, his expression didn't betray his thoughts.

"Are you going to keep the man standing in the doorway, Stuart?" In the far corner of the room Mary Ellen carefully removed a pie from the oven and slid it onto a sideboard. Tucking the length of cloth she had used to insulate her hand from the hot pan into her waistband, she came forward and reached behind Stuart to shut the door. "Welcome, Tony."

Stuart grinned sheepishly. "Sorry, honey. I was just a little surprised, that's all."

"Look, if I'm disturbing you folks, I could just . . ."

"Don't you dare!" Stuart thumped Tony on his back. "We're delighted to see you. Let me take your coat, and you can fill us in on what brings you our way."

Stuart took Tony's coat, heavy with dampness, and hung it on a hook behind the door while Tony eased off his wet boots. He inhaled the sweet, spicy aromas that filled the small cabin. "Sure smells good in here."

Mary Ellen smoothed her white apron. "Just getting

a head start on Christmas dinner. Oh, what have I been thinking? You must be starved. Can I get you a sample?"

"That wasn't a hint, Mary Ellen." Tony winked at her. "But, since you asked . . ."

With a grateful sigh, Tony settled into a chair by the large, rough-hewn table and glanced around the cabin. The tiny room was nearly filled with a small kitchen area and the big wooden table and a few chairs. An oversized bed with a carved wood headboard, covered by a colorful blue and red patchwork quilt, took up one corner. Above a stone fireplace, where the fire was dying to glowing embers, hung three thickly knit homemade stockings.

Mary Ellen slid a mug of coffee and a plate of star-shaped cookies in front of him. He picked up one of the cookies and bit off a point. Its buttery sweetness nearly melted on his tongue.

"Mmm . . . wonderful. Nice place you have here." Somewhat to his surprise, he meant it. The rough cabin couldn't be more different from the house he had grown up in, but it still felt like home.

He took a swig of coffee to wash down the cookie, nearly scalding his tongue. He wondered if he'd ever again have a place of his own that felt like home to him.

"Where are the kids?"

Stuart chuckled and pointed toward the low ceiling. "The twins are up in the loft, asleep. I threatened them with dire consequences—no presents—if they didn't go right to bed tonight."

Mary Ellen went over to the corner by the bed and brushed aside a green curtain suspended from the ceiling.

Tony shuffled over to her and stared down at the small cradle the curtain had hidden.

Jedediah was sleeping peacefully, his cheeks smooth and pink, his tiny mouth occasionally making sucking motions as if he was dreaming of sweet milk. Tony nibbled absently on his cookie while he watched the baby.

"He's beautiful, Mary Ellen." He couldn't resist reaching out to gently trace one delicate ear with his finger. "So beautiful," he whispered.

Mary Ellen looked up at him, her eyes dark with concern. "What happened, Tony?"

He didn't even try to pretend not to know what she meant. "I had some business to attend to. I left Jess to visit with her brother." He shrugged. "I didn't know it would take this long. Then, when it was almost Christmas and I found myself in the area . . ."

She slipped her hand into his. "I know you'd rather be with her for the holidays. But, if you can't, I'm glad you're with us."

"Oof." Tony was awakened the next morning by two blond whirlwinds landing squarely on his stomach. From Susannah and Sam's yelps and screeches, he judged that his arrival was only slightly less thrilling than Christmas, and he was inordinately pleased at their excitement.

The twins scurried to retrieve their stockings. Tony rubbed a hand over the stubble of his beard and blinked twice, trying to clear the fog from his eyes.

He hadn't got much sleep the night before. He had made a pallet in front of the fireplace, and he was certainly warmer and more comfortable than he had been for many nights. But Mary Ellen and Stuart had talked for a bit after they had retired for the evening. Their voices had been too low for him to understand their words, but he recognized the tone: loving, companionable, comfortable, punctuated by an occasional giggle and the rustle of crisp sheets. He had stared into the embers of the fire a long time after they had quieted, wondering if he and Jessie had sounded like that, like two people who belonged together, who were somehow more when they were side by side than when they were apart.

He had just fallen asleep when he was awakened by Jed, who was clearly angered by the delay of his night feeding. His wails had reverberated off the log walls until he was soothed by Mary Ellen's soft lullaby, her sweet voice mingling with the suckling sounds of a feeding baby. The quiet, domestic sounds caused a bittersweet ache to grow in his chest, delaying his rest even further.

When the twins had fetched their stockings they plopped back on his legs, and spilled the contents of their stockings across his blanket. Tony reached for his shirt and shrugged into it, buttoning it quickly but not bothering to stuff it into the breeches he hadn't removed the night before.

He wrapped an arm around each child, pulled them onto his lap, and settled into exclaiming over their new treasures. He had tucked an extra present into each of their stockings the night before. For Sam, there was a carved wooden horse he quickly dubbed General, and for Susannah Tony had brought a small, cloth-and-porcelain doll with red-gold hair and big blue eyes. Susannah's eyes were as round as the doll's, and Tony received two very wet, smacking kisses as a reward. He was glad that two days ago, after he'd decided to visit them, he'd taken the time to stop at a small town and pick up the presents.

The delectable aroma of roasting chicken already filled the air, and if he didn't turn around he could pretend that Jessie was in the kitchen cooking while he played with the children.

It was almost enough to ease the pain in his chest, if only a little bit.

The bang of the front door and a chorus of shouted "Merry Christmas!" announced Ginnie and Andrew's arrival.

Tony deposited the twins on his pallet and rose to his feet just in time to catch Ginnie, hurtling forward in the excitement of seeing him, in a huge hug that swept her off her feet. He twirled her around, laughing, and then set her back on her unsteady feet.

She raised a palm to her forehead. "Honey, you still know how to make a girl's head spin!"

Tony smiled, his dimples denting his cheeks. "Only for you, sweetheart. Only for you."

Andrew hugged his wife from behind, one hand resting on her belly, and gave a mock scowl. "Better watch it, Winchester. That's a pregnant woman you're flirting with there."

"Pregnant?" One look at their beaming faces told him all he needed to know. He gave Ginnie an exuberant kiss of congratulations and then turned to pump Andrew's hand. "That's wonderful, you two. I know Jessie will be so happy for you when I tell her."

"Thank you," Ginnie said, her eyes shining with happiness. "And speakin' of Jessie, where—"

"Ah, Ginnie, could you give me a hand with the potatoes?" Mary Ellen called from the corner that served as a kitchen.

"But I was just—"

"Please?"

Ginnie sighed. "Sure." She waggled a finger in Tony's face. "But I'll be talkin' to you later."

"I never doubted it for a minute."

Ginnie cuffed him lightly and bustled off to join Mary Ellen.

The morning passed pleasantly. Thankfully, Ginnie hadn't asked again about Jessie, and he wondered if Mary Ellen had warned her. To tide them over until it was time to eat, Mary Ellen served warm apple cider and small, delectable cinnamon buns, so heavily iced in vanilla glaze that they looked like hills after a record-breaking blizzard. Tony guessed that Ginnie had done the frosting.

He munched contentedly, listening to the men's plans for their farms and the twins' bickering over their new treasures. Maybe it wasn't Winchester Meadows, but it was a hundred times better than being out in the cold.

Mary Ellen called them for dinner, and Tony settled into his place around the crowded table with a twin on each side of him. She tried to entice the children away, leaving Tony to eat in peace, but Tony asked her to let them stay. He figured he wouldn't have too much time to think about Jessie with a child chattering at him from both directions.

There wasn't a spare inch on the table. It was covered with a rough-woven white cloth and lots and lots of food. There were two golden roasted chickens with herb-scented stuffing, vegetable casseroles, large bowls of gravy, two baskets of fragrant hot breads and biscuits, and a bewildering array of homemade jellies, relishes, and pickles. Sam stood guard over a big bowl of "smashed potatoes" that he clearly had no intention of sharing.

Tony looked around the table. He didn't miss his family nearly as much as he had expected to. Surrounded by people with whom he had shared so much, he realized that, in a way, they were also his family.

If only Jessie were here, too. It took no effort at all to picture her there, laughing as she pulled one more dish from the oven, ruffling Sam's hair as she passed him. It was almost as easy to imagine squeezing in a couple more children, a little girl with reddish hair and freckles across her nose, maybe a baby boy as sweet as Jed, only with dark curls this time. Their children.

God, would it ever happen? What had he ever done to deserve it? If only he could go back and do it all over again, live a life worthy of happiness, worthy of her.

He bowed his head for prayer, glad of the opportunity to hide his face, not knowing if his expression gave away his pain. He didn't want to spoil their Christmas.

He didn't hear Stuart's words. He could only add a plea of his own: please, God, let me get back to her . . . and let her still be there, waiting for me. I need her so much.

With a heave, Tony threw the saddle onto General's back. He tugged on it, adjusting it automatically before bending down to secure the straps.

"Are you sure you have to leave so soon?"

It was the third time Stuart had asked the question —after Mary Ellen, Ginnie, Andrew, Susannah, and Samuel. The only one who hadn't tried to talk him into staying was the baby.

Maybe it was a little crazy. The sun would be going down in just a few hours, and it was still Christmas Day. Why didn't he wait until tomorrow and leave in the morning?

Because he couldn't take it anymore, that's why. Couldn't stay in a house that shouted domestic bliss, seeing Mary Ellen coo to Jed, listening to Ginnie babble about their baby, watching Stuart and Andrew look at their wives with such pride and love. He missed Jessie more with every damn second that passed.

The sooner he left, the sooner this was over, and the sooner he got on with the rest of his life—not that he'd have much of a life if Jessie wasn't in it.

He gave the leather strap a final, sharp jerk and then stood straight. His eyes were very black, and his jaw set at a determined angle. Stuart had enough sense not to question.

"Yes," Tony said. "I have to leave. Now."

28

Smoothing the fine linen tablecloth, Jessie kept a close watch out of the corner of her eye on Rose as she muttered and stirred a steaming pot. Standing on tiptoe, Rose peered in the pot until a bubble of liquid burst abruptly, sending her jumping back with a start.

"Damn!"

Jessie giggled. Rose had been repeating the expletive at least every five minutes all morning. "What is it now, Rose?"

"Damn stuff almost burned me. Dropped my spoon in the pot, too." She cast a beleaguered eye toward Jessie. "Are you sure J.J. likes oyster stew for Christmas dinner?"

"It's his absolute favorite." Jessie set two long red tapers in brass candlesticks in the center of the table. "Sure you don't want me to cook it?"

Rose squared her shoulders stubbornly. "No, I want to do it. I think!" she wailed as the soup boiled over the side of the pot. The scent of scorched cream and burned seafood filled the kitchen as they scurried to avert disaster.

The stew was unsalvageable, but after scrubbing the stove clean of the congealed mess they sank gratefully into the kitchen chairs and poured themselves well-deserved cups of tea.

Rose fanned her flushed face with the hem of her apron. "The things I do for your brother! Damned if I know why."

Jessie blew on her mug of hot tea. "Because you love him, of course."

"Is it that obvious?"

"It is to me."

Rose chuckled. "And here I thought I was hidin' it so well." The bold confidence in her eyes softened to wistful yearning. "You don't suppose he knows, do you?"

Jessie waited a long moment before shaking her head in answer. Men could be so blind.

"I don't know why I keep hopin' . . . I suppose it's better this way."

Tracing the rim of her cup, Jessie asked what she had wondered for so long. "Why do you put up with it?"

Rose's eyes clouded. "Because I know what life is like without him." Her fingers tightened around her cup. "After my husband died—"

Jessie lowered her mug to the table with a thump. "I didn't know you'd been married!"

"When I was sixteen." Rose stared into her tea. "I'd known Johnny all my life. We grew up together, and I loved him like . . . well, more than life itself. A year after we got married he got it into his head we could strike it rich gold minin' like everybody else, and I followed him out here." Her hand trembled, and hot tea sloshed over the rim of the cup, but she didn't seem to feel it. "It was rough, trying to work a claim, but it didn't seem to matter much, 'cause we had each other. Then we started panning out a bit of gold, and just afterwards I found out I was pregnant. Seemed like the world was finally ours." She swallowed heavily. "Then some claim jumpers . . . they . . ." Her voice cracked. "When it was over, John was dead, and I'd lost the baby. I still don't know why I didn't die with them, too. Lord knows I thought about it enough."

Jessie lay a hand on Rose's arm. "I'm so sorry. That doesn't say it, I know—"

Rose shrugged. "It was a long time ago. It's all right now," she said, her words belied by the sheen of moisture in her eyes.

She took a long pull of tea. "I remember the first time I saw your brother," she said, smiling. "I was workin' in this run-down little bar down by the harbor. I was singin' a little and drinkin' a lot, and sometimes one of the customers and I . . . well, I'd do just about anythin' to keep from rememberin'. Then, one day, your brother walked in and smiled at me. You know the smile I mean?"

Jessie nodded.

"An' suddenly I knew. There was life worth livin' out there after all. We've been together ever since."

Jessie wondered if J.J. had any idea what he had in Rose. "Don't you ever worry about what happens . . ."

"After it's over?"

"Yes."

"I'll hurt a lot, I guess. But it's worth it. I don't know if I can make you understand . . ."

"I understand."

Rose looked at Jessie curiously. "You do understand, don't you?"

"Yes."

"Tony?"

"Tony."

* * *

The dinner—minus oyster stew—was delicious, and the gifts were thoughtful. David gave Jessie a complete set of new paints and canvases, and Rose gave her a lacy little ice-blue nightgown that had J.J. scowling for a good twenty minutes.

J.J. stunned Jessie with a pair of gorgeous—and obviously expensive—diamond earrings. As she tried to stammer her thanks, he tugged her earlobe playfully.

"They're worth every penny just to see you speechless, brat," he teased. Then he sobered. "I'm sorry you had to be alone last Christmas, Jessie. I wanted to make it up to you."

Jessie had few memories of last Christmas. Numbed by her father's recent death, she had closeted herself in their house, ignoring any reminders of the impending holiday when she was forced to go out. As happy as she should have been this Christmas, with her brother and friends at last, Tony's absence dulled her pleasure, stripping the joy from the day. She tried hard to hide her depression from J.J. He already felt enough guilt over leaving her alone to cope with their father, and she didn't want him to take on responsibility for this mood, too.

She forced what she hoped was a believable approximation of gaiety into her voice. "If this is what I get for spending last Christmas alone, I'm going to run away and hide every other Christmas for the rest of my life." Rising to her toes, she kissed his cheek. "You know what I'd really like?"

"What?" he asked warily.

"Don't look so suspicious. I'd like you to read us the Christmas story like Daddy used to do."

"Ah . . . Bibles are in short supply around here, Jess."

She tried unsuccessfully to ruffle the perfect

strands of his hair. It fell back into precise array. "Lucky for you I brought one with me, then."

She fetched the large, black-bound leather family Bible she had brought from Chicago, and they settled in a private sitting room on the second floor in between J.J.'s and David's bedrooms. The room had cream-colored walls and carpets and was furnished with large, sturdily elegant furniture of dark wood, covered in burgundy, forest-green, and cream striped fabric.

Jessie sat on a love seat facing Rose and J.J. and accepted the small glass of wine David offered her as he sank down beside her and stretched his arm on the back of the sofa behind her.

"You look absolutely gorgeous," he said, his gaze resting on her face.

"Thank you." Her gown, bottle-green satin trimmed with snowy lace, was new, and she thought she looked rather well herself. Adjusting the lace at her cuff, she studied her old friend. David wore a distinguished-looking gray suit she had never seen before, and when he saw her attention he self-consciously smoothed the mustache he'd just grown. He looked more mature and sophisticated than she'd ever seen him, but the friendly gleam in his eye was pure David. "You look mighty fine, yourself. I can't figure out why some bright young woman hasn't snatched you up yet."

"Maybe I haven't wanted to be snatched."

"Yeah, that's a great idea," J.J. said. "Instead of sitting around here, we'll go hunt down a woman for David. That'd make a great Christmas present."

"Hush up, Johnston. I can find my own woman, thank you very much. You just want to get out of reading."

"Who, me? I love to read Bible stories. Do it all the time. But, since I'm so generous, I'd be willing to make the supreme sacrifice and allow you the pleasure."

"Come on now, J.J.," Jessie said. "Would you want us to think you couldn't handle all those big words?"

"I'll have you know I have a most extensive vocabulary."

"Of course you do."

"Brat," he muttered under his breath. He opened the large book and flipped rapidly through the pages. "Now if I can just remember where Luke is . . . what's this?" He held up an unidentifiable clump of sorry-looking pressed flowers.

"It's mine." Jessie snatched them from his hand and returned to her seat before he even realized she had moved. "I'd forgotten I put it there."

"What the hell is it?"

Jessie looked down at the brittle remains of her wedding bouquet. The light fuchsia stalks had faded to brown and muddy purple. "It's called blazing star. Just something I picked up on the trip. Nothing . . . important."

"If it's not important, why are you keeping it? It's pretty pitiful looking, Jess."

She gave him the exasperated look a sister reserves for her brother. "Would you just shut up and read?"

"All right, all right." He skimmed through a few more pages. "Ah, here we are." He settled himself more comfortably. "The angel Gabriel was sent from God to a town of Galilee named Nazareth, to a virgin betrothed to a man named Joseph, of the house of David. The virgin's name was Mary . . ."

His words faded, and her vision blurred as Jessie stared at the dried bouquet, remembering another voice and other words.

"I'm counting your freckles."

"Tell me about your father."

"Don't look so stricken, Jess. It was just a kiss."

"The only trip worth takin' . . . is a journey home."

"I want you so much it hurts every time I look at you."

"I won't leave you tonight."

She felt every muscle in her body go tight with the effort not to reach out to someone who wasn't there.

"I do."

"You're . . . radiant."

"That's my woman."

"I am coming back for you."

She blinked twice to clear her eyes of moisture. The tears dropped to her lap, leaving dark blotches on the green silk. In her agitation, she had clenched her fingers, crumbling the delicate flowers. Frantically, she tried to piece them back together, the tiny dried petals and broken leaves. They were destroyed.

She felt a warm hand on her shoulder. David's voice was gentle with concern. "Jessie, is something wrong?"

Her voice was hoarse. "I'm . . . not feeling well. Please excuse me." She stood, tiny bits of crushed vegetation drifting from her lap to the thick carpets, and ran from the room.

J.J. jumped up to follow her, but Rose grabbed his arm to stop him.

"Let her go," she said.

He pulled his arm free. "But she's my little sister, damn it!"

"She's a woman now, J.J. There are things big brothers just can't fix."

29

The pines were dark, standing out in bold relief against the tarnished pewter sky which looked ready at any minute to unleash rain, sleet, snow, or an unpleasant combination of all three. Tony headed General farther up the trail in the foothills of the mountains, breathing in the sharp, distinctive scent of the evergreens.

Had he found Benjamin this time? God, he hoped so. How ironic it would be, after searching through half of the central California territory, to find him here, so near the valley where the Wrightmans and Walkers had settled.

A thick layer of fallen needles carpeted the trail and muffled General's hoofbeats. He doubted that anyone could hear his approach, but when he saw the unmistakable curl of smoke drifting above the trees ahead, he dismounted and tethered General in a thick copse of trees a fair distance from the trail and continued on foot.

He debated for a moment, weighing his rifle in his

hand before deciding to bring it along. There were more things than just Ben to worry about out here.

Then he sauntered almost lazily up the path. An observer might have thought he was out for a casual stroll. Only someone who knew him very well would have noticed the quiet alertness in his steps.

The trail curved sharply to the left, entering a small clearing. He slipped behind a large tree in order to study the area unobserved. The source of the smoke was a tiny cabin, smaller than the Walkers' but with a shaded porch running the length of the front. The cleared land before the cabin was a tangle of meadow grasses and winter-dead wildflowers.

There was no movement, and, other than the smoke, no sign of human activity. He wondered if the owner had gone off into the woods for a while. Farther to the left of the cabin was a wide path, which Tony figured led to the valley just below the crest of the hill. He'd seen it in his scout of the area before he'd attempted to approach the cabin.

Behind the house was a barnlike structure almost twice as big as the house. A huge corral was built off to the side, taking up all the space from the barn to the top of the trail and back to a few yards from the house.

"Lady," he whispered.

He moved to the corral like a sleepwalker, inexorably drawn, no longer aware of his surroundings. He reached the fence, leaned his rifle against it, and grasped the top rail, gripping it so tightly that his knuckles whitened and the rough boards cut into his palms.

He never noticed the pain. They were there. His babies, his dreams. His horses.

The looked wonderful, sleek and well muscled, as always with fire in their eyes. Gingerbread and Blaze, Wildflower and Temptation. Off to either end of the enclosure, in smaller, separate spaces, were the two stallions, Falcon and Mercury. Of the six mares and two magnificent stallions he had planned to build his business—their business—around, only one mare was gone. In her place were two young fillies and a colt.

Forgetting his caution, he laughed aloud at the pure joy of seeing his horses again. It had been more than nine months—such a long time to wait and worry, to hope and pray, and here they were.

One of the horses whinnied in response and took a few steps toward him.

Tony stood still, waiting, silently encouraging the beautiful chestnut mare with the white stockings to approach. He had no idea if, after all this time, the horse would remember him.

She ambled closer, stopping an arm's length away. Tony slowly reached out his hand. She bent her head and nuzzled his palm, finally nickering in welcome. He grinned and caressed her muzzle.

"Lady, my Scandalous Lady." He leaned forward, resting his forehead against her soft nose. "You always were the biggest flirt."

"So. You finally got here."

Tony spun, retrieved his rifle, and lifted it to his shoulder in the same motion. He sighted down the barrel—straight at his cousin, whose pistol was pointed squarely back at him.

Neither moved. Neither heard the caw of a crow flying overhead. Neither gun wavered a fraction of an inch.

Ben smiled coldly. "It seems we are at an impasse."

"So it seems."

Tony studied Benjamin, who was standing at the end of the porch just a few steps away. Once, they had looked so much alike that people had taken them for brothers. Tony had gotten his mother's coloring and dimples, but their features were otherwise nearly identical, and Ben, ten months younger, had been only an inch or so shorter and slightly thinner.

Ben had changed, though. His leanness had turned to gauntness, and the hollows beneath his cheeks were deep. His hair was long and unkempt, his blond beard scraggly, and there were deep purple shadows under his eyes, eyes that looked haunted and remote.

Perhaps revenge had cut both ways.

Ben suddenly laughed, the sound strangely cold and humorless.

"Well, Tony? Are we going to stand here until we freeze solid or are we going to shoot each other?"

"Neither, I hope." Tony narrowed his gaze. "Put the gun down, Ben."

"And why should I go first?"

"Because you know I won't shoot at you unless you shoot at me."

"And you don't know that about me?"

Tony clenched his jaw. "No. Not anymore, I don't."

Ben didn't answer. Not so much as a muscle twitched, and their eyes never wavered. They could have been statues carved from the hardest granite. Finally, the corner of Ben's mouth lifted, his arm lowered, and he placed the pistol on a nearby table.

Tony approached the cabin cautiously, keeping his rifle leveled on Ben. He circled the porch, sliding his feet to locate the steps, not daring to look down. Reaching a point no more than a yard from Ben, he stopped.

Ben swept his arm to indicate a chair and battered stool that sat beside the hand-hewn table—the table on which the gleaming pistol rested next to a half-empty bottle of whiskey.

"Welcome to my humble abode, cousin. Won't you sit down?"

Tony lowered himself to the stool, laying his gun across his thighs, as Ben sank into the chair.

Ben waited patiently. And waited. And, finally, not so patiently.

"Well? What are you going to do with me now?"

"Damned if I know." Tony shook his head, disbelief lighting his features. "Do you know, all this time I was concentrating on finding you, I never thought about what happened then? I guess I sort of figured I'd just *know* what to do. But I don't." His gaze fixed on the corral. "Looks like you been takin' good care of our . . . of *my* horses."

Ben lifted the bottle to his mouth and drank, a motion so automatic that Tony knew he had repeated it hundreds of times before. He wiped his lips with the back of his hand before he spoke again. "Duchess didn't make it. The trip was more than she could take." He set the bottle carefully back down on the table.

"That's what I figured when she wasn't in the corral with the others. Still, losing only one is better than I expected, especially with some of the mares carrying." Tony's smile was empty. "Seems we did a good job selecting stock."

"Seems so."

Silence reigned again. An empty, wasteful silence, punctuated only by the whistling of the cold wind through the pines.

Tony leaned forward, his bleak eyes focusing on Ben's.

"Why?" His voice grew stronger. "Oh God, Ben. Why?"

Ben's eyes were dark with misery and hopeless pain. "I loved her."

"So?" Tony brought his fist down hard on the table. "So? You loved her. But I loved you too! We were closer than brothers. You were part of me as long as I can remember."

"Brothers! We weren't brothers! You were Edward Winchester's son. My old man was Jeb Mattson, a little too fond of cards and a lot too fond of whiskey. You got everything you ever wanted. All I got was a heavy fist against the side of my head."

"I never knew you felt like that."

"You weren't supposed to know. Your place was the only good thing in my life. So I ignored the pity in your father's eyes every time he looked at me and thought of what his little sister married."

"I didn't know." Tony shook his head slowly. "I didn't know you loved her, either."

"How could I let you know?" Ben closed his eyes, then opened them again, and they were even darker and emptier than before. "Once Liza grew up enough to look at us as more than playmates, she took one look at you and you were all she ever saw. And you never even cared."

"If I had known how you felt, I would never have touched her."

"Can you tell me that?" Ben's mouth tightened, the flesh surrounding it becoming taut and white. "Can you honestly tell me that?"

Tony thought back, remembering what it was like when he was sixteen with his blood running high and hot, when he felt like he was going to die if he didn't get to touch the sweet, soft skin of a woman, when he never bothered to stop and think about the consequences. He was compelled to answer truthfully.

"No."

Ben pryed a splinter off the arm of his chair and snapped it into tiny bits. "You know what I don't get?"

"What?"

"Why the hell aren't you trying to rip me to shreds? I know you've always been the Winchester without a temper, but after everything I stole from you . . . why aren't you furious with me?"

"I don't know." Tony raked his fingers through his hair and crossed his arms over his chest. He wondered the same thing himself. "I was, at first. But then . . . maybe I thought I deserved some of it."

Ben sat up straight, a hint of speculation in his eyes. "You love someone."

Tony gave a noncommittal shrug and didn't answer. Was that the reason? He only knew that if some man had done to Jessie what he had done to Liza, the man would be damned lucky to lose only his life's savings and his life's work.

Ben's voice grew more certain. "That's it, isn't it. You love someone."

Tony had no intention of discussing Jessie with Ben. If much of his anger was gone, the pain and sense of betrayal remained. He leaned forward, bracing his palms on his knees.

"I still don't understand. How could you do it? How could you work with me every day for eight god-damn years and never let on that you hated me? To choose horses together, to look at land together, to save every last penny we could until we were ready to buy our own place . . . and then just take the money and the horses and disappear?"

"I never hated you." At Tony's look of utter disbelief, he repeated it. "I never hated you, not when we were together. When it was just you and me . . . it was just you and me. You were my best friend. But at night, I'd go home and I'd remember. I'd remember the way the sun used to glint off her hair, or the way she'd laugh, and I . . ."

"Your best friend." Tony shook his head. *"Dio,* Ben, why didn't you come to me? How could you not even give me a chance to explain?"

The first hint of fire appeared in Ben's empty eyes. "What was there to explain?" He dropped his head back, as if he couldn't bear to look at Tony anymore. "I saw you two together, you know."

"What?"

"That day, in the cave. It was raining like crazy—I got sick from the cold, but I didn't care, 'cause I hurt so much worse inside. Anyway, I knew I shouldn't be out in it, but I knew you were together somewhere. I could see the way she'd been looking at you, and I knew you were starting to notice she was growing up. I couldn't stand the idea of you two being alone together."

"And where else would you look for us but the cave."

"Where else?" He took a deep breath, as if fortifying himself against a memory he still couldn't bear. "You never knew I was there. You were too . . . occupied. God, I can still see it, as if it were carved into my brain. I tried to obliterate that picture so many times, blot it out, drown it out, anything, but it's still there, as clear as the day it happened. Her skirts were up around her hips, her legs wrapped around you, and she was holding on to you like she never wanted to let you go . . . and I knew she didn't."

"God, Ben, I'm so sorry."

"Even that I think I could have forgiven you, Tony. If you had loved her."

"But I didn't."

"No . . . you didn't."

They didn't speak of what had happened then. Even now, some things hurt too much to put into words.

There was one more thing Tony had to know.

"Was it worth it, Ben?"

"No." Ben lifted his head, finally looking again at him. Tony had never seen such deep agony, such palpable, desperate pain, in the eyes of another human being. "No. Not for one fucking minute. For you see, she's still gone . . . and I lost you, too."

Unprepared for Ben's sudden move to the table, Tony's reaction was a split-second late.

He dove for the gun and shouted.

"No!"

In the corral, ten magnificent horses raised their heads as the unfamiliar sound of a gunshot rent the air. They paused, motionless, but the sound was not repeated.

Soon they resumed their contented cropping of the grass.

30

Jessie lowered herself into the chair in the corner of her room and raised a trembling hand to her forehead.

God, she was tired. Tired of feeling sick, tired of dreaming and wondering about Tony, tired of avoiding her brother's questions, and tired of being tired.

Maybe it was time to get on with the rest of her life. It was certainly time to get out of here.

Desperate for some fresh air, she tugged on a thick winter coat, tying a knitted scarf snugly around her neck for good measure. She tiptoed down the back staircase, hoping to slip out to the tiny rear garden before anyone saw her.

It was too late.

"Jessie!"

She muffled her groan of disappointment before turning to face her brother. She wasn't ready for this yet.

He leaned against the wall and grinned down at her. "Where ya goin', brat?"

"Out to the garden."

"The garden!" He pushed himself off the wall. "But it's the middle of winter!"

She forced a smile. "I'm aware of that, J.J. I *am* capable of reading a calendar."

"But it's cold outside."

"That's why I'm wearing a coat."

"Oh. So you are. Well, then." He touched her arm and stopped her as she turned to go. "Wait a second. I wanted to talk to you about an idea I had. With February almost here, I thought we could advertise your portraits as Valentine gifts. Bring in a little more business."

"I don't know if I'm going to be here that long."

"What!" He looked astonished. "What do you mean you're not going to be here? Of course you're going to be here. You live here."

"No, I don't." She sighed. She hadn't wanted to get into this with J.J. now. She wasn't sure she had the strength. He'd never understand, and she wasn't going to tell him the one thing that would make him understand.

"I've loved visiting here, J.J. But the portrait business is going well now, and I'm ready to get a place of my own."

J.J. frowned, looking as hurt as a little boy who was just rejected by his new puppy. "If I've done something that makes you want to leave—"

"No." She smoothed the collar of his white jacket. "Of course not. But I never intended to spend the rest of my life in a saloon. Especially not now."

He drew himself up in mock grandeur. "We're not just a saloon. We're the finest entertainment establishment in San Francisco. The Naked Rose is—" He stopped as if the impact of her words had just penetrated. "What do you mean, especially not now?"

"Never mind," Jessie said quickly. "I promise, I'll think about Valentine's Day, O.K? As long as you promise to be reasonable about me getting a place of my own."

"I'm always reasonable." He gave her a quick squeeze before she could dispute his claim. "Now go dig in the dead flowers, brat."

He gave her a tiny push toward the door but lingered in the hallway, watching her leave and thinking.

His mind made up, he ran lightly up the stairs, humming.

Perhaps he couldn't do anything to prevent her leaving. But maybe David could.

Sitting back on her heels, Jessie tugged off her muddy gardening gloves and surveyed the remains of The Naked Rose's miniscule back garden. No one had bothered to clean it after the growing season, and it was a sad tangle of dried, overgrown weeds and the black remains of barely identifiable flowers.

She loosened the scarf around her neck and raised her face to the sun. It was a rare, clear winter day. Compared to the Chicago winters she was accustomed to, the weather in San Francisco was practically balmly, but she wasn't sure she'd ever get used to the continuous fog and clouds. Today there was sunlight, though. It was watery and weak, but it was enough to heat her as she grubbed in the heavy, damp earth. It felt good. She rubbed an itchy spot on her nose with the back her hand, then pulled her gloves back on. Grabbing the dried stalk of a large, dead marigold, she gave a sharp yank. The roots were deep, and it wouldn't come free, so she balanced on her heels for better leverage, wrapped both hands around the stubborn plant, and gave a mighty heave.

It let go. Clumps of earth showered around her as she fell back and landed square on her rump.

Hearty laughter made her spine stiffen. Why were

people always sneaking up on her when she was at her worst?

David watched the glint of battle light her eyes. How well he remembered that look, when she was ready to tear into someone for the smallest of reasons. There were always fireworks when Jessie was around.

Large smudges of dirt decorated her cheeks, her leaf-studded hair tumbled in wild tangles around her, and her legs stuck straight out in front of her beneath a raggedy, faded brown dress.

He sure did like fireworks.

"You look exactly like you did when you were twelve."

Jessie grimaced up at him. "Oh, thanks a lot. Now I know why you haven't got a woman. You scare them away with all your silver-tongued flattery."

He chuckled and extended a hand, lifting her easily from the ground and setting her on her feet. "It is a compliment. You were beautiful at twelve."

She snorted in disbelief, removing her gloves and tossing them to the ground. "Of course I was. Everyone's taste runs to scrawny, redheaded, awkward little squirrels."

"I'm serious."

Something in his voice made her look more closely at him. His beautiful gold and green eyes were intent.

"You are, aren't you?"

"Absolutely. Any idiot could have seen what you were going to be in a few years, when your outside started to match your insides." He moved closer and gently untangled a dead leaf from her hair. "Didn't you ever wonder why I left with J.J.?"

"Well, a little. I knew you were never interested in gold."

"I couldn't stand to be around you anymore, waiting for you to grow up. I didn't have enough patience, and I didn't want to hurt you by rushing you into something you weren't ready for."

She stared at him in amazement. "I had no idea."

"You weren't meant to. You were just a child."

Her eyes clouded. "Not for long."

"No. Not for long," he said regretfully. Lightly, almost reverently, he brushed his knuckles down her smudged cheekbone. "And you're certainly not a child now, are you?" He leaned down to kiss her gently.

Her eyes remained open in surprise. It was so different. There was no heat, no passion, no little nerves jumping up and down all over her body. Just two mouths meeting. Just a kiss.

He pulled back. His eyes were filled with a bit of acceptance, a bit of pain, and a lot of regret.

"It's just not there for you, is it?"

The back of her nose stung, and she dropped her gaze. David was the last person in the world she ever wanted to hurt. "I'm sorry, it's not you, it's—"

"Hush." He lifted one finger to her lips to silence her. "It's nothing you need to apologize for. No one can make their heart feel something it doesn't. It doesn't work that way. It's nobody's fault, it's just the way it is."

She felt his gentleness as he laid his palm against her cheek while she tried to think of something worth saying.

"I hope Winchester knew what a lucky bastard he was."

"What?" Her gaze flew to his. "How did you know?"

"I don't sleep well. Sometimes I wander around at night. I saw you go into his room the first night you were here. You didn't come out."

She searched his face for some hint of accusation or revulsion but found none. "But you never said anything."

"What was I supposed to do? Call you a fallen woman and try to save you?"

"You wouldn't have been the first."

"I'm a grown man, Jessie. I can't say I've never spent the night with a woman."

"Most people seem to think it's different for a man."

A corner of his mouth lifted. "That's just another one of those things about 'most people' I've never been able to figure out." Reluctantly, he let his hand drop from her face.

She nudged a clump of dirt with her toe. "Are you going to tell J.J.?"

"Did I ever let on that you were the one who told Cheryl Carson and Sandra Mitchelson that he went to see both of them in one night?"

She wrinkled her nose. "No."

"Did I tell him that you spied on him when he was on the porch swing with Colleen O'Malley?"

She giggled. "No."

He looked her in the eye, his expression serious. "He's going to know soon, Jessie."

"How did you—"

"When could you ever keep anything from me?"

She brushed an errant lock of sandy hair from his brow. "Never."

"He may be obtuse, Jessie, but he's not blind and stupid. J.J.'s going to figure it out."

"I know." She sighed heavily. "I was hoping his current overbearing, overprotective stage would wear off a bit first."

"Ain't never gonna happen, Jess."

"I guess not." She narrowed her eyes. "Did he send you out here to try and get me to change my mind about moving out?"

"Maybe."

"Did he?" she persisted.

"Yes. But I was planning to talk to you, anyway." He shifted, leaning a bit closer. "What *are* you going to do, Jessie?"

She turned away, her gaze focusing on the distant hills. They were bumpy, damp, and brown, not a hint of life or spring. "What everybody does, I guess. Make a life for myself."

"He's not coming back, Jess."

She squeezed her eyes shut. "I know."

"It's been three months." He stepped closer.

Her voice rose. "I know."

"If he was coming back, he'd be here by now."

"I know!" she shouted.

Coming up behind her, he placed his big, warm hands on her shoulders, rubbed them gently, and waited.

Finally he said, "I love you, Jess."

She whirled and threw herself against his chest, feeling his arms come around her to hold her there. It wasn't thrilling. It wasn't exciting. It wasn't Tony. But it was safe and warm and comforting, and she stayed.

"Marry me, Jessie."

She leaned back to look at him, tears leaving pale streaks down the dirt on her face.

"How can you suggest that? Even when you know I . . . ?"

Linking his hands at the back of her waist, he smiled sadly. "Part of you is better than all of anybody else."

She twisted her hands in the fabric of his shirt. "You deserve better, David."

He kissed her temple and rested his cheek against the top of her head, feeling the softness of her curls against his skin. "This isn't about what I deserve. It's about what I want."

She leaned against his chest. He was so safe. She was so tired. "But—"

"No buts." His embrace tightened. "What else are you going to do, Jessie?"

No, it wasn't exciting and passionate. It wasn't Tony. It would never be Tony.

But it was something.

"I do love you, David."

31

"Well, well. Isn't this friendly."

He had ridden constantly for what seemed like days, not worrying about whether he was pushing General too hard, not aware of the scenery or his hunger or his fatigue, knowing only that, with each hoofbeat, with each matching beat of his heart, he was getting closer to Jessie.

A sense of hope and overwhelming anticipation filled him as he came out of the winter-chilled foothills, through the slick, muddy streets of San Francisco, up the brutal slopes . . . *Jessie*. He was almost there.

He had rounded the side of the Naked Rose, intending to drop General in the stables—just this once, he'd tend to him later—when he heard the murmur of a familiar voice in the secluded garden. He stepped through the portal, visualizing what he would say, how she would look, and there she was. In David's arms.

The blood froze in his veins—ice, fury, and wrenching loss. His vision clouded, his breathing stopped. Hell, maybe his *life* stopped. Did it matter if it did?

He saw her jolt of surprise. Saw her jerk from David's arms, saw her turn toward him with shock on her face. Saw her eyes.

It was there, in her beaming, luminous, blue-gray eyes. It was quickly masked, but it had been there for an instant, and it was enough.

Joy.

The ice was gone as quickly as it came, and the angry winter left his heart.

"Tony." Her lips formed his name, but no sound came out.

He was there, really there in the flesh, not some conjuring of her desperate imagination. His feet, encased in muddy black boots, were planted solidly on the same plot of earth as hers. His arms, the ones that had held her with such tenderness, were crossed over the broad chest she knew so well. His dark brows were drawn together over his eyes, eyes that snapped and sparked with tangible power. And she knew that every image she had dreamed of him over the long, lost months was a pallid imitation of the real thing.

Although his features were familiar, it seemed as if some stranger—angry, cold, and remote—had taken over his body. He looked like some ancient god, come to mete out judgment on foolish and misguided mortals.

Their eyes met, and she saw the subtle release of tension, the relaxation of those massive muscles. She watched him grin slowly, effortlessly. The twin creases in his cheeks were deeper than ever, but otherwise he was suddenly transformed into *her* Tony, familiar and beloved.

Having forgotten his presence, she was surprised when she felt David shift by her side.

"You can unruffle all those cock feathers, Winchester. The lady already told me no."

Tony's gaze didn't waver from Jessie. "I know."

They remained still, not moving closer together, as if they were afraid that if they touched it would be less real. They didn't notice David move to the door and open it, didn't see him look back at them, two people three yards apart but obviously, completely, connected. They didn't hear him whisper, "Good-bye, Jessie," before he slipped through the door and let it close slowly behind him.

Tony was a handbreadth from her before he realized that his feet had moved. His mouth was on hers before he realized his intent. Her lips were soft, trembling slightly, unbearably sweet.

It didn't settle anything. Not one damn thing. But, God, it felt good.

He opened his mouth to tell her that he loved her, but the words never had a chance to be heard. A hand wheeled him around, and a blow came from nowhere, sudden, vicious, with the force only fury can impart. It caught him underneath his chin, spinning him around, laying him out on the ground with his face in a clump of rotting pansies.

"You goddamn sonofabitch."

The voice was vaguely familiar. Good hook, he thought in a daze. It'd been a long time since anyone had caught him that unaware. He'd better move, or he was going to get walloped again.

He felt someone kneel next to him, felt that someone give a heave and roll him over. He felt gentle fingers probe the injury to his jaw and lift his head to a lap.

Jessie's lap. He closed his eyes and settled himself more comfortably. Maybe he'd stay here for a while after all.

"Jessie, get away from that bastard."

"J.J., you idiot, you hit him!"

"Damn right, I hit him. Now if you'd just move away a little bit, I'd hit him again."

Tony dragged himself to his feet. Not too woozy. He balanced his weight on both feet and took a good look at Jessie's brother.

J.J. looked furious. His face was red, his impeccable tie askew. His hair was even slightly mussed.

"I'm warning you, Johnston," Tony said calmly. "You just got one free shot, and the only reason you got that one was because you're Jessie's brother. One more swing, and I'm swinging back."

"Go right ahead." J.J. took a half step forward, his fists raised in preparation, and stopped when a large clump of dirt smacked him square in the chest. He looked down at his formerly pristine white shirt front in disbelief, then at his sister, who was hastily scooping up another clod. "Whatja do that for, brat?"

"Just evening up the odds. I would have thought attacking from behind was beneath you, J.J."

"He deserved it, Jess."

"I did, did I?" Tony brushed the remaining earth off his face. "And what, precisely, did I do to deserve it?"

J.J. clenched his fists, clearly wishing that he could ram them down Tony's throat. "You seduced my baby sister!"

"I did?" He flashed a charming grin and winked at Jessie. "And here I thought she seduced me."

"You made her a . . . a . . . a . . ."

Tony's eyes narrowed. "Don't say it."

"Why shouldn't I say it? You're the one who did it."

Tony lowered his gaze to Jessie. "Oh, good job, Jess. Told your guard dog we slept together, but you neglected to mention we were married at the time."

"Don't talk to her like that! She didn't tell me, I know because of the baby . . ." his voice trailed off in confusion. "Married?"

"Baby?"

Jessie put a hand over her mouth in an attempt to

cover her smile. Poor men. Their eyes were wide and glazed, their jaws hanging loose. "You both look like you've been run over by a mule train."

"I'm beginning to feel like it." Tony rubbed the growing bruise on his jaw.

J.J. glared at Jessie. "Are you *really* married?"

"Yes, I'm *really* married."

"Well, you could have told me," he grumbled. "Would have saved me months of worry."

"Why were you worried?"

"Why? I thought my little sister's virtue had been stolen, that's why."

"And what would be so wrong with that, Mr. Sleeps-with-his-mistress-every-night?"

"That's different."

She arched an eyebrow. "Oh? How?"

"You're a woman."

"And what is Rose?"

"Well . . . she's . . . it's just . . ."

"Yes?"

J.J. knew that silky tone. It was time to cut his losses. "Never mind, Jessie."

"Oh, but I do mind. And, just so you know, I *was* the one who did the seducing. Did a pretty good job of it, too, don't you think, Tony?"

"Better than pretty good. Absolutely the best," he said. "Course, it didn't take much. I think I was seduced the instant I laid eyes on you."

Unbelievable. Her sophisticated brother was turning as red as a young man confronted with his first woman. She took pity on him and changed the subject. "J.J., how did you know I was pregnant, anyway?"

"Contrary to prevailing opinion, I'm not stupid, Jess. I know what it means when a woman is throwing up every morning for three months."

"You're sick, *cara*?" Tony had been content to watch Jessie put her brother in his place, but suddenly he became serious. He cradled Jessie's head in his hands, tipping up her face and looking down at her with such a sweetly tender gaze that it made her heart melt. "Is something wrong, Jessie?"

She lifted her hands and placed them on his wrists, her fingertips tracing the strong, powerful muscles just beneath his skin. "It's normal, Tony, and it's going away already. You needn't look so worried."

"I can't help it. It seems to be a chronic condition where you're concerned."

"Well, how sweet." J.J.'s voice dripped with sarcasm. "I guess the two of you won't be needing me anymore, so I'll just go in and see to making tonight's fortune."

"You do that, big brother," Jessie said without glancing his way.

"I will. And, while the you're at it, why don't you have Winchester explain where he's been the last three months while you've been here chucking up your breakfast."

Tony saw the doubt cloud her beautiful eyes, saw skepticism and perhaps a hint of fear, and he felt a palpable pain in his chest. Not yet, he wanted to scream. Not yet! Let her look at him with happiness and trust for just a little longer.

"Jessie . . ."

"No." She dropped her gaze and her arms, leaning slightly away. "You don't owe me any explanations."

"Yes, I do. I owe you everything I can give you, everything you want to take."

A frown crinkled her brow. *Dio*, what had he said now? This wasn't how he'd planned on telling her. He'd imagined showering her with expressions of his feelings, convincing her of his love, before he had to tell her what a bastard he'd been before he met her. But it was too late. He'd put it off too long.

There was a small granite bench in one corner of the garden, perched under a decrepit orange tree. He led her to it, settling them on the mottled stone, and tucked her red woolen scarf carefully under her chin.

"Are you warm enough? If you want to go inside—"

"No. I'm warm enough."

He wasn't. The bench was cold under his thighs, the chill seeping through fabric and skin into his bones. Wanting to draw her close and share her warmth, he tucked his hands under his legs to prevent temptation. He hadn't earned the right to touch her.

He let his gaze trace over her face. He didn't see planes and curves and angles, the classic features that made up some arbitrary standard of beauty, not anymore. What he saw now was fire and strength, courage and humor. What he saw now was, simply, Jessie.

"I love you," he said, unable to hold it in any longer.

He saw her eyes darken, filled with pain, hope, and, yes, love. He looked away, unable to watch that love evaporate. Jessie had left her gloves in a heap near the dead pansies, and he focused on their muddied whiteness.

"You know I went to find someone." He paused, searching for the proper words. How was he going to explain it all? "It was my cousin, Benjamin. My father's sister's son. He was much more than my cousin, really. More than a brother even would have been, I expect. His father was . . . not a good one so Ben spent most of his time with us when we were growing up. We were blood brothers from the time we were old enough to know what that meant.

"We'd always planned to go into business together. When we were fourteen, we started to make it a reality. Working here and there, training horses, trading, keeping the best ones for ourselves, saving every bit of money we had.

"Finally, early last spring, we were ready. We had a great string of breeding stock, not too many, but enough to start. Found a good piece of land fifty miles from home. I had to go up to Ohio to check out a new stallion. I left Ben with the money to buy the land before somebody else snatched it up."

Pulling his hands free, he rubbed them together, trying to warm them, but the coldness had penetrated to the bone. He remembered the chill he had felt in his soul when he had returned from his buying trip.

"When I got back, Ben was gone. Took the horses, the money, everything. Everything we'd worked for, everything we'd planned, everything we'd dreamed."

So that was why he came to California. She'd always wondered why. She waited for him to continue. When he didn't, she said, "Did you find him?"

"Yes." Tony seemed remote, his customary openness absent. "He was in a valley at the edge of the mountains. We passed near it on the way here, as a matter of fact." His skin grew pale under his tan, as if he were physically ill. "He'd . . . changed so much. What he'd done didn't seem to sit well with him, but I wasn't expecting it when he went for his gun." He rubbed his hands over his face, as if it could erase painful memories. "I'm still not sure what he meant to shoot—the horses, himself, or me. I don't think I want to know.

"I went for the gun, too. It went off, I don't know how, but Ben got hit in the side of his chest." He dared one quick glance at Jessie, but her face revealed nothing. "I . . . felt responsible. I had to stay and take care of him. That's why it took me so long to come back."

"Is he all right now?"

Tony nodded slowly. "Physically, I guess. The rest of him . . ." His shoulders sagged as if under a great weight. "He's gone. Left the horses with me. I . . . _Dio_, I hope he's going to be O.K."

He braced himself for the inevitable question, and

she didn't disappoint him. "Why did he do it, Tony? There has to be more to it."

"Yes." The skin of his face was pulled tight, stretched so tautly over his cheekbones that light glanced off the planes. Jessie wondered how long someone could remain so tense without shattering. "It wasn't just the two of us when we were kids. There was Liza. The Carlyles had the place next to ours. Liza was just a year younger than Ben and me. She was our buddy. I never really thought of her as a girl, not for a long time."

His hands gripped the edge of the bench with crushing force, his knuckles white with the effort. "I didn't know that he loved her." He slammed a hand down on the seat with such abrupt violence that Jessie jumped. "Damn it, I should have known!"

He closed his eyes, his head sagging tiredly. "I have to tell you how it was for me, Jessie. Not an excuse, not a defense, just an . . . explanation. The first time I slept with a woman was my fifteenth birthday. She was a regular customer of my father's. She was also married. She said she had a birthday present for me and took me into the tack room." He laughed hollowly. "The goddamn tack room! Not that I wasn't willing, mind you. I wasn't some injured innocent. I was just . . . young.

"All the other women I knew were like that. Sex to them was just . . . recreation, no more important than a well-played hand of cards. I didn't have any idea what it could be. Never did, really, until I met you."

She shifted closer to him, wanting to be near, to comfort him, but he slid away. "One day Liza and I snuck away without Benjamin. We wanted to make plans to surprise him for his sixteenth birthday. There was this cave we always used to hide out in, and we went there. A big summer thunderstorm blew in, and we decided to wait it out.

"We . . . it just happened, Jessie. I swear to God I didn't plan it. But afterwards, she started talking about our wedding. I couldn't believe it. It had never even occurred to me what it would mean to her, and she just assumed we would get married. But I did care about her, and it seemed like the right thing to do, so I went along with the engagement.

"But it really didn't seem real to me. I was so stupid. Careless, I guess. I couldn't imagine never touching another woman again. So . . . I did."

His silence was long. The sounds of the city, the street—horses' hooves and clambering vehicles, shouting merchants and playing children—seemed far away and insignificant.

"She came to my room to see me. I think she wanted to talk about flowers or music for the ceremony, something like that . . . I wasn't alone. One of our maids was there with me. I'll never forget how she looked. She was so pale, she looked like all the blood was sucked right out of her face.

"The next day she married somebody else, a storekeeper from town. He seemed old to me at the time, but I suppose he wasn't more than forty. I just remember he had these cruel little eyes, like a weasel or something.

"She . . ." He shuddered, the tremor running throughout his body. "I never knew what he did to her. I only know the morning after her wedding, she climbed into her bathtub and slit her wrists. I wasn't there, I didn't see it, but, *Dio,* I saw it for so long, every time I tried to go to sleep. Her blue eyes empty, her skin as white as when she walked in on me in bed with another woman, the ends of her yellow hair floating in water stained red with her blood."

He took a great gulp of air. What would he see when he looked into Jessie's eyes? Fear, disappointment, revulsion? Please, God, don't let it be revulsion.

It was none of those. Her eyes were clear, brilliantly blue.

"I love you," she said.

"You shouldn't."

"Should doesn't have anything to do with it. It just is, Tony." She tenderly stroked his face, feeling the rough stubble of his beard under her fingertips. "It just is."

"It was my fault, Jessie."

"Did you force her to sleep with you? Did you drag her to the church to marry that man? Did you put the knife to her flesh?" Her face was afire with determination to make him understand. "Her life was her own, Tony. She made her own choices. You were young. You hurt her. That is your responsibility. But the rest belongs to her."

He wanted to believe her. God, he wanted to, but he couldn't. Not until he was sure that she understood. "Jessie, I wish I'd never—"

She shook her head vehemently. "If you could change your past, you'd be changing you. I want the man you are now, Tony. Just you."

He felt the sudden release of pressure, the absence of a heavy burden he hadn't known he carried. He felt giddy, weightless, as if the sun was shining just for him. "I love you, Jessie."

She smiled but looked sad.

"I do, Jessie," he said more forcefully.

"You've done a lot of things because you *should*, not because you wanted to. First with the wedding, now with the baby. I don't want you out of honor or duty, only out of love. I deserve nothing less."

"Maybe it's better if fate makes the choices for me. She seems to do a helluva lot better job of it than I do." He reached out a forefinger and tipped up her chin, forcing her to look at him. *See it in my eyes, Jessie,* he silently begged. *See it!* "Do you honestly think I'm not happy about the baby, about us?"

His eyes were dark and gleaming. She saw no uncertainty, no apprehension. Only vivid exultation.

Her answering smile was bright and jubilant. He scooped her up and pulled her down on his lap, settling her solidly against him.

"Now see here." Although she wanted nothing more than to curl into his embrace, Jessie pushed herself up, scowled at him severely. "There's one more thing."

"Yes?"

"Remember after our wedding? What you said about not being faithful?"

"What about it?"

She grabbed his shirt, pulling him close until they were nose to nose. "You can just forget it. I'm not sharing you."

"Is that a threat?"

"You'd better believe it, Winchester."

"God, I love it when you're tough." He tilted his chin just enough for his mouth to meet hers. He meant it to be just a taste, a tiny treat, but once he felt the warmth of her lips he returned to kiss her again and again, lingering, reacquainting, savoring. It had always been exceptional between them, but there was a new element now, lush warmth and security, love both magnifying and mellowing their attraction, leaving him stunned by its power.

He thought of all the other women he had known. He could admire them in the abstract. He could think they were beautiful, enjoy their company, but have no desire to touch them. For, in the end, they weren't Jessie.

He drew back, regarding her seriously. "Other women aren't going to be a problem, Jess."

She smiled and snuggled closer, laying her head in the curve of his shoulder. They sat there quietly, each simply grateful for the other's presence. Tony felt replete, suffused with happiness, all shadows of guilt and pain swept away by the sunshine of Jessie's love.

It was such a simple thing, she thought, to be held close in another's arms, but how different when it was someone you love. Then it became no longer simple. It took on textures and hues composed of passion and gentleness, heat and comfort.

"When do we leave for Kentucky?" she asked.

He rubbed his cheek against the fine softness of her hair. "What would you think if we didn't?"

"Not go?" Bewildered, she leaned back slightly to look in his face. "Why?"

His big hands were warm on her back, rubbing her gently, and she could feel their magic even through the thick cloth of her coat.

"Though I can't for the life of me figure out why you're so fond of the fellow, I thought you might like to stay nearer your brother."

"Well, yes, but—"

"Ben gave me the land, Jess. It's beautiful, up near the mountains, clean and shiny and new. You could paint the most incredible pictures. The horses are thriving. And it's only a day's ride from Ginnie's and Mary Ellen's places."

"That's wonderful, but what about Winchester Meadows? Your family? Your home?"

"Winchester Meadows is just a piece of land, nothing more, nothing less. As for my family, the government has started surveying for the transcontinental railroad. Getting back and forth for visits will be much easier." He slid one hand down over her belly and grinned at her. "Besides, in a couple of years I figure we'll have all the family we can handle."

He dropped light, cherishing kisses on her nose, the curve of her cheek, the angle of her jaw. "And my home?" He cupped her face in his hands, holding her as if she were the most fragile, precious object.

"I'm with you, *cara*. I am home."

In the tiny garden, the grip of winter was fast and cruel. Decomposing flowers lay on cold, congealed earth, and the winter sunlight was weak. But under a limp, solitary orange tree, on an icy gray bench, a woman in a frayed brown coat was tucked securely in the lap of a man whose clothes were travel streaked and rumpled. A dark head bent to one of sun-kissed gold silk, and they murmured of dreams and love and forever. Here, in this sheltered corner of a faded Eden, it was already spring.

Here, it was home.

Author's Note

The people who went West in the great overland migration of the mid-1800s must have had some idea that they were part of history, for a great many of them kept diaries recording their adventures. Some of the scenes in this book were taken directly from these journals. There was indeed a woman who made supper for her family by standing over the camp fire for hours with an umbrella, as well as a young man who stopped a buffalo charge by slashing a beast across the nose with a bowie knife.

Most history must be embellished for fiction; but I was rather restrained in writing this book. The trip *was* extraordinarily difficult and dangerous. It would have been unusual for a train to experience as few deaths as Tony and Jessie's did, and a great many of those who died were children. But I couldn't bring myself to kill off a child, and 1853 was, comparatively, one of the safest years to travel West. The hordes who had gone to California in the gold-rush years of 1849 and 1850 had left well-blazed trails and numerous ferries and bridges, while the violent Indian attacks that characterized the late 1850s had not yet begun in force.

I tried to give some sense of the courage and fortitude the families who expanded our country must have had, and I hope you enjoyed Tony and Jessie's *Journey Home*.

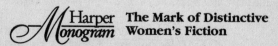

COMING NEXT MONTH

COMING UP ROSES by Catherine Anderson

From the bestselling author of the Comanche trilogy, comes a sensual historical romance. When Zach McGovern was injured in rescuing her daughter from an abandoned well, Kate Blakely nursed him back to health. Kate feared men, but Zach was different, and only buried secrets could prevent their future from coming up roses.

HOMEBODY by Louise Titchener

Bestselling author Louise Titchener pens a romantic thriller about a young woman who must battle the demons of her past, as well as the dangers she finds in her new apartment.

BAND OF GOLD by Zita Christian

The rush for gold in turn-of-the-century Alaska was nothing compared to the rush Aurelia Breighton felt when she met the man of her dreams. But then Aurelia discovered that it was not her he was after but her missing sister.

DANCING IN THE DARK by Susan P. Teklits

A tender and touching tale of two people who were thrown together by treachery and found unexpected love. A historical romance in the tradition of Constance O'Banyon.

CHANCE McCALL by Sharon Sala

Chance McCall knows that he has no right to love Jenny Tyler, the boss's daughter. With only his monthly paycheck and checkered past, he's no good for her, even though she thinks otherwise. But when an accident leaves Chance with no memory, he has no choice but to return to his past and find out why he dare not claim the woman he loves.

SWEET REVENGE by Jean Stribling

There was nothing better than sweet revenge when ex-Union captain Adam McCormick unexpectedly captured his enemy's stepdaughter, Letitia Ramsey. But when Adam found himself falling in love with her, he had to decide if revenge was worth the sacrifice of love.

HIGHLAND LOVE SONG by Constance O'Banyon

Available in trade paperback! From the bestselling author of *Forever My Love,* a sweeping and mesmerizing story continues the DeWinter legacy begun in *Song of the Nightingale.*

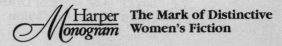

Harper Monogram   **The Mark of Distinctive Women's Fiction**

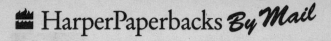

YESTERDAY'S SHADOWS
by Marianne Willman

Bettany Howard was a young orphan traveling west searching for the father who left her years ago. Wolf Star was a Cheyenne brave who longed to know who abandoned him—a white child with a jeweled talisman. Fate decreed they'd meet and try to seize the passion promised. 0-06-104044-4

MIDNIGHT ROSE by Patricia Hagan

From the rolling plantations of Richmond to the underground slave movement of Philadelphia, Erin Sterling and Ryan Youngblood would pursue their wild, breathless passion and finally surrender to the promise of a bold and unexpected love. 0-06-104023-1

WINTER TAPESTRY
by Kathy Lynn Emerson

Cordell vows to revenge the murder of her father. Roger Allington is honor bound to protect his friend's daughter but has no liking for her reckless ways. Yet his heart tells him he must pursue this beauty through a maze of plots to win her love and ignite their smoldering passion.
0-06-100220-8